KU-374-570

PENGUIN ENGLISH LIBRARY

CONY-CATCHERS AND BAWDY BASKETS

Gāmini Salgādo is a Reader in the School of English and American Studies at the University of Sussex. In addition to editing *Three Jacobean Tragedies* and *Three Restoration Comedies* for the Penguin English Library, he has written a short study of *Sons and Lovers* and edited a collection of essays on the same novel.

CONY-CATCHERS
AND BAWDY BASKETS

AN ANTHOLOGY OF
ELIZABETHAN LOW LIFE

edited with
an Introduction and Notes by

GĀMINI SALGĀDO

PENGUIN BOOKS

Penguin Books Ltd, Harmondsworth, Middlesex, England
Penguin Books Inc., 7110 Ambassador Road, Baltimore, Maryland 21207, U.S.A.
Penguin Books Australia Ltd, Ringwood, Victoria, Australia

—

A Manifest Detection of Dice-Play first published *c.* 1552
The Fraternity of Vagabonds first published 1561
A Caveat for Common Cursitors first published 1566
A Notable Discovery of Cozenage first published 1591
The Second Part of Cony-Catching first published 1592
The Third and Last Part of Cony-Catching first published 1592
A Disputation first published 1592
The Defence of Cony-Catching first published 1592
The Black Book's Messenger first published 1592
Parson Haberdyne's Sermon first published 1880
Published in Penguin English Library 1972

—

Introduction and Notes copyright © Gāmini Salgādo, 1972

—

Made and printed in Great Britain by
Hazell Watson & Viney Ltd
Aylesbury, Bucks
Set in Linotype Plantin

This book is sold subject to the condition
that it shall not, by way of trade or otherwise,
be lent, re-sold, hired out, or otherwise circulated
without the publisher's prior consent in any form of
binding or cover other than that in which it is
published and without a similar condition
including this condition being imposed
on the subsequent purchaser

FOR 'DITH

benshyp autem-mort for twenty years,
lightmans and darkmans.

CONTENTS

INTRODUCTION

ONE of the most memorable entrances in the plays of Shakespeare is that of Autolycus in *The Winter's Tale.* After the claustrophobic gloom of the court and the sour scenes of Leontes' mistrust and its aftermath, this cheerful scoundrel comes in, singing a song full of the freshness and freedom of the English countryside. Or does he?

> When daffodils begin to peer,
> With heigh the doxy over the dale,
> Why, then comes in the sweet o' the year,
> For the red blood reigns in the winter's pale.

As so often in Shakespeare, the effect is never single or simple. The sense of the open country is certainly there, but so also is another note, suggested by the second line. The words 'heigh the doxy over the dale' are usually explained as referring to the vagrant's mistress (doxy) coming over field or valley. But 'dale' was often written as 'dell' and a 'dell' was Elizabethan rogues' cant for a beggar's wench who had not yet matured into a doxy. In the words of Thomas Harman, one of the earliest and best-informed inquirers into the subject, 'A dell is a young wench, able for generation, and not yet known or broken by the upright man.' It is possible, therefore, that Autolycus is not merely singing about a young man's fancy but stating a preference for the mature 'doxy' over the inexperienced 'dell'. Certainly it would be more in keeping with his character and background. For Autolycus and all his quality comprise a ragged and motley band whose names in their own private tongue are as variously fascinating as their tricks and trades – patriarchos, palliards and priggers of prancers, autem-morts and walking morts, fraters, Abraham men and rufflers, nipping, foisting and crossbiting – the list is all but endless. Where did they come from and whither were they bound? And above all what could honest law-abiding citizens, men of rank and substance who had everything handsome about them do to protect themselves from the unscrupulous activities of this vast army of wandering parasites? These questions, and especially the last, were asked with increasing urgency during the reign of the first Elizabeth.

*

Tudor observers as well as modern historians are agreed that the problem of the idle poor was one of the most acute and widespread in the sixteenth and early seventeenth centuries. 'The most immediate and pressing concern of government ... for something more than a century (1520–1640) was the problem of vagrancy.' [1] Writing in the fifteen-seventies, William Harrison in his *Description of England* tells us that:

> It is not yet full threescore years since this trade began: but how it hath prospered since that time it is easy to judge, for they are now supposed, of one sex and another, to amount unto above ten thousand persons, as I have heard reported.

Harrison's remark places the source of the troubles at the beginning of the sixteenth century, but hindsight makes it clear that the roots of the problem go back well beyond that. Perhaps the decisive impetus was provided by the havoc caused within the body politic by the Wars of the Roses; at any rate Harrison is right to the extent that the opening years of the sixteenth century saw vagabondage as a constant feature of social life all over England, though particularly in the larger towns.

Writers of the period tried, not always successfully, to draw a clear line between the deserving and the undeserving poor. The aged, the blind, the lame and the sick, as well as orphans and those wounded in war, were recognized to be the responsibility of the more fortunate members of the community, though it is fair to say that it was a responsibility acknowledged oftener than it was discharged. On the other side of the dividing line, beyond the pale of any but the most enlightened observer's compassion, were the 'sturdy beggars', those who seemed to suffer from no obvious physical or other handicap and who seemed to have joined the ranks of beggary simply because it seemed to offer a soft and easy

1. Jordan, W. K., *Philanthropy in England*, 1959, p. 78.

life. The complaints directed against these are almost indistinguishable in tone and content from present-day objections to those who live off the social security services at the expense of the hard-working taxpayer; however well-founded or otherwise the Elizabethan criticisms of able-bodied vagrants may have been, one thing will be clear to the reader before he has gone through many pages of this volume: the life of the sturdy beggar may not have been work in the nine-to-five sense but by no stretch of the imagination could it be described as soft and easy. This was not because the apparatus of law enforcement was efficient or even adequate (Dogberry and his fellows are, incredibly, typical) but because it was haphazard, arbitrary and brutal. Though only heretics were burned alive and boiling to death had been abolished even for poisoners, this still left open a wide repertory of penalties which included branding, burning through the ears, whipping, and of course, hanging.

The vast majority of sturdy beggars may (as Marx believed) have been recruited from the ranks of discharged serving-men and ex-soldiers. Henry VII's campaign to abolish private armies had been successful enough to swell the bands of the unemployed with 'masterless men' from many noble households, men who often had as much experience in arms as soldiers who had seen active service. Together, these two groups formed the most potentially dangerous class of vagrants. The discharged soldier was a common figure in earlier periods, but he seems to be better organized and his activities more widespread at this time. Thus, on a celebrated occasion, soldiers returning from Drake's unsuccessful expedition against Portugal in 1589 arrived in London at the time of the great Bartholomew Fair, causing a panic in the streets which did not wholly die down for six months. Perhaps the fact that soldiers were often ill-paid or not paid at all and allowed only their arms and uniform on discharge had something to do with their tendency to turn to vagabondage and armed robbery as a way of life, though demobilization was the cause of particular crises rather than a permanent element in the situation. As for discharged retainers, it is difficult to see what else they could do to keep alive but take to the open road and rely on their wits in a society where the population was expanding much faster than opportunities for employment. For in the hundred years before the end of Elizabeth's reign it is probable that the population increased by nearly half as much again.

Other recruits to the ever-growing army of the homeless came from poorer servants of the state whose livelihood often depended on the favour of a rich patron who was himself liable to be blown down by the winds of political change, and young gentlemen up from the country who had little difficulty in squandering in months what it may have taken generations to accumulate (a recurrent theme in contemporary drama). There was also a large number of poorer tenants turned out of their holdings either by forcible eviction or by inability to pay increased rents; these were imposed by landowners, either to keep up with inflation or to encourage tenants to quit arable land which could then be used for more profitable purposes, such as cattle-breeding.

By the time the first of the writers represented in this collection begins to set down his observations, vagrancy has become an established feature of the social landscape; so much so that we must count among the sources of supply those who are to the manner born, sons and daughters of vagrants most of whom follow in their parents' footsteps either by necessity or inclination. Perhaps, too, the dissolution of the monasteries contributed its own share to the vagrant population, though it is unlikely that many monks became vagrants themselves as most of them had pensions. Nor, in all probability, did the cessation of monastic charity make a great deal of difference, as it had been random and intermittent at the best of times. The real sufferers from the Dissolution were the large numbers of servants, butchers, bakers, gardeners and the like who were thrown out of jobs when the monasteries were dissolved.

These, then, were the tributary streams which fed the ever-widening river of Elizabethan vagrancy until, if we are to believe most of the writers of the time, its flood-tide threatened to engulf civilized life altogether. The measures which the authorities took to protect the established order from this ragged throng do not directly concern us; they range from penal laws of imaginative savagery to a grudging recognition, first at parish and later at national level, that the poor are always with us, and that some-

thing more would have to be done with them by way of reliev-
ing their condition than chopping off their hands or burning
their ears. The reader will get more than a glimpse of how these
measures worked in practice and will be able to form his own
judgement of their efficacy. What I shall try to do here is to out-
line briefly those measures which the dispossessed took to or-
ganize and protect themselves against the forces of law and order.

*

Elizabethan society had its own equivalent of the welfare state.
If one had a definite and recognized place in the complicated
hierarchical system, life could be reasonably secure and comfortable. Thus the wife was assured of food, clothing, shelter and a
place in the community as long as her husband was alive. But if
he died without making adequate provision for her she risked
passing into the limbo of widowhood, her place in society unde-
fined or defined only (if she had private means) by her being the
target of fortune-hunters. Again, the elder son came under the
shade of the welfare umbrella while the younger might not. An
actor could sleep at night, warm in the protection of the patron
whose livery he wore; without that protection he was no better
than a vagrant. A skilled craftsman normally had the strength of
his craft guild behind him; if he did not, all his skill would not
serve to get him a secure livelihood. Even a poor beggar was entitled to charity if he lived in his own parish; if not what charity
he got could be very cold indeed. At every point the line between
those inside and those outside the social establishment was clear
and crucial.

The mass of rogues and vagabonds I have referred to earlier was
by definition outside the social pale. They were treated by the
parishes only as nuisances to be got rid of as speedily as possible.
Seen through the disapproving eyes of respectable citizens they
were nothing but a disorderly and disorganized rabble, dropouts
from the social ladder. But seen from within, they appear to be
like nothing so much as a mirror-image of the Elizabethan world-
picture: a little world, tightly organized into its own ranks and
with its own rules, as rigid in its own way as the most elaborate
protocol at court or ritual in church. Thus Thomas Harman, in

a memorable spasm of alliteration, refers to 'these rowsey, ragged rabblement of rakehells' and hopes piously that as a result of the revelations made in his treatise,

the honourable will abhor them, the worshipful will reject them, the yeomen will sharply taunt them, the husbandmen utterly defy them, the labouring men bluntly chide them, the women with a loud exclamation wonder at them, and all children with clapping hands cry out at them.

The very arrangement of the clauses, moving from passive abhorrence to open mockery, here represents the protest of all classes in organized and respectable society against the ragged mob. But what makes Harman's little tract so interesting is that much of it is based on first-hand conversations with such vagrants as passed by his door when he was confined to his house by illness. As a country magistrate in Kent he came into official contact with many rogues and vagabonds; but his book is based on inside information and incidentally, as the reader will soon see, became a rich hunting ground for later writers on roguery (Robert Greene included). And reading through Harman's elaborate and painstaking lists of the vagabonds and their ways, we become aware of a society, a community with its rules and ranks, aspirations and taboos. Thus, as soon as Harman begins to classify the various types of sturdy beggar, he recognizes a certain hierarchical pattern. 'The ruffler, because he is first in degree of this odious order ... he shall be first placed, as the worthiest of this unruly rabblement.' And he goes on to describe the privileges of the 'upright men' in terms which imply a generally acknowledged pecking order:

These upright men will seldom or never want; for what is gotten by any mort, or doxy, if it please him, he doth command the same. And if he meet any beggar, whether he be sturdy or impotent, he will demand of him, whether ever he was stalled to the rogue [i.e. formally initiated] or no. If he say he was, he will know of whom, and his name that stalled him.

To return to Autolycus, we see now that he is relatively small fry:

My revenue is the silly cheat [i.e. petty theft]. Gallows and knock are too powerful on the highway. Beating and hanging are terrors to me.

Indeed, so far is he from being one of the élite of the thieving classes that he even resorts to the more or less honest practice of selling ballads and ribbons. In Harman's classification, Autolycus is merely a swadder, almost the humblest of the male vagrants, a long way behind in the lordly procession of rufflers, upright men and fraters.

To some extent, no doubt, this impression of an ordered anti-social society comes to us as a result of the Elizabethan passion for classifying everything into groups and classes. Thus the second section of Awdeley's *Fraternity of Vagabonds*, entitled 'A Quarterne of Knaves', appears to owe more to imagination than observation. Its elaborate catalogue of the different types of (bad) servant is nicely compounded of implausibility and artificiality:

Munch-Present is he that is a great gentleman, for when his master sendeth him with a present, he will take a taste thereof by the way. This is a bold knave, that sometime will eat the best and leave the worst for his master.

And a bare ten years after Greene's pamphlets Samuel Row-lands, in *Green's Ghost Haunting Cony-Catchers* (1602), takes leave no doubt whether the barnard's law, so painstakingly set forth in *A Notable Discovery of Cozenage*, ever had any basis in fact. But when every allowance has been made for contemporary habits of mind it is difficult to believe that the hierarchies of rogues and vagrants mentioned by Harman and others are merely figments of incensed imaginations. Rather they suggest a degree of professionalism and organization in the ranks of the outsiders which may have been the minimum condition for survival.

The very first of the commentators represented here puts the point cogently:

And hereof it riseth that, like as law, when the term is truly con-sidered, signifieth an ordinance of good men established for the com-monwealth to repress all vicious living, so these cheaters turned the cat in the pan, giving to divers vile patching shifts an honest and godly title, calling it by the name of a law; because, by a multitude of hateful rules, a multitude of dregs and draff (as it were all good learning) govern and rule their idle bodies, to the destruction of the good labouring people.

Gilbert Walker is here satisfied that the anti-commonwealth can exist only to the detriment of ordinary folk, but a little later in his tract he puts into the mouth of one of his villains words which were to be echoed and re-echoed in the literature of roguery, and which suggest a quite different relationship between civil society and those who threatened it:

Though your experience in the world be not so great as mine, yet am I sure ye see that no man is able to live an honest man unless he have some privy way to help himself withal, more than the world is witness of. Think you the noblemen could do as they do, if in this hard world they should maintain so great a port only upon their rent? Think you the lawyers could be such purchasers [i.e. of land] if their pleas were short, and all their judgements, justice and conscience? Suppose ye that offices would be so dearly bought, and the buyers so soon enriched, if they counted not pillage an honest point of purchase? Could merchants, without lies, false making their wares, and selling them by a crooked light, to deceive the chapman in the thread or colour, grow so soon rich and to a baron's possessions, and make all their posterity gentlemen? What will ye more? Whoso hath not some anchorward way to help himself, but followeth his nose, as they say, always straight forward, may well hold up the head for a year or two, but the third he must needs sink and gather the wind into beggars' haven.

This uncertainty of attitude as to whether rogues and vagrants are a threat to society (the orthodox view) or whether they reflect at a higher temperature the disorders of society runs right through to Greene, where it finds expression in a definite tendency to glamorize the rogue and the con-man, forgetting the pious moralizings of the opening address to the reader. More than once we are reminded of Brecht's question: 'What is the crime of burgling a bank compared to the crime of building one?'

Perhaps the uncertainty stems from an uneasy awareness – in Greene at any rate – that the writer himself is in a position in society not dissimilar to that of the Elizabethan vagrant. This is the point at which the professional writer is emerging as a distinct and recognizable figure in English society. The older system of patronage by the nobility is beginning to crack under the strain of inflation and an excess of demand over supply. Only a few, such as Samuel Daniel, were lucky enough to obtain a more or less permanent position in a great household. On the other hand, the writer as a fully-fledged professional able to negotiate for himself with publishers and booksellers was still a figure in the distant future. Many writers carried on the fiction of being Renaissance gentlemen practising the craft of letters not for gain but as one of many accomplishments of the gentleman-amateur, but the real situation was far otherwise. Like the vagrant, the writer too was a masterless man. (Shakespeare was able to retire to Stratford and buy the biggest house in the town not because he was a successful writer, but because he was a shareholder in the most popular theatrical company of his day.) Like the confidence trickster, the writer relied entirely on his wits. Neither had the protection of a craft guild. And perhaps we may add that both were graduating into professionalism at about the same time. The point is not lost on 'Cuthbert Cony-Catcher' who in *The Defence of Cony-Catching* accuses Robert Greene of being no better than the tricksters whom he affects to despise (and if, as is possible, Greene and 'Cuthbert Cony-Catcher' are one and the same, the situation takes on added piquancy):

But now sir by your leave a little, what if I should prove you a cony-catcher, Master R.G., would it not make you blush at the matter? I'll go as near to it as the friar did to his hostess's maid, when the clerk of the parish took him at Leatem at midnight. Ask the Queen's Players, if you sold them not Orlando Furioso for twenty nobles, and when they were in the country, sold the same play to the Lord Admiral's men for as much more. Was not this plain cony-catching, Master R.G.?

Everything we know about the Elizabethan writer at this time suggests that this incident is typical not only of Greene himself but of many of his fellows. Perhaps in the Protean figure of the confidence trickster, ever ready to change his personality and his part to suit the present situation, protected by no one and depending only on his wit and address for his livelihood, the Elizabethan hack uneasily saluted his double.

A high degree of professional organization implies not only a considerable amount of internal discipline but some tradition of apprenticeship and training. Not the least fascinating aspect of these pamphlets is the insight they give us into the methods used by the older craftsmen to transmit their skill and experience to the younger generation. Again, it is not fanciful to see a distorted mirror-image of the Elizabethan system of masters and prentices. We hear of a veteran cutpurse showing his protégé how a near-impossible piece of pocket-picking is done (p. 215); there is evidence of the need to be formally initiated as a fully fledged villain ('stalled to the rogue'); there is also a record (not reproduced here) of a school for pick-pockets that seems to have anticipated Fagin by several centuries.[2] And more than once we hear the note of professional pride, the craftsman's satisfaction in being master of his mystery:

I promise you, I disdain these base and petty paltries, and, may my fortune jump with my resolution, ye shall hear, my boys, within a day or two, that I will accomplish a rare stratagem indeed, of more value than forty of yours, and when it is done shall carry some credit with it.

This sense of a common bond between writer and rogue affects not only the tone of the various tracts but the presentation of their content. In the case of Walker (if it was indeed Walker who wrote *A Manifest Detection of Dice-Play*) the intention and the presentation are alike straightforward. The author sincerely wishes to warn possible victims of the wiles of city swindlers, and the naïvely handled device of the dialogue enables him to set forth the various tricks in their clearest forms. He even prefaces the text with a glossary of technical terms relating to different varieties of false dice. The justification of the cheater quoted earlier – namely that it is by cheating in all walks of life that the commonwealth flourishes – while undeniably eloquent, goes very much against the general tenor of the tract, which is clearly hostile to the swindling classes. When we turn to Awdeley, on the other hand, the simple relish for cataloguing appears to be the dominant motive, at least in the first section devoted to rogues and vagabonds. (Indeed, Awdeley's moral disapprobation is much more severe in the second part, dealing with varieties of idle servant.) As he states, in verse which anticipates the real McGonigall:

2. Tawney and Power, eds., *Tudor Economic Documents* II, pp. 337–8.

> He did declare as here is read,
> Both names and states of most and least,
> Of this their vagabonds' brotherhood.
> Which at the request of a worshipful man
> I have set it forth as well as I can.

The absence of moral censure where we (and even more the Elizabethan reader) would expect it constitutes in itself a step towards sympathy for the vagrant. Another sign of this incipient sympathy is the obvious relish with which the author narrates some of the stories which illustrate the wiles of Elizabethan rogues. (See, for instance, the account of the ring-faller, p. 70). In *A Caveat for Common Cursitors*, classification is no longer mere classification. The didactic intention is made clear not only in the elaborate dedicatory letter to a noble lady (itself a finely judged rhetorical manoeuvre to reinforce the intention of the tract), but also continuously in the terms in which Harman conducts his cataloguing. A single example may serve for many:

A upright man, the second in sect of this unseemly sort, must be next placed, of these ranging rabblement of rascals; some be servingmen, artificers, and labouring men traded up in husbandry. These, not minding to get their living with the sweat of their face, but casting off all pain, will wander, after their wicked manner, through the most shires of this realm.

The honest gentleman's scorn for the idle layabout is evident in almost every phrase of this passage. Harman is at least as anxious to tell us what he thinks of these good-for-nothings as he is to identify them. And this is certainly the note that is struck loudest and most often in his work. The anecdotes he recounts, even when they tell of near-farcical events (as in the walking mort's story, p. 129) never stray far from their moralizing objective. In the question which Harman asks the walking mort at the end of the story we can hear the tight-lipped moralist as well as the curious social investigator: ' "It was prettily handled," quoth I. "And is here all?" ' and the first is even more prominent in the conclusion to an earlier tale: ' "Well" quoth I, "thank God of all, and repair home into thy native country." ' But even Harman cannot quite suppress a sort of interest in the life-style of the vagrant almost for its own sake – which is as near to sympathetic identification as the worthy country gentleman ever gets. We see this in the snatch of dialogue in rogues' cant which comes almost at the end of the tract. The utilitarian value of this contrivance was surely minimal, since it is unlikely that two vagrants would talk to each other at length in their own argot where others could overhear them, the penalties for vagrancy being what they were. But Harman the social moralist has here succumbed to Harman the proto-novelist. The characters and their talk have taken hold of his imagination, so much so that in his translation he seems to make a curious error. At one point in the dialogue, the upright man says 'Yonder dwelleth a queer cuffin. It were beneship to mill him' which Harman renders as 'Yonder dwelleth a hoggish and churlish man. It were very well done to rob him.' Now 'queer' in thieves' cant did mean 'worthless' and 'cuffin' meant 'fellow'. But together 'queer cuffin' meant a 'Justice of the Peace' and the context almost certainly seems to require this sense here. But from the speaker's point of view a J.P. would be 'a hoggish and churlish man'. Harman's mistake, if that is what it is, seems to be a sign of a sympathy which goes below the author's conscious intention.

It is only with Greene's work, however, that sympathy for his subjects and identification with their activities threaten almost to make nonsense of the high-minded moral purpose which Greene frequently affects (the sincerity of which is often called into question when we realize that many of these moral sentiments are lifted more or less verbatim from Walker and Harman). We may note, for instance, the contrast between Greene's didactic protestations and the constant references to the stories he tells as 'merry jests' and 'pleasant tales'. Even allowing for some change in the connotation of the two epithets since Greene's day, it is clear that his interest is not single-mindedly on the edifying aspect of the narrative. And this becomes even clearer when we turn to the tales themselves. For example, the various escapades of Ned Browne (an early wife-swapper) are recorded in *The Black Book's Messenger* with something not very far from admiration. The very device of having Ned himself tell the story enables Greene to have the best of both worlds – to adopt a tone of admiration for the adventures and at the same time to take refuge behind the persona of his hero:

> If you think, Gentlemen, to hear a repentent man speak, or to tell a large tale of his penitent sorrows, ye are deceived. For as I have ever lived lewdly, so I mean to end my life as resolutely, and not by a cowardly confession to attempt the hope of a pardon. Yet, in that I was famous in my life for my villainies, I will at my death profess myself as notable, by discoursing to you all merrily the manner and method of my knaveries, which, if you hear without laughing, then after my death call me base knave, and never have me in remembrance.

Whether, as he claims, Greene had first-hand experience of the rogues he describes is less important than the obvious sympathy he has for them. Nothing in *The Black Book's Messenger* rings as false as Ned Browne's final confession, when he tries to squeeze a conventional moral lesson out of the misdeeds he has been recounting with such evident enthusiasm in the rest of the book. It is as if Ned (and Greene) were suddenly remembering, before it was too late, the moral purpose which was supposed to be the *raison d'être* of the whole work:

> 'Scorn not labour, Gentlemen, nor hold not any course of life bad or servile, that is profitable and honest, lest in giving yourselves over to idleness, and having no yearly maintenance, you fall into many prejudicial mischiefs ... And so, Lord, into thy hands I commit my spirit.' – And with that he himself sprung out at the window and died.

As well he might, the reader may feel. The final leap is much more in keeping with the rest of his dramatic existence than the pious rodomontade which precedes it.

Considered from this standpoint *The Defence of Cony-Catching* is the next logical step in the identification between the author and his subjects. The element of justification – cony-catching seen as a more honest because less hypocritical expression of the underlying basis of all social activity – which was an isolated and often unassimilated feature in earlier tracts now becomes the core of the work. The fully-fledged anti-hero is born. We no longer have to read between the lines to feel the author's sympathy for the villains and his contempt for the victims; it speaks to us in every line:

Thus have I proved to your masterships, how there is no estate, trade, occupation, nor mystery, but lives by cony-catching, and that our shift at cards, compared to the rest, is the simplest of all, and yet forsooth, you could bestow the pains to write two whole pamphlets against us poor cony-catchers.

The wheel is come full circle when the writer goes on to point out that it is the guardians of law and order who are the only begetters of all kinds of cozenage,

for the occasion of most mischief, of greatest nipping and foisting, and of all villainies, comes through the extorting bribery of some cozening and counterfeit keepers and companions [i.e. jailers and law officers] that carry unlawful warrants about them to take up men.

All that is needed is a public acknowledgement by the forces of orthodoxy that those who are outside the pale of society are not only as good, but indeed better men than they; and this is provided by the solemnly hilarious sermon which concludes this volume in which Parson Haberdyne, whom God preserve, undertakes to prove that thieves are the only true Christians, a paradox which would have delighted John Donne himself.

*

The reader who is familiar with Elizabethan and Jacobean drama, particularly the 'city comedies' of the period, will have no difficulty in recognizing in the pages that follow the real-life counterparts of many of the characters in Jonson, Middleton, Massinger and many lesser dramatists – from more or less earth-bound figures such as Touchwood, Tapwell and Cocledemoy to such supreme spirits as Face and Subtle, not forgetting Auto-lycus himself. On the other hand, the reader who knows some-thing of the beginnings of the English novel in Defoe and Fielding will see how closely some of these pamphlets anticipate the early novel – so closely, indeed, as to raise the question why the fully-fledged novel wasn't born a century earlier than it was. I have deliberately left these two points to the end and shall do no more than mention them even now. This is partly because they

have been fully discussed elsewhere – in Ernest Barker's volu-
minous history of the novel, for instance, and in Walter Raleigh's
shorter study, as well as in the appropriate volumes of the *Cambridge History of English Literature*. But my chief reason for
not stressing the matter of the historical importance of these
writings or their influence is that I want to place the emphasis
squarely where I believe it ought to be put – namely on the
intrinsic richness and variety of these tracts, not simply as documents of a fascinating segment of society at a fascinating moment
of English history but also as works of considerable literary
accomplishment. Where Greene is concerned, the case no longer
needs arguing. His skill in the delineation of character, the
creation of dramatic suspense and the maintaining of narrative
pace has long been recognized. But, as the reader will see for himself, the earlier and lesser-known writers from whom Greene took
so much are by no means despicable. The naïvest of them,
Awdeley, has a crispness of phrase and an eye for detail that
sparks his catalogue into life over and over again:

An Abraham man is he that walketh bare-armed, and bare-legged,
and feigneth himself mad, and carrieth a pack of wool, or a stick
with bacon on it, or suchlike toy, and nameth himself Poor Tom.

As for Walker, he has a sharp ear for contemporary speech and a
sense of narrative tempo which often puts us in mind of Greene
himself; see, for example, the opening story of the encounter in
St Paul's. Harman's great strength comes from his determination
to be scrupulously accurate and to document each of his exhibits
as fully as possible. His work has the vividness and impact of a
first-rate documentary, and, as a first-rate documentary should,
has a well-defined point of view. As for Parson Haberdyne's sermon, its distinctive flavour and sparkle need no bush: Swift
would have been proud of it.

Taken as a whole, this collection portrays a society within a
society, or rather outside it, an anti-society with its own rules
and rulers. The dominant orthodox attitude to this anti-society
is hostility springing from fear, the fear of rebellion which is the
ground bass of all Elizabethan thinking on social and political
questions and which runs through Shakespeare's history plays.

But we can also see the emergence of another attitude, compounded of defiance for established society and sympathy for those outside it. I have tried to suggest that in part this sympathy stemmed from an awareness of a similar position in society occupied by the writer and the rogue. I shall end by firmly resisting the temptation to draw modern parallels, reminding the reader that he need not, of course, impose any such self-denying ordinance on himself.

GĀMINI SALGĀDO

University of Sussex
September 1971

A NOTE ON THE TEXTS

1. *A Manifest Detection of Dice-Play*: As many as three editions of this pamphlet may have been published about 1552. My text is based on the Bodleian Library copy.

2. *The Fraternity of Vagabonds*: First published in 1561 by John Awdeley who was probably the author. The text is based on the Bodleian Library copy (1575) and I have consulted the version in Furnivall's *Rogues and Vagabonds of Shakespeare's Youth* (1880); Furnivall also used the 1575 Bodleian text.

3. *A Caveat for Common Cursitors*: First published in 1566, two more editions of this tract appeared two years later. The edition of 1592 was called *The Groundwork of Cony-Catching*. The first edition is unknown. I have used the British Museum copy of the third edition, which I have checked against Furnivall's reprint.

4. *A Notable Discovery of Cozenage*: The text is based on the British Museum copy of the 1591 edition which I have checked against the facsimile reprint in the Bodley Head Quarto series edited by G. B. Harrison.

5. *The Second Part of Cony-Catching*: The text is based on the Bodleian Library copy of the second edition (1592) which I have checked against the Bodley Head Quarto reprint.

6. *The Third and Last Part of Cony-Catching*: The one known edition appeared in 1592. My text is based on the Bodleian Library copy, checked against the Bodley Head Quarto reprint.

7. *A Disputation*: Text is based on the Bodleian Library copy (1592) checked against the Bodley Head Quarto reprint.

8. *The Black Book's Messenger*: Text is based on the Bodleian Library copy (1592) checked against the Bodley Head Quarto reprint.

9. *The Defence of Cony-Catching*: Text is based on the British Museum copy (1592). I have followed the Bodley Head Quarto reprint in restoring the original *Address*, not found in the British Museum copy but present in the Huntington Library copy.

10. *Parson Haberdyne's Sermon*: The text is based on Furnivall's reprint of the Cotton MS version in *Rogues and Vagabonds of Shakespeare's Youth*. There is a slightly different version in the Lansdowne MS (98, leaf 210), also reprinted by Furnivall.

*

A NOTE ON THE TEXTS

Spelling and punctuation have been conservatively modernized, though a very few Elizabethan spellings of special interest have been retained. Square brackets indicate editorial emendation, usually mentioned in the notes. Like everyone else who has worked on this subject recently, I am indebted to A. V. Judges's *The Elizabethan Underworld*, which I have consulted continuously, and to the invaluable Bodley Head Quartos. I am also indebted to my colleague Michael Hawkins for saving me from many historical blunders. Any that remain are my own. Grateful thanks to Janet Cohen and Roger Moss for help with proof-reading, and to my colleague Stephen Medcalf for tracking down some classical allusions.

G.S.

❡ A manifest de-
tection of the moste vyle and detestable
vse of Diceplay, and other practises lyke
the same. a Myrrour very necessary for
all yonge Gentilmen & others sodenly
enabled by worldly abudace,
to loke in. Newly set forth
for their behoufe.

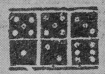 

❡ Democritus.

Si ie ris vous estes plus folz que ne ries
be me veoir rire
De vous et de voz actes sont plus que mon
rire plus dire
Tant ilya a vous redire et aulx plus sages
de vous tous.
Qui est piene sol qui ne rit de vous.

❡ Fortune vient a point.

GENTLE READER, when you shall read this book, devised as a mean to show and set forth such naughty practices as hath been, and be peradventure yet used in houses of dice-play, think it not to be written in dispraise of offence of the honest, but for that, under colour and cloak of friendship, many young gentlemen be drawn to their undoing. And to the intent that such as have not yet fed of that sour-sweet or hungry bait (wherewith they at length unawares be choked), shall learn, not only to avoid the danger thereof by knowing their mischievous and most subtle practice in getting a prey to spoil the same; but shall also by mean thereof see, as it were in a glass, the miserable ends that a sort of handsome gentlemen hath by this crafty and subtle device come to, imputing, for want of knowledge, their cause of misery to ill fortune. Thus, having in a few words showed the effect of that which the book shall declare with some more circumstance, I bid you farewell.

The Names of [the] Dice

A bale of barred cinque-deuces.
A bale of flat cinque-deuces.
A bale of flat sice-aces.
A bale of barred sice-aces.
A bale of barred cater-treys.
A bale of flat cater-treys.
A bale of fullans of the best making.
A bale of light graviers.
A bale of langrets contrary to the vantage.
A bale of gourds with as many high men as low men for passage.
A bale of demies.
A bale of long dice for even and odd.
A bale of bristles.
A bale of direct contraries.

Interlocutors: R. and M.

R. speaketh:
Haply as I roamed me in the church of Paul's now twenty days
ago, looking for certain my companions that hither might have
stalled a meeting, there walked up and down by me in the body
of the church a gentleman, fair dressed in silks, gold, and jewels,
with three or four servants in gay liveries all 'broidered with
sundry colours, attending upon him. I advised him well, as one
that pleased me much for his proper personage, and more for the
wearing of his gear, and he again, at each check made in our
walking, cast earnest looks upon me, not such as by his hollow
frownings and piercing aspect might pretend any malice or disdain, but rather should signify by his cheerful countenance that
he noted in me something that liked him well, and could be content to take some occasion to embrace mine acquaintance. Anon,

advised: observed.

30

while I devised with myself what means I might make to understand his behaviour, and what sort he was of – for man's nature,
as ye know, is in those things curious, specially in such as profess
courting – he humbled himself far beneath my expectation, and
began to speak first after this manner:

'Sir, it seemeth to me that we have both one errand hither, for
I have marked you well now more than half an hour, stalking up
and down alone without any company, sometime with such heavy
and uncheerful countenance as if ye had some hammers working
in your head, and that breach of company had moved your
patience. And I, for my part, what face soever I set on the matter,
am not all in quiet; for had all promises been kept, I should, or
this hour, have seen a good piece of money told here upon the
front, and as many indentures, obligations and other writings
sealed, as cost me twice forty shillings for the drawing and
counsel. But as to me, let them that be a-cold blow the coals, for
I am already on the sure side, and if I miss of my hold this way, I
doubt not to pinch them as near by another shift; though indeed
I must confess that unkindness and breach of promise is so much
against my nature that nothing can offend me more. And you,
on the other side, if your grief in tarrying be the same that I take
it, ye cannot do better than to make little of the matter, for ye
seem to be a man that wadeth not so unadvisedly in the deep but
that always ye be sure of an anchorhold. And therefore let us by
mine advice forget such idle griefs, and while noontide draweth
on, talk of other matters that may quicken our spirits to make a
merry dinner. Perchance this occasion may confirm a joyful
acquaintance between us.'

'Sir,' quoth I, 'as touching the cause of my long abiding here,
it is not very great, neither is it tied to any such thrift as ye speak
of, but lack of company will soon lead a man into a brown study.'

'Well then,' quoth he, 'if your head be fraught with no heavier
burden, it is an easy matter to lighten your load, for a little
grief is soon forgotten. But I pray you, sir, 'long ye not to the
Court? Methinks I have seen you ere now, and cannot call it
home where it should be.'

or this hour: before (ere) this hour.
'long: belong.

M. A good workman, by St Mary! Now do I easily foresee, without any instruction further, whereto this matter tendeth. But yet tell what further talk had ye?

R. I told him I was yet but a raw courtier, as one that came from school not many months afore, and was now become servant to my Lord Chancellor of England; partly to see experience of things, the better to govern myself hereafter; and, chiefly, to have a staff to lean unto to defend mine own. And he again commended me much therein, declaring how divers notable persons, rashly by ignorance misguiding themselves, were suddenly shaken asunder, and fallen on the rocks of extreme penury; and how some other, even goodly wits, circumspectly working in all their doings, have by want of such a leaning-stock, been overthrown with tyrants' power. 'For which cause,' quoth he, 'like as I cannot but praise your wary working in this your first courting, so for my lord your master's sake you shall not lack the best that I may do for you. For, albeit that I am much beholden to all the Lords of the Council, as [one] whom they stick not at all times to take to their board, and use sometime for a companion at play, yet is he my singular good lord above all the rest. And, if I shall confess the truth, a great part of my living hath risen by his friendly preferment. And, though I say it myself, I am too old a courtier, and have seen too much to bear nothing away; and, in case our acquaintance hold, and by daily company gather deep root, I shall now and then show you a lesson worth the learning; and to th'end hereafter each of us may be the bolder of the other, I pray you, if ye be not otherwise bespoken, take a capon with me at dinner. Though your fare be but homely and scant, yet a cup of good wine I can promise you, and all other lacks shall be supplied with a friendly welcome.'

'I thank you, sir,' quoth I. 'Ye offer me more gentleness than I can deserve; but, since I have tarried all this while, I will abide the last hour, to prove how well my companions will hold their appointment; and for that cause, I will forbear to trouble you till another time.'

'Nay, not so,' quoth he. 'Yet had I rather spend twenty pounds than that my lord your master should know but that the worst

prove: test.

groom of his stable is as dear to me as any kinsman I have. And therefore, lay all excuses aside, and shape yourself to keep me company for one dinner, while your man and mine shall walk here together till twelve of the clock; and, if your friends happen to come hither, he shall bring them home to us. I love to see gentlemen swarm and cleave together like burrs.'

M. How then? Went ye home together?

R. What else? Would ye have me forsake so gentle a friend, and so necessary acquaintance?

M. Go to. Say on. Lo, how gentle lambs are led to the slaughter-man's fold! How soon reckless youth falleth in snare of crafty dealing!

R. Soon after, we came home to his house. The table was fair spread with diaper cloths, the cupboard garnished with much goodly plate. And last of all came forth the gentlewoman his wife, clothed in silks and embroidered works; the attire of her head 'broidered with gold and pearl; a carcanet about her neck, agreeable thereto, with a flower of diamonds pendant thereat, and many fair rings on her fingers. 'Bess,' quoth he, 'bid this gentleman welcome.' And with that she courteously kissed me; and, after, moved communication of my name, my natural country, what time my father died, and whether I were married yet or not, always powdering our talk with such pretty devices, that I saw not a woman in all my life whose fashions and entertainment I liked better.

The goodman, in the mean season, had been in the kitchen, and suddenly returning, and breaking our talk, somewhat sharply blamed his wife that the dinner was no further forward. And while she withdrew her from us, belike to put things in a good readiness, 'Come on,' quoth he, 'you shall see my house the while. It is not like your large country houses. Rooms, ye wot, in London be strait, but yet the furniture of them is costly enough; and victuals be here at such high prices, that much money is soon consumed, specially with them that maintain an idle household. Nevertheless, assure yourself that no man is welcomer than you

natural country: native county.
strait: small.

33

to such cheer as ye find.' And, consequently, bringing me through divers well-trimmed chambers, the worst of them apparelled with verdures, some with rich cloth of Arras, all with beds, chairs and cushions of silk and gold, of sundry colours, suitably wrought, 'Lo here,' quoth he, 'a poor man's lodging; which if ye think it may do you any pleasure – for the inns of London be the worst of England – take your choice, and heartily welcome, reserving but one for my lord my wife's cousin, whom I dare not disappoint, lest haply he should lour, and make the house too hot for us.'

I gave him thanks, as meet it was I should, neither yet refusing his gentle offer – for, indeed, mine own lodging is somewhat loathsome, and pestered with company – nor yet embracing it, because hitherto I had not by any means deserved so great a pleasure.

So down we came again into the parlour, and found there divers gentlemen, all strangers to me. And what should I say more, but to dinner we went.

M. Let me hear, then, what matters were moved at dinner-time, and how ye passed the afternoon till the company brake up and sundered themselves.

R. That can I readily tell you. I have not yet forgotten it, since done it was so late. As touching our fare, though partridge and quail were no dainties, and wines of sundry grapes flowed abundantly, yet spare I to speak thereto, because ye have demanded a contrary question. So soon as we had well victualled ourselves, I wot not how, but easily it came to pass that we talked of news, namely, of Boulogne,[1] how hardly it was won, what policy then was practised to get it, and what case the soldiers had in the siege of it, insomuch that the least progress the king maketh into the inland parts of the realm, dislodgeth more of his train, and leaveth them to their own provision, with less relief of victuals than had the worst unwaged adventurer there. From this the goodman led us to talk of home pleasures, enlarging the beauties of peace and London pastimes, and made so jolly a discourse thereof, that to my judgement he seemed skilful in all things.

consequently: afterwards.
unwaged: unpaid.

'Methinks,' quoth he, 'such simple fare as this, taken in peace, without fear and danger of gunshot, is better than a prince's purveyance in war, where each morsel he eateth shall bring with it a present fear of sudden mischance or violent hostility. And though that in the open camp none might have more familiar access to the nobility than here at home, yet, for my part, I thank God, I have no cause to complain either, because of their gentleness; no usher keeps the door between me and them when I come to visit them, or that the greatest princes refuse not sometimes to hallow my poor table and house with their person; which – be it spoken without boast, or imbraiding – doth sometime cost me twenty pounds a day. I am sure that some of this company do remember what a brave company of lords supped with me the last term, and I think how ye have heard how some of them got an hundred pounds or two by their coming.'

With this and that like talk, consumed was our dinner. And, after the table was removed, in came one of the waiters with a fair silver bowl, full of dice and cards.

'Now masters,' quoth the goodman, 'who is so disposed, fall to. Here is my twenty pounds. Win it and wear it.'

Then each man chose his game. Some kept the goodman company at the hazard, some matched themselves at a new game called 'primero'.

M. And what did you the while?

R. They egged me to have made one at dice, and told me it was a shame for a gentleman not to keep gentlemen company for his twenty or forty crowns. Nevertheless, because I alleged ignorance, the gentlewoman said I should not sit idle, all the rest being occupied, and so we two fell to sant, five games a crown.

M. And how sped you in the end?

R. In good faith, I passed not for the loss of twenty or forty shillings for acquaintance, and so much I think it cost me; and then I left off. Marry, the dice-players stuck well by it, and made very fresh play, saving one or two that were clean shriven, and had no more money to lose. In the end, when I should take my leave to depart, I could not by any means be suffered so to break com-

imbraiding: taunting, boasting.
sant: card game with hundred (cent) as winning score.

pany, unless I would deliver the gentlewoman a ring, for a gage of my return to supper. And so I did. And, to tell you all in a few words, I have haunted none other since I got that acquaintance. My meat and drink and lodging is every way so delicate, that I make no haste to change it.

M. And what, pay you nothing for it? Have ye not an ordinary charge for your meals?

R. None at all. But this device we have, that every player, at the first hand he draweth, payeth a crown to the box by way of a relief towards the house charges.

M. Ye may fare well of that price at the stark staring stews.

R. In good faith, and methinketh it an easy burthen for him that will put his forty pounds in adventure to pay the tribute of a crown and fare well for it, whose chance is to lose a hundred crowns or two, would never have spared one to make a new stock withal, and whose hap is to win, were a very churl to be a niggard of so little.

M. Is every man a player there, or do some go scot-free?

R. Whoso listeth not to put much in hazard playeth at mum-chance for his crown with some one or other: so some goeth free, and some be at double charge; for always we have respect that the house be relieved, and it standeth so much the more with good reason, because that besides the great charges of victuals, and great attendance of the servants, and great spoil of napery and household stuff, the goodman also loseth his twenty or forty pounds to keep us company.

M. And what do you the while? I am sure ye be not yet so cunning as to keep such workmen company.

R. And why not, I pray you? Is it so hard a thing to tell twenty, or to remember two or three chances? But yet indeed I play little myself, unless it be at the cards. Otherwise I am the goodman's half for the most part, and join both our lucks together.

M. How sped ye there for the most part?

R. Not always so well as I would wish. I will be plain with you, as with my friend: it hath cost me forty pounds within this

ordinary: eating-house.
scot-free: without paying their share (scot).
tell: count.

sennight. But I vouchsafe my loss the better, I had such fair play for it; and who would not hazard twenty pounds among such quiet company, where no man gives a foul word? At one good hand a man may chance, as I have often seen, to make his forty pound a hundred; and I have seen a man begin to play with five hundred mark lands, and once yet, ere the year went about, would have sold land if he had it.

M. Perchance so too.

R. But his luck was too bad; the like falleth scarcely once in a hundred years.

M. That is but one doctor's opinion. I see it betide every day, though not in this so large a proportion. And because I see you so raw in these things, that ye account that for most unfeigned friendship, where most deceit is meant, and, being already given to play, may in a few days come further behind than all your travail of your latter years can overtake again; I can neither forbear thee, for the zeal I bear unto you, or the hatred I bear to the occupation, to make you understand some parts of the sleights and falsehoods that are commonly practised at dice and cards; opening and overturning the things, not so that I would learn you to put the same in use, but open their wicked snares.

R. I thank you for your gentle offer. I would be glad to know the worst, lest haply I should fall in such crafty company. But yonder at my lodging cometh none but men of worship, some mounted upon mules fair trapped, some upon fine hackneys with foot-cloths; all such as, I dare say, would not practise a point of legerdemain for an hundred pound.

M. Well, as to that, there lay a straw, till anon that the matter lead us to speak more of it. And in the mean season, let this be sufficient; that so soon as ye began your declaration of the first acquaintance in Paul's, I felt aforehand the hooks were laid to pick your purse withal.

R. Wist I that, I would from henceforth stand in doubt of mine own hands, the matter hath such appearance of honesty.

M. Well, hearken to me awhile. There is no man I am sure, that hath experience of the world, and by reading of histories con-

sennight: week.
lay a straw: defer.

ferreth our time to the days of our elders, but will easily grant, that, as time hath grown and gathered increase by running, so wit, first planted in a few, hath in time taken so many roots, that in every corner ye may find new branches budding and issuing from the same. For proof whereof, to speak of one thing among many that at this time may serve our purpose, although the Greek and Latin histories be full of notable examples of good princes that utterly exiled dicing out of their seigniories and countries, or at the least held them as infamed persons; yet find I not that in those our forefathers' days, any the like sleight and crafty deceit was practised in play, as now is common in every corner. Yea, and he, namely Hodge Setter,[2] whose surname witnesseth what opinion men had of him, though forty years agone was thought peerless in crafty play, and had, as they say, neither mate nor fellow, yet now towards his death was so far behind some younger men in that knowledge, that I myself have known more than twenty that could make him a fool, and cannot suffer him to have the name of a workman in that faculty.

And it is not yet twenty years agone since all that sought their living that way, as then were few in number – scarcely so many as were able to maintain a good fray – so were they much of Hodge Setter's estate, the next door to a beggar. Now, such is the misery of our time, or such is the licentious outrage of idle misgoverned persons, that of only dicers a man might have half an army, the greatest number so gaily beseen and so full of money, that they bash not to insinuate themselves into the company of the highest, and look for a good hour to creep into a gentleman's room of the Privy Chamber. And hereof you may right well assure yourself, that if their cost were not exceeding great, it were not possible by the only help thereof to lead so sumptuous a life as they do, always shining like blazing stars in their apparel, by night taverning with [s]trumpets, by day spoiling gentlemen of their inheritance. And to speak all at once, like as all good and liberal sciences had a rude beginning, and by the industry of good men, being augmented by little and by little, at last grew to a just perfection; so this detestable privy robbery,

conferreth: compares.
good fray: daunting appearance (dial.).

from a few and deceitful rules is in few years grown to the body of an art, and hath his peculiar terms, and thereof as great a multitude applied to it, as hath grammar or logic, or any other of the approved sciences.

Neither let this seem strange unto you, because the thing is not commonly known, for this faculty hath one condition of juggling, that if the sleight be once discovered, marred is all the market. The first precept thereof is to be as secret in working as he that keepeth a man company from London to Maidenhead, and makes good cheer by the way, to the end in the thicket to turn his prick upwards, and cast a weaver's knot on both his thumbs behind him. And they, to the intent that ever in all companies they may talk familiarly in all appearance, and yet so covertly indeed that their purpose may not be espied, they call their worthy art by a new-found name, calling themselves cheaters, and the dice-cheaters, borrowing the term from among our lawyers, with whom all such casuals as fall unto the lord at the holding his leets, as waifs, strays and suchlike, be called cheats, as are accustomably said to be escheated to the lord's use.
R. Trow ye, then, that they have any affinity with our men of law?
M. Never with those that be honest. Marry! with such as be ambidexters, and use to play on both the hands, they have a great league; so have they also with all kind of people that from a good order of civility are fallen, and resolved, as it were from the hardness of virtuous living, to the delicacy and softness of uncareful idleness and gainful deceit; for gain and ease be the only pricks that they shoot at. But by what right or honest means they might acquire it, that part never cometh in question among them. And hereof it riseth that, like as law, when the term is truly considered, signifieth an ordinance of good men established for the commonwealth to repress all vicious living, so these cheaters turned the cat in the pan, giving to divers vile patching shifts an honest and godly title, calling it by the name of a law; because, by a multitude of hateful rules, a multitude of dregs and draff (as it were all good learning) govern and rule their idle bodies, to

turn his prick upwards: threaten with dagger or sword.
leets: manorial courts.
pricks: centre(s) of target.

the destruction of the good labouring people. And this is the cause that divers crafty sleights, devised only for guile, hold up the name of the law, ordained, ye wot, to maintain plain dealing. Thus give they their own conveyance the name of cheating law; so do they other terms, as sacking law, high law, figging law, and suchlike.

R. What mean ye hereby? Have ye spoken broad English all this while, and now begin to choke me with mysteries and quaint terms?

M. No, not for that. But always ye must consider that a carpenter hath many terms, familiar enough to his prentices, that other folk understand not at all; and so have the cheaters, not without great need, for a falsehood, once detected, can never compass the desired effect. Neither is it possible to make you grope the bottom of their art, unless I acquaint you with some of their terms. Therefore note this at the first, that sacking law signifieth whoredom; high law, robbery; figging law, pickpurse craft.

R. But what is this to the purpose; or what have cheaters to do with whores or thieves?

M. As much as with their very entire friend, that hold all of one corporation. For the first and original ground of cheating is a counterfeit countenance in all things, a study to seem to be, and not to be in deed; and because no great deceit can be wrought but where special trust goeth before, therefore the cheater, when he pitcheth his hay to purchase his profit, enforceth all his wits to win credit and opinion of honesty and uprightness.

Who hath a great[er] outward show of simplicity than the pickpurse, or what woman will seem so fervent in love as will the common harlot? So, as I told you before, the foundation of all those sorts of people is nothing else but mere simulation and bearing in hand. And like as they spring all from one root, so tend they all to one end: idly to live by rape and ravin, devouring the fruit of other men's labours. All the odds between them be in the mean actions, that lead towards the end and final purpose.[3]

R. I am almost weary of my trade already to hear that our gay gamesters are so strongly allied with thieves and pickpurses. But

conveyance: trickery.

I pray you proceed, and let me hear what sundry shifts of deceit they have to meet all well together at the close.

M. That is more than I promised you at the beginning, and more than I intend to perform at this time; for every of them keepeth as great schools in their own faculty as the cheaters do; and if I should make an open discourse of every wrinkle they have to cover and work deceit withal, I should speak of more sundry quaint conveyances than be rocks in Milford Haven to defend the ships from the boisterous rage of the weather. But I will first go forward with that I have in hand, and by the way, as occasion shall serve, so touch the rest that ye may see their workmanship, as it were afar off more than half a kenning. The cheater, for the most part, never receiveth his scholar, to whom he will discover the secrets of his art, but such one as before he had from some wealth and plenty of things made so bare, and brought to such misery, that he will refuse no labour, nor leave no stone unturned, to pick up a penny underneath. And this he doth not but upon a great skill. For, like as it is an old proverb and a true, that he must needs go whom the devil driveth, so is there not such a devil to force a man to an extreme refuge as is necessity and want, specially where it hath proceeded of abundance. Therefore the cheater, using necessity for a great part of persuasion, when he hath sucked this needy companion so dry that there remaineth no hope to press any drop of further gain by him, taketh some occasion to show him a glimpse of his faculty. And if, haply, he find him eagle-eyed, and diligent to mark, anon shapeth him in such a fashion, as that he will raise a new gain in him, and, withal, somewhat relieve his urgent poverty. Then, walking aside into some solitary place, he maketh the first way to his purpose after this, or the like manner:

'I am sure it is not yet out of your remembrance how late it is since ye first fell into my company; how great loss ye had at play before we entered in any acquaintance, and how little profit redounded unto me since ye first haunted my house. Neither can ye forget, on the other side, how friendly I have entertained you in every condition, making my house, my servants, my horses, mine apparel, and other things whatsoever I had, rather common to

kenning: range of vision, recognition.

us both than private to myself. And now I perceive that of a youthful wantonness and, as it were, a childish oversight, ye have suddenly brought yourself, unaware to me, so far under the hatches, and are shaken with lavish dispense, that ye cannot find the way to rise again, and bear any sail among men, as heretofore you have done. Which thing, whiles I deeply consider with myself, I cannot but lament much your negligence, and, more, the harm that is like to ensue upon it. For, first, your friends being, as I have heard, many in number, and all of worship, shall conceive such inward grief of your unthriftiness, that not one will vouchsafe a gentle plaster to quench the malice of this fretting corsie that penury hath applied; and I, again, because my hap was to have you in my house, and to gain a little of other men's leavings, shall be counted the cause of your undoing, and slandered for taking a few feathers out of the nest when other had stolen the birds already. For which causes, and specially to help you to maintain yourself like a gentleman, as hitherto of yourself ye have been able, I can be content to put you in a good way, so as, treading the steps that I shall appoint you, neither shall yet need to run to your friends for succour, and all men shall be glad to use you for a companion. But wist I that I should find you crafting with me in any point, and void of that fidelity and secretness, some sparks whereof I have noted in your nature, assure yourself that I would never make you privy to the matter, but give you over to your own provision, perchance to end your life with infamy and wretchedness.'

The young man, that lately flowed in plenty and pleasures, and now was pinched to the quick with lack of all things, humbled himself anon to be wholly at his devotion, and gave him a thousand thanks for his great kindness. Then forth goeth the cheater, and further says:

'Though your experience in the world be not so great as mine, yet am I sure ye see that no man is able to live an honest man unless he have some privy way to help himself withal, more than the world is witness of. Think you the noblemen could do as they do, if in this hard world they should maintain so great a port

corsie: grievance (corrosive).

only upon their rent? Think you the lawyers could be such purchasers if their pleas were short, and all their judgements, justice
and conscience? Suppose ye that offices would be so dearly
bought, and the buyers so soon enriched, if they counted not
pillage an honest point of purchase? Could merchants, without
lies, false making their wares, and selling them by a crooked light,
to deceive the chapman in the thread or colour, grow so soon rich
and to a baron's possessions, and make all their posterity gentlemen? What will ye more? Whoso hath not some anchorward
way to help himself, but followeth his nose, as they say, always
straight forward, may well hold up the head for a year or two, but
the third he must needs sink and gather the wind into beggars'
haven. Therefore mine advice shall be, that ye beat all your wits,
and spare not to break your brains always to save and help one.
Your acquaintance, I know, is great amongst your countrymen,
such as be rich and full of money, nevertheless, more simple than
that they know what good may be done in play, and better it is that
each man of them smart a little, than you to live in lack. Therefore seek them out busily at their lodgings; but always bear them
in hand that ye met them by chance. Then will it not be hard to
call them hither to take part of a supper; and, having them once
within the house doors, doubt ye not but they shall have a blow at
one pastime or other, that shall lighten their purses homeward.
Myself will lend you money to keep them company, and, nevertheless, make you partaker of the gain. And, to the end ye shall
not be ignorant by what means I will compass the matter, come
on go we unto my closet, and I shall give you a lesson worth the
learning.' Then bringeth he forth a great box with dice, and first
teacheth him to know a langret.

R. A God's name, what stuff is it? I have often heard men talk of
false dice; but I never yet heard so dainty a name given them.

M. So much the sooner may ye be deceived. But suffer me a while,
and break not my talk, and I shall paint you anon a proper kind
of pulling.

'Lo, here,' saith the cheater to this young novice, 'a well-

anchorward: secure (crooked?).
langret: dice with greater length along one axis.

favoured die that seemeth good and square; yet is the forehead longer on the cater and trey than any other way, and therefore, holdeth the name of a langret. Such be also called barred cater-treys, because commonly, the longer end will, of his own sway, draw downwards, and turn up to the eye sice, cinque, deuce, or ace. The principal use of them is at novem quinque. So long as a pair of barred cater-treys be walking on the board, so long can ye cast neither 5 nor 9, unless it be, by a great mischance, that the roughness of the board, or some other stay, force them to stay and run against their kind; for without cater-trey ye wot that 5 nor 9 can never fall.

R. By this reason, he that hath the first dice is like always to strip and rob all the table about!

M. True it is, were there not another help. And for the purpose an odd man is at hand, called a flat cater-trey, and none other number. The[n] granting that trey or cater be always one upon the one die, if there is no chance upon the other die but may serve to make 5 or 9, and so cast forth and lose all. 'Therefore,' saith the master, 'mark well your flat and learn to know him surely when he runneth on the board. The whiles he is abroad, ye forbear to cast at much; and, keeping this rule to avoid suspicion, because I am known for a player, ye shall see me bring all the gain into your hands.'

R. But what shift have they to bring the flat in and out?

M. A jolly fine shift, that properly is called foisting; and it is nothing else but a sleight to carry easily within the hand as often as the foister list. So that when either he or his partner shall cast the dice, the flat comes not abroad till he have made a great hand and won as much as him list. Otherwise the flat is ever on, unless at few times that, of purpose, he suffer the silly souls to cast in a hand or two to give them courage to continue their play and live in hope of winning.

R. This gear seemeth very strange unto me, and it sinketh not yet into my brain how a man might carry so many dice in one hand, and chop them and change them so often, and the thing not espied.

trey and cater: 3 and 4.
sice: 6.

44

M. So jugglers' conveyance seemeth to exceed the compass of reason till ye know the feat. But what is it that labour overcometh not?

And true it is, to foist finely and readily, and with the same hand to tell money to and fro, is a thing hardly learned, and asketh a bold spirit and long experience, though it be one of the first he learned. But to return to the purpose. If haply this young scholar have not so ready and so skilful an eye to discern the flat at every time that he is foisted in – for use maketh mastery, as well in this as in other things – then partly to help this ignorance withal, and partly to teach the young cock to crow, all after the cheaters' kind, the old cole instructeth the young in the terms of his art after this manner:

'Ye know that this outrageous swearing and quarrelling that some use in play, giveth occasion to many to forbear, that else would adventure much money at it; for this we have a device amongst us, that rather we relent and give place to a wrong, than we would cause the play, by strife, to cause any company to break. Neither have we any oaths in use but lightly these: "of honesty", "of truth", "by salt", "[St] Martin"; which, when we use them affirmatively, we mean always directly the contrary. As for example: if haply I say unto you, when the dice cometh to your hands, "Of honesty, cast at all," my meaning is, that ye shall cast at the board or else at very little. If, when a thing is offered in gage, I swear by St Martin I think it fine gold, then mean I the contrary, that it is but copper. And like as it is a gentle and old proverb, "Let losers have their words," so, by the way, take forth this lesson ever to show gentleness to the silly souls, and creep if ye can into their very bosoms. For harder it is to hold them when ye have them than for the first time to take them up. For these young wits be so light, and so wavering, that it requireth great travail to make them always dance after one pipe. But to follow that we have in hand: be they young, be they old, that falleth into our laps, and be ignorant of our art, we call them all by the name of a cousin, as men that we make as much of as if they were of our kin indeed. The greatest wisdom of our faculty resteth in this point, diligently to foresee to make the cousin

cole: sharper at dice.

sweat, that is, to have a will to keep play and company, and always to beware that we cause him not to smoke, lest that having any feel or savour of guile intended against him, he slip the collar as it were a hound, and shake us off for ever. And whensoever ye take up a cousin, be sure, as near as ye can, to know aforehand what store of bit he hath in his buy, that is, what money he hath in his purse, and whether it be in great cogs or in small, that is, gold or silver; and at what game he will soonest stoop, that we may feed him with his own humour, and have cauls ready for him; for thousands there be that will not play a groat at novem, and yet will lose a hundred pound at the hazard; and he that will not stoop a dodkin at the dice, perchance at cards will spend God's cope; therefore they must be provided for every way.

'Generally, your fine cheats, though they be good made both in the King's Bench and in the Marshalsea, yet Bird, in Holborn, is the finest workman. Acquaint yourself with him, and let him make you a bale or two of squariers of sundry sizes, some less, some more, to throw into the first play, till ye perceive what your company is; then have in a readiness, to be foisted in when time shall be, your fine cheats of all sorts. Be sure to have in store of such as these be: a bale of barred cinque-deuces, and flat cinque-deuces, a bale of barred sice-aces and flat sice-aces, a bale of barred cater-treys and flat cater-treys; the advantage whereof is all on the one side, and consisteth in the forging. Provide also a bale or two of fullans, for they have great use at the hazard; and, though they be square outward, yet being within at the corner with lead or other ponderous matter stopped, minister as great an advantage as any of the rest. Ye must also be furnished with high men and low men for a mumchance and for passage. Yea, and a long die for even and odd is good to strike a small stroke withal, for a crown or two, or the price of a dinner. As for gourds and

smoke: suspect.
cauls: nets, traps.
dodkin: small coin.
squariers: dice.
fullans: weighted dice.
high and low men: dice with faces wrongly numbered.
gourds: (*graviers*) hollowed dice.

bristle dice [these] be now too gross a practice to be put in use; light graviers there be, demies, contraries, and of all sorts, forged clean against the apparent vantage, which have special and sundry uses.

'But it is enough at this time to put you in a remembrance what tools ye must prepare to make you a workman. Hereafter, at more leisure, I shall instruct you of the several uses of them all, and in the mean season take with you also this lesson: that when fine squarers only be stirring, there rests a great help in cogging; that is, when the undermost die standeth dead by the weighty fall of his fellow, so that if 6 be my chance, and 10 yours, grant that, upon the die, I cog and keep always an ace, deuce, or trey, I may perhaps soon cast 6, but never 10. And there be divers kind of cogging, but of all other the Spanish cog bears the bell, and seldom raiseth any smoke.'

'Gramercy,' saith the scholar, and now thinketh he himself so ripely instructed, that though he be not yet able to beguile others, yet he supposeth himself sufficiently armed against all falsehood that might be wrought to bring him to an afterdeal, and little seeth he the while how many other ends remain, how many points there be in slippery cheaters' science, that he shall not yet be skilful enough to tag in their kind, perchance in four or five years' practice.

R. Why, have they any deeper reaches to lift a man out of his saddle, and rid him of his money, than ye have opened already?
M. Alas! this is but a warning and, as it were, the shaking of a rod to a young boy to scare him from places of peril. All that I have told you yet, or that I have minded to tell you, 'greeth not to the purpose to make you skilful in cheaters' occupation. For as soon would I teach you the next way to Tyburn as to learn you the practice of it! Only my meaning is to make you see as far into it as should a cobbler into a tanner's faculty; to know whether his leather be well liquored, and well and workmanly

bristle dice : dice with a short bristle on one edge.
demies : false dice with less than the normal bias.
contraries : false dice with a bias opposite to those in play.
vantage : bias (of a die).
cogging : manipulation of dice.

dressed or not. And, like as I would not wish a cobbler a currier, lest two sundry occupations running together into one, might, perhaps, make a lewd London medley in our shoes, the one using falsehood in working, the other facing and lying in uttering; so seek I to avoid, that ye should not both be a courtier, in whom a little honest, moderate play is tolerable, and, withal, a cheater, that with all honesty hath made an undefensible dormant defiance. For, even this new-nurtured novice, notwithstanding he is received into the college of these double dealers, and is become so good a scholar that he knoweth readily his flats and bars, and hath been snapper with the old cole at two or three deep strokes; yea, and though he have learned to verse, and lay in the reason well favouredly, to make the cousin stoop all the cogs in his buy, yet if he once wax slow in seeking out cousins, and be proud of his new thrift, and so goodly a passage to recover his old losses, the knap of the case, the goodman of the house calleth secretly unto him the third person, for the most part a man that might be warden of his company, and talketh with him after this manner:

'Here is a young man in my house, if ye know him, that hath been one of the sweetest cousins alive, so long as he was able to make a groat. Now at the last, I wot not how he came by it, he hath gotten some knowledge, and talks of a great deal more than he can in deed. Marry! a langret he knoweth metely well, and that is all his skill. I made much of him all this month, because he hath great acquaintance of men of the country, and specially the cloth-men of the west parts; and, at the beginning, would every day fill the case with jolly fat cousins. And, albeit he had no knowledge to work any feat himself, yet did I use him always honestly, and gave him his whole snap, to the end he should be painful and diligent to take the cousins up, and bring them to the blow. Now waxen is he so proud of his gain, because he hath gotten a new chain, fire-new apparel, and some store of bit, that

uttering : putting goods on the market.
verse : cheat.
knap of the case : leader of the gang.
snap : share of spoils.
bit : money.

I cannot get him once out of the door to go about anything. "Take some pains yourself," saith he, "and bring some of your own cousins home, or else let all alone for me." Thus if ye see that nothing mars him, but that he is too fat, and might we make him once lean again, as he was within this month, then should we see the hungry whoreson trudge. There should not be stirring a cousin in any quarter but he would wind him straight. Therefore come you in anon like a stranger, and ye shall see him take you up roundly. If ye lack contraries to crossbite him withal, I shall lend you a pair of the same size that his cheats be.'

R. Is there no more fidelity among them? Can they not be content, one false knave to be true to his fellow, though they conspire to rob all other men?

M. Nothing less. Did not I warn you in the beginning, that the end of the science is mere deceit? And would ye have themselves, against their kind, to work contrary to their profession? Nay, they be ever so like themselves, that, when all other deceits fail, look which of them in play gets any store of money into his hands, he will every foot, as he draweth a hand, be figging more or less and rather than fail, cram it and hide it in his hose, to make his gain greatest. Then when they fall to the division of the gain, and the money that the cousin hath lost is not forthcoming, nor will be confessed among them, it is a world to hear what rule they make, and how the one imbraideth the other with dishonesty, as if there were some honesty to be found among them. What should I then speak of swearing and staring, were they always as liberal of alms as they be of oaths! I had rather bring a beggar to have the reward of a cheater, than to the best alms-knight's room that the king gives at Windsor.[4] But these storms never fall but in secret councils within themselves, and then peradventure the stronger part will strip the weaker out of his clothes rather than he should flock away with the stuff and make them louts to labour for his lucre.

R. Then is it but folly to recover my losses in yonder company. And, if there cannot be one faithful couple found in the whole band, how might I hope, that am but a stranger, to win an unfeigned friend amongst them?

figging: cheating.

M. As for in that case, never speak more of the matter, and be as sure as ye are of your creed that all the friendly entertainment ye have at your lodging is for no other end but for to persuade you to play, and bring you to loss. Neither was it any better than falsehood in fellowship, when the goodman got you to be half, and seemed unwillingly to lose both your moneys.

R. By these means, either must I utterly forbear to hazard anything at the dice, or live in doubt and suspection of my friend, whensoever I fall to play.

M. No question thereof. For the contagion of cheating is now so universal that they swarm in every quarter, and therefore ye cannot be in safety from deceit, unless ye shun the company of hazarders, as a man would fly a scorpion.

R. Then am I sufficiently lessoned for the purpose. But, because at the first our talk matched dice and cards together, like a couple of friends that draw both in a yoke, I pray you, is there much craft at cards as ye have rehearsed at the dice?

M. Altogether, I would not give a point to choose; they have such a sleight in sorting and shuffling of the cards, that play at what game ye will, all is lost aforehand. If two be confederate to beguile the third, the thing is compassed with the more ease than if one be but alone. Yet are there many ways to deceive. Primero, now, as it hath most use in Court, so is there most deceit in it. Some play upon the prick; some pinch the cards privily with their nails; some turn up the corners; some mark them with fine spots of ink. One fine trick brought in a Spaniard; a finer than this invented an Italian, and won much money with it by our doctors, and yet, at the last, they were both over-reached by new sleights devised here at home. At trump, sant, and such other like, cutting at the neck is a great vantage, so is cutting by a bum card (finely) under and over, stealing the stock of the decarded cards, if their broad laws be forced aforehand. At decoy, they draw easily twenty hands together, and play all upon assurance when to win or lose. Other helps I have heard of besides: as, to set the cousin upon the bench with a great looking-glass be-

play upon the prick: ? play with pricked cards.
cutting at the neck: ? using a pack with some nicked cards (Judges).
cutting by a bum card: dividing pack at card with slightly raised surface.

hind him on the wall, wherein the cheater might always see what cards were in his hand. Sometimes they work by signs made by some of the lookers-on. Wherefore methinks this, among the rest, proceeded of a fine invention: a gamester, after he had been oftentimes bitten among the cheaters, and after much loss, grew very suspicious in his play, that he could not suffer any of the sitters-by to be privy to his game. For this the cheaters devised a new shift. A woman should sit sewing beside him, and by the shift, or slow drawing her needle, give a token to the cheater what was the cousin's game. So that, a few examples instead of infinite that might be rehearsed, this one universal conclusion may be gathered, that, give you to play, and yield yourself to loss.

R. I feel well that if a man happen to put his money in hazard, the odds is great that he shall rise a loser. But many men are so continent of their hands, that nothing can cause them to put aught in adventure; and some, again, be unskilful, that lack of [c]unning forceth them to forbear.

M. I grant you well both. But, nevertheless, I never yet saw man so hard to be vanquished, but they would make him stoop at one law or other. And for that purpose, their first travail is, after that they have taken up the cousin, and made him somewhat sweat, to seek by all means they can to understand his nature, and where-unto he is inclined. If they find that he taketh pleasure in the company of females, then seek they to strike him at the sacking law. And take this always for a maxim, that all the bawds in a country be of the cheaters' familiar acquaintance. Therefore it shall not be hard, at all times, to provide for this amorous knight a lewd, lecherous lady to keep him loving company. Then fall they to banqueting, to minstrels, masking; and much is the cost that the silly cousin shall be at in jewels, apparel, and otherwise. He shall not once get a grant to have scarcely a lick at this dainty lady's lips; and ever anon she layeth in this reason: for her sake to put his twenty or forty crowns in adventure. 'Ye wot not,' saith she, 'what may be a woman's luck.' If he refuse it, Lord! how unkindly she taketh the matter, and cannot be reconciled with less than a gown, or a kirtle of silk, which commonly is a reward unto her by knap of the case, and the cut-throats, his com-

lips: original 'laps'.

plices, to whom the matter is put in daying. Yea, and the more is, if haply they perceive that he esteemed not bruised ware, but is enamoured with virginity, they have a fine cast, within an hour's warning, to make Joan Silverpin as good a maid as if she had never come at stews, nor opened to any man her quiver. The mystery thereof ye shall understand by this my tale, which I myself saw put in experience.

A young roisterly gentleman, desiring a maiden make to content his wanton lust, resorted to a bawd and promised her good wages to provide him a maid against the next day. He declared unto her that he took more pleasure in virginity than beauty, but if both came together the pleasure was much the more thankful, and her reward should be the better. This mother bawd undertook to serve his turn according to his desire, and having at home a well-painted, mannerly harlot, as good a maid as Fletcher's mare, that bare three great foals, went in the morning to the apothecary's for half a pint of sweet water, that commonly is called surfling water, or clinker-device, and on the way homeward turned into a nobleman's house to visit his cook, an old acquaintance of hers. Uneath had she set her feet within the kitchen, and set down her glass, the more handsomely to warm her afore the range, but anon the cook had taken her in his arms, and whiles they wrestled, more for manner's sake of the light than for any squeamish business, had she been behind the door, down fell the glass and spilt was the water. 'Out, alas!' quoth the woman. – 'Quiet yourself,' quoth the cook, 'let us go into the buttery to breakfast, and I will buy you a new glass, and pay for the filling.'

Away they went out of the kitchen; and the boy, that turned a couple of spits, delighting with the savour of the water, let first one spit stand, and after another, always with one hand taking up the water as it dropped from the board by him and washed his eyes, his mouth, and all his face withal. Soon after that this liquor was with the heat of the fire dried, and soaked up in the boy's face, down came the cook again into the kitchen and finding

put in daying: passed for arbitration.
make: mate.
uneath: scarcely.

the breast of the capon all burnt for lack of turning, caught up a great basting-stick to beat the turnspit. And, haply casting a sour look upon him, espied the boy's mouth and eyes drawn so together and closed, that neither had he left an eye to look withal, and scarcely might ye turn your little finger in his mouth. The cook abashed with the sudden change, ran about the house half out of his wit, and cried, 'The kitchen-boy is taken. He can neither see nor speak.' And so the poor boy, with his starched face, continued more than half an hour a wondering-stock to all the house, till a man of experience bade bathe his face with hot fat beef broth, whereby, forthwith, he was restored to as wide a mouth, and as open eyes as he had before.

R. A good miracle, and soon wrought. If maids be so easy to make, no marvel it is we have such store in London. But forth, I pray you, with your purpose. When whoredom hath no place, what other shifts have they to raise their thrift upon?

M. A hundred more than I can rehearse; but most commonly one of these that follow. If it be winter season, when masking is most in use, then, missing of their cheaped helps, they spare not for cost of the dearer. Therefore, first do they hire, in one place or other, a suit of right masking apparel, and after, invite divers guests to a supper – all such as be then of estimation, to give them credit by their acquaintance, or such as they think will be liberal, to hazard some thing in a mumchance. By which means they assure themselves at the least to have the supper shot-free, perchance, to win twenty pounds, about. And, howsoever the common people esteem the thing, I am clean out of doubt that the more half of your gay masques in London are grounded upon such cheating crafts, and tend only the pulling and robbing of the king's subjects.

Another jolly shift, and for the subtle invention and fineness of wit exceedeth far all the rest, is the barnard's law,[5] which, to be exactly practised, asketh four persons at the least, each of them to play a long several part by himself.

The first is the taker-up, of a skilful man in all things, who hath by long travail conned, without the book, a hundred reasons to insinuate himself into a man's acquaintance. Talk of matters in law: and he hath plenty of cases at his fingers' ends that he hath seen tried and ruled in every of the king's courts. Speak of grazing and husbandry: no man knoweth more shires than he; no man knoweth better where to raise a gain, and how the abuses and overture of prices [6] might be redressed. Finally, enter into what discourse of things they list, were it into a broom-man's faculty, he knoweth what gain they have for old boots and shoes, and whence their gain cometh. Yea, and it shall escape him hard, but that ere your talk break off, he will be your countryman at least, and, peradventure, either of kin, or ally or some sole sib unto you – if your reach surmount not his too far. In case he bring to pass that ye be glad of his acquaintance, and content with his company, played is the chief of his part, and he giveth place to the principal player, the barnard. Nevertheless, he lightly hath in his company a man of more worship than himself, that hath the countenance of a possessioner of land, and he is called the verser; and though it be a very hard thing to be a perfect taker-up, and as it were, a man universally practised in all accidents of a man's life, yet doth the barnard go so far beyond him in cunning, as doth the sun's summer brightness exceed the glimmering light of the winter stars.

This body's most common practice is to come stumbling into your company like some rich farmer of the country, a stranger to you all, that had been at some market town thereabouts, buying and selling, and there tippled so much malmsey, that he had never a ready word in his mouth, and is so careless for his money that out he throweth an hundred or two of old angels upon the board's end, and, standing somewhat aloof, calleth for a pot of ale, and saith, 'Masters, I am somewhat bold with you. I pray you be not aggrieved that I drink my drink by you,' and minister such idle drunken talk, that the verser, who counterfeiteth the gentleman, cometh stoutly and sits at your elbow, praying you to call him [the barnard] near to laugh at his folly. Between them two the matter shall be so workmanly conveyed, and so finely argued, that out cometh a pair of old cards, whereat the barnard teacheth the verser a new game, that he supposeth cost him two pots of ale for the learning not past an hour or two before. The first wager is drink, the next twopence, or a groat, and lastly to make the tale short, they use the matter so that he that hath eighty years of his back, and never played for a groat in his life, cannot refuse to be the verser's half and consequently, at one cutting of the cards, to lose all they play for, be it an hundred pound.

And if, perhaps, when the money is lost, the cousin begins to smoke, and swear that the drunken knave shall not get his money so, then standeth the rubber[7] at the door, and draweth his sword, and picketh a quarrel to his own shadow if he lack an ostler or a tapster or some other to fall out withal; that, whiles the street and company gather to the fray, as the manner is, the barnard steals away with all the stuff, and picks him to one blind tavern or other, such as before is appointed among them, and there abideth the coming of his companions to make an equal portion of the gain. And whensoever these shifts may not take place, then lead they the cousin to the gaze of an interlude, or the bear-baiting at Paris Garden, or some other place of throng, where, by [a] fine-fingered fig-boy, a grounded disciple of James Ellis,[8] picked shall be his purse, and his money lost in a moment. Or else they run to the last refuge of all, and, by a knot of lusty companions of the high law, not only shake the harmless body out of all his clothes, but bind him or bob him to boot, that less had been his harm to have stooped low at the first, and so to have stopped their greedy mouths, than to save himself so long, and in the end to be fleeced as bare as a new-born sheep, and perchance so far from his friends, that he shall be forced to trip on his ten toes homeward, for lack of a hackney to ride on, and beg for his charges on the way.

R. Now speak ye indeed of a ready way to thrift, but it hath an ill-favoured success many times.

M. I wot what you mean. You think they come home by Tyburn or St Thomas of Waterings; and so they do indeed, but nothing so soon as a man would suppose. They be but petty figgers and unlessoned lads that have such ready passage to the gallows. The old thieves go through with their vices [?] well twenty or thirty years together, and be seldom taken or tainted, specially the fig bodies that have a goodly corporation for the relief. Their craft,

bob: rob or mock.
Tyburn or St Thomas: sites of gallows.
vices: original, 'usies' (?)

of all others, requireth most sleight, and hath marvellous plenty of terms and strange language; and therefore no man can attain to be a workman thereat, till he have had a good time of schooling, and by that means they do not only know each other well, but they be subject to an order such as the elders shall prescribe. No man so sturdy to practise his feat but in the place appointed, nor for any cause once to put his foot in another's walk. Some two or three hath Paul's Church in charge; other hath Westminster Hall in term-time; divers Cheapside with the flesh and fish shambles; some the Borough and bear-baiting; some the Court; and part follow markets and fairs in the country with pedlars' foot-packs; and generally to all places of assembly. Some of them are certainly 'pointed, as it were, by their wardens to keep the haunt, with commission but a short while, and to interchange their places as order shall be made, to avoid suspicion. By occasion, whereof whensoever any stroke is workmanly stricken, though it were at Newcastle, the rest of the fig-boys that keeps resident in London, [can] forthwith prognosticate by whom the worthy feat was wrought; and one great provision they have, that is a sovran salve at all times of need; a treasurer they choose in some blind corner, a trusty secret friend; and whensoever there cometh any jewels, plate, or such gear to their share, the present sale whereof might chance to discover the matter, the same [is] committed into his hands in pledge as it were of money lent; and ʒe taketh a bill of sale in default of repayment, as if all things were done by good faith and plain dealing. So that whensoever he shall seek to make money of these gages, at the end of two or three months, if any question arise how he came by them, he showeth anon a fair bill of sale for his discharge, from John a Knock or John a Stile, a man that never was, never shall be, found. And such theft by this occasion is ever mannerly covered.

Another help they have, that of every purse that is cleanly conveyed a rateable portion is duly delivered into the treasurer's hands, to the use, that whensoever by some misadventure any of them happen to be taken and laid in prison, this common stock may serve to satisfy the party grieved, and to make friends to save them from hanging.

term-time: when courts were in session.

Now have ye a calendar, as it were, to put you in remembrance of these chief points and practices of cheating; enough, I suppose, to serve for a warning that ye withdraw yourself from yonder costly company, wherein, if my experience may serve to give you occasion to eschew such evils, I shall be glad of this our happy meeting.

R. Yes, doubt ye not thereof but that this talk hath wrought already such effects in me, that, though I live a hundred years, I shall not lightly fall into the cheaters' snares. But because ye spake of the principal points, whereby I conceive that yet some small sparks remain untouched, I pray you put me out of doubt thereof; and then, on God's name, ye shall gladly depart, with as many thanks as if you had disbursed a large sum of money for redemption of my land and saved it from selling. For had not forewarning come, the merchant and I must within a few days have coped together, as did my bed-fellow but now the last week; whose losses I pity so much the more, as that now I understand by what cheatery it was won.

M. The feat of losing is easily learned, and, as I told you in the beginning that the cheaters beat and busy their brains only about fraud and subtlety, so can it not be chosen but give themselves over all to that purpose, and must every day forge out one new point of knavery or other to deceive the simple withal. As of late I knew a young gentleman so wary in his doings, that neither by dice or cards, nor by damosels of dalliance, nor of the ways afore rehearsed, could be made stoop one penny out of his purse. For this the cheater [who] consulted with the lewd lady, in this case devised that she should dally with the gentleman and, playing with his chain, should find the mean to keep it awhile, till they might fig a link or two to make a like by. Done it was anon, and within a few days after, another made of copper, equal in length to that. At the gentleman's next returning to the house, the damosel dallied so long with the chain, sometime putting it about her neck, and sometimes about his, that in the end she foisted the copper chain in the other's place, and thereby robbed him of better than forty pounds.

This and the like shifts I forbear to remember, sooner because the deceit resteth not in any slight practice at dice and cards;

nevertheless, because cheaters were the first inventors as well of this as of all other falsehood in fellowship, that now daily is put in use at all manner of games: as when one man lost, not many years ago, an hundred pound land at shooting, by occasion that some that shot with him on his side were booty fellows against him; another was rid of six hundred pounds at the tennis in a week by the fraud of his stopper. Methink they cannot be better rewarded than sent home to the place they come from.

And, since cheaters were the first authors thereof, let them also bear the blame. And, having disclosed unto you, as briefly as I can, the principal practice of the cheaters' crafty faculty, and other workmen of their alliance, I will bid you farewell for this time.

¶ The Fraternitye of Uacabondes.

As wel of ruflyng Uacabonds, as of beggerly, as
wel of wemen as of men, and as wel of Gyles, as of
Boyes, with their proper names and qualityes.
¶ Also the .xxv. Orders of Knaues, otherwyse
called a Quartern of Knaues. Confirmed thys
yere by Cocke Lorel.

The Upright man speaketh.

Our brotherhode of Uacab ondes,
If you would know where dwel:
In Graues end Barge which seldom stands
The talke wyl shew right wel.

Cocke Lorel speaketh.

Some orders of my Knaues also
In that Bar shall ye fynde,
For no where shal ye walke (I know)
But ye shall see their kinde,

¶ Imprinted at London,
by John Awdely, dwelling in lytle Brittain
streete, beyond Aldersgate,
The .13. day of December.
Anno. do. 1565.

The Upright Man Speaketh:

Our brotherhood of vagabonds,
  If you would know where dwell,
In Gravesend barge which seldom stands,
  The talk will show right well.

Cock Lorel[1] Answereth:

Some orders of my knaves also
  In that barge shall ye find:
For nowhere shall ye walk, I trow,
  But ye shall see their kind.

The Printer to the Reader

This brotherhood of vagabonds,
To show that there be such indeed,
Both justices and men of lands,
Will testify it if it need.
    For at a Sessions as they sat,
    By chance a vagabond was got.

Who promised if they would him spare,
And keep his name from knowledge, then,
He would as strange a thing declare,
As ever they knew since they were men.
    'But if my fellows do know,' said he,
    'That thus I did, they would kill me.'

They granting him this his request,
He did declare as here is read,
Both names and states of most and least,
Of this their vagabonds' brotherhood.
    Which at the request of a worshipful man
    I have set it forth as well as I can.

FINIS

The Fraternity of Vagabonds

An Abraham Man

An Abraham man is he that walketh bare-armed, and bare-legged, and feigneth himself mad, and carrieth a pack of wool, or a stick with bacon on it, or suchlike toy, and nameth himself Poor Tom.

Abraham man: perhaps derived from the Abraham ward of Bethlehem (Bedlam) Hospital (cf. Poor Tom in *King Lear*).

A Ruffler

A ruffler goeth with a weapon to seek service, saying he hath been a servitor in the wars, and beggeth for his relief. But his chiefest trade is to rob poor wayfaring men and market-women.

A Prigman

A prigman goeth with a stick in his hand like an idle person. His property is to steal clothes off the hedge, which they call storing of the rogueman; or else filch poultry, carrying them to the ale-house, which they call the boozing inn, and there sit playing at cards and dice, till that is spent which they have so filched.

A Whip-Jack

A whip-jack is one, that by colour of a counterfeit licence (which they call a gybe, and the seals they call jarks) doth use to beg like a mariner; but his chiefest trade is to rob booths in a fair, or to pilfer ware from stalls, which they call heaving of the booth.

A Frater

A frater goeth with a like licence to beg for some spitalhouse or hospital. Their prey is commonly upon poor women as they go and come to the markets.

A Queer-Bird

A queer-bird is one that came lately out of prison and goeth to seek service. He is commonly a stealer of horses, which they term a prigger of palfreys.

An Upright Man

An upright man is one that goeth with the truncheon of a staff, which staff they call a filchman. This man is of so much authority that, meeting with any of his profession, he may call them to account and command a share or snap unto himself of all that they have gained by their trade in one month. And if he do them wrong, they have no remedy against him, no, though he beat them, as he useth commonly to do. He may also command any of their women, which they call doxies, to serve his turn. He hath the chief place at any market walk and other assemblies, and is not of any to be controlled.

A Curtal

A curtal is much like to the upright man, but his authority is not fully so great. He useth commonly to go with a short cloak, like to grey friars and his woman with him in like livery, which he calleth his altham, if she be his wife, and if she be his harlot, she is called his doxy.

A Palliard

A palliard is he that goeth in a patched cloak; and his doxy goeth in like apparel.

An Irish Toyle

An Irish toyle is he that carrieth his ware in his wallet, as laces, pins, points and suchlike. He useth to show no wares until he have his alms; and if the goodman and wife be not in the way, he procureth of the children or servants a fleece of wool, or the worth of twelve pence of some other thing, for a pennyworth of his wares.

A Jackman

A jackman is he that can write and read, and sometime speak Latin. He useth to make counterfeit licences which they call gybes, and sets to seals, in their language called jarks.

A Swigman

A swigman goeth with a pedlar's pack.

A Washman

A washman is called a palliard, but not of the right making. He useth to lie in the highway with lame or sore legs or arms to beg. These men the right palliards will oftentimes spoil, but they dare not complain. They be bitten with spickworts and sometime with ratsbane.

A Tinkard

A tinkard leaveth his bag a-sweating at the ale-house, which they term their boozing inn, and in the mean season goeth abroad a-begging.

points: lace for attaching hose to doublet.

A Wild Rogue

A wild rogue is he that hath no abiding place, but by his colour of going abroad to beg is commonly to seek some kinsman of his, and all that be of his corporation be properly called rogues.

A Kitchin Co

A kitchin co is called an idle runagate boy.

A Kitchin Morts

A kitchin morts is a girl; she is brought at her full age to the upright man to be broken, and so she is called a doxy, until she come to the honour of an altham.

Doxies

Note especially all which go abroad working laces and shirt-strings; they name them doxies.

A Patriarch Co

A patriarch co doth make marriages, and that is until death depart the married folk, which is after this sort: when they come to a dead horse or any dead cattle, then they shake hands and so depart, every one of them a several way.

The Company of Cozeners and Shifters

A Courtesy-Man

A courtesy-man is one that walketh about the back lanes in London in the day-time, and sometime in the broad streets in the night-season, and when he meeteth some handsome young man cleanly apparelled, or some other honest citizen, he maketh humble salutations and low courtesy, and showeth him that he hath a word or two to speak with his mastership. This child can behave himself mannerly, for he will desire him that he talketh withal to take the upper hand, and show him much reverence, and at last like his familiar acquaintance will put on his cap, and walk side by side, and talk on this fashion:

'Oh, sir, you seem to be a man, and one that favoureth men, and therefore I am the more bolder to break my mind unto your good mastership. Thus it is, sir, there is a certain of us (though I say it, both tall and handsome men of their hands) which have come lately from the wars, and, as God knoweth, have nothing to take to, being both masterless and moneyless, and knowing no way whereby to earn one penny. And further, whereas we have been wealthily brought up, and we also have been had in good estimation, we are ashamed now to declare our misery, and to fall a-craving as common beggars, and as for to steal and rob, God is our record, it striketh us to the heart to think of such a mischief, that ever any handsome man should fall into such a danger for this worldly trash. Which if we had to suffice our want and necessity, we should never seek thus shamefastly to crave on such good pitiful men as you seem to be, neither yet so dangerously to hazard our lives for so vile a thing. Therefore, good sir, as you seem to be a handsome man yourself, and also such a one as pitieth the miserable case of handsome men, as now your eyes and countenance showeth to have some pity upon this my miserable complaint; so in God's cause I require your mastership, and in the behalf of my poor afflicted fellows, which though here in sight, they cry not with me to you, yet, wheresoever they be, I am sure they cry unto God to move the hearts of some good men to show forth their liberality in this behalf. All which, and I with them, crave now the same request at your good mastership's hand.'

With these or suchlike words he frameth his talk. Now if the party, which he thus talketh withal, proffereth him a penny or twopence, he taketh it, but very scornfully, and at last speaketh on this sort:

'Well sir, your good will is not to be refused. But yet you shall understand, good sir, that this is nothing for them, for whom I do thus shamefastly entreat. Alas sir, it is not a groat or twelve pence I speak for, being such a company of servitors as we have been: yet nevertheless, God forbid I should not receive your gentle offer at this time, hoping hereafter through your good motions to some such like good gentleman as you be, that I, or some of my fellows in my place, shall find the more liberality.'

These kind of idle vagabonds will go commonly well apparelled without any weapon, and in place where they meet together, as at their hostelries or other places, they will bear the port of right good gentlemen, and some are the more trusted, but commonly they pay them with stealing a pair of sheets or coverlet, and so take their farewell early in the morning, before the master or dame be stirring.

A Cheater or Fingerer

These commonly be such kind of idle vagabonds as scarcely a man shall discern, they go so gorgeously, sometime with waiting men and sometime without. Their trade is to walk in such places whereas gentlemen and other worshipful citizens do resort, as at Paul's, or at Christ's Hospital, and sometime at the Royal Exchange.[2] These have very many acquaintances, yea, and for the most part will acquaint themselves with every man and feign a society in one place or other. But chiefly they will seek their acquaintance of such (which they have learned by diligent enquiring where they resort) as have received some portion of money of their friends, as young gentlemen which are sent to London to study the laws, or else some young merchantman or other kind of occupier, whose friends hath given them a stock of money to occupy withal. When they have thus found out such a prey, they will find the means by their familiarity as very courteously to bid him to breakfast at one place or other, where they are best acquainted, and closely among themselves will appoint one of their fraternity, which they call a fingerer, an old-beaten child, not only in such deceits, but also such a one as by his age is painted out with grey hairs, wrinkled face, crooked back, and most commonly lame, as it might seem with age; yea, and such

occupy: engage in business (often with quibble on sexual intercourse).
old-beaten: experienced, mature.

a one as to show a simplicity shall wear a homely cloak and hat scarce worth sixpence. This nimble-fingered knight, being appointed to this place, cometh in as one not known of these cheaters, but as unawares shall sit down at the end of the board where they sit, and call for his penny pot of wine, or a pint of ale, as the place serveth. Thus, sitting as it were alone, mumbling on a crust or some such thing, these other younkers will find some kind of merry talk with him, sometimes questioning where he dwelleth, and sometimes inquiring what trade he useth, which commonly he telleth them he useth husbandry. And talking thus merrily, at last they ask him, 'How sayest thou, father, wilt thou play for thy breakfast with one of us, that we may have some pastime as we sit?'

This old carl, making it strange at the first, saith: 'My masters, Ich am an old man and half blind, and can skill of very few games, yet for that you seem to be such good gentlemen as to proffer to play for that of which you had no part, but only I myself, and therefore of right Ich am worthy to pay for it, I shall with all my heart fulfil your request': and so falleth to play, sometime at cards, and sometime at dice; which, through his counterfeit simplicity in the play, sometimes overcounteth himself, or playeth sometimes against his will, so as he would not, and then counterfeiteth to be angry, and falleth to swearing, and so, losing that, proffereth to play for a shilling or two. The other threat having good sport, seeming to mock him, falleth again to play, and so by their legerdemain and counterfeiting winneth each of them a shilling or twain, and at last whispereth the young man in the ear to play with him also, that each one might have a fling at him.

This young man, for company, falleth again to play also with the said fingerer, and winneth as the other did; which, when he had lost a noble or six shillings, maketh as though he had lost all his money, and falleth a-entreating for part thereof again to bring him home, which the other knowing his mind and intent, stoutly denyeth, and jesteth and scoffeth at him. This fingerer, seeming then to be in a rage, desireth them, as they are true

younkers: literally 'novices'; here used satirically.
noble: gold coin worth between 6s 8d. and 10s.

gentlemen, to tarry till he fetcheth more store of money, or else to point some place where they may meet. They seeming greedy hereof, promiseth faithfully and clappeth hands so to meet. They, thus tickling the young man in the ear, willeth him to make as much money as he can, and they will make as much as they can, and consent as though they will play booty against him. But in the end they so use the matter, that both the young man loseth his part, and, as it seemeth to him, they losing theirs also, and so maketh as though they would fall together by the ears with this fingerer, which by one wile or other at last conveyeth himself away, and they, as it were raging like mad bedlams, one runneth one way, another another way, leaving the loser indeed all alone. Thus these cheaters at their accustomed hostelries meet closely together, and there receive each one his part of this their vile spoil.

Of this fraternity there be that be called helpers, which commonly haunt taverns or ale-houses, and cometh in as men not acquainted with none in the company, but spying them at any game will bid them God-speed and God-be-at-their-game, and will so place himself that he will show his fellow by signs and tokens, without speech commonly, but sometime with far-fetched words, what cards he hath in his hand, and how he may play against him. And those between them both getteth money out of the other's purse.

A Ring-Faller

A ring-faller is he that getteth fair copper rings, some made like signets and some after other fashions, very fair gilded, and walketh up and down the streets, till he spyeth some man of the country, or some other simple body whom he thinketh he may deceive, and so goeth a little before him or them, and letteth fall one of these rings, which, when the party that cometh after spyeth and taketh it up, he having an eye backward, cryeth, 'Half part!' The party that taketh it up, thinking it to be of great value, proffereth him some money for his part, which he not fully denyeth, but willeth him to come into some ale-house

play booty: conspire to defraud.

or tavern, and there they will common upon the matter. Which, when they come in and are set in some solitary place (as commonly they call for such a place), there he desireth the party that found the ring to show it him. When he seeth it, he falleth a-entreating the party that found it, and desireth him to take money for his part, and telleth him that if ever he may do him any friendship hereafter he shall command him, for he maketh as though he were very desirous to have it. The simple man, seeing him so importune upon it, thinketh the ring to be of great value, and so is the more loather to part from it. At last this ring-faller asketh him what he will give him for his part, 'For,' saith he, 'seeing you will not let me have the ring, allow me my part, and take you the ring.' The other asketh what he counteth the ring to be worth, he answereth, 'Five or six pound.' – 'No,' saith he, 'it is not so much worth.' – 'Well,' saith this ring-faller, 'let me have it, and I will allow you forty shillings for your part.' The other party, standing in a doubt and looking on the ring, asketh if he will give the money out of hand. The other answereth, he hath not so much ready money about him, but he will go fetch so much for him, if he will go with him. The other, that found the ring, thinking he meaneth truly, beginneth to proffer him twenty shillings for his part, sometimes more or less, which he very scornfully refuseth at the first, and still entreateth that he might have the ring, which maketh the other more fonder of it, and desireth him to take the money for his part, and so profferth him money. This ring-faller seeing the money, maketh it very strange, and first questioneth with him where he dwelleth, and asketh him what is his name, and telleth him that he seemeth to be an honest man, and therefore he will do somewhat for friendship's sake, hoping to have as friendly a pleasure at his hand hereafter, and so profferth him for ten shillings more he should have the ring. At last, with entreaty on both parts, he giveth the ring-faller the money and so departeth, thinking he hath gotten a very great jewel.

These kind of deceiving vagabonds have other practices with their rings, as sometimes to come to buy wares of men's prentices, and sometimes of their masters, and when he hath agreed

common upon: discuss.

of the price, he saith he hath not so much money about him, but pulleth off one of these rings from his fingers, and proffereth to leave it in pawn till his master or his friends hath seen it, so promising to bring the money. The seller, thinking he meaneth truly, letteth him go, and never seeth him after, till perhaps at Tyburn or at suchlike place.

There is another kind of these ring-choppers, which commonly carry about them a fair gold ring indeed, and these have other counterfeit rings made so like this gold ring, as ye shall not perceive the contrary, till it be brought to the touchstone. This child will come to borrow money of the right gold ring. The party mistrusting the ring not to be good, goeth to the goldsmith with the party that hath the ring and tryeth it whether it be good gold, and also weigheth it to know how much it is worth. The goldsmith tryeth it to be good gold, and also to have his full weight like gold, and warranteth the party which shall lend the money that the ring is worth so much money, according to the weight. This younker, coming home with the party which shall lend the money, and having the gold ring again, putteth up the gold ring, and pulleth out a counterfeit ring very like the same, and so delivereth it to the party which lendeth the money, they thinking it to be the same which they tried, and so delivereth the money or sometimes wares, and thus vilely be deceived.

The XXV Orders of Knaves

Otherwise Called
a Quarterne of Knaves,
Confirmed For Ever by Cock Lorel

1. Troll and Troll By

Troll and Troll By is he that setteth naught by no man, nor no man by him. This is he that would bear rule in a place, and hath none authority nor thank, and at last is thrust out of the door like a knave.

2. Troll With

Troll With is he that no man shall know the servant from the master. This knave, with his cap on his head like Capon Hardy, will sit down by his master, or else go cheek by cheek with him in the street.

3. Troll Hazard of Trace

Troll Hazard of Trace is he that goeth behind his master as far as he may see him. Such knaves commonly use to buy spice-cakes, apples, or other trifles, and do eat them as they go in the streets like vagabond boys.

4. Troll Hazard of Tritrace

Troll Hazard of Tritrace, is he that goeth gaping after his master, looking to and fro till he have lost him. This knave goeth gazing about like a fool at every toy, and then seeketh in every house like a masterless dog, and when his master needeth him, he is to seek.

5. Chafe-Litter

Chafe-Litter is he that will pluck up the feather-bed or mattress, and piss in the bedstraw, and will never rise uncalled. This knave berayeth many times in the corner of his master's chamber, or other places inconvenient, and maketh clean his shoes with the coverlet or curtains.

6. Obloquium

Obloquium is he that will take a tale out of his master's mouth and tell it himself. He of right may be called a malapert knave.

Capon Hardy: saucy scamp.
berayeth: befouls.
obloquium: from Latin 'to interrupt'.

7. Rinse Pitcher

Rinse Pitcher is he that will drink out his thrift at the ale or wine, and be ofttimes drunk. This is a licorish knave that will swill his master's drink and bribe his meat that is kept for him.

8. Jeffrey God's Foe

Jeffrey God's Foe is he that will swear and maintain oaths. This is such a lying knave that none will believe him, for the more he sweareth, the less he is to be believed.

9. Nichol Heartless

Nichol Heartless is he that when he should do ought for his master his heart faileth him. This is a truant knave that feigneth himself sick when he should work.

10. Simon Soon-Agone

Simon Soon-Agone is he that when his master hath any thing to do, he will hide him out of the way. This is a loitering knave that will hide him in a corner and sleep or else run away.

11. Green Winchard

Green Winchard is he that when his hose is broken and hangs out at his shoes, he will put them into his shoes again with a stick, but he will not amend them. This is a slothful knave, that had leaver go like a beggar than cleanly.

12. Proctor

Proctor is he that will tarry long, and bring a lie, when his master sendeth him on his errand. This is a stibber-gibber knave that doth feign tales.

    licorish: greedy.
    bribe: take dishonestly.

13. Committer of Tidings

Committer of Tidings is he that is ready to bring his master novels and tidings, whether they be true or false. This is a tale-bearer knave, that will report words spoken in his master's presence.

14. Gyle Hather

Gyle Hather is he that will stand by his master when he is at dinner, and bid him beware that he eat no raw meat, because he would eat it himself. This is a pickthank knave that would make his master believe that the cow is wood.

15. Bawd Physic

Bawd Physic is he that is a-cock when his master's meat is evil dressed, and he challenging him therefore, he will say he will eat the rawest morsel thereof himself. This is a saucy knave, that will contrary his master alway.

16. Munch-Present

Munch-Present is he that is a great gentleman, for when his master sendeth him with a present, he will take a taste thereof by the way. This is a bold knave, that sometime will eat the best and leave the worst for his master.

17. Cole Prophet

Cole Prophet is he that when his master sendeth him on his errand, he will tell his answer thereof to his master ere he depart from him. This tittivell knave commonly maketh the worst of the best between his master and his friend.

---

novels : news.
wood : mad (or possibly here in modern sense 'wooden').
tittivell : tell-tale.

18. Curry Favell

Curry Favell is he that will lie in his bed, and curry the bed boards in which he lieth instead of his horse. This slothful knave will buskill and scratch when he is called in the morning, for any hest.

19. Dyng Thrift

Dyng Thrift is he that will make his master's horse eat pies and ribs of beef, and drink ale and wine. Such false knaves ofttimes will sell their master's meat to their own profit.

20. Esen Droppers

Esen Droppers be they that stand under men's walls or windows, or in any other place, to hear the secrets of a man's house. These misdeeming knaves will stand in corners to hear if they be evil spoken of, or wait a shrewd turn.

21. Choplogic

Choplogic is he that when his master rebuketh him of his fault he will give him twenty words for one, else bid the devil's pater noster in silence. This proud prating knave will maintain his naughtiness when he is rebuked for them.

22. Unthrift

Unthrift is he that will not put his wearing clothes to washing, nor black his own shoes, nor amend his own wearing clothes. This reckless knave will alway be lousy, and say that he hath no more shift of clothes, and slander his master.

buskill: ? wriggle (cf. *busk*: 'to shift about').
devil's pater noster: Lord's Prayer recited backwards.

23. Ungracious

Ungracious is he that by his own will will hear no manner of service, without he be compelled thereunto by his rulers. This knave will sit at the alehouse drinking or playing at dice, or at other games at service time.

24. Nunquam

Nunquam is he that when his master sendeth him on his errand he will not come again of an hour or two where he might have done it in half an hour or less. This knave will go about his own errand or pastime and saith he cannot speed at the first.

25. Ingratus

Ingratus is he that when one doth all that he can for him, he will scant give him a good report for his labour. This knave is so ingrate or unkind that he considereth not his friend from his foe, and will requite evil for good and being put most in trust, will soonest deceive his master.

FINIS

Nunquam: Latin 'never'.

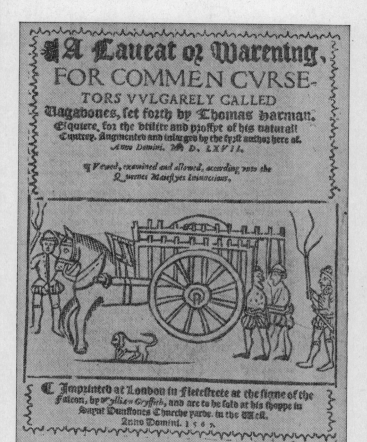

cursitors : explained in Epistle to the Reader (p. 87).

To the Right Honourable and my singular good lady, Elizabeth, Countess of Shrewsbury,[1] Thomas Harman wisheth all joy and perfect felicity, here and in the world to come.

As of ancient and long time there hath been, and is now at this present, many good, godly, profitable laws and acts made and set forth in this most noble and flourishing realm for the relief, succour, comfort and sustentation of the poor, needy, impotent and miserable creatures being and inhabiting in all parts of the same; so is there, Right Honourable and mine especial good lady, most wholesome statutes, ordinances, and necessary laws, made, set forth and published, for the extreme punishment of all vagrants and sturdy vagabonds, as passeth through and by all parts of this famous isle, most idly and wickedly; and I well, by good experience understanding and considering your most tender, pitiful, gentle, and noble nature, – not only having a vigilant and merciful eye to your poor, indigent, and feeble parishioners; yea, not only in the parish where your honour most happily doth dwell, but also in others environing or nigh adjoining to the same; as also abundantly pouring out daily your ardent and bountiful charity upon all such as cometh for relief unto your luckly gates – I thought it good, necessary, and my bounden duty, to acquaint your goodness with the abominable, wicked, and detestable behaviour of all these rowsey, ragged rabblement of rakehells, that – under the pretence of great misery, diseases, and other innumerable calamities which they feign – through great hypocrisy do win and gain great alms in all places where they wil[il]y wander, to the utter deluding of the good givers, deceiving and impoverishing of all such poor householders, both sick and sore, as neither can or may walk abroad for relief and comfort (where, indeed, most mercy is to be showed). And for that I, most honourable lady, being placed as a poor gentleman, have kept a house these twenty years, whereunto poverty daily hath and doth repair, not without some relief, as my poor calling and ability may and doth extend, I have of late years gathered a great suspicion that all should not be well, and, as the proverb saith: 'Something lurk and lay hid that did not plainly appear.' For I, having more occasion, through sickness, to tarry and remain at home than I have been accustomed, do, by my there abiding, talk and confer daily with many of these wily wanderers of both sorts, as well men and women, as boys and girls, by whom I have gathered and understand their deep dissimulation and detestable dealing, being marvellous subtle and crafty in their kind, for not one amongst twenty will discover, either declare their scelerous secrets. Yet with fair flattering words, money, and good cheer, I have attained to the tip by such as the meanest of them hath wandered these thirteen years, and most sixteen and some twenty and upward, and not without faithful promise made unto them never to discover their names or anything they showed me. For they would all say, if the upright men should understand thereof, they should not be only grievously beaten, but put in danger of their lives, by the said upright men.

There was a few years since a small brief set forth of some zealous man to his country, of whom I know not, that made a little show of their names and usage, and gave a glimpsing light, not sufficient to persuade of their peevish, pelting, and picking practices, but well worthy of praise. But, good madam, with no less travail than good will, I have repaired and rigged the ship of knowledge, and have hoist up the sails of good fortune, that she may safely pass about and through all parts of this noble realm, and there make port sale of her wished wares, to the confusion of their drowsy demeanour and unlawful language, pilfering picking, wily wandering, and liking lechery of all these rabblement of rascals that ranges about all the coasts of the same, so that their undecent, doleful dealing and execrable exercises

scelerous: abominably wicked.
a small brief: probably Awdeley's, first published in 1561.
port sale: ? sale at each port, quick sale (auction sale – Judges).

may appear to all, as it were in a glass, that thereby the Justices and shrieves may in their circuits be more vigilant to punish these malefactors, and the constables, bailiffs and borsholders, setting aside all fear, sloth, and pity, may be more circumspect in executing the charge given them by the aforesaid Justices. Then will no more this rascal rabblement range about the country; then greater relief may be showed to the poverty of each parish; then shall we keep our horses in our pastures unstolen; then our linen clothes shall and may lie safely on our hedges untouched; then shall we not have our clothes and linen hooked out at our windows as well by day as by night; then shall we not have our houses broken up in the night, as of late one of my neighbours had, and two great bucks of clothes stolen out, and most of the same fine linen; then shall we safely keep our pigs and poultry from pilfering; then shall we surely pass by the highways leading to markets and fairs unharmed; then shall our shops and booths be unpicked and spoiled; then shall these uncomely companies be dispersed and set to labour for their living, or hastily hang for their demerits; then shall it encourage a great number of gentlemen and others, seeing this security, to set up houses and keep hospitality in the country,[2] to the comfort of their neighbours, relief of the poor, and to the amendment of the commonwealth; then shall not sin and wickedness so much abound among us; then will God's wrath be much the more pacified towards us; then shall we not taste of so many and sundry plagues, as now daily reigneth over us; and then shall this famous empire be in more wealth and better flourish, to the inestimable joy and comfort of the Queen's most excellent Majesty, whom God of His infinite goodness, to His great glory, long and many years make most prosperously to reign over us, to the great felicity of all the peers and nobles, and to the unspeakable joy, relief, and quietness of mind of all her faithful commons and subjects.

Now, methinketh, I see how these peevish, perverse, and

shrieves: sheriffs.
borsholders: high-ranking constables.
bucks: baskets.
surely: safely.

pestilent people begin to fret, fume, swear, and stare at this my book, their life being laid open and apparently painted out, that their confusion and end draweth on apace. Whereas indeed, if it be well weighted, it is set forth for their singular profit and commodity, for the sure safeguard of their lives here in this world, that they shorten not the same before their time, and that by their true labour and good life, in the world to come they may save their souls, that Christ, the second Person in [the] Trinity, hath so dearly bought with His most precious blood. So that hereby I shall do them more good than they could have devised for themselves. For behold, their life being so manifest wicked and so apparently known, the honourable will abhor them, the worshipful will reject them, the yeomen will sharply taunt them, the husbandmen utterly defy them, the labouring men bluntly chide them, the women with a loud exclamation wonder at them, and all children with clapping hands cry out at them.

I many times musing with myself at these mischievous mislivers, marvelled when they took their original and beginning; how long they have exercised their execrable wandering about. I thought it meet to confer with a very old man that I was well acquainted with, whose wit and memory is marvellous for his years, being about the age of fourscore, what he knew when he was young of these lousy loiterers. And he showed me, that when he was young he waited upon a man of much worship in Kent, who died immediately after the last Duke of Buckingham was beheaded.[3] At his burial there was such a number of beggars, besides poor householders dwelling thereabouts, that uneath they might lie or stand about the house. Then was there prepared for them a great and a large barn, and a great fat ox sod out in frumenty[4] for them, with bread and drink abundantly to furnish out the premises; and every person had twopence, for such was the dole. When night approached, the poor householders repaired home to their houses: the other wayfaring bold beggars remained all night in the barn; and the same barn being searched with light in the night by this old man (and then young), with others they told seven score persons of men, every of them having his woman, except it were two women that lay

apparently: fully and clearly.

alone together for some especial cause. Thus having their makes to make merry withal, the burial was turned to boozing and belly-cheer, mourning to mirth, fasting to feasting, prayer to pastime and pressing of paps, and lamenting to lechery.

So that it may appear this uncomely company hath had a long continuance, but then nothing given so much to pilfering, picking, and spoiling; and, as far as I can learn or understand by the examination of a number of them, their language – which they term pedlars' French or Canting – began but within these thirty years, little above; and that the first inventor thereof was hanged, all save the head; for that is the final end of them all, or else to die of some filthy and horrible diseases. But much harm is done in the mean space by their continuance, as some ten, twelve and sixteen years [may pass] before they be consumed and the number of them doth daily renew. I hope their sin is now at the highest; and that as short and as speedy a redress will be for these, as hath been of late years for the wretched, wily, wandering vagabonds calling and naming themselves Egyptians,[5] deeply dissembling and long hiding and covering their deep, deceitful practices, feeding the rude common people, wholly addicted and given to novelties, toys, and new inventions; delighting them with the strangeness of the attire of their heads, and practising palmistry to such as would know their fortunes; and, to be short, all thieves and whores, as I may well write, as some have had true experience, a number can well witness, and a great sort hath well felt it. And now, thanks be to God, through wholesome laws, and the due execution thereof, all be dispersed, banished, and the memory of them clean extinguished; that when they be once named hereafter our children will much marvel what kind of people they were. And so, I trust, shall shortly happen of these. For what thing doth chiefly cause these rowsey rakehells thus to continue and daily increase? Surely a number of wicked persons that keep tippling houses in all shires where they have succour and relief; and whatsoever they bring, they are sure to receive money for the same, for they sell good pennyworths. The buyers have the greatest gain. Yea, if they have neither money nor ware, they will be trusted; their credit is much. I have taken a note of a good many of them, and will send their names and dwelling-places to such Justices as dwelleth near or next unto them, that they by their good wisdoms may displace the same, and authorize such as have honesty. I will not blot my book with their names, because they be resident. But as for this fleeting fellowship, I have truly set forth the most part of them that be doers at this present,' with their names that they be known by. Also, I have placed in the end thereof their lewd language, calling the same pedlars' French or Canting.

And now shall I end my prologue, making true declaration, Right Honourable Lady, as they shall fall in order of their untimely trifling time, lewd life, and pernicious practices, trusting that the same shall neither trouble or abash your most tender, timorous, and pitiful nature, to think the small meed should grow unto you for such alms so given. For God, our merciful and most loving Father, well knoweth your hearts and good intent. The giver never wanteth his reward, according to the saying of St Augustine: 'As there is, neither shall be, any sin unpunished, even so shall there not be any good deed unrewarded.' But how comfortably speaketh Christ our Saviour unto us in His Gospel: 'Give ye, and it shall be given you again.' Behold farther, good madam, that for a cup of cold water Christ hath promised a good reward. Now St Austin properly declareth why Christ speaketh of cold water, because the poorest man that is shall not excuse himself from that charitable work, lest he would, peradventure, say that he hath neither wood, pot, nor pan to warm any water with. See farther what God speaketh in the mouth of His prophet Isaiah: 'Break thy bread to him that is a-hungered.' He saith not give him a whole loaf, for peradventure the poor man hath it not to give: then let him give a piece. This much is said, because the poor that hath it should not be excused: now how much more then the rich? Thus you see, good madam, for your treasure here dispersed, where need and lack is, it shall be heaped up abundantly for you in Heaven, where neither rust or moth shall corrupt or destroy the same. Unto which triumphant place, after many good, happy and fortunate years prosperously here dispended, you may for ever and ever there most joyfully remain. Amen.

FINIS

The Epistle to the Reader

Although, good reader, I write in plain terms – and not so plainly as truly – concerning the matter, meaning honestly to all men, and wish them as much good as to mine own heart, yet, as there hath been, so there is now, and hereafter will be curious heads to find faults. Wherefore I thought it necessary, now at this second impression to acquaint thee with a great fault, as some taketh it (but none as I mean it), calling these vagabonds *cursitors* in the entitling of my book, as runners or rangers about the country, derived of this Latin word, *curro*. Neither do I write it *cooresetores*, with a double *oo*, or *cowresetors*, with a *w*, which hath another signification. Is there no diversity between a *gardein* and a *garden*, *maynteynaunce* and *maintenance*, *streytes* and *stretes*? Those that have understanding know there is a great difference. Who is so ignorant by these days as knoweth not the meaning of a *vagabond*? And if an idle loiterer should be so called of any man, would not he think it both odious and reproachful? Will he not shun the name? Yea, and whereas he may and dare, with bent brows will revenge that name of ignominy. Yet this plain name *vagabond* is derived, as others be, of Latin words, and now use makes it common to all men. But let us look back four hundred years sithence, and let us see whether this plain word *vagabond* was used or no. I believe not: and why? Because I read of no such name in the old statutes of this realm, unless it be in the margin of the book, or in the table, which in the collection and printing was set in. But these were then the common names of these lewd loiterers: *faitours*, *Roberdsmen*, *draw-latches*, and *valiant beggars*. If I should have used such words, or the same order of writing as this realm used in King Henry the Third or Edward the First's time – Oh, what a gross barbarous fellow have we here! His writing is both homely and dark, that we had need to have an interpreter. Yet then it was very well, and in short season a great change we see. Well, this delicate age shall have his time on the other side. Eloquence have I none; I never was acquainted with the Muses; I never tasted of

Helicon. But according to my plain order, I have set forth this work, simply and truly, with such usual words and terms as is among us well known and frequented. So that, as the proverb saith, 'Although truth be blamed it shall never be shamed.' Well, good reader, I mean not to be tedious unto thee, but have added five or six more tales, because some of them were done while my book was first in the press. And, as I trust I have deserved no rebuke for my good will, even so I desire no praise for my pain, cost, and travail. But faithfully for the profit and benefit of my country I have done it, that the whole body of the realm may see and understand their lewd life and pernicious practices, that all may speedily help to amend that is amiss. Amen say all with me.

FINIS

Chapter 1

A Ruffler

THE ruffler, because he is first in degree of this odious order, and is so called in a statute made for the punishment of vagabonds in the twenty-seventh year of King Henry the Eighth, late of most famous memory, he shall be first placed, as the worthiest of this unruly rabblement. And he is so called when he goeth first abroad. Either he hath served in the wars, or else he hath been a serving man; and weary of well-doing, shaking off all pain doth choose him this idle life, and wretchedly wanders about the most shires of this realm. And with stout audacity demandeth where he thinketh he may be bold, and circumspect enough as he seeth cause to ask charity, ruefully and lamentably that it would make a flinty heart to relent, and pity his miserable estate, how he hath been maimed and bruised in the wars; and, peradventure, some will show you some outward wound, which he got at some drunken fray, either halting of some privy wound festered with a filthy fiery flankard. For be well assured that the hardiest soldiers be either slain or maimed, either and they escape all hazards, and return home again. If they be without relief of their friends they will surely desperately rob and steal, and either shortly be hanged or miserably die in prison. For they be so much ashamed and disdain to beg or ask charity, that rather they will as desperately fight for to live and maintain themselves, as manfully and valiantly they ventured themselves in the Prince's quarrel. Now these rufflers, the outcasts of servingmen, when begging or craving fails, then they pick and pilfer from other inferior beggars that they meet by the way, as rogues, palliards, morts, and doxies. Yea, if they meet with a woman alone riding to the market, either old man or boy, that he well knoweth will not resist, such they filch and spoil. These rufflers, after a year or two at the farthest, become upright men, unless they be prevented by twined hemp.

flankard: ? spark of fire (flanker) or wound at side.
twined hemp: hangman's noose.

I had of late years an old man to my tenant, who customably a great time went twice in the week to London, either with fruit or with peasecods, when time served therefore. And as he was coming homeward on Blackheath, at the end thereof next to Shooters Hill, he overtook two rufflers, the one mannerly waiting on the other, as one had been the master, and the other the man or servant, carrying his master's cloak. This old man was very glad that he might have their company over the hill, because that day he had made a good market; for he had seven shillings in his purse, and an old angel, which this poor man had thought had not been in his purse, for he willed his wife overnight to take out the same angel, and lay it up until his coming home again; and he verily thought that his wife had so done, which indeed forgot to do it. Thus, after salutations had, this master ruffler entered into communication with this simple old man, who, riding softly beside them, commoned of many matters. Thus feeding this old man with pleasant talk until they were on the top of the hill, where these rufflers might well behold the coast about them clear, quickly steps unto this poor man, and taketh hold of his horse bridle, and leadeth him into the wood and demandeth of him what and how much money he had in his purse.

'Now, by my troth,' quoth this old man, 'you are a merry gentleman. I know you mean not to take away anything from me, but rather to give me some if I should ask it of you.'

By and by this servant thief casteth the cloak that he carried on his arm about this poor man's face, that he should not mark or view them, with sharp words to deliver quickly that he had, and to confess truly what was in his purse. This poor man, then all abashed, yielded, and confessed that he had but just seven shillings in his purse. And the truth is he knew of no more. This old angel was fallen out of a little purse into the bottom of a great purse. Now, this seven shillings in white money they quickly found, thinking indeed that there had been no more; yet farther groping and searching, found this old angel. And with great admiration, this gentleman thief began to bless him saying, 'Good Lord, what a world is this! How may,' quoth he, 'a man believe or trust in the same? See you not,' quoth he, 'this old knave

angel: coin equivalent to noble (see p. 69).

told me that he had but seven shillings, and here is more by an angel. What an old knave and a false knave have we here!' quoth this ruffler. 'Our Lord have mercy on us! Will this world never be better?' – and therewith went their way, and left the old man in the wood, doing him no more harm. But sorrowfully sighing, this old man, returning home, declared his misadventure, with all the words and circumstances above showed. Whereat for the time was great laughing, and this poor man for his losses among his loving neighbours well considered in the end.

Chapter 2

A Upright Man

A UPRIGHT man, the second in sect of this unseemly sort, must be next placed, of these ranging rabblement of rascals; some be servingmen, artificers, and labouring men traded up in husbandry. These, not minding to get their living with the sweat of their face, but casting off all pain, will wander, after their wicked manner, through the most shires of this realm: as Somersetshire, Wiltshire, Berkshire, Oxfordshire, Hertfordshire, Middlesex, Essex, Suffolk, Norfolk, Sussex, Surrey and Kent, as the chief and best shires of relief. Yea, not without punishment by stocks, whippings, and imprisonment, in most of these places abovesaid. Yet, notwithstanding, they have so good liking in their lewd, lecherous loiterings, that full quickly all their punishments is forgotten. And repentance is never thought upon until they climb three trees with a ladder.

These unruly rascals, in their roiling, disperse themselves into several companies, as occasion serveth, sometime more and sometime less. As, if they repair to a poor husbandman's house, he will go alone, or one with him, and stoutly demand his charity, either showing how he hath served in the wars, and there maimed, either that he seeketh service, and sayeth that he would be glad to take pain for his living, although he meaneth nothing

not minding to : not being inclined to.
roiling : wandering.

less. If he be offered any meat or drink, he utterly refuseth scorn-fully, and will nought but money; and if he espy young pigs or poultry, he well noteth the place, and the[n] the next night, or shortly after, he will be sure to have some of them, which they bring to their stalling kens, which is their tippling houses, as well known to them according to the old proverb, 'as the beggar knows his dish'. For, you must understand, every tippling ale-house will neither receive them or their wares, but some certain houses in every shire, especially for that purpose, where they shall be better welcome to them than honester men. For by such have they most gain, and shall be conveyed either into some loft out of the way, or other secret corner not common to any other. And thither repair at accustomed times their harlots, which they term morts and doxies – not with empty hands. For they be as skilful in picking, rifling, and filching as the upright men, and nothing inferior to them in all kind of wickedness, as in other places hereafter they shall be touched. At these foresaid pelting, peevish places and unmannerly meetings, oh, how the pots walk about! Their talking tongues talk at large. They boll and booze one to another, and for the time boozing belly-cheer. And after their roisting recreation, if there be not room enough in the house, they have clean straw in some barn or backhouse near adjoining, where they couch comely together, an it were dog and bitch. And he that is hardest may have his choice, unless for a little good manner. Some will take their own that they have made promise unto, until they be out of sight, and then, according to the old adage, out of mind.

Yet these upright men stand so much upon their reputation, as they will in no case have their women walk with them, but separate themselves for a time, a month or more, and meet at fairs, or great markets, where they meet to pilfer and steal from stalls, shops, or booths. At these fairs the upright men use com-monly to lie and linger in highways, by lanes some pretty way or distance from the place, by which ways they be assured that company passeth still to and fro. And there they will demand, with cap in hand and comely courtesy, the devotion and charity of the people. They have been much lately whipped at fairs. If

boll: drink.

they ask at a stout yeoman's or farmer's house his charity, they will go strong as three or four in a company; where, for fear more than good will, they often have relief. They seldom or never pass by a Justice's house, but have by-ways, unless he dwell alone, and but weakly manned. Thither will they also go strong, after a sly, subtle sort, as with their arms bound up with kercher or list, having wrapped about the same filthy clothes, either their legs in such manner be wrapped, halting downright; not unprovided of good cudgels, which they carry to sustain them, and, as they feign, to keep dogs from them, when they come to such good gentlemen's houses.

If any search be made, or they suspected for pilfering clothes off hedges, or breaking of houses, which they commonly do when the owners be either at the market, church, or other ways occupied about their business – either rob some silly man or woman by the highway, as many times they do – then they hie them into woods, great thickets, and other rough corners, where they lie lurking three or four days together, and have meat and drink brought them by their morts and doxies. And while they thus lie hidden in covert, in the night they be not idle, neither, as the common saying is, 'well occupied'. For then as the wily fox, creeping out of his den, seeketh his prey for poultry, so do these for linen and anything else worth money that lieth about or near a house, as sometime a whole buck of clothes, carried away at a time. When they have a greater booty than they may carry away quickly to their stalling kens, as is abovesaid, they will hide the same for a three days in some thick covert, and in the night time carry the same, like good water-spaniels, to their foresaid houses; to whom they will discover where or in what places they had the same, where the marks shall be picked out clean, and conveyed craftily far off to sell if the man or woman of the house want money themselves. If these upright men have neither money nor wares, at these houses they shall be trusted for their victuals an it amount to twenty or thirty shillings. Yea, if it fortune any of these upright men to be taken, either suspected or charged with felony or petty bribery, done at such a time or such a place, he will say he was in his host's house. And if the man or wife of that house be examined by an officer, they boldly vouch, that they lodged him such a time, whereby the truth cannot appear.

And if they chance to be retained into service, through their lamentable words, with any wealthy man, they will tarry but a small time either robbing his master or some of his fellows. And some of them useth this policy, that although they travel into all these shires abovesaid, yet will they have good credit especially in one shire, where at divers good farmers' houses they be well known, where they work a month in a place or more and will for that time behave themselves very honestly and painfully, and may at any time, for their good usage, have work of them. And to these at a dead lift, or last refuge, they may safely repair unto, and be welcome when in other places, for a knack of knavery that they have played, they dare not tarry.

These upright men will seldom or never want; for what is gotten by any mort, or doxy, if it please him, he doth command the same. And if he meet any beggar, whether he be sturdy or impotent, he will demand of him, whether ever he was stalled to the rogue or no. If he say he was, he will know of whom, and his name that stalled him. And if he be not learnedly able to show him the whole circumstance thereof, he will spoil him of his money, either of his best garment, if it be worth any money, and have him to the boozing ken which is to some tippling house next adjoining, and layeth there to gage the best thing that he hath for twenty pence or two shillings. This man obeyeth for fear of beating. Then doth this upright man call for a gage of boozè, which is a quart pot of drink, and pours the same upon his peld pate, adding these words: 'I, G.P., do stall thee, W.T., to the rogue, and that from henceforth it shall be lawful for thee to cant' – that is, to ask or beg – 'for thy living in all places.' Here you see that the upright man is of great authority. For all sorts of beggars are obedient to his hests, and [he] surmounteth all others in pilfering and stealing.

I lately had standing in my well-house, which standeth on the back-side of my house, a great cauldron of copper, being then full of water, having in the same half a dozen of pewter dishes, well marked, and stamped with the cognizance of my arms which, being well noted when they were taken out, were set aside,

stalled to the rogue: ceremonially admitted to thieves' order.

the water poured out and my cauldron taken away, being of such bigness that one man, unless he were of great strength, was not able far to carry the same. Notwithstanding, the same was one night within this two years conveyed more than half a mile from my house, into a common or heath, and there bestowed in a great fir-bush. I then immediately the next day sent one of my men to London, and there gave warning in Southwark, Kent Street, and Bermondsey Street,[6] to all the tinkers there dwelling, that if any such cauldron came thither to be sold, the bringer thereof should be stayed; and promised twenty shillings for a reward. I gave also intelligence to the watermen that kept the ferries, that no such vessel should be either conveyed to London or into Essex, promising the like reward to have understanding thereof. This my doing was well understood in many places about, and that the fear of espying so troubled the conscience of the stealer, that my cauldron lay untouched in the thick fir-bush more than half a year after, which, by a great chance, was found by hunters for conies; for one chanced to run into the same bush where my cauldron was and being perceived, one thrust his staff into the same bush, and hit my cauldron a great blow, the sound whereof did cause the man to think and hope that there was some great treasure hidden, whereby he thought to be the better while he lived; and in farther searching he found my cauldron. So had I the same again unlooked for.

Chapter 3

A Hooker, or Angler

THESE hookers, or anglers, be perilous and most wicked knaves, and be derived or proceed forth from the upright men. They commonly go in frieze jerkins and gallyslops, pointed beneath the knee. These when they practise their pilfering, it is all by night; for, as they walk a day-times from house to house to de-

frieze : cheap woollen cloth.
gallyslops : wide hose.
pointed : fastened with lace.

mand charity, they vigilantly mark where or in what place they may attain to their prey, casting their eyes up to every window, well noting what they see there, whether apparel or linen, hanging near unto the said windows, and that will they be sure to have the next night following. For they customably carry with them a staff of five or six foot long, in which, within one inch of the top thereof, is a little hole bored through, in which hole they put an iron hook, and with the same they will pluck unto them quickly anything that they may reach therewith, which hook in the day-time they covertly carry about them, and is never seen or taken out till they come to the place where they work their feat. Such have I seen at my house, and have oft talked with them and have handled their staves, not then understanding to what use or intent they served, although I had and perceived by their talk and behaviour great likelihood of evil suspicion in them. They will either lean upon their staff, to hide the hole thereof, when they talk with you, or hold their hand upon the hole. And what stuff, either woollen or linen, they thus hook out, they never carry the same forthwith to their stalling kens, but hide the same a three days in some secret corner, and after convey the same to their houses abovesaid, where their host or hostess giveth them money for the same, but half the value that it is worth, or else their doxies shall afar off sell the same at the like houses. I was credibly informed that a hooker came to a farmer's house in the dead of the night, and putting back a draw window of a low chamber, the bed standing hard by the said window, in which lay three persons (a man and two big boys), this hooker with his staff plucked off their garments which lay upon them to keep them warm, with the coverlet and sheet, and left them lying asleep naked saving their shirts, and had away all clean, and never could understand where it became. I verily suppose that when they were well waked with cold, they surely thought that Robin Goodfellow, according to the old saying, had been with them that night.

Robin Goodfellow: Puck, a mischievous sprite (cf. *A Midsummer Night's Dream*, II, i, 42–57).

Chapter 4

A Rogue

A ROGUE is neither so stout or hardy as the upright man. Many of them will go faintly and look piteously when they see, either meet any person; having a kercher, as white as my shoes, tied about their head, with a short staff in their hand, halting, although they need not, requiring alms of such as they meet, or to what house they shall come. But you may easily perceive by their colour that they carry both health and hypocrisy about them whereby they get gain, when others want that cannot feign and dissemble. Others there be that walk sturdily about the country, and feigneth to seek a brother or kinsman of his, dwelling within some part of the shire. Either that he hath a letter to deliver to some honest householder, dwelling out of another shire, and will show you the same fair sealed, with the superscription to the party he speaketh of, because you shall not think him to run idly about the country; either have they this shift: they will carry a certificate or passport about them from some Justice of the Peace, with his hand and seal unto the same, how he hath been whipped and punished for a vagabond according to the laws of this realm, and that he must return to T—, where he was born or last dwelt, by a certain day limited in the same, which shall be a good long day. And all this feigned, because without fear they would wickedly wander, and will renew the same where or when it pleaseth them; for they have of their affinity that can write and read.

These also will pick and steal as the upright men, and hath their women and meetings at places appointed, and nothing to them inferior in all kind of knavery. There be of these rogues curtals, wearing short cloaks, that will change their apparel as occasion serveth. And their end is either hanging, which they call trining in their language, or die miserably of the pox.

There was not long sithence two rogues that always did associate themselves together, and would never separate themselves, unless it were for some especial causes, for they were sworn brothers, and were both of one age, and much like of favour. These two, travelling into East Kent, resorted unto an ale-house there, being wearied with travelling, saluting with short courtesy, when they came into the house, such as they saw sitting there, in which company was the parson of the parish; and, calling for a pot of the best ale, sat down at the table's end: the liquor liked them so well, that they had pot upon pot, and sometime, for a little good manner, would drink and offer the cup to such as they best fancied; and, to be short, they sat out all the company, for each man departed home about their business. When they had well refreshed themselves, then these rowsey rogues requested the goodman of the house with his wife to sit down and drink with them, of whom they inquired what priest the same was, and where he dwelt. Then they, feigning that they had an uncle a priest, and that he should dwell in these parts, which by all presumptions it should be he, and that they came of purpose to speak with him, but, because they had not seen him sithence they were six years old, they durst not be bold to take acquaintance of him until they were farther instructed of the truth, and began to inquire of his name, and how long he had dwelt there, and how far his house was off from the place they were in. The goodwife of the house, thinking them honest men without deceit, because they so far inquired of their kinsman, was but of a good zealous natural intent, showed them cheerfully that he was an honest man and well beloved in the parish, and of good wealth, and had been there resident fifteen years at the least.

'But,' saith she, 'are you both brothers?' – 'Yea surely,' said they; 'we have been both in one belly, and were twins.' – 'Mercy, God!' quoth this foolish woman; 'It may well be, for ye be not much unlike,' – and went unto her hall window, calling these young men unto her, and looking out thereat, pointed with her finger and showed them the house standing alone, no house near the same by almost a quarter of a mile. 'That,' said she, 'is your uncle's house.' – 'Nay,' saith one of them, 'he is not only my uncle, but also my godfather.' – 'It may well be,' quoth she. 'Nature will bind him to be the better unto you.' – 'Well,' quoth they, 'we be weary, and mean not to trouble our uncle tonight.

favour: countenance.

But tomorrow, God willing, we will see him and do our duty. But, I pray you, doth our uncle occupy husbandry? What company hath he in his house?' – 'Alas!' saith she, 'but one old woman and a boy. He hath no occupying at all. Tush,' quoth this goodwife, 'you be madmen. Go to him this night, for he hath better lodging for you than I have, and yet I speak foolishly against my own profit, for by your tarrying here I should gain the more by you.'

'Now, by my troth,' quoth one of them, 'we thank you, good hostess, for your wholesome counsel and we mean to do as you will us. We will pause awhile, and by that time it will be almost night. And, I pray you, give us a reckoning.' So, mannerly paying for that they took, bade their host and hostess farewell, with taking leave of the cup, marched merrily out of the doors towards this parson's house, viewed the same well round about, and passed by two bowshots off into a young wood, where they lay consulting what they should do until midnight.

Quoth one of them, of sharper wit and subtler than the other, to his fellow, 'Thou seest that this house is stone-walled about, and that we cannot well break in, in any part thereof. Thou seest also that the windows be thick of mullions, that there is no creeping in between. Whereof we must of necessity use some policy, when strength will not serve. I have a horse-lock here about me,' saith he; 'and this I hope shall serve our turn.'

So when it was about twelve of the clock, they came to the house and lurked near unto his chamber window. The dog of the house barked a-good, that with the noise this priest waketh out of his sleep, and began to cough and hem. Then one of these rogues steps forth nearer the window and maketh a rueful and pitiful noise, requiring for Christ sake some relief, that was both hungry and thirsty and was like to lie without the doors all night and starve for cold, unless he were relieved by him with some small piece of money. 'Where dwellest thou?' quoth this parson – 'Alas! sir,' saith this rogue, 'I have small dwelling, and have come out of my way. An I should now,' said he, 'go to any town now at this time of night, they would set me in the stocks and punish me.' – 'Well,' quoth this pitiful parson, 'away from my house, either lie in some of my out-houses until the morning. And hold – here is a couple of pence for thee.' – 'A God reward you,' quoth this rogue, 'and in Heaven may you find it!' The parson openeth his window, and thrusteth out his arm to give his alms to this rogue that came whining to receive it, and quickly taketh hold of his hand, and calleth his fellow to him, which was ready at hand with the horse-lock, and clappeth the same about the wrist of his arm, that the mullions standing so close together for strength, that for his life he could not pluck in his arm again and made him believe, unless he would at the least give them three pounds, they would smite off his arm from the body. So that this poor parson, in fear to lose his hand, called up his old woman that lay in the loft over him, and willed her to take out all the money he had, which was four marks, which he said was all the money in his house, for he had lent six pounds to one of his neighbours not four days before.

'Well,' quoth they, 'Master Parson, if you have no more, upon this condition we will take off the lock, that you will drink twelve pence for our sakes tomorrow at the ale-house where we found you, and thank the goodwife for the good cheer she made us.'

He promised faithfully that he would do so. So they took off the lock, and went their way so far ere it was day, that the parson could never have any understanding more of them. Now this parson, sorrowfully slumbering that night between fear and hope, thought it was but folly to make two sorrows of one. He used contentation for his remedy, not forgetting in the morning to perform his promise, but went betimes to his neighbour that kept tippling, and asked angrily where the same two men were that drank with her yesterday. 'Which two men?' quoth this goodwife. 'The strangers that came in when I was at your house with my neighbours yesterday.' – 'What! your nephews?' quoth she. 'My nephews?' quoth this parson; 'I trow thou art mad.' – 'Nay, by God!' quoth this goodwife, 'as sober as you. For they told me faithfully that you were their uncle. But, in faith, are you not so indeed? For, by my troth, they are strangers to me. I never saw them before.' – 'Oh, out upon them!' quoth the parson; 'they be false thieves, and this night they compelled me to give them all the money in my house.' – '*Benedicite!*' quoth this goodwife, 'and have they so indeed? As I shall answer before God, one of them told me besides that you were godfather to him, and that he trusted to have your blessing before he departed.' – 'What! did he?' quoth this parson; 'a halter bless him for me!' – 'Methinketh, by the mass, by your countenance you looked so wildly when you came in,' quoth this goodwife, 'that something was amiss.' – 'I use not to jest,' quoth this parson, 'when I speak so earnestly.' – 'Why, all your sorrows go with it!' quoth this goodwife. 'And sit down here, and I will fill a fresh pot of ale shall make you merry again.' – 'Yea,' saith this parson, 'fill in, and give me some meat. For they made me swear and promise them faithfully that I should drink twelve pence with you this day.' – 'What! did they?' quoth she; 'Now, by the Marymass, they be merry knaves. I warrant you they mean to buy no land with your money. But how could they come into you in the night, your doors being shut fast? Your house is very strong.' Then this parson showed her all the whole circumstance, how he gave them his alms out at the window: they made such lamentable cry that it pitied him at the heart; for he saw but one when he put out his hand at the window.

'Be ruled by me,' quoth this goodwife. 'Wherein?' quoth this parson. 'By my troth, never speak more of it. When they shall understand of it in the parish, they will but laugh you to scorn.' 'Why, then,' quoth this parson, 'the devil go with it.' And there an end.

Chapter 5

A Wild Rogue

A WILD rogue is he that is born a rogue. He is a more subtle and more given by nature to all kind of knavery than the other, as beastly begotten in barn or bushes, and from his infancy traded up in treachery; yea, and before ripeness of years doth permit, wallowing in lewd lechery – but that is counted amongst them no sin. For this is their custom, that when they meet in barn at night, every one getteth a make to lie withal, and there chance to be twenty in a company as there is sometime more and sometime less. For to one man that goeth abroad, there are at the least two women, which never make it strange when they be called, although she never knew him before. Then, when the day doth appear he rouses him up, and shakes his ears, and away wandering where he may get aught to the hurt of others. Yet before he skippeth out of his couch and departeth from his darling, if he like her well, he will appoint her where to meet shortly after, with a warning to work warily for some cheats, that their meeting might be the merrier.

Not long sithence, a wild rogue chanced to meet a poor neighbour of mine, who for honesty and good nature surmounteth many. This poor man, riding homeward from London, where he had made his market, this rogue demanded a penny for God's sake, to keep him a true man. This simple man, beholding him well, and saw he was of tall personage with a good quarterstaff in his hand, it much pitied him, as he said, to see him want; for he was well able to serve his prince in the wars. Thus, being moved with pity, and looked in his purse to find out a penny; and, in looking for the same, he plucked out eight shillings in white money and raked therein to find a single penny; and at the last finding one, doth offer the same to this wild rogue. But he, seeing so much money in this simple man's hand, being stricken to the heart with a covetous desire, bid him forthwith deliver all that he had, or else he would with his staff beat out his brains. For it was not a penny would now quench his thirst, seeing so much as he did. Thus, swallowing his spittle greedily down, [he] spoiled this poor man of all the money that he had, and leapt over the hedge into a thick wood, and went his way as merrily as this good simple man came home sorrowfully. I, once rebuking a wild rogue because he went idly about, he showed me that he was a beggar by inheritance. His grandfather was a beggar, his father was one, and he must needs be one by good reason.

cheats: things.

Chapter 6

A Prigger of Prancers

A PRIGGER of prancers be horse-stealers; for to prig signifieth in their language to steal, and a prancer is a horse. So being put together, the matter is plain. These go commonly in jerkins of leather, or of white frieze, and carry little wands in their hands, and will walk through grounds and pastures to search and see horses meet for their purpose. And if they chance to be met and asked by the owners of the ground what they make there, they feign straight that they have lost their way, and desire to be instructed the best way to such a place. These will also repair to gentlemen's houses and ask their charity, and will offer their service. And if you ask them what they can do, they will say that they can keep two or three geldings, and wait upon a gentleman. These have also their women, that, walking from them in other places, mark where and what they see abroad, and showeth these priggers thereof when they meet, which is within a week or two. And look, where they steal anything, they convey the same at the least three score miles off or more.

There was a gentleman, a very friend of mine, riding from London homeward into Kent, having within three miles of his house business, alighted off his horse, and his man also, in a pretty village, where divers houses were, and looked about him where he might have a convenient person to walk his horse, because he would speak with a farmer that dwelt on the back-side of the said village, little above a quarter of a mile from the place where he lighted, and had his man to wait upon him, as it was meet for his calling. Espying a prigger there standing, thinking the same to dwell there, charging this pretty prigging person to walk his horse well, and that they might not stand still for taking of cold, and at his return, which he said should not be long, he would give him a penny to drink, and so went about his business.

This pelting prigger, proud of his prey, walketh his horse up and down till he saw the gentleman out of sight, and leaps him into the saddle, and away he goeth amain. This gentleman return-

CONY-CATCHERS AND BAWDY BASKETS

ing, and finding not his horses, sent his man to the one end of
the village, and he went himself unto the other end, and inquired
as he went for his horses that were walked, and began somewhat
to suspect, because neither he nor his man could see nor find
him. Then this gentleman diligently inqured of three or four
town dwellers there whether any such person [passed by], declaring his stature, age, apparel, with so many lineaments of his body
as he could call to remembrance. And *una voce* all said that no
such man dwelt in their street, neither in the parish, that they
knew of. But some did well remember that such a one they saw
there lurking and huggering two hours before the gentleman
came thither, and a stranger to them. 'I had thought', quoth this
gentleman, 'he had here dwelled' – and marched home mannerly
in his boots. Far from the place he dwelt not. I suppose at his
coming home he sent such ways as he suspected or thought meet
to search for this prigger, but hitherto he never heard any tidings
again of his palfreys. I had the best gelding stolen out of my
pasture that I had, amongst others, while this book was first a-
printing.

Chapter 7

A Palliard

THESE palliards be called also clapperdudgeons. These go with
patched cloaks, and have their morts with them, which they call
wives. And if he go to one house to ask his alms, his wife shall go
to another; for what they get, as bread, cheese, malt and wool,
they sell the same for ready money; for so they get more [than]
if they went together. Although they be thus divided in the day,
yet they meet jump at night. If they chance to come to some
gentleman's house standing alone, and be demanded whether
they be man and wife, and if he perceive that any doubteth
thereof, he showeth them a testimonial with the minister's name,
and others of the same parish, naming a parish in some shire far
distant from the place where he showeth the same. This writing
he carryeth to salve that sore. There be many Irishmen [7] that go

huggering : lying concealed.

about with counterfeit licences. And if they perceive you will straitly examine them, they will immediately say they can speak no English.

Farther understand for truth that the worst and wickedest of all this beastly generation are scarce comparable to these prating palliards. All for the most part of these will either lay to their legs an herb called spearwort, either arsenic, which is called ratsbane. The nature of this spearwort will raise a great blister in a night upon the soundest part of his body. And if the same be taken away, it will dry up again and no harm. But this arsenic will so poison the same leg or sore, that it will ever after be incurable. This do they for gain and to be pitied. The most of these that walk about be Welshmen.

Chapter 8

A Frater

SOME of these fraters will carry black boxes at their girdle, wherein they have a brief of the Queen's Majesty's letters patents, given to such [a] poor spital-house for the relief of the poor there, which brief is a copy of the letters patents, and utterly feigned if it be in paper or in parchment without the great seal. Also, if the same brief be in print, it is also of authority. For the printers will see and well understand, before it come in press, that the same is lawful. Also, I am credibly informed that the chief proctors of many of these houses, that seldom travel abroad themselves, but have their factors to gather for them, which look very slenderly to the impotent and miserable creatures committed to their charge, and die for want of cherishing; whereas they and their wives are well crammed and clothed, and will have of the best. And the founders of every such house, or the chief of the parish where they be, would better see unto these proctors, that they might do their duty: they should be well spoken of here, and in the world to come abundantly therefore rewarded.

I had of late an honest man, and of good wealth, repaired to my house to common with me about certain affairs. I invited the same to dinner, and, dinner being done, I demanded of him some news of th[o]se parts where he dwelt. 'Thanks be to God, sir,' saith he; 'all is well and good now.' – 'Now!' quoth I, 'this same "now" declareth that some things of late hath not been well.' – 'Yes, sir,' quoth he, 'the matter is not great. I had thought I should have been well beaten within this seventh night.' – 'How so?' quoth I.

'Marry, sir,' said he, 'I am Constable for fault of a better, and was commanded by the Justice to watch. The watch being set, I took an honest man, one of my neighbours, with me, and went up to the end of the town as far as the spital-house, at which house I heard a great noise, and, drawing near, stood close under the wall, and this was at one of the clock after midnight.' Where he heard swearing, prating, and wagers laying, and the pot apace walking, and forty pence gaged upon a match of wrestling, pitching of the bar, and casting of the sledge. And out they go, in a fustian fume, into the back-side, where was a great axle-tree, and there fell to pitching of the bar, being three to three. The moon did shine bright, the Constable with his neighbour might see and behold all that was done, and how the wife of the house was

proctors: those licensed to collect for almshouses.

roasting of a pig, while her guests were in their match. At the last they could not agree upon a cast, and fell at words, and from words to blows. The Constable with his fellow runs unto them to part them, and in the parting licks a dry blow or two. Then the noise increased. The Constable would have had them to the stocks. The wife of the house runs out with her goodman to entreat the Constable for her guests, and leaves the pig at the fire alone. In cometh two or three of the next neighbours, being waked with this noise, and into the house they come, and find none therein, but the pig well roasted, and carrieth the same away with them, spit and all, with such bread and drink also as stood upon the table.

When the goodman and the goodwife of the house had entreated and pacified the Constable, showing unto him that they were proctors and factors all of spital-houses, and that they tarried there but to break their fast, and would ride away immediately after, for they had far to go, and therefore meant to ride so early. And, coming into their house again, finding the pig with bread and drink all gone, made a great exclamation, for they knew not who had the same.

The Constable returning, and hearing the lamentable words of the goodwife, how she had lost both meat and drink and saw it was so indeed, he laughed in his sleeve, and commanded her to dress no more at unlawful hours for any guests. For he thought it better bestowed upon those smell-feasts his poor neighbours than upon such sturdy lubbers. The next morning betimes the spit and pots were set at the spital-house door for the owner. Thus were these factors beguiled of their breakfast, and one of them had well beaten another. 'And, by my troth,' quoth this Constable, 'I was glad when I was well rid of them.' – 'Why,' quoth I, 'could they cast the bar and sledge well?' – 'I will tell you, sir,' quoth he. 'You know there hath been many games this summer. I think verily that if some of these lubbers had been there, and practised amongst others, I believe they would have carried away the best games. For they were so strong and sturdy, that I was not able to stand in their hands.' – 'Well,' quoth I, 'at these games you speak of, both legs and arms be tried.' – 'Yea,' quoth this

dress: prepare food.

officer, 'they be wicked men. I have seen some of them sithence with clouts bound about their legs, and halting with their staff in their hands. Wherefore some of them, by God, be nought all.'

Chapter 9

A Abraham Man

THESE Abraham men be those that feign themselves to have been mad, and have been kept either in Bethlem[8] or in some other prison a good time, and not one amongst twenty that ever came in prison for any such cause. Yet will they say how piteously and most extremely they have been beaten and dealt withal. Some of these be merry and very pleasant; they will dance and sing. Some others be as cold and reasonable to talk withal. These beg money. Either when they come at farmers' houses, they will demand bacon, either cheese, or wool, or anything that is worth money. And if they espy small company within, they will with fierce countenance demand somewhat. Where for fear the maids will give them largely, to be rid of them.

If they may conveniently come by any cheat, they will pick and steal, as the upright man or rogue, poultry or linen. And all women that wander be at their commandment. Of all that ever I saw of this kind, one naming himself Stradling is the craftiest and most dissemblingest knave. He is able with his tongue and usage to deceive and abuse the wisest man that is. And surely for the proportion of his body, with every member thereunto appertaining, it cannot be amended. But as the proverb is, 'God hath done his part.' This Stradling saith he was the Lord Sturton's man;[9] and when he was executed, for very pensiveness of mind he fell out of his wit, and so continued a year after and more; and that with the very grief and fear, he was taken with a marvellous palsy, that both head and hands will shake when he talketh with any and that apace or fast, whereby he is much pitied, and getteth greatly. And if I had not demanded of others, both men and women that commonly walketh as he doth, and known by them his deep dissimulation, I never had understand the same. And thus I end with these kind of vagabonds.

Chapter 10

A Fresh-Water Mariner or Whipjack

THESE fresh-water mariners, their ships were drowned in the plain of Salisbury. These kind of caterpillars counterfeit great losses on the sea. These be some western men, and most be Irishmen. These will run about the country with a counterfeit licence, feigning either shipwreck, or spoiled by pirates, near the coast of Cornwall or Devonshire, and set a-land at some haven town there, having a large and formal writing, as is abovesaid, with the names and seals of such men of worship, at the least four or five, as dwelleth near or next to the place where they feign their landing. And near to those shires will they not beg, until they come into Wiltshire, Hampshire, Berkshire, Oxfordshire, Hertfordshire, Middlesex, and so to London and down by the river to seek for their ship and goods that they never had. Then pass they through Surrey, Sussex, by the sea-coasts, and so into Kent, demanding alms to bring them home to their country.

Sometime they counterfeit the seal of the Admiralty. I have divers times taken away from them their licences, of both sorts, with such money as they have gathered, and have confiscated the same to the poverty nigh adjoining to me. And they will not be long without another. For at any good town they will renew the same. Once with much threatening and fair promises, I required to know of one company who made their licence. And they swear that they bought the same at Portsmouth of a mariner there, and it cost them two shillings. With such warrants to be so good and effectual, that if any of the best men of law, or learned, about London, should peruse the same, they were able to find no fault therewith, but would assuredly allow the same.

Chapter 11

A Counterfeit Crank

THESE that do counterfeit the crank be young knaves and young harlots, that deeply dissemble the falling sickness. For the crank in their language is the falling evil. I have seen some of these with fair writings testimonial, with the names and seals of some men of worship in Shropshire and in other shires far off, that I have well known, and have taken the same from them. Many of these do go without writings, and will go half naked, and look most piteously. And if any clothes be given them, they immediately sell the same, for wear it they will not, because they would be the more pitied, and wear filthy cloths on their heads and never go without a piece of white soap about them, which, if they see cause or present gain, they will privily convey the same into their mouth, and so work the same there that they will foam as it were a boar, and marvellously for a time torment themselves. And thus deceive they the common people, and gain much. These have commonly their harlots as the other.

Upon Allhallow Day in the morning last, *Anno Domini* 1566, ere my book was half printed, I mean the first impression, there came early in the morning a counterfeit crank under my lodging at the Whitefriars, within the cloister, in a little yard or court, whereabouts lay two or three great ladies being without the liberties of London, whereby he hoped for the greater gain. This crank there lamentably lamenting and pitifully crying to be relieved, declared to divers there his painful and miserable disease. I being risen and not half ready heard his doleful words and rueful moanings; hearing him name the falling sickness, thought assuredly to myself that he was a deep dissembler. So, coming out at a sudden, and beholding his ugly and irksome attire, his loathsome and horrible countenance, it made me in a marvellous perplexity what to think of him, whether it were feigned or truth. For after this manner went he: he was naked from the waist upward, saving he had a old jerkin of leather patched, and that was loose about him that all his body lay bare. A filthy foul cloth he wear on his head, being cut for the purpose, having a narrow place to put out his face, with a beaver made to truss up his beard, and a string that tied the same down close about his neck; with an old felt hat which he still carried in his hand to receive the charity and devotion of the people, for that would he hold out from him; having his face from the eyes downward, all smeared with fresh blood, as though he had new fallen, and been tormented with his painful pangs; his jerkin being all berayed with dirt and mire, and his hat and hosen also, as though he had wallowed in the mire. Surely the sight was monstrous and terrible! I called him unto me, and demanded of him what he ailed. 'Ah, good master,' quoth he, 'I have the grievous and painful disease called the falling sickness.' – 'Why,' quoth I, 'how cometh thy jerkin, hose and hat so berayed with dirt and mire, and thy skin also?' 'Ah, good master, I fell down on the backside here in the foul lane hard by the waterside; and there I lay almost all night, and have bled almost all the blood out in my body.' It rained that morning very fast; and, while I was thus talking with him, a honest poor woman that dwelt thereby brought him a fair linen cloth, and bid him wipe his face therewith, and there being a tub standing full of rain-water, offered to give him some in a dish that he might make himself clean. He refuseth the same. 'Why does thou so?' quoth I. 'Ah, sir,' saith he, 'if I should wash myself, I should fall to bleeding afresh again, and then I should not stop myself.' These words made me the more to suspect him.

Then I asked of him where he was born, what his name was, how long he had this disease, and what time he had been here about London, and in what place. 'Sir,' saith he, 'I was born at Leicester. My name is Nicholas Jennings; and I have had this falling sickness eight years, and I can get no remedy for the same; for I have it by kind. My father had it, and my friends before me; and I have been these two years here about London, and a year and a half in Bethlem.' – 'Why? Wast thou out of thy wits?' quoth I. 'Yea, sir, that I was.' – 'What is the keeper's name of the house?' – 'His name is,' quoth he, 'John Smith.' – 'Then,' quoth I, 'he must understand of thy disease. If thou hadst the same for the time thou wast there, he knoweth it well.' – 'Yea, not only he, but all the house beside,' quoth this crank; 'for I came thence but within this fortnight.'

I had stand so long reasoning the matter with him that I was a-cold, and went into my chamber and made me ready, and commanded my servant to repair to Bethlem, and bring me true word from the keeper there whether any such man hath been with him as a prisoner having the disease aforesaid, and gave him a note of his name and the keeper's also. My servant, returning to my lodging, did assure me that neither was there ever any such man there, neither yet any keeper of any such name. But he that was there keeper, he sent me his name in writing, affirming that he letteth no man depart from him unless he be fet away by his friends, and that none that came from him beggeth about the City.

Then I sent for the printer of this book, and showed him of this dissembling crank, and how I had sent to Bethlem to understand the truth, and what answer I received again, requiring him that I might have some servant of his to watch him faithfully that day, that I might understand trustily to what place he would repair at night unto; and thither I promised to go myself to see their order, and that I would have him to associate me thither. He gladly granted to my request, and sent two boys that both diligently and vigilantly accomplished the charge given them, and found the same crank about the Temple, whereabout the most part of the day he begged, unless it were about twelve of the clock he went on the back-side of Clement's Inn without Temple Bar. There is a lane that goeth into the fields. There he renewed his face again with fresh blood which he carried about him in a bladder, and daubed on fresh dirt upon his jerkin, hat and hosen; and so came back again unto the Temple, and sometime to the waterside, and begged of all that passed by. The boys beheld how some gave groats, some sixpence, some gave more. For he looked so ugly and irksomely, that every one pitied his miserable case that beheld him. To be short, there he passed all the day till night approached. And when it began to be somewhat dark, he went to the waterside, and took a sculler, and was set over the water into St George's Fields, contrary to my expectation; for I had thought he would have gone into Holborn, or to St Giles in the Field. But these boys, with Argus' and lynxes' eyes, set sure watch upon him, and the one took a boat and followed him, and the other went back to tell his master.

The boy that so followed him by water, had no money to pay for his boat hire, but laid his penner and his inkhorn to gage for a penny. And by that time the boy was set over, his master, with all celerity, had taken a boat and followed him apace. Now had they still a sight of the crank, which crossed over the fields towards Newington, and thither he went, and by that time they came thither it was very dark. The printer had there no acquaintance neither any kind of weapon about him; neither knew he how far the crank would go, because he then suspected that they dogged him of purpose. He there stayed him and called for the Constable, which came forth diligently to inquire what the matter was. This zealous printer charged this officer with him as a malefactor and a dissembling vagabond. The Constable would have laid him all night in the cage that stood in the street. 'Nay,' saith this pitiful printer, 'I pray you have him into your house. For this is like to be a cold night, and he is naked. You keep a victualling house. Let him be well cherished this night, for he is well able to pay for the same. I know well his gains hath been great today, and your house is a sufficient prison for the time, and we will there search him.'

The Constable agreed thereunto. They had him in, and caused him to wash himself. That done, they demanded what money he had about him. Saith this crank, 'So God help me I have but twelve pence,' and plucked out the same of a little purse. 'Why, have you no more?' quoth they. 'No,' saith this crank, 'as God shall save my soul at the day of judgement.' – 'We must see more,' quoth they, and began to strip him. Then he plucked out another purse, wherein was forty pence. 'Tush,' saith this printer, 'I must see more.' Saith this crank, 'I pray God I be damned both body and soul if I have any more.' 'No?' saith this printer, 'Thou false knave; here is my boy that did watch thee all this day, and saw when such men gave thee pieces of sixpence, groats, and other money. And yet thou hast showed us none but small money.' When this crank heard this, and the boy vowing it to his face, he relented, and plucked out another purse, wherein was eight shillings and odd money. So had they in the whole that he begged that day 13s 3½d. Then they stripped him stark naked; and as many as saw him said they never saw a handsomer man, with a

cage: lock-up.

yellow flaxen beard, and fair-skinned, without any spot or grief. Then the goodwife of the house fet her goodman's old cloak, and caused the same to be cast about him, because the sight should not abash her shamefast maidens, neither loath her squeamish sight.

Thus he set [him] down at the chimney's end, and called for a pot of beer and drank off a quart at a draft, and called for another, and so the third, that one had been sufficient for any reasonable man, the drink was so strong. I myself the next morning tasted thereof. But let the reader judge what and how much he would have drunk an he had been out of fear! Then when they had thus wrung water out of a flint in spoiling him of his evil-gotten goods, his passing pence, and fleeting trash, the printer with this officer were in jolly jealousy, and devised to search a barn for some rogues and upright men, a quarter of a mile from the house, that stood alone in the fields, and went out about their business, leaving this crank alone with his wife and maidens. This crafty crank, espying all gone, requested the goodwife that he might go out on the back-side to make water, and to exonerate his paunch. She bade him draw the latch of the door and go out, neither thinking or mistrusting he would have gone away naked. But, to conclude, when he was out, he cast away the cloak, and, as naked as ever he was born, he ran away over the fields to his own house, as he afterwards said.

Now the next morning betimes, I went unto Newington, to understand what was done, because I had word ere it was day that there my printer was. And at my coming thither I heard the whole circumstance, as I above have written. And I, seeing the matter so fall out, took order with the chief of the parish that this 13s 3½d. might the next day be equally distributed by their good discretions to the poverty of the same parish, whereof this crafty crank had part himself, for he had both house and wife in the same parish, as after you shall hear. But this lewd loiterer could not lay his bones to labour, having got once the taste of this lewd

grief: sore or skin blemish.
jolly jealousy: great eagerness.
ran away: 1567 ed. has 'that he could never be heard of again'.
the same parish: 1567 ed. concludes 'and so it was done'.

lazy life, for all this fair admonition, but devised other subtle
sleights to maintain his idle living, and so craftily clothed himself
in mariners' apparel and associated himself with another of his
companions. They, having both mariners' apparel, went abroad
to ask charity of the people, feigning they had lost their ship with
all their goods by casualty on the seas, wherewith they gained
much. This crafty crank, fearing to be mistrusted, fell to another
kind of begging, as bad or worse, and apparelled himself very
well with a fair black frieze coat, a new pair of white hose, a fine
felt hat on his head, a shirt of Flanders work esteemed to be
worth sixteen shillings; and upon New Year's Day came again
into the Whitefriars to beg.

The printer, having occasion to go that ways, not thinking
of this crank, by chance met with him, who asked his charity for
God's sake. The printer, viewing him well, did mistrust him to
be the counterfeit crank which deceived him upon Allhallow
Day at night, demanded of whence he was, and what was his
name. 'Forsooth,' saith he, 'my name is Nicholas Jennings, and
I came from Leicester to seek work, and I am a hat-maker by my
occupation, and all my money is spent; and if I could get money
to pay for my lodging this night, I would seek work tomorrow
amongst the hatters.'

The printer, perceiving his deep dissimulation, putting his
hand into his purse, seeming to give him some money, and with
fair allusions brought him into the street, where he charged the
Constable with him, affirming him to be the counterfeit crank
that ran away upon Allhallow Day last. The Constable being
very loath to meddle with him, but the printer knowing him and
his deep deceit, desired he might be brought before the Deputy
of the ward, which straight was accomplished, which when he
came before the Deputy, he demanded of him whence he was,
and what was his name. He answered as before he did unto the
printer. The Deputy asked the printer what he would lay unto
his charge. He answered and alleged him to be a vagabond and
deep deceiver of the people, and the counterfeit crank that ran

Whitefriars: at this time a prosperous residential area.
Deputy of the ward: ward alderman's deputy rather than deputy
constable.

away upon Allhallow Day last from the Constable of Newington and him, and requested him earnestly to send him to ward. The Deputy, thinking him to be deceived, but nevertheless laid his commandment upon him, so that the printer should bear his charges if he could not justify it. He agreed thereunto, and so he and the Constable went to carry him to the Counter. And as they were going under Ludgate, this crafty crank took his heels and ran down the hill as fast as he could drive, the Constable and the printer after him as fast as they could. But the printer of the twain being lighter of foot, overtook him at Fleet Bridge, and with strong hand carried him to the Counter and safely delivered him.

In the morrow, the printer sent his boy that stripped him upon Allhallow Day at night to view him, because he would be sure, which boy knew him very well. This crank confessed unto the Deputy that he had hosted the night before in Kent Street in Southwark, at the sign of 'The Cock', which thing to be true, the printer sent to know, and found him a liar; but further inquiring, at length found out his habitation, dwelling in Master Hill's rents, having a pretty house, well stuffed, with a fair joint-table, and a fair cupboard garnished with pewter, having an old ancient woman to his wife. The printer being sure thereof, repaired unto the Counter, and rebuked him for his beastly behaviour, and told him of his false feigning, willed him to confess it, and ask forgiveness. He perceived him to know his deep dissimulation, relented, and confessed all his deceit; and so remaining in the Counter three days, was removed to Bridewell, where he was stripped stark naked, and his ugly attire put upon him before the masters thereof, who wondered greatly at his dissimulation. For which offence he stood upon the pillory in Cheapside, both in his ugly and handsome attire; and after that went in the mill while his ugly picture was a-drawing; and then was whipped at a cart's tail through London, and his displayed banner carried before him unto his own door, and so back to Bridewell again, and there

Counter: prison for debtors and prisoners awaiting magistrates' sentence.
Bridewell: house of correction.
mill: ? treadmill (O.E.D. records no usage before 1842).

remained for a time and at length let at liberty, on that condition he would prove an honest man, and labour truly to get his living. And his picture remaineth in Bridewell for a monument.

Chapter 12

A Dummerer

THESE dummerers are lewd and most subtle people. The most part of these are Welshmen, and will never speak, unless they have extreme punishment, but will gape, and with a marvellous force will hold down their tongues doubled, groaning for your charity, and holding up their hands full piteously, so that with their deep dissimulation they get very much. There are of these many, and but one that I understand of hath lost his tongue indeed. Having on a time occasion to ride to Dartford, to speak with a priest there, who maketh all kind of conserves very well, and useth stilling of waters, and, repairing to his house, I found a dummerer at his door and the priest himself perusing his licence under the seals and hands of certain worshipful men, which priest had thought the same to be good and effectual. I, taking the same writing, and reading it over, and noting the seals, found one of the seals like unto a seal that I had about me, which seal I bought besides Charing Cross, that I was out of doubt it was none of those gentlemen's seals that had subscribed; and, having understanding before of their peevish practices, made me to conceive that all was forged and nought.

I made the more haste home; for well I wist that he would and must of force pass through the parish where I dwelt; for there was no other way for him. And coming homeward, I found them in the town, according to my expectation, where they were stayed. For there was a palliard associate with the dummerer and partaker of his gains, which palliard I saw not at Dartford. The stayers of them was a gentleman called Chayne, and a servant of my Lord Keeper's called Wostestowe, which was the chief causer of the staying of them, being a surgeon, and cunning in his science, had seen the like practices, and, as he said, had caused one to speak afore that was dumb. It was my chance to come at the beginning of the matter.

'Sir,' quoth this surgeon, 'I am bold here to utter some part of my cunning. I trust', quoth he, 'you shall see a miracle wrought anon. For I once,' quoth he, 'made a dumb man to speak.'

Quoth I, 'You are well met, and somewhat you have prevented me. For I had thought to have done no less ere they had passed this town. For I well know their writing is feigned, and they deep dissemblers.'

The surgeon made him gape, and we could see but half a tongue. I required the surgeon to put his finger in his mouth, and to pull out his tongue, and so he did, notwithstanding he held strongly a pretty while. At the length he plucked out the same, to the great admiration of many that stood by. Yet when we saw his tongue, he would neither speak nor yet could hear.

Quoth I to the surgeon, 'Knit two of his fingers together, and thrust a stick between them, and rub the same up and down a little, and for my life he speaketh by and by.'

'Sir,' quoth this surgeon, 'I pray you let me practise another way.'

I was well contented to see the same. He had him into a house, and tied a halter about the wrists of his hands, and hoisted him up over a beam, and there did let him hang a good while. At the length, for very pain he required for God's sake to let him down. So he that was both deaf and dumb could in short time both hear and speak. Then I took that money I could find in his purse, and distributed the same to the poor people dwelling there, which was fifteen pence halfpenny, being all that we could find. That done, and this merry miracle madly made, I sent them with my servant to the next Justice, where they preached on the pillory for want of a pulpit, and were well whipped, and none did bewail them.

Chapter 13

A Drunken Tinker

THESE drunken tinkers, called also priggs, be beastly people, and these young knaves be the worst. These never go without their doxies, and if their women have anything about them, as apparel or linen, that is worth the selling, they lay the same to gage, or sell it outright, for bene booze at their boozing ken. And full soon will they be weary of them, and have a new. When they happen on work at any good house, their doxies linger aloof, and tarry for them in some corner; and if he tarryeth long from her, then she knoweth he hath work, and walketh near, and sitteth down by him. For besides money he looketh for meat and drink for doing his dame pleasure. For if she have three or four holes in a pan, he will make as many more for speedy gain. And if he see any old kettle, chafer, or pewter dish abroad in the yard where he worketh, he quickly snappeth the same up, and into the budget it goeth round. Thus they live with deceit.

I was credibly informed by such as could well tell, that one of these tippling tinkers with his dog robbed by the highway four palliards and two rogues, six persons together, and took from them above four pound in ready money, and hid him after in a thick wood a day or two, and so escaped untaken. Thus with picking and stealing, mingled with a little work for a colour, they pass their time.

Chapter 14

A Swadder or Pedlar

THESE swadders and pedlars be not all evil, but of an indifferent behaviour. These stand in great awe of the upright men, for they have often both wares and money of them. But forasmuch as they

bene : good (see p. 147).
budget : bag.

seek gain unlawfully against the laws and statutes of this noble realm, they are well worthy to be registered among the number of vagabonds. And undoubtedly, I have had some of them brought before me, when I was in Commission of the Peace, as malefactors, for bribering and stealing. And now of late it is a great practice of the upright man, when he hath gotten a booty, to bestow the same upon a packful of wares, and so goeth a time for his pleasure, because he would live without suspicion.

Chapter 15

A Jarkman and a Patrico

FORASMUCH as these two names, a jarkman and a patrico, be in the old brief of vagabonds, and set forth as two kinds of evil-doers, you shall understand that a jarkman hath his name of a jark, which is a seal in their language, as one should make writings and set seals for licences and passports. And for truth there is none that goeth about the country of them that can either write so good and fair a hand, either indite so learnedly, as I have seen and handled a number of them, but have the same made in good towns where they come; as what can not be had for money? As the proverb saith, *Omnia venalia Roma.* And many hath confessed the same to me.

Now, also, there is a patrico, and not a patriarcho, which in their language is a priest that should make marriages till death did depart. But they have none such, I am well assured. For I put you out of doubt that not one amongst a hundred of them are married; for they take lechery for no sin, but natural fellow-ship and good liking love: so that I will not blot my book with these two that be not.

handled: i.e. as Justice of the Peace.
Omnia venalia Roma: 'Everything is for sale in Rome.'

Chapter 16

A Demander for Glimmer

THESE demanders for glimmer be for the most part women; for glimmer, in their language, is fire. These go with feigned licences and counterfeited writings, having the hands and seals of such gentlemen as dwelleth near to the place where they feign themselves to have been burnt, and their goods consumed with fire. They will most lamentably demand your charity, and will quickly shed salt tears, they be so tender-hearted. They will never beg in that shire where their losses (as they say) was. Some of these go with slates at their backs (which is a sheet to lie in a-nights). The upright men be very familiar with these kind of women, and one of them helps another.·

A demander for glimmer came unto a good town in Kent, to ask the charity of the people, having a feigned licence about her, that declared her misfortune by fire, done in Somersetshire; walking with a wallet on her shoulders, wherein she put the devotion of such as had no money to give her, that is to say malt, wool, bacon, bread, and cheese. And always, as the same was full, so was it ready money to her, when she emptied the same, wheresoever she travelled. This harlot was, as they term it, snout-fair, and had an upright man or two always attending on her watch (which is on her person), and yet so circumspect, that they would never be seen in her company in any good town unless it were in small villages where tippling houses were, either travelling together by the highways. But the truth is, by report, she would weekly be worth six or seven shilling with her begging and bitchery.

This glimmering mort, repairing to an inn in the said town, where dwelt a widow of fifty winter old of good wealth – but she had an unthrifty son, whom she used as a chamberlain to attend guests when they repaired to her house. This amorous man, beholding with ardent eyes this glimmering glancer, was presently piteously pierced to the heart, and lewdly longed to be clothed under her livery, and, bestowing a few fond words with her, understood straight that she would be easily persuaded to liking lechery, and, as a man mazed, mused how to attain to his purpose, for he had no money. Yet, considering with himself that wares would be welcome where money wanted, he went with a wanion to his mother's chamber, and there seeking about for odd ends, at length found a little whistle of silver that his mother did use customably to wear on, and had forgot the same for haste, that morning, and offers the same closely to this mannerly Marian, that if she would meet him on the back-side of the town and courteously kiss him without constraint, she should be mistress thereof, and it wear much better.

'Well,' saith she, 'you *are* a wanton'; and beholding the whistle, was farther in love therewith than ravished with his person, and agreed to meet him presently, and to accomplish his fond fancy. To be short and not tedious, a quarter of a mile from the town, he merrily took measure of her under a bawdy bush. So she gave him that she had not, and he received that he could not, and, taking leave of each other with a courteous kiss, she pleasantly passed forth on her journey, and this untoward lickerous chamberlain repaired homeward.

But ere these two turtles took their leave, the good wife missed her whistle, and sent one of her maidens into her chamber for the same, and being long sought for, none could be found. Her mistress hearing that, diligent search was made for the same, and that it was taken away, began to suspect her unblessed babe, and demanded of her maidens whether none of them saw her son in her chamber that morning. And one of them answered that she saw him not there, but coming from thence. Then had she enough, for well she wist that he had the same, and sent for him, but he could not be found. Then she caused her ostler, in whom she had better affiance in for his truth (and yet not one amongst twenty of them but have well left their honesty, as I hear a great sort say) to come unto her, which attended to know her pleasure. 'Go, seek out', saith she, 'my untoward son, and bid him come speak with me.' – 'I saw him go out,' saith he, 'half an hour sithence on the back-side. I had thought you had sent him of your errand.' – 'I sent him not,' quoth she. 'Go, look him out.'

with a wanion : with a vengeance or with a curse.

This hollow ostler took his staff in his neck, and trudged out apace that way he saw him before go, and had some understanding, by one of the maidens, that his mistress had her whistle stolen and suspected her son. And he had not gone far but that he espied him coming homeward alone, and, meeting him, asked where he had been.

'Where have I been?' quoth he, and began to smile.

'Now, by the mass, thou hast been at some bawdy banquet.'

'Thou hast even told truth,' quoth this chamberlain.

'Surely,' quoth this ostler, 'thou hadst the same woman that begged at our house today, for the harms she had by fire. Where is she?' quoth he.

'She is almost a mile by this time,' quoth this chamberlain.

'Where is my mistress's whistle?' quoth this ostler. 'For I am well assured that thou hadst it, and I fear me thou hast given it to that harlot.'

'Why, is it missed?' quoth this chamberlain.

'Yea,' quoth this ostler, and showed him all the whole circumstance, what was both said and thought on him for the thing.

'Well, I will tell thee,' quoth this chamberlain. 'I will be plain with thee. I had it indeed, and have given the same to this woman, and I pray thee make the best of it, and help now to excuse the matter. And yet surely, an thou wouldst take so much pain for me as to overtake her, for she goeth but softly, and is not yet far off, and take the same from her, and I am ever thine assured friend.'

'Why, then go with me,' quoth this ostler.

'Nay, in faith,' quoth this chamberlain. 'What is freer than a gift? And I had pretty pastime for the same.'

'Hadst thou so?' quoth this ostler. 'Now, by the mass and I will have some too, or I will lie in the dust ere I come again.' Passing with haste to overtake this paramour, within a mile from the place where he departed he overtook her, having an upright man in her company, a strong and a sturdy vagabond. Somewhat amazed was this ostler to see one familiarly in her company, for he had well hoped to have had some delicate dalliance, as his fellow had. But, seeing the matter so fall out, and being of good courage, and thinking to himself that one true man was better than two false knaves, and being on the highway, thought upon help if need had been, by such as had passed to and fro, demanded fiercely the whistle that she had even now of his fellow.

'Why, husband,' quoth she, 'can you suffer this wretch to slander your wife?'

'Avaunt varlet!' quoth this upright man, and lets drive with all his force at this ostler, and after half a dozen blows, he strikes his staff out of his hand, and as this ostler stepped back to have taken up his staff again, his glimmering mort flings a great stone at him, and struck him on the head that down he falls, with the blood about his ears, and while he lay th[u]s amazed, the upright man snatches away his purse, wherein he had money of his mistress's as well as of his own, and there let him lie, and went away with speed that they were never heard of more.

When this dry-beaten ostler was come to himself, he faintly wandereth home, and creepeth in to his couch, and rests his idle head. His mistress heard that he was come in, and laid him down on his bed, repaired straight unto him, and asks him what he ailed, and what the cause was of his so sudden lying on his bed.

'What is the cause?' quoth this ostler. 'Your whistle, your whistle!' – speaking the same piteously three or four times.

'Why, fool,' quoth his mistress, 'take no care for that, for I do not greatly weigh it; it was worth but three shillings fourpence.'

'I would it had been burnt for four years agone.'

'I pray thee, why so?' quoth his mistress. 'I think thou art mad.'

'Nay, not yet,' quoth this ostler; 'but I have been madly handled.'

'Why, what is the matter?' quoth his mistress, and was more desirous to know the case.

'An you will forgive my fellow and me, I will show you. Or else I will never do it.'

She made him presently faithful promise that she would.

'Then,' saith he, 'send for your son home again, which is ashamed to look you in the face.'

'I agree thereto,' saith she.

'Well, then,' quoth this ostler, 'your son hath given the same mort that begged here for the burning of her house a whistle, and you have given her five shillings in money, and I have given her ten shillings of my own.'

'Why, how so?' quoth she.

Then he sadly showed her of his mishap with all the circumstance that you have heard before, and how his purse was taken away and fifteen shillings in the same, whereof five shillings was her money, and ten shillings his own money.

'Is this true?' quoth his mistress.

'Ay, by my troth,' quoth this ostler, 'and nothing grieves me so much, neither my beating, neither the loss of my money, as doth my evil and wretched luck!'

'Why, what is the matter?' quoth his mistress.

'Your son,' saith this ostler, 'had some cheer and pastime for that whistle for he lay with her, and I have been well beaten, and have had my purse taken from me. And you know your son is merry and pleasant, and can keep no great counsel. And then shall I be mocked and laughed to scorn in all places when they shall hear how I have been served.'

'Now, out upon you, knaves both!' quoth his mistress, and laughs out the matter; for she well saw it would not otherwise prevail.

Chapter 17

A Bawdy Basket

THESE bawdy baskets be also women, and go with baskets and cap-cases on their arms, wherein they have laces, pins, needles, white inkle, and round silk girdles of all colours. These will buy conyskins, and steal linen clothes off on hedges. And for their trifles they will procure of maiden-servants, when their mistress or dame is out of the way, either some good piece of beef, bacon, or cheese, that shall be worth twelvepence, for twopence of their toys. And as they walk by the way, they often gain some money with their instrument by such as they suddenly meet withal. The

cap-case : wallet.
inkle : linen thread or tape.
with their instrument : i.e. by whoring.

upright men have good acquaintance with these, and will help and relieve them when they want. Thus they trade their lives in lewd loathsome lechery. Amongst them all is but one honest woman, and she is of good years. Her name is Joan Messenger. I have had good proof of her, as I have learned by the true report of divers.

There came to my gate the last summer, *Anno Domini* 1566, a very miserable man, and much deformed, as burnt in the face, blear-eyed, and lame of one of his legs, that he went with a crutch. I asked him where he was born, and where he dwelt last, and showed him that thither he must repair and be relieved, and not to range about the country; and seeing some cause of charity, I caused him to have meat and drink, and when he had drunk, I demanded of him whether he was never spoiled of the upright man or rogue.

'Yes, that I have,' quoth he; 'and not this seven years, for so long I have gone abroad, I had not so much taken from me, and so evil handled, as I was within these four days.'

'Why, how so?' quoth I.

'In good faith, sir,' quoth he, 'I chanced to meet with one of these bawdy baskets which had an upright man in her company, and as I would have passed quietly by her, "Man," saith she unto her make, "do you not see this ill-favoured, windshaken knave?" "Yes," quoth the upright man. "What say you to him?" "This knave oweth me two shillings for wares that he had of me, half a year ago, I think it well." Saith this upright man, "Sirrah," saith he, "pay your debts." Saith this poor man, "I owe her none; neither did I ever bargain with her for anything, and as I am advised I never saw her before in all my life." "Mercy, God!" quoth she, "what a lying knave is this! An he will not pay you, husband, beat him surely." And the upright man gave me three or four blows on my back and shoulders, and would have beat me worse an I had not given him all the money in my purse; and, in good faith, for very fear, I was fain to give him fourteen pence, which was all the money that I had. "Why," saith this bawdy basket, "hast thou no more? Then thou owest me ten pence still; and, be well assured that I will be paid the next time I meet with thee." And so they let me pass by them. I pray God save and bless me, and all other in my case, from such wicked persons,' quoth this poor man.

'Why, whither went they then?' quoth I.

'Into East Kent, for I met with them on this side of Rochester. I have divers times been attempted, but I never lost much before. I thank God there came still company by afore this unhappy time.'

'Well,' quoth I, 'thank God of all, and repair home into thy native country.'

Chapter 18

A Autem-Mort

THESE autem-morts be married women, as there be but a few. For autem in their language is a church. So she is a wife married at the church. And they be as chaste as a cow I have, that goeth to bull every noon, with what bull she careth not. These walk most times from their husband's company a month and more together, being associate with another as honest as herself. These will pilfer clothes off hedges. Some of them go with children of ten or twelve years of age. If time and place serve for their purpose, they will send them into some house at the window, to steal and rob, which they call in their language, milling of the ken; and will go with wallets on their shoulders and slates at their backs.

There is one of these autem-morts, she is now a widow, of fifty years old. Her name is Alice Milson. She goeth about with a couple of great boys; the youngest of them is fast upon twenty years of age. And these two do lie with her every night, and she lieth in the midst. She saith that they be her children, that betelled be babes born of such abominable belly.

slates: sheets.
betelled: cursed.

Chapter 19

A Walking Mort

THESE walking morts be not married. These for their unhappy years doth go as a autem-mort, and will say their husbands died either at Newhaven, Ireland, or in some service of the Prince. These make laces upon staves, and purses, that they carry in their hands, and white valance for beds. Many of these hath had and have children. When these get ought, either with begging, bitchery, or bribery, as money or apparel, they are quickly shaken out of all by the upright men, that they are in a marvellous fear to carry anything about them that is of any value. Wherefore, this policy they use: they leave their money now with one and then with another trusty householders, either with the goodman or goodwife, sometime in one shire, and then in another, as they travel. This have I known, that four or five shillings, yea, ten shillings, left in a place, and the same will they come for again within one quarter of a year, or sometime not in half a year; and all this is to little purpose, for all their peevish policy; for when they buy them linen or garments, it is taken away from them, and worse given them, or none at all.

The last summer, *Anno Domini* 1566, being in familiar talk with a walking mort that came to my gate, I learned by her what I could, and I thought I had gathered as much for my purpose as I desired. I began to rebuke her for her lewd life and beastly behaviour, declaring to her what punishment was prepared and heaped up for her in the world to come for her filthy living and wretched conversation.

'God help!' quoth she, 'how should I live? None will take me into service. But I labour in harvest-time honestly.'

'I think but a while with honesty,' quoth I.

'Shall I tell you?' quoth she. 'The best of us all may be amended. But yet, I thank God, I did one good deed within this twelve months.'

Newhaven: Le Havre.
conversation: sexual intimacy.

'Wherein?' quoth I.

Saith she, 'I would not have it spoken of again.'

'If it be meet and necessary,' quoth I, 'it shall lie under my feet.'

'What mean you by that?' quoth she.

'I mean,' quoth I, 'to hide the same, and never to discover it to any.'

'Well,' quoth she, and began to laugh as much as she could, and swear by the mass that if I disclosed the same to any, she would never more tell me anything. 'The last summer,' quoth she, 'I was great with child, and I travelled into East Kent by the sea-coast, for I lusted marvellously after oysters and mussels, and gathered many, and in the place where I found them, I opened them and ate them still. At the last, in seeking more, I reached after one, and stepped into a hole and fell in into the waist, and there did stick, and I had been drowned if the tide had come, and espying a man a good way off, I cried as much as I could for help. I was alone. He heard me, and repaired as fast to me as he might, and finding me there fast sticking, I required for God's sake his help. And whether it was with striving and forcing myself out, or for joy I had of his coming to me, I had a great colour in my face, and looked red and well-coloured. And, to be plain with you, he liked me so well as he said that I should there lie still, an I would not grant him that he might lie with me. And, by my troth, I wist not what to answer, I was in such a perplexity. For I knew the man well. He had a very honest woman to his wife, and was of some wealth; and, on the other side, if I were not holp out, I should there have perished, and I granted him that I would obey to his will. Then he plucked me out. And because there was no convenient place near hand, I required him that I might go wash myself, and make me somewhat cleanly, and I would come to his house and lodge all night in his barn, whither he might repair to me, and accomplish his desire. "But let it not be", quoth he, "before nine of the clock at night for then there will be small stirring." "And I may repair to the town," quoth I, "to warm and dry myself"; for this was about two of the clock in the afternoon. "Do so," quoth he; "for I must be busy to look out my cattle hereby before I can come home." So I went away from him, and glad was I.'

'And why so?' quoth I.

'Because,' quoth she, 'his wife, my good dame, is my very friend, and I am much beholden to her. And she hath done me so much good ere this, that I were loath now to harm her any way.'

'Why,' quoth I, 'what an it had been any other man, and not your good dame's husband?'

'The matter had been the less,' quoth she.

'Tell me, I pray thee,' quoth I, 'who was the father of thy child?'

She studied a while, and said that it had a father.

'But what was he?' quoth I.

'Now, by my troth, I know not,' quoth she. 'You bring me out of my matter, so you do.'

'Well, say on,' quoth I.

'Then I departed straight to the town, and came to my dame's house, and showed her of my misfortune, also of her husband's usage in all points, and that I showed her the same for good will, and bid her take better heed to her husband, and to herself. So she gave me great thanks, and made me good cheer, and bid me in any case that I should be ready at the barn at that time and hour we had appointed. "For I know well," quoth this goodwife, "my husband will not break with thee. And one thing I warn thee, that thou give me a watchword aloud when he goeth about to have his pleasure of thee, and that shall be 'Fie, for shame, fie,' and I will be hard by you with help. But I charge thee, keep this secret until all be finished. And hold," saith this goodwife; "here is one of my petticoats I give thee." "I thank you, good dame," quoth I, "and I warrant you I will be true and trusty unto you." So my dame left me sitting by a good fire with meat and drink; and with the oysters I brought with me, I had great cheer. She went straight and repaired unto her gossips dwelling thereby, and, as I did after understand, she made her moan to them, what a naughty, lewd, lecherous husband she had, and how that she

naughty: promiscuous.

could not have his company for harlots, and that she was in fear to take some filthy disease of him, he was so common a man, having little respect whom he had to do withal. "And," quoth she, "now here is one at my house, a poor woman that goeth about the country, that he would have had to do withal. Wherefore, good neighbours and loving gossips, as you love me, and as you would have help at my hand another time, devise some remedy to make my husband a good man that I may live in some surety without disease, and that he may save his soul that God so dearly bought." After she had told her tale, they cast their piercing eyes all upon her. But one stout dame amongst the rest had these words: "As your patient bearing of troubles, your honest behaviour among us your neighbours, your tender and pitiful heart to the poor of the parish, doth move us to lament your case, so the unsatiable carnality of your faithless husband doth instigate and stir us to devise and invent some speedy redress for your case and the amendment of his life. Wherefore, this is my counsel, an you will be advertised by me, for I say to you all, unless it be this goodwife, who is chiefly touched in this matter, I have the next cause; for he was in hand with me not long ago, an company had not been present, which was by a marvellous chance, he had, I think, forced me. For often he hath been tampering with me, and yet have I sharply said him nay. Therefore, let us assemble secretly into the place where he hath appointed to meet this gillot that is at your house, and lurk privily in some corner till he begin to go about his business. And then methought I heard you say even now that you had a watchword, at which word we will all step forth, being five of us besides you, for you shall be none because it is your husband, but get you to bed at your accustomed hour. And we will carry each of us a good birchen rod in our laps, and we will all be muffled for knowing. And see that you go home and acquaint that walking mort with the matter; for we must have her help to hold, for always four must hold and two lay on." "Alas!" saith this goodwife, "he is too strong for you all. I would be loath for my sake you should receive

tampering: 1573 ed. has 'tempting'.
gillot: wanton.
muffled: masked.

harm at his hand." "Fear you not," quoth these stout women. "Let her not give the watchword until his hosen be about his legs. And I trow we all will be with him to bring before he shall have leisure to pluck them up again." They all with one voice agreed to the matter, that the way she had devised was the best. So this goodwife repaired home. But before she departed from her gossips, she showed them at what hour they should privily come in on the back-side, and where to tarry their good hour. So by the time she came in, it was almost night, and found the walking mort still sitting by the fire, and declared to her all this new device abovesaid, which promised faithfully to fulfil to her small power as much as they had devised. Within a quarter of an hour after, in cometh the goodman, who said that he was about his cattle. "Why, what have we here, wife, sitting by the fire? An if she have eat and drunk, send her into the barn to her lodging for this night, for she troubleth the house." "Even as you will, husband," saith his wife. "You know she cometh once in two years into these quarters. Away," saith this goodwife, "to your lodging!" "Yes, good dame," saith she, "as fast as I can." Thus, by looking one on the other, each knew other's mind, and so departed to her comely couch.

'The goodman of the house shrugged him for joy, thinking to himself, "I will make some pastime with you anon"; and, calling to his wife for his supper, set him down, and was very pleasant, and drank to his wife, and fell to his mammerings, and munched apace, nothing understanding of the banquet that was a-preparing for him after supper, and, according to the proverb, that sweet meat will have sour sauce. Thus, when he was well refreshed, his spirits being revived, entered into familiar talk with his wife of many matters, how well he had spent that day to both their profits, saying some of his cattle were like to have been drowned in the ditches, driving others of his neighbours' cattle out that were in his pastures, and mending his fences that were broken down. Thus profitably he had consumed the day, nothing talking of his helping out of the walking mort out of the mire, neither of his request nor yet of her promise. Thus feeding her with friendly fantasies, consumed two hours and more. Then

mammerings: mumblings.

feigning how he would see in what case his horse were in and how they were dressed, repaired covertly into the barn, whereas his friendly foes lurked privily, unless it were this mannerly mort, that comely couched on a bottle of straw. "What, are you come?" quoth she. "By the mass, I would not for a hundred pound that my dame should know that you were here, either any else of your house." "No, I warrant thee," saith this goodman, "they be all safe and fast enough at their work, and I will be at mine anon"; and lay down by her, and straight would have had to do with her. "Nay, fie," saith she, "I like not this order. If ye lie with me, you shall surely untruss you and put down your hosen, for that way is most easiest and best." "Sayest thou so?" quoth he, "Now, by my troth, agreed." And when he had untrussed himself and put down, he began to assault the unsatiable fort. "Why," quoth she, that was without shame, saving for her promise, "and are you not ashamed?" "Never a whit," saith he. "Lie down quickly." "Now, fie, for shame, fie," saith she aloud, which was the watchword. At the which word, these five furious, sturdy, muffled gossips flings out, and takes sure hold of this betrayed person, some plucking his hosen down lower, and binding the same fast about his feet; then binding his hands, and knitting a handkercher about his eyes, that he should not see. And when they had made him sure and fast, then they laid him on until they were windless. "Be good," saith this mort, "unto my master, for the passion of God!" and laid on as fast as the rest and still ceased not to cry upon them to be merciful unto him and yet laid on apace. And when they had well beaten him, that the blood brast plentifully out in most places, they let him lie still bound – with this exhortation, that he should from that time forth know his wife from other men's, and that this punishment was but a fleabiting in respect of that which should follow if he amended not his manners. Thus leaving him blustering, blowing, and foaming for pain and melancholy that he neither might or could be revenged of them, they vanished away, and had this mort with them, and safely conveyed her out of the town. Soon after cometh into the barn one of the goodman's boys, to fet some hay for his

bottle: bundle.
brast: burst.

horse; and finding his master lying fast bound and grievously beaten with rods, was suddenly abashed and would have run out again to have called for help. But his master bade him come unto him and unbind him; "and make no words," quoth he, "of this. I will be revenged well enough." Yet notwithstanding, after better advice, the matter being unhonest, he thought it meeter to let the same pass, and not, as the proverb saith, to awake the sleeping dog. And, by my troth,' quoth this walking mort, 'I come now from that place, and was never there sithence this part was played, which is somewhat more than a year. And I hear a very good report of him now, that he loveth his wife well, and useth himself very honestly. And was not this a good act, now? How say you?'

'It was prettily handled,' quoth I. 'And is here all?'

'Yea,' quoth she, 'here is the end.'

Chapter 20

A Doxy

THESE doxies be broken and spoiled of their maidenhead by the upright men, and then they have their name of doxies and not afore. And afterward she is common and indifferent for any that will use her, as *homo* is a common name to all men. Such as be fair and somewhat handsome keep company with the walking morts, and are ready always for the upright men, and are chiefly maintained by them for others shall be spoiled for their sakes. The other inferior sort will resort to noblemen's places, and gentlemen's houses, standing at the gate either lurking on the back-side about back-houses, either in hedgerows, or some other thicket, expecting their prey which is for the uncomely company of some courteous guest, of whom they be refreshed with meat and some money, where exchange is made, ware for ware. This bread and meat they use to carry in their great hosen; so that these beastly bribering breeches serve many times for bawdy purposes.

I chanced, not long sithence, familiarly to common with a

doxy that came to my gate, and surely a pleasant harlot, and not so pleasant as witty, and not so witty as void of all grace and goodness. I found by her talk that she had passed her time lewdly eighteen years in walking about. I thought this a necessary instrument to attain some knowledge by. And before I would grope her mind, I made her both eat and drink well. That done, I made her faithful promise to give her some money if she would open and discover to me such questions as I would demand of her, and never beray her neither to disclose her name.

'An you should,' saith she, 'I were undone.'

'Fear not that,' quoth I. 'But, I pray thee,' quoth I, 'say nothing but truth.'

'I will not,' saith she.

'Then first tell me,' quoth I, 'how many upright men and rogues dost thou know, or hast thou known and been conversant with, and what their names be?'

She paused awhile, and said, 'Why do you ask me, or wherefore?'

'For nothing else,' as I said, 'but that I would know them when they came to my gate.'

'Now by my troth,' quoth she, 'then are ye never the near, for, all mine acquaintance for the most part are dead.'

'Dead!' quoth I, 'how died they? For want of cherishing, or of painful diseases?'

Then she sighed, and said they were hanged.

'What, all?' quoth I, 'And so many walk abroad, as I daily see!'

'By my troth,' quoth she, 'I know not past six or seven by their names' – and named the same to me.

'When were they hanged?' quoth I.

'Some seven years agone, some three years and some within this fortnight' – and declared the place where they were executed, which I knew well to be true by the report of others.

'Why,' quoth I, 'did not this sorrowful and fearful sight much grieve thee, and for thy time long and evil spent?'

'I was sorry,' quoth she, 'by the mass. For some of them were good loving men. For I lacked not when they had it, and they

beray: asperse.

wanted not when I had it, and divers of them I never did forsake, until the gallows departed us.'

'O merciful God!' quoth I, and began to bless me.

'Why bless ye?' quoth she. 'Alas! good gentleman, every one must have a living.'

Other matters I talked of. But this now may suffice to show the reader, as it were in a glass, the bold beastly life of these doxies. For such as hath gone any time abroad will never forsake their trade, to die therefore. I have had good proof thereof. There is one, a notorious harlot of this affinity called Bess Bottomly. She hath but one hand, and she hath murdered two children at least.

Chapter 21

A Dell

A DELL is a young wench, able for generation and not yet known or broken by the upright man. These go abroad young, either by the death of their parents and nobody to look unto them, or else by some sharp mistress that they serve do run away out of service; either she is naturally born one, and then she is a wild dell. These are broken very young. When they have been lain withal by the upright man, then they be doxies, and no dells. These wild dells, being traded up with their monstrous mothers, must of necessity be as evil, or worse, than their parents, for neither we gather grapes from green briars, neither figs from thistles. But such buds, such blossoms, such evil seed sown, well worse being grown.

able for generation: able to conceive.
traded up: brought up.

Chapter 22

A Kinchin Mort

A KINCHIN mort is a little girl. The morts their mothers carries them at their backs in their slates, which is their sheets, and brings them up savagely, till they grow to be ripe: and soon ripe, soon rotten.

Chapter 23

A Kinchin Co

A KINCHIN CO is a young boy, traden up to such peevish purposes as you have heard of other young imps before, that when he groweth unto years, he is better to hang than to draw forth.

Chapter 24

Their Usage in the Night

NOW I think it not unnecessary to make the reader understand how and in what manner they lodge a-nights in barns or backhouses, and of their usage there, forasmuch as I have acquainted them with their order and practices a-daytimes. The arch and chief walkers, that hath walked a long time, whose experience is great because of their continuing practice, I mean all morts and doxies for their handsomeness and diligence for making of their couches. The men never trouble themselves with that thing, but takes the same to be the duty of the wife. And she shuffles up a quantity of straw or hay into some pretty corner of the barn where she may conveniently lie and well shaketh the same, making the head somewhat high, and drives the same upon the sides and feet like a bed: then she layeth her wallet, or some other little pack of rags or scrip under her head in the straw, to bear up the same, and layeth her petticoat or cloak upon and over the straw, so made like a bed, and that serveth for the blanket. Then she layeth her slate (which is her sheet) upon that. An she have no sheet, as few of them go without, then she spreadeth some large clouts or rags over the same and maketh her ready, and layeth her drowsily down. Many will pluck off their smocks and lay the same upon them instead of their upper sheet, and all her other pelt and trash upon her also; and many lyeth in their smocks. And if the rest of her clothes in cold weather be not sufficient to keep her warm, then she taketh straw or hay to perform the matter. The other sort, that have not slates, but tumble down and couch a hogshead in their clothes, these be still lousy, and shall never be without vermin, unless they put off their clothes, and lie as is abovesaid. If the upright man come in where they lie, he hath his choice, and creepeth in close by his doxy. The rogue hath his leavings. If the morts or doxies lie or be lodged in some farmer's barn, and the door be either locked or made fast to them, then will not the upright man press to come in, unless it be in barns and out-houses standing alone, or some distance from houses which be commonly known to them, as St Quinten's, 'Three Cranes of the Vintry', St Tybbes, and Knapsbery. These four be within one mile compass near unto London. Then have you four more in Middlesex: 'Draw the Pudding out of the Fire' in Harrow-on-the-Hill parish, 'The Cross Keys' in Cranford parish, St Julian's in Thistleworth [10] parish, 'The House of Pity' in Northall parish. These are their chief houses near about London where commonly they resort unto for lodging, and may repair thither freely at all times. Some-time shall come in some rogue, some picking knave, a nimble prig. He walketh in softly a-nights, when they be at their rest, and plucketh off as many garments as be aught worth that he may come by, and worth money, and may easily carry the same, and runneth away with the same with great celerity, and maketh port-sale at some convenient place of theirs, that some be soon

scrip: small bag.
couch a hogshead: sleep (see p. 148).

ready in the morning, for want of their casters and togmans:
where instead of blessing is cursing; in place of praying, pestilent
prating with odious oaths and terrible threatenings.

The upright men have given all these nicknames to the places
abovesaid. Yet have we two notable places in Kent, not far from
London. The one is between Deptford and Rotherhithe, called
the 'King's Barn', standing alone, that they haunt commonly;
the other is Ketbroke, standing by Blackheath, half a mile from
any house. There will they boldly draw the latch of the door, and
go in when the goodman with his family be at supper and sit
down without leave, and eat and drink with them, and either lie
in the hall by the fire all night, or in the barn, if there be no room
in the house for them. If the door be either bolted or locked, if it
be not opened unto them when they will, they will break the same
open to his farther cost. And in this barn sometime do lie forty
upright men, with their doxies together at one time. And this
must the poor farmer suffer, or else they threaten him to burn
him and all that he hath.

The Names of the Upright Men,
Rogues, and Palliards

Here followeth the unruly rabblement of rascals, and the most
notorious and wickedest walkers that are living now at this
present, with their true names as they be called and known by.
And, although I set and place here but three orders, yet, good
reader, understand that all the others above-named are derived
and come out from the upright men and rogues. Concerning
the number of morts and doxies, it is superfluous to write of
them. I could well have done it, but the number of them is great,
and would ask a large volume.

casters and togmans : cloaks and coats.

Upright Men

A

Anthony Heymer
Anthony Jackson

B

Burfet
Brian Medcalfe

C

Core the Cuckold
Christopher Cooke

D

Dowzabell (skilful in fence)
David Coke
Dick Glover
Dick Abrystowe
David Edwardes
David Holland
David Jones

E

Edmund Dun (a singing man)
Edward Skinner (alias Ned
    Skinner)
Edward Browne

F

Follentine Hylles
Ferdinando Angell
Francis Daughton

G

Griffin
Great John Graye
George Marrinar
George Hutchinson

H

Harry Hylles (alias Harry
    Godepar)
Harry Agglyntine
Harry Smith (he drivelleth
    when he speaketh)
Harry Jonson

I

James Barnard
John Myllar
John Welshman
John Jones
John Teddar
John Braye
John Cutter
John Bell
John Stephens
John Graye
John Whyte
John Rewe
John Mores
John a Fernando
John Newman
John Wyn (alias Williams)
John a Pycons
John Thomas
John Arter

Upright Men (*cont.*)
John Palmer (alias Tod)
John Geoffrey
John Goddard
John Graye the little
John Graye the great
John Williams the longer
John Horwood (a maker of wells; he will take half his bargain in hand, and when he hath wrought two or three days, he runneth away with his earnest)
John Peter
John Porter
John Ap Powis
John Arter
John Bates
John Comes
John Chyles (alias great Chyles)
John Levet (he maketh taps and faucets)
John Lovedall (a master of fence)
John Lovedale
John Mekes
John Ap Powell
John Chapell
John Griffen
John Mason
John Humphrey (with the lame hand)
John Stradling (with the shaking head)
John Frank
John Baker
John Bascafeld

K

L

Leonard Just
Long Greene
Laurence Ladd
Laurence Marshall

M

N

Nicholas Wilson
Ned Barington
Ned Wetherdon
Ned Holmes

O

P

Philip Greene

Q

R

Robert Gravener
Robert Gerse
Robert King
Robert Egerton
Robert Bell (brother to John Bell)
Robert Maple
Robert Langton
Robin Bell
Robin Toppe
Robert Brownswerd (he weareth his hair long)

Robert Curtis
Richard Brymmysh
Richard Justice
Richard Barton
Richard Constance
Richard Thomas
Richard Cadman
Richard Scategood
Richard Ap Price
Richard Walker
Richard Coper

S

Stephen Nevet

T

Thomas Bullock
Thomas Cutter
Thomas Garret
Thomas Newton
Thomas Webb
Thomas Graye (his toes be gone)
Tom Bodel
Thomas Wast
Thomas Dawson (alias Thomas Jacklin)
Thomas Bassett
Thomas Marchant

Thomas Webb
Thomas Awefeld
Thomas Gybbins
Thomas Lacon
Thomas Bate
Thomas Allen

V

W

Well-arrayed Richard
William Chamborne
William Pannell
William Morgan
William Belson
William Ebes
William Garret
William Robinson
William Umberville
William Davids
Will Penn
William Jones
Will Powell
William Clarke
Wa[l]ter Wirral
William Browne
Wa[l]ter Martin
William Grace
William Pickering

Rogues

A
Archie Douglas (a Scot)

B
Black Dick

C

D

Dick Durram

Rogues (*cont.*)
David Dew Nevet (a
  counterfeit crank)

E

Edward Ellis
Edward Anseley

F

G

George Belberby
Goodman
Gerard Gybbin (a counterfeit
  crank)

H

Harry Walles (with the little
  mouth)
Humphrey Ward
Harry Mason

I

John Warren
John Donne (with one leg)
John Elson
John Reynolds (Irishman)
John Harris
James Monkaster (a
  counterfeit crank)
John Dewe
John Crew (with one arm)
John Browne (great
  stammerer)

L

Little Dick
Little Robin

Lambert Rose

M

More (burnt in the hand)

N

Nicholas Adams (a great
  stammerer)
Nicholas Crispin
Nicholas Blunt (alias
  Nicholas Jennings, a
  counterfeit crank)
Nicholas Lynch

R

Richard Brewton
Richard Horwood (well near
  eighty years old; he will bite
  a sixpenny nail asunder with
  his teeth; and a bawdy
  drunkard)
Richard Crane (he carryeth a
  kinchen co at his back)
Richard Jones
Ralph Ketley
Robert Harrison

S

Simon King

T

Thomas Paske
Thomas Bere
Thomas Shawnean (Irishman)
Thomas Smith (with the scald
  skin)

W

William Carew
William Wastfield
Wilson
William Jinks (with a white
  beard, a lusty and strong
man; he runneth about the
country to seek work, with
a big boy his son carrying
his tools as a dauber or
plasterer but little work
serveth him)

Palliards

B

Bashford

D

Dick Sehan (Irish)
David Powell
David Jones (a counterfeit
  crank)

E

Edward Hayward (hath his
  mort following him, which
  feigned the crank)
Edward Lewes (a dummerer)

H

Hugh Jones

I

John Perse (a counterfeit
  crank)
John Davids
John Harrison
John Carew
James Lane (with one eye;
  Irish)

John Fisher
John Dewe
John Gylford (Irish with a
  counterfeit licence)

L

Laurence (with the great leg)

N

Nicholas Newton (carrieth a
  feigned licence)
Nicholas Decase

P

Prestove

R

Robert Lackley
Robert Canloke
Richard Hilton (carrieth two
  kinchen-morts about him)
Richard Thomas

S

Soth Gard
Swanders

Palliards (*cont.*)

T

Thomas Edwards
Thomas Davids

W

William Thomas

William Coper (with the
hare-lip)
Will Pettyt (beareth a
kinchin mort at his back)
William Bowmer

There is above an hundred of Irishmen and women that wander about to beg for their living, that hath come over within these two years. They say they have been burned and spoiled by the Earl of Desmond,[11] and report well of the Earl of Ormonde.

All these above written for the most part walk about Essex, Middlesex, Sussex, Surrey, and Kent. Then let the reader judge what number walks in other shires; I fear me too great a number, if they be well understand.

Here followeth their pelting speech:

Here I set before the good reader the lewd, lousy language of these loitering lusks and lazy lorels, wherewith they buy and sell the common people as they pass through the country; which language they term pedlars' French, an unknown tongue only but to these bold, beastly, bawdy beggars and vain vagabonds, being half mingled with English when it is familiarly talked. And first placing things by their proper names as an introduction to this peevish speech:

nab, a head
nab-cheat, a hat or cap
glaziers, eyes
a smelling-cheat, a nose
gan, a mouth
a prattling-cheat, a tongue
crashing-cheats, teeth
hearing-cheats, ears
fambles, hands

a fambling-cheat, a ring on thy
hand
quarroms, a body
prat, a buttock
stamps, legs
a caster, a cloak
a togman, a coat
a commission, a shirt
drawers, hosen

lusks: useless scoundrels.

stampers, shoes
a muffling-cheat, a napkin
a belly-cheat, an apron
duds, clothes
a lag of duds, a buck of clothes
a slate or slates, a sheet or sheets
libbege, a bed
bung, a purse
lour, money
mint, gold
a bord, a shilling
half-a-bord, sixpence
flag, a groat
a win, a penny
a make, a halfpenny
booze, drink
bene, good
beneship, very good
queer, nought
a gage, a quart pot
a skew, a cup
pannam, bread
cassan, cheese
yarrum, milk
lap, buttermilk or whey
peck, meat
poplars, porridge
ruff-peck, bacon
a grunting-cheat or a patrico's kinchin, a pig
a cackling-cheat, a cock or capon
a margery-prater, a hen
a Roger or tib of the buttery, a goose
a quacking-cheat or a redshank, a drake or duck

grannam, corn
a lowing-cheat, a cow
a bleating-cheat, a calf or sheep
a prancer, a horse
autem, a church
Solomon, a altar or mass
patrico, a priest
nosegent, a nun
a gybe, a writing
a jark, a seal
a ken, a house
a stalling-ken, a house that will receive stolen ware
a boozing ken, a ale-house
a libken, a house to lie in
a libbege, a bed
glimmer, fire
Rome-booze, wine
lage, water
a skipper, a barn
strummel, straw
a gentry cove's ken, a noble or gentleman's house
a jigger, a door
bufe, a dog
the lightmans, the day
the darkmans, the night
Rome-vill, London
dewse-a-vill, the country
Rome-mort, the Queen
a gentry cove, a noble or gentleman
gentry mort, a noble or gentlewoman
the Queer Cuffin, the Justice of Peace
the harman-beck, the constable
the harmans, the stocks

queer-ken, a prison-house
queer cramp-rings, bolts or fetters
trining, hanging
chats, the gallows
the high-pad, the highway
the ruffmans, the woods or bushes
a smelling-cheat, a garden or orchard
crassing-cheats, apples, pears, or any other fruit
to filch, to beat, to strike, to rob
to nip a bung, to cut a purse
to scour the cramp-rings, to wear bolts or fetters
to heave a bough, to rob or rifle a booth
to cly the jerk, to be whipped
to cut benely, to speak gently
to cut bene whids, to speak, or give good words
to cut queer whids, to give evil words or evil language
to cut, to say
to tour, to see
to booze, to drink
to maund, to ask or require
to stall, to make or ordain
to cant, to speak
to mill a ken, to rob a house
to prig, to ride
to dup the jigger, to open the door
to couch a hogshead, to lie down and sleep
to niggle, to have to do with a woman carnally
stow you, hold your peace
bing a waste, go you hence
to the ruffian, to the devil
the ruffian cly thee, the devil take thee

The upright cove canteth to the rogue: The upright man speaketh to the rogue

UPRIGHT MAN. *Bene lightmans to thy quarroms! In what libken hast thou libbed in this darkmans, whether in a libbege or in the strummel?*
Good-morrow to thy body! In what house hast thou lain in all night, whether in a bed or in the straw?

ROGUE. *I couched a hogshead in a skipper this darkmans.*
I laid me down to sleep in a barn this night.

UPRIGHT MAN. *I tour the strummel trine upon thy nab-cheat and togman.*
I see the straw hang upon thy cap and coat.

ROGUE. *I say by the Solomon I will lage it off with a gage of bene booze. Then cut to my nose watch.*

I swear by the mass I will wash it off with a quart of good drink. Then say to me what thou wilt.

MAN. *Why, hast thou any lour in thy bung to booze?*

Why, hast thou any money in thy purse to drink?

ROGUE. *But a flag, a win, and a make.*

But a groat, a penny, and a halfpenny.

MAN. *Why, where is the ken that hath the bene booze?*

Where is the house that hath good drink?

ROGUE. *A bene-mort hereby at the sign of the Prancer.*

A goodwife hereby at the sign of the Horse.

MAN. *I cut it is queer booze. I boozed a flag the last darkmans.*

I say it is small and naughty drink. I drank a groat there the last night.

ROGUE. *But booze there a bord, and thou shalt have beneship.*

But drink there a shilling, and thou shalt have very good.

Tour ye. Yonder is the ken. Dup the jigger and maund that is beneship.

See you. Yonder is the house. Open the door and ask for the best.

MAN. *This booze is as beneship as Rome-booze.*

This drink is as good as wine.

Now I tour that bene booze makes nase nabs.

Now I see that good drink makes a drunken head.

Maund of this mort what bene peck is in her ken.

Ask of this wife what good meat she hath in her house.

ROGUE. *She hath a cackling-cheat, a grunting-cheat, ruff-peck, cassan, and poplar of yarrum.*

She hath a hen, a pig, bacon, cheese, and milk-porridge.

MAN. *That is beneship to our watch.*

That is very good for us.

[ROGUE]. *Now we have well boozed, let us strike some cheat.*

Now we have well drunk, let us steal something.

[MAN]. *Yonder dwelleth a queer cuffin.*[12] *It were beneship to mill him.*

Yonder dwelleth a hoggish and churlish man. It were very well done to rob him.

ROGUE. *Now bing we a waste to the high-pad; the ruffmans is by.*

Nay, let us go hence to the highway; the woods is at hand.

MAN. *So may we happen on the harmans, and cly the jerk, or to the queer-ken and scour queer cramp-rings, and so to trining on the chats.*

So we may chance to set in the stocks, either be whipped, either had to prison-house, and there be shackled with bolts and fetters, and then to hang on the gallows.

[ROGUE]. *Gerry gan! the ruffian cly thee!*

A turd in thy mouth! the devil take thee!

MAN. *What! Stow your bene, cove, and cut benat whids! And bing we to Rome-vill, to nip a bung. So shall we have lour for the boozing ken. And when we bing back to the dewse-a-vill, we will filch some duds off the ruffmans, or mill the ken for a lag of duds.* What! Hold your peace, good fellow, and speak better words! And go we to London, to cut a purse. Then shall we have money for the ale-house. And when we come back again into the country, we will steal some linen clothes off some hedges, or rob some house for a buck of clothes.

*

By this little ye may wholly and fully understand their untoward talk and pelting speech, mingled without measure. And as they have begun of late to devise some new terms for certain things, so will they in time alter this, and devise as evil or worse. This language now being known and spread abroad, yet one thing more I will add unto, not meaning to English the same, because I learned the same of a shameless doxy. But for the phrase of speech I set it forth only.

There was a proud patrico and a nosegent. He took his jockam in his famble, and a wapping he went; he docked the dell; he prig to prance; he binged a waste into the darkmans; he filched the cove without any filchman.

*

While this second impression was in printing, it fortuned that Nicholas Blunt, who called himself Nicholas Jennings, a counterfeit crank, that is spoken of in this book, was found begging in the Whitefriars on New Year's Day last past, *Anno Domini* 1567 [–8] and committed unto a officer, who carried him unto the Deputy of the ward which committed him unto the Counter; and as the Constable and another would have carried him thither, this counterfeit crank ran away, but one lighter of foot than the other overtook him, and so leading him to the Counter, where he remained three days, and from thence to Bridewell, where before the Master he had his disguised apparel put upon him, which was monstrous to behold, and after stood in Cheapside with the same apparel on a scaffold.

> A stocks to stay sure, and safely detain
> Lazy lewd loiterers, that laws do offend,
>   Impudent persons, thus punished with pain,
> Hardly for all this, do mean to amend.

> Fetters or shackles serve to make fast
> Male malefactors that on mischief do muse,
>   Until the learned laws do quit or do cast
> Such subtle searchers as all evil do use.

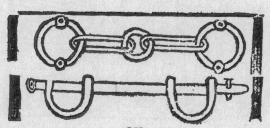

A whip is a whisker that will wrest out blood,
Of back and of body, beaten right well.
 Of all the other it doth the most good;
Experience teacheth, and they can well tell.

 O doleful day! now death draweth near,
His bitter sting doth pierce me to the heart.
 I take my leave of all that be here,
Now piteously playing this tragical part.
 Neither stripes nor teachings in time could convert;
Wherefore an ensample let me to you be,
 And all that be present, now pray you for me.

This counterfeit crank,[13] now view and behold,
  Placed in pillory, as all may well see.
This was he, as you have heard the tale told,
  Before recorded with great subtlety,
Abused many with his impiety,
  His loathsome attire, in most ugly manner,
Was through London carried with displayed banner.

Thus I conclude my bold beggars' book,
That all estates most plainly may see,
As in a glass well polished to look,
Their double demeanour in each degree;
Their lives, their language, their names as they be,
That with this warning their minds may be warmed [14]
To amend their misdeeds, and so live unharmed.

FINIS

A
Notable Discouery of Coosnage.

Now daily practised by sundry lewd per-
sons , called Connie-catchers, and
Crosse-biters.

Plainely laying open those pernitious sleights that hath brought many ignorant men to confusion.

Written for the generall benefit of all Gentlemen, Citizens, Aprentises, Countrey Farmers
and yeomen, that may hap to fall into the company of such coosening campanions.

With a delightsull discourse of the coosnage of Colliers.

Nascimur propatria.   By R. Greene, Maister of Arts.

LONDON
Printed by Iohn Wolfe for T.N. and are to be sold ouer
against the great South doore of Paules. 1591.

To the young gentlemen, merchants, apprentices, farmers, and plain countrymen, health.

Diogenes, Gentlemen, from a counterfeit coiner of money, became a current corrector of manners, as absolute in the one, as dissolute in the other. Time refineth men's affects, and their humours grow different by the distinction of age. Poor Ovid that amorously writ in his youth the art of love, complained in his exile amongst the Getes [1] of his wanton follies; and Socrates' age was virtuous though his prime was licentious. So, Gentlemen, my younger years had uncertain thoughts, but now my ripe days calls on to repentant deeds, and I sorrow as much to see others wilful, as I delighted once to be wanton. The odd madcaps I have been mate to, not as a companion, but as a spy to have an insight into their knaveries, that seeing their trains I might eschew their snares, those mad fellows I learned at last to loath, by their own graceless villainies; and what I saw in them to their confusion I can forewarn in others to my country's commodity. None could decipher tyrannism better than Aristippus; not that his nature was cruel, but that he was nurtured with Dionysius. The simple swain that cuts the lapidary's stones, can distinguish a ruby from a diamond only by his labour. Though I have not practised their deceits, yet conversing by fortune and talking upon purpose with such copesmates, hath given me light into their conceits, and I can decipher their qualities, though I utterly mislike of their practices. To be brief, Gentlemen, I have seen the world and rounded it, though not with travel, yet with experience, and I cry out with Solomon, *Omnia sub sole vanitas*. I have smiled with the Italian, and worn the viper's head in my hand, and yet

affects : passions.
copesmates : associates.
conceits : mentalities.
Omnia . . . vanitas : 'Everything under the sun is vanity.'

157

stopped his venom. I have eaten Spanish myrobalans, and yet am nothing the more metamorphosed. France, Germany, Poland, Denmark, I know them all, yet not affected to any in the form of my life; only I am English-born, and I have English thoughts, not a devil incarnate because I am Italianate, but hating the pride of Italy, because I know their peevishness. Yet in all these countries where I have travelled, I have not seen more excess of vanity than we Englishmen practise through vainglory: for as our wits be as ripe as any, so our wills are more ready than they all to put in effect any of their licentious abuses. Yet amongst the rest, letting ordinary sins pass, because custom hath almost made them a law, I will only speak of two such notable abuses, which the practitioners of them shadow with the name of arts, as never have been heard of in any age before. The first and chief is called the art of cony-catching; the second, the art of crossbiting; two such pestilent and prejudicial practices, as of late have been the ruin of infinite persons, and the subversion and overthrow of many merchants, farmers and honest-minded yeomen. The first is a deceit at cards, which, growing by enormity into a cozenage, is able to draw (by the subtle show thereof) a man of great judgement to consent to his own confusion. Yet, Gentlemen, when you shall read this book, written faithfully to discover these cozening practices, think I go not about to disprove or disallow the most ancient and honest pastime or recreation of card-play, for thus much I know by reading: when the city of Thebes was besieged by them of Lacedaemonia, being girt within strong fenced walls, and having men enough, and able to rebate the enemy, they found no inconvenience of force to breed their ensuing bane but famine, in that, when victuals waxed scant, hunger would either make them yield by a fainting composition, or a miserable death. Whereupon to weary the foe with wintering at the siege, the Thebans devised this policy: they found out the method of cards and dice, and so busied their brains with the pleasantness of that new invention, passing away the time with strange recreations and pastimes, beguiling hunger with the delight of the new sports, and eating but every third day and playing two, so their frugal sparing of victuals kept them from

myrobalans: astringent dried fruit formerly used medicinally.

famine, the city from sacking, and raised the foe from a mortal
siege. Thus was the use of cards and dice first invented, and
since amongst princes highly esteemed, and allowed in all com-
monwealths, as a necessary recreation for the mind. But as in
time and malice of man's nature hatcheth abuse, so good things
by ill wits are wrested to the worse, and so in cards; for from an
honest recreation it is grown to a prejudicial practice and most
high degree of cozenage, as shall be discovered in my *Art of
Cony-catching*; for not only simple swains, whose wits is in
their hands, but young gentlemen and merchants, are all caught
like conies in the hay, and so led like lambs to their confusion.

The poor man that cometh to the Term to try his right, and
layeth his land to mortgage to get some crowns in his purse to
see his lawyer, is drawn in by these devilish cony-catchers, that
at one cut at cards loseth all his money, by which means, he, his
wife and children, is brought to utter ruin and misery. The poor
prentice, whose honest mind aimeth only at his master's profits,
by these pestilent vipers of the commonwealth is smoothly enticed to the hazard of this game at cards, and robbed of his
master's money, which forceth him ofttimes either to run away,
or bankrupt all, to the overthrow of some honest and wealthy
citizen. Seeing then such a dangerous enormity groweth by them
to the discredit of the estate of England, I would wish the Justices
appointed as severe censors of such fatal mischiefs, to show
themselves *patres patriae*, by weeding out such worms as eat away
the sap of the tree, and rooting this base degree of cozeners out of
so peaceable and prosperous a country, for of all devilish practices this is the most prejudicial. The high-lawyer that challengeth a purse by the highway side, the foist, the nip, the stale, the
snap – I mean the pickpockets and cutpurses – are nothing so
dangerous to meet withal as these cozening cony-catchers. The
cheaters that with their false dice make a hand and strike in at
hazard or passage with their dice of advantage, are nothing so
dangerous as these base-minded caterpillars. For they have their
vies and their revies upon the poor cony's back, till they so ferret-
beat him, that they leave him neither hair on his skin nor hole to

Term: court sessions.
patres patriae : fathers of (their) country.

harbour in. There was before this, many years ago,[2] a practice put in use by such shifting companions, which was called the barnard's law, wherein, as in the art of cony-catching, four persons were required to perform their cozening commodity: the taker-up, the verser, the barnard and the rutter; and the manner of it indeed was thus. The taker-up seemeth a skilful man in all things, who hath by long travail learned without book a thousand policies to insinuate himself into a man's acquaintance. Talk of matters in law, he hath plenty of cases at his fingers' ends, and he hath seen, and tried, and ruled in the king's courts. Speak of grazing and husbandry, no man knoweth more shires than he, nor better which way to raise a gainful commodity, and how the abuses and overture of prices might be redressed. Finally, enter into what discourse they list, were it into a broom-man's faculty, he knoweth what gains they have for old boots and shoes; yea, and it shall escape him hardly, but that ere your talk break off, he will be your countryman at least, and peradventure either of kin, ally or some stale sib to you, if your reach far surmount not his. In case he bring to pass that you be glad of his acquaintance, then doth he carry you to the taverns, and with him goes the verser, a man of more worship than the taker-up, and he hath the countenance of a landed man. As they are set, comes in the barnard stumbling into your company, like some aged farmer of the country, a stranger unto you all, that had been at some market town thereabout, buying and selling, and there tippled so much malmsy that he had never a ready word in his mouth, and is so careless of his money that out he throweth some forty angels on the board's end, and, standing somewhat aloof, calleth for a pint of wine, and saith, 'Masters, I am somewhat bold with you; I pray you be not grieved if I drink my drink by you'; and thus ministers such idle drunken talk that the verser, who counterfeited the landed man, comes and draws more near to the plain honest-dealing man, and prayeth him to call the barnard more near to laugh at his folly. Between them two the matter shall be so workmanly conveyed and finely argued that out cometh an old pair of cards, whereat the barnard teacheth the verser a new game, that he says cost him for the learning two pots of ale not two hours ago. The first wager is drink, the next twopence or a groat, and lastly, to be brief, they use the matter so, that he that were an hundred year old and never played in his life for a penny, cannot refuse to be the verser's half, and consequently, at one game at cards he loseth all they play for, be it a hundred pound. And if perhaps, when the money is lost (to use their word of art), the poor countryman begin to smoke them and swears the drunken knave shall not get his money so, then standeth the rutter at the door and draweth his sword and picketh a quarrel at his own shadow, if he lack an ostler or a tapster or some other to brabble with, that while the street and company gather to the fray, as the manner is, the barnard steals away with all the coin, and gets him to one blind tavern or other, where these cozeners had appointed to meet.

Thus, Gentlemen, I have glanced at the barnard's law, which though you may perceive it to be a prejudicial insinuating cozenage, yet is the art of cony-catching so far beyond it in subtlety, as the Devil is more honest than the holiest angel: for so unlikely is it for the poor cony to lose, that might he pawn his stake to a pound, he would lay it that he cannot be cross-bitten in the cut at cards, as you shall perceive by my present discovery. Yet, Gentlemen, am I sore threatened by the hacksters of that filthy faculty that if I set their practices in print, they will cut off that hand that writes the pamphlet; but how I fear their bravados, you shall perceive by my plain painting out of them; yea, so little do I esteem such base-minded braggards that, were it not I hope of their amendment, I would in a schedule set down the names of such cozening cony-catchers.

Well, leaving them and their course of life to the honourable and the worshipful of the land to be censors of with justice, have about for a blow at the art of crossbiting. I mean not crossbiters at dice, when the cheater with a langret, cut contrary to the vantage, will crossbite a barred cater-trey; nor I mean not when a broking knave crossbiteth a gentleman with a bad commodity;[3] nor when the foist, the pickpocket (sir, reverence I mean), is cross-bitten by the snap, and so, smoked for his purchase; nor when the nip, which the common people call a cutpurse, hath a crossbite by some bribing officer, who, threatening to carry him to prison,

blind: obscure.

takes away all the money, and lets him slip without any punishment; but I mean a more dishonourable art, when a base rogue, either keepeth a whore as his friend, or marries one to be his maintainer, and with her not only crossbites men of good calling, but especially poor ignorant country farmers, who, God wot, be by them led like sheep to the slaughter. Thus, gentle readers, have I given you a light in brief what I mean to prosecute at large, and so with an humble suit to all Justices, that they will seek to root out these two roguish arts, I commit you to the Almighty.

Yours, Rob. Greene.

The Art of Cony-Catching

There be requisite effectually to act the art of cony-catching three several parties, the setter, the verser, and the barnacle. The nature of the setter is to draw any person familiarly to drink with him, which person they call the cony, and their method is according to the man they aim at. If a gentleman, merchant or apprentice, the cony is the more easily caught, in that they are soon induced to play, and therefore I omit the circumstance which they use in catching of them. And for because the poor country farmer or yeoman is the mark which they most of all shoot at, who they know comes not empty to the Term, I will discover the means they put in practice to bring in some honest, simple and ignorant men to their purpose.

The cony-catchers, apparelled like honest civil gentlemen or good fellows, with a smooth face, as if butter would not melt in their mouths, after dinner when the clients are come from Westminster Hall and are at leisure to walk up and down Paul's, Fleet Street, Holborn, the Strand, and such common-haunted places, where these cozening companions attend only to spy out a prey; who, as soon as they see a plain country fellow, well and cleanly apparelled, either in a coat of homespun russet, or of frieze, as the time requires, and a side-pouch at his side – 'There is a cony,' saith one. At that word out flies the setter, and overtaking the man, begins to salute him thus: 'Sir, God save you, you are welcome to London! How doth all our good friends in the

162

country? I hope they be all in health?' The countryman, seeing a man so courteous he knows not, half in a brown study at this strange salutation, perhaps makes him this answer: 'Sir, all our friends in the country are well, thanks be to God; but truly I know you not. You must pardon me.' 'Why sir,' saith the setter, guessing by his tongue what countryman he is, 'are you not such a countryman?' If he say, 'Yes,' then he creeps upon him closely. If he say, 'No,' then straight the setter comes over him thus: 'In good sooth, sir, I know you by your face and have been in your company before. I pray you, if without offence, let me crave your name and the place of your abode.' The simple man straight tells him where he dwells, his name and who be his next neighbours, and what gentlemen dwell about him. After he hath learned all of him, then he comes over his fallows kindly: 'Sir, though I have been somewhat bold to be inquisitive of your name, yet hold me excused, for I took you for a friend of mine, but since by mistaking I have made you slack your business, we'll drink a quart of wine or a pot of ale together.' If the fool be so ready as to go, then the cony is caught; but if he smack the setter, and smells a rat by his clawing, and will not drink with him, then away goes the setter, and discourseth to the verser the name of the man, the parish he dwells in, and what gentlemen are his near neighbours. With that, away goes he, and, crossing the man at some turning, meets him full in the face, and greets him thus:

'What, Goodman Barton, how fare all our friends about you? You are well met. I have the wine for you. You are welcome to town.' The poor countryman hearing himself named by a man he knows not, marvels, and answers that he knows him not, and craves pardon.

'Not me, Goodman Barton, have you forgot me? Why, I am such a man's kinsman, your neighbour not far off. How doth this or that good gentleman, my friend? Good Lord, that I should be out of your remembrance! I have been at your house divers times.'

'Indeed, sir,' saith the farmer, 'are you such a man's kinsman? Surely, sir, if you had not challenged acquaintance of me, I

comes over his fallows: ? covers neglected ground.
clawing: fawning.

should never have known you. I have clean forgot you, but I know the good gentleman your cousin well, he is my very good neighbour.'

'And for his sake,' saith the verser, 'we'll drink afore we part.'

Haply the man thanks him, and to the wine or ale they go; then, ere they part, they make him a cony and so ferret-claw him at cards, that they leave him as bare of money as an ape of a tail. Thus have the filthy fellows their subtle fetches to draw on poor men to fall into their cozening practices. Thus, like consuming moths of the commonwealth, they prey upon the ignorance of such plain souls as measure all by their own honesty, not regarding either conscience, or the fatal revenge that's threatened for such idle and licentious persons, but do employ all their wits to overthrow such as with their handy thrift satisfy their hearty thirst; they preferring cozenage before labour, and choosing an idle practice before any honest form of good living.

Well, to the method again of taking up their conies: if the poor countryman smoke them still, and will not stoop unto either of their lures, then one, either the verser, or the setter, or some of their crew – for there is a general fraternity betwixt them – steppeth before the cony as he goeth, and letteth drop twelve-pence in the highway, that of force the cony must see it. The countryman, spying the shilling, maketh not dainty, for *quis nisi mentis inops oblatum respuit aurum?* but stoopeth very mannerly and taketh it up. Then one of the cony-catchers behind crieth, 'Half part!' and so challengeth half of his finding. The country-man, content, offereth to change the money. 'Nay, faith! friend,' saith the verser, ''tis ill luck to keep found money; we'll go spend it in a pottle of wine, or in a breakfast' (*dinner* or *supper* – as the time of day requires). If the cony say he will not, then answers the verser, 'Spend my part.' If still the cony refuse, he taketh half and away.

If they spy the countryman to be of a having and covetous mind, then have they a further policy to draw him on. Another that knoweth the place of his abode, meeteth him and saith, 'Sir, well met! I have run hastily to overtake you. I pray you, dwell you

ferret-claw: strip (of money).
quis . . . aurum? : 'Who but a fool rejects offered gold?'

not in Derbyshire, in such a village?' – 'Yes, marry, do I, friend,' said the cony. Then replies the verser, 'Truly, sir, I have a suit to you; I am going out of town, and must send a letter to the parson of your parish. You shall not refuse to do a stranger such a favour as to carry it him. Haply, as men may in time meet, it may lie in my lot to do you as good a turn, and for your pains I will give you twelvepence.' The poor cony in mere simplicity saith, 'Sir, I'll do so much for you with all my heart. Where is your letter?' – 'I have it not, good sir, ready written; but may I entreat you to step into some tavern or alehouse. We'll drink the while, and I will write but a line or two.' At this the cony stoops, and for greediness of the money, and upon courtesy goes with the setter unto the tavern. As they walk they meet the verser, and then they all three go into the tavern together.

See, Gentlemen, what great logicians these cony-catchers be, that have such rhetorical persuasions to induce the poor country-man to his confusion, and what variety of villainy they have to strip the poor farmer of his money! Well, imagine the cony is in the tavern. Then sits down the verser, and saith to the setter, 'What, sirrah, wilt thou give me a quart of wine, or shall I give thee one?'

'We'll drink a pint,' saith the setter, 'and play a game at cards for it, respecting more the sport than the loss.'

'Content,' quoth the verser. 'Go call for a pair.' And while he is gone to fetch them, he saith to the cony, 'You shall see me fetch over my young master for a quart of wine finely; but this you must do for me: when I cut the cards, as I will not cut above five off, mark then of all the greatest pack which is undermost, and when I bid you call a card for me, name that, and you shall see, we'll make him pay for a quart of wine straight.'

'Truly,' saith the cony, 'I am no great player at cards, and I do not well understand your meaning.'

'Why,' saith he, 'it is thus: I will play at mumchance, or decoy, that he shall shuffle the cards, and I will cut. Now, either of us must call a card. You shall call for me, and he for himself, and whose card comes first wins. Therefore, when I have cut the cards, then mark the nethermost of the greatest heap, that I set upon the cards which I cut off, and always call that for me.'

'Oh now,' saith the cony, 'I understand you. Let me alone, I warrant I'll fit your turn.'

With that in comes the setter with his cards and asketh at what game they shall play. 'Why,' saith the verser, 'at a new game called mumchance, that hath no policy nor knavery, but plain as a pikestaff. You shall shuffle and I'll cut. You shall call a card, and this honest man, a stranger almost to us both, shall call another for me, and which of our cards comes first, shall win.'

'Content,' saith the setter, 'for that's but mere hazard.' And so he shuffles the cards, and the verser cuts off some four cards, and then, taking up the heap to set upon them, giveth the cony a glance of the bottom card of that heap and saith, 'Now, sir, call for me.'

The cony, to blind the setter's eyes, asketh as though he were not made privy to the game: 'What shall I call?'

'What card?' saith the verser. 'Why, what you will, either heart, spade, club or diamond, court-card or other.'

'Oh, is it so?' saith the cony. 'Why then, you shall have the four of hearts' (which was the card he had a glance of); and saith the setter (holding the cards in his hand, and turning up the uppermost card, as if he knew not well the game), 'I'll have the knave of trumps.'

'Nay,' saith the verser, 'there is no trump; you may call what card you will.'

'Then,' saith he, 'I'll have the ten of spades.' With that he draws and the four of hearts comes first.

'Well,' saith the setter, ' 'tis but hazard; mine might have come as well as yours; five is up, I fear not the set.' So they shuffle and cut, but the verser wins.

'Well,' saith the setter, 'no butter will cleave on my bread. What! not one draught among five? Drawer, a fresh pint. I'll have another bout with you.'

'But, sir, I believe,' saith he to the cony, 'you see some card, that it goes so cross on my side.'

'I?' saith the cony. 'Nay, I hope you think not so of me; 'tis but hazard and chance, for I am but a mere stranger unto the game. As I am an honest man, I never saw it before.'

'What shall I call?': (original,) 'What shall I cut?'

Thus this simple cony closeth up smoothly to take the verser's part, only for greediness to have him win the wine.

'Well,' answers the setter, 'then I'll have one cast more.' And to it they go, but he loseth all, and beginneth to chafe in this manner; 'Were it not,' quoth he, 'that I care not for a quart of wine, I could swear as many oaths for anger, as there be hairs on my head. Why should not my luck be as good as yours, and fortune favour me as well as you? What! Not one called card in ten cuts? I'll foreswear the game for ever.'

'What! chafe not, man,' saith the verser, 'seeing we have your quart of wine, I'll show you the game'; and with that, discourseth all to him, as if he knew it not.

The setter, as simply as if the knave were ignorant, saith, 'Ay, marry! I think so; you must needs win when he knows what card to call. I might have played long enough before I had got a set.'

'Truly,' says the cony, ' 'tis a pretty game, for 'tis not possible for him to lose that cuts the cards. I warrant the other that shuffles may lose St Peter's cope if he had it. Well, I'll carry this home with me into the country, and win many a pot of ale with it.'

'A fresh pint,' saith the verser, 'and then we'll away. But seeing, sir, you are going homeward, I'll learn you a trick worth the noting, that you shall win many a pot with in the winter nights.' With that he culls out the four knaves, and pricks one in the top, one in the midst, and one in the bottom. 'Now sir,' saith he, 'you see these three knaves apparently. Thrust them down with your hand, and cut where you will, and, though they be so far asunder, I'll make them all come together.'

'I pray you, let's see that trick,' saith the cony; 'methinks it should be impossible.'

So the verser draws, and all the three knaves comes in one heap. This he doth once or twice; then the cony wonders at it, and offers him a pint of wine to teach it him.

'Nay,' saith the verser, 'I'll do it for thanks, and therefore mark me where you have taken out the four knaves, lay two together above and draw up one of them that it may be seen, then prick the other in the midst, and the third in the bottom, so when any cuts, cut he never so warily, three knaves must of force come together, for the bottom knave is cut to lie upon both the upper knaves.'

'Ay, marry,' saith the setter, 'but then the three knaves you showed come not together.'

'Truth,' said the verser, 'but one among a thousand mark not it; it requires a quick eye, a sharp wit, and a reaching head to spy at the first.'

'Now gramercy, sir, for this trick,' saith the cony, 'I'll domineer with this amongst my neighbours.'

Thus doth the verser and the setter feign friendship to the cony, offering him no show of cozenage, nor once to draw him in for a pint of wine, the more to shadow their villainy. But now begins the sport. As thus they sit tippling, comes the barnacle and thrusts open the door, looking into the room where they are, and as one bashful steppeth back again and saith, 'I cry you mercy, gentlemen, I thought a friend of mine had been here; pardon my boldness.'

'No harm,' saith the verser, 'I pray you drink a cup of wine with us and welcome.'

So in comes the barnacle and, taking the cup, drinks to the cony, and then saith 'What! at cards gentlemen? Were it not I should be offensive to the company, I would play for a pint till my friend come that I look for.'

'Why sir,' saith the verser, 'if you will sit down you shall be taken up for a quart of wine.'

'With all my heart,' saith the barnacle. 'What will you play at, at primero, prima-vista, cent, one-and-thirty, new cut, or what shall be the game?'

'Sir,' saith the verser, 'I am but an ignorant man at cards, and I see you have them at your fingers' end. I will play with you at a game wherein can be no deceit; it is called mumchance at cards, and it is thus: you shall shuffle the cards, and I will cut, you shall call one, and this honest country yeoman shall call a card for me, and which of our cards comes first shall win. Here you see is no deceit, and this I'll play.'

'No, truly,' saith the cony, 'methinks there can be no great craft in this.'

'Well,' saith the barnacle, 'for a pint of wine, have at you.' So they play as before, five up, and the verser wins. 'This is hard luck,' saith the barnacle, 'and I believe the honest man spies some card in the bottom, and therefore I'll make this, always to prick the bottom card.'

'Content,' saith the verser; and the cony, to cloak the matter, saith, 'Sir, you offer me injury to think that I can call a card, when I neither touch them, shuffle, cut, nor draw them.'

'Ah sir,' saith the barnacle, 'give losers leave to speak.' Well, to it they go again and then the barnacle, knowing the game best, by chopping a card wins two of the five, but lets the verser win the set; then in a chafe he sweareth 'tis but his ill luck, and he can see no deceit in it, and therefore he will play twelvepence a cut. The verser is content, and wins two or three shillings of the barnacle. Whereat he chafes, and saith, 'I came hither in an ill hour; but I will win my money again, or lose all in my purse.' With that he draws out a purse with some three or four pound, and claps it on the board. The verser asketh the cony secretly by signs if he will be his half; he says 'Ay', and straight seeks for his purse. Well, the barnacle shuffles the cards thoroughly, and the verser cuts as before. The barnacle, when he hath drawn one card, saith, 'I'll either win something or lose something; therefore I'll vie and revie every card at my pleasure, till either yours or mine come out, and therefore twelve pence upon this card; my card comes first for twelve pence.' 'No,' saith the verser. 'Ay,' saith the cony, 'and I durst hold twelve pence more.' 'Why, I hold you,' saith the barnacle. And so they vie and revie till some ten shillings be on the stake. And then next comes forth the verser's card, that the cony called, and so the barnacle loseth.

Well, this flesheth the cony; the sweetness of gain maketh him frolic, and no man is more ready to vie and revie than he. Thus for three or four times the barnacle loseth, at last to whet on the cony, he striketh his chopped card and winneth a good stake. 'Away with the witch!' cries the barnacle, 'I hope the cards will turn at last.' 'Ay, much,' thinketh the cony, ''twas but a chance that you asked so right, to ask one of the five that was cut off; I am sure there was forty to one on my side, and I'll have you on the lurch anon.'

chopped card: card whose place in pack has been secretly changed.

So still they vie and revie, and for once that the barnacle wins, the cony gets five. At last when they mean to shave the cony clean of all his coin, the barnacle chafeth, and upon a pawn borroweth some money of the tapster, and swears he will vie it to the uttermost. Then thus he chops his card to crossbite the cony: he first looks on the bottom card, and shuffles often, but still keeping that bottom card, which he knows, to be uppermost; then sets he down the cards, and the verser to encourage the cony, cut[s] off but three cards, whereof the barnacle's card must needs be the uppermost; then shows he the bottom card of the other heap cut off to the cony, and sets it upon the barnacle's card which he knows, so that of force the card that was laid uppermost must come forth first, and then the barnacle calls that card. They draw a card, and then the barnacle vies, and the countryman vies upon him; for this is the law, as often as one vies or revies, the other must see it, else he loseth the stake. Well, at last the barnacle plies it so, that perhaps he vies more money than the cony hath in his purse. The cony, upon this, knowing his card is the third or fourth card, and that he hath forty to one against the barnacle, pawns his rings, if he have any, his sword, his cloak or else what he hath about him, to maintain the vie; and when he laughs in his sleeve, thinking he hath fleeced the barnacle of all, then the barnacle's card comes forth, and strikes such a cold humour unto his heart that he sits as a man in a trance, not knowing what to do, and sighing while his heart is ready to break, thinking on the money that he hath lost.

Perhaps the man is very simple and patient, and, whatsoever he thinks, for fear goes his way quiet with his loss (while the cony-catchers laugh and divide the spoil), and being out of the doors, poor man, goes to his lodging with a heavy heart, pensive and sorrowful, but too late, for perhaps his state did depend on that money, and so he, his wife, his children and his family, are brought to extreme misery.

Another, perhaps, more hardy and subtle, smokes the cony-catchers, and smelleth cozenage, and saith they shall not have his money so. But they answer him with braves, and though he bring them before an officer, yet the knaves are so favoured, that the man never recovers his money, and yet he is let slip unpunished.

Thus are the poor conies robbed by these base-minded cater-pillars; thus are servingmen oft enticed to play, and lose all; thus are prentices induced to be conies, and so are cozened of their masters' money; yea, young gentlemen, merchants and others, are fetched in by these damnable rakehells, a plague as ill as hell, which is present loss of money, and ensuing misery. A lamentable case in England, when such vipers are suffered to breed, and are not cut off with the sword of justice! This enormity is not only in London, but now generally dispersed through all England, in every shire, city and town of any receipt, and many complaints are heard of their egregious cozenage. The poor farmer, simply going about his business or unto his attorney's chamber, is catched up and cozened of all. The serving-man sent with his lord's treasure, loseth ofttimes most part to these worms of the commonwealth. The prentice, having his master's money in charge, is spoiled by them, and from an honest servant either driven to run away, or to live in discredit for ever. The gentle-man loseth his land, the merchant his stock, and all to these abominable cony-catchers, whose means is as ill as their living, for they are all either wedded to whores, or so addicted to whores, that what they get from honest men they spend in bawdy-houses among harlots, and consume it as vainly as they get it villain-ously. Their ears are of adamant, as pitiless as they are treacher-ous, for be the man never so poor, they will not return him one penny of his loss.

I remember a merry jest done of late to a Welshman, who, being a mere stranger in London, and not well acquainted with the English tongue, yet chanced amongst certain cony-catchers, who [e]spying the gentleman to have money, they so dealt with him, that what by signs and broken English, they got him in for a cony, and fleeced him of every penny that he had, and of his sword; at last the man smoked them, and drew his dagger upon them at Ludgate (for thereabouts they had catched him), and would have stabbed one of them for his money. People came and stopped him, and the rather because they could not understand him, though he had a card in one hand and his dagger in the other, and said, as well as he could, 'a card, a card, mon Dieu'. In the meanwhile the cony-catchers were got into Paul's, and so away. The Welshman followed them, seeking them there up and down in the church, still with his naked dagger and the card in his hand, and the gentlemen marvelled what he meant thereby. At last one of his countrymen met him, and inquired the cause of his choler; and then he told him how he was cozened at cards, and robbed of all his money, but as his loss was voluntary, so his seeking them was mere vanity, for they were stepped into some blind ale-house to divide the shares.

Near to St Edmundsbury in Suffolk, there dwelt an honest man, a shoemaker, that having some twenty marks in his purse, long a-gathering and nearly kept, came to the market to buy a dicker of hides, and by chance fell among cony-catchers, whose names I omit, because I hope of their amendment. This plain countryman, drawn in by these former devices, was made a cony, and so straight stripped of all his twenty mark, to his utter undoing. The knaves 'scaped, and he went home a sorrowful man. Shortly after, one of these cony-catchers was taken for a suspected person, and laid in Bury jail. The sessions coming and he produced to the bar, it was the fortune of this poor shoemaker to be there, who spying this rogue to be arraigned, was glad and said nothing unto him, but looked what would be the issue of his appearance. At the last he was brought before the Justices, where he was examined of his life and, being demanded what occupation he was, said none.

'What profession then are you of? How live you?'

'Marry,' quoth he, 'I am a gentleman, and live of my friends.'

'Nay, that is a lie,' quoth the poor shoemaker. 'Under correction of the worshipful of the bench, you have a trade, and are by your art a cony-catcher.'

'A cony-catcher,' said one of the Justices, and smiled. 'What is he, a warrener, fellow? Whose warren keepeth he, canst thou tell?'

'Nay sir, your worship mistaketh me,' quoth the shoemaker. 'He is not a warrener, but a cony-catcher.'

The bench, that never heard this name before, smiled, attributing the name to the man's simplicity, thought he meant a warrener; which the shoemaker spying, answered, that some conies

dicker: ten.

this fellow catched were worth twenty mark apiece: 'And for proof,' quoth he, 'I am one of them'; and so discoursed the whole order of the art and the baseness of the cozening; whereupon the Justices looking into his life, appointed him to be whipped, and the shoemaker desired that he might give him his payment, which was granted. When he came to his punishment, the shoemaker laughed, saying, ' 'Tis a mad world when poor conies are able to beat their catchers.' But he lent him so friendly lashes, that almost he made him pay an ounce of blood for every pound of silver.

Thus we see how the generation of these vipers increase[s], to the confusion of many honest men, whose practices to my poor power I have discovered, and set out, with the villainous sleights they use to entrap the simple. Yet have they cloaks for the rain, and shadows for their villainies, calling it by the name of *art* or *law*: as cony-catching art, or cony-catching law. And hereof it riseth,[4] that like as law, when the term is truly considered, signifieth the ordinance of good men, established for the commonwealth, to repress all vicious living, so these cony-catchers turn the cat in the pan, giving to divers vile patching shifts, an honest and godly title, calling it by the name of a *law*, because by a multitude of hateful rules, as it were in good learning, they exercise their villainies to the destruction of sundry honest persons. Hereupon they give their false conveyance the name of cony-catching law, as there be also other laws, as high law, sacking law, figging law, cheating law and barnard's law. If you marvel at these mysteries and quaint words, consider, as the carpenter hath many terms familiar enough to his prentices, that others understand not at all, so have the cony-catchers; not without great cause, for a falsehood once detected, can never compass the desired effect. Therefore will I presently acquaint you with the signification of the terms in a table; but leaving them till time and place.

Coming down Turnmill Street the other day, I met one whom I suspected a cony-catcher. I drew him on to the tavern, and after a cup of wine or two, I talked with him of the manner of his life, and told him I was sorry for his friends' sake that he took so bad a course as to live upon the spoil of poor men, and specially to deserve the name of cony-catching, dissuading him from that base kind of life, that was so ignominious in the world, and so loathsome in the sight of God.

'Tut, sir,' quoth he, calling me by my name, 'as my religion is small, so my devotion is less. I leave God to be disputed on by divines. The two ends I aim at are gain and ease; but by what honest gains I may get, never comes within the compass of my thoughts. Though your experience in travel be great, yet in home matters mine be more. Yea, I am sure you are not so ignorant, but you know that few men can live uprightly, unless he have some pretty way, more than the world is witness to, to help him withal. Think you some lawyers could be such purchasers, if all their pleas were short, and their proceedings justice and conscience? that offices would be so dearly bought, and the buyers so soon enriched, if they counted not pillage an honest kind of purchase? or do you think that men of handy trades make all their commodities without falsehood, when so many of them are become daily purchasers? Nay, what will you more? Whoso hath not some sinister way to help himself, but followeth his nose always straight forward, may well hold up the head for a year or two, but the third he must needs sink, and gather the wind into beggars' haven. Therefore, sir, cease to persuade me to the contrary, for my resolution is to beat my wits and spare not to busy my brains to save and help me, by what means soever I care not, so I may avoid the danger of the law.'

Whereupon, seeing this cony-catcher resolved in his form of life, leaving him to his lewdness, I went away, wondering at the baseness of their minds, that would spend their time in such detestable sort. But no marvel, for they are given up into a reprobate sense and are in religion mere atheists, as they are in trade flat dissemblers. If I should spend many sheets in deciphering their shifts, it were frivolous, in that they be many and full of variety, for every day they invent new tricks and such quaint devices as are secret, yet passing dangerous, that if a man had Argus' eyes, he could scant pry into the bottom of their practices.

Thus for the benefit of my country I have briefly discovered the law of cony-catching, desiring all justices, if such cozeners

sinister: literally 'left-handed'.

light in their precinct, even to use *summum jus* against them, because it is the basest of all villainies; and that London prentices, if they chance in such cony-catchers' company, may teach them 'London law', that is, to defend the poor men that are wronged, and learn the caterpillars the highway to Newgate, where, if Hind favour them with the heaviest irons in all the house and give them his unkindest entertainment, no doubt his other petty sins shall be half pardoned for his labour. But I would it might be their fortune to happen into Nobles Northward in Whitechapel; there, in faith, Round Robin,[5] his deputy, would make them, like wretches, feel the weight of his heaviest fetters. And so desiring both honourable and worshipful, as well justices, as other officers, and all estates, from the prince to the beggar, to rest professed enemies to these base-minded cony-catchers, I take my leave.

Nascimur pro patria

A Table of the Words of Art, Used in the Effecting These Base Villainies

Wherein is Discovered the Nature of Every Term, being Proper to None but to the Professors thereof.

1. *High law* (robbing by the highway side).
2. *Sacking law* (lechery).
3. *Cheating law* (play at false dice).
4. *Crossbiting law* (cozenage by whores).
5. *Cony-catching law* (cozenage by cards).
6. *Versing law* (cozenage by false gold).
7. *Figging law* (cutting of purses and picking of pockets).
8. *Barnard's law* (a drunken cozenage by cards).

These are the eight laws of villainy, leading the highway to infamy.

summum jus: full force of law.
Hind: possibly a Newgate jailer.
Nascimur ... patria: 'We are born for (the good of) the country.'

In High Law

The thief is called a *high-lawyer*;
he that setteth the watch, a *scrippet*;
he that standeth to watch, *an oak*;
he that is robbed, the *martin*;
when he yieldeth, *stooping*.

In Sacking Law

The bawd, if it be a woman, a *pander*;
the bawd, if a man, an *apple-squire*;
the whore, a *commodity*;
the whore-house, a *trugging-place*.

In Cheating Law

Pardon me, Gentlemen, for although no man could better than myself discover this law and his terms, and the names of their cheats, barred dice, flats, forgers, langrets, gourds, demies, and many other, with their nature, and the crosses and contraries to them upon advantage, yet for some special reasons herein I will be silent.

In Crossbiting Law

The whore, the *traffic*;
the man that is brought in, the *simpler*;
the villains that take them, the *crossbiters*.

In Cony-Catching Law

The party that taketh up the cony, the *setter*;
he that playeth the game, the *verser*;
he that is cozened, the *cony*;
he that comes in to them, the *barnacle*;
the money that is won, *purchase*.

for some special reasons : ? lack of first-hand knowledge.

In Versing Law

He that bringeth him in, the *verser*;
the poor countryman, the *cousin*;
and the drunkard that comes in, the *suffier*.

In Figging Law

The cutpurse, a *nip*;
he that is half with him, the *snap*;
the knife, the *cuttle-bung*;
the pickpocket, a *foin*;
he that faceth the man, the *stale*;
taking the purse, *drawing*;
spying of him, *smoking*;
the purse, the *bung*;
the money, the *shells*;
the act doing, *striking*.

In Barnard's Law

He that fetcheth the man, the *taker*;
he that is taken, the *cousin*;
the landed man, the *verser*;
the drunken man, the *barnard*;
and he that makes the fray, the *rutter*.

Cum multis aliis quae nunc praescribere longum est

These quaint terms do these base arts use to shadow their villainy withal; for, *multa latent quae non patent*, obscuring their filthy crafts with these fair colours, that the ignorant may not espy what their subtlety is; but their end will be like their beginning, hatched with Cain, and consumed with Judas. And so, bidding them adieu to the devil, and you farewell to God, I end. And now to the art of crossbiting.

Cum multis . . . longum est: 'With much else too long to set down here'.
multa . . . patent: 'much is here that does not appear'.

The Art of Crossbiting

The crossbiting law is a public profession of shameless cozenage, mixed with incestuous whoredoms, as ill as was practised in Gomorrah or Sodom, though not after the same unnatural manner. For the method of their mischievous art (with blushing cheeks and trembling heart let it be spoken) is, that these villainous vipers, unworthy the name of men, base rogues – yet why do I term them so well – being outcasts from God, vipers of the world and an excremental reversion of sin, doth consent, nay constrain their wives to yield the use of their bodies to other men, that, taking them together, he may crossbite the party of all the crowns he can presently make. And that the world may see their monstrous practices, I will briefly set down the manner.

They have sundry preys that they call 'simplers', which are men fondly and wantonly given, whom for a penalty of their lust, they fleece of all that ever they have; some merchants, prentices, serving-men, gentlemen, yeomen, farmers and all degrees. And this is their form: there are resident in London and the suburbs certain men attired like gentlemen, brave fellows, but basely minded, who living in want, as their last refuge, fall unto this crossbiting law, and to maintain themselves either marry with some stale whore, or else forsooth keep one as their friend; and these persons be commonly men of the eight laws before rehearsed, either high-lawyers, versers, nips, cony-catchers, or such of the like fraternity. These, when their other trades fail – as the cheater when he has no cousin to grime with his stop dice, or the high-lawyer, when he hath no set match to ride about, and the nip when there is no Term, fair, nor time of great assembly – then, to maintain the main chance, they use the benefit of their wives or friends to the crossbiting of such as lust after their filthy enormities. Some simple men are drawn on by subtle means, which never intended such a bad matter.

In summer evenings and in the winter nights, these traffics, these common trulls I mean, walk abroad either in the fields or streets that are commonly haunted, as stales to draw men into hell, and afar off, as attending apple-squires, certain crossbiters stand aloof, as if they knew them not. Now so many men, so many affections! Some unruly mates that place their content in lust, letting slip the liberty of their eyes on their painted faces, feed upon their unchaste beauties, till their hearts be set on fire. Then come they to these minions, and court them with many sweet words. Alas, their loves needs no long suits, for they are forthwith entertained, and either they go to the tavern to seal up the match with a pottle of hippocras, or straight she carries him to some bad place, and there picks his pocket, or else the cross-biters come swearing in, and so outface the dismayed companion, that, rather than he would be brought in question, he would disburse all that he hath present. But this is but an easy cozenage.

Some other, meeting with one of that profession in the street, will question if she will drink with him a pint of wine. Their trade is never to refuse, and if for manners they do, it is but once; and then, scarce shall they be warm in the room, but in comes a terrible fellow with a side hair and a fearful beard, as though he were one of Polyphemus' cut,[6] and he comes frowning in and saith: 'What hast thou to do, base knave, to carry my sister (or my wife) to the tavern: by His 'ounds, you whore, 'tis some of your companions. I will have you both before the Justice, Deputy, or Constable, to be examined.'

The poor serving-man, apprentice, farmer, or whatsoever he is, seeing such a terrible huff-snuff, swearing with his dagger in his hand, is fearful both of him and to be brought in trouble, and therefore speaks kindly and courteously unto him, and desires him to be content, he meant no harm. The whore, that hath tears at command, falls a-weeping, and cries him mercy. At this submission of them both he triumphs like a braggard, and will take no compassion. Yet at last, through entreaty of other his companions coming in as strangers, he is pacified with some forty shillings, and the poor man goes sorrowful away, sighing out that which Solomon hath in his proverbs: *A shameless woman*

apple-squires: male bawds.
hippocras: spiced wine cordial.
by His 'ounds: by (God's) wounds.

hath honey in her lips, and her throat as sweet as honey, her throat as soft as oil: but the end of her is more bitter than aloes, and her tongue is more sharp than a two-edged sword, her feet go unto death, and her steps lead unto hell.

Again these trulls, when they have got in a novice, then straight they pick his purse, and then have they their crossbiters ready, to whom they convey the money and so offer themselves to be searched. But the poor man is so outfaced by these crossbiting ruffians that he is glad to go away content with his loss; yet are these easy practices. Oh, might the justices send out spials in the night! They should see how these streetwalkers will jet in rich guarded gowns, quaint periwigs, ruffs of the largest size, quarter- and half-deep, gloried richly with blue starch, their cheeks dyed with surfling water – thus are they tricked up, and either walk like stales up and down the streets, or stand like the devil's *Si quis* at a tavern or ale-house, as if who should say:

'If any be so minded to satisfy his filthy lust, to lend me his purse, and the devil his soul, let him come in and be welcome.'

Now, sir, comes by a country farmer, walking from his inn to perform some business and, seeing such a gorgeous damsel, he, wondering at such a brave wench, stands staring her on the face, or perhaps doth but cast a glance, and bid her good speed, as plain simple swains have their lusty humours as well as others.

The trull, straight beginning her exordium with a smile, saith: 'How now, my friend! What want you? Would you speak with anybody here?'

If the fellow have any bold spirit, perhaps he will offer the wine, and then he is caught. 'Tis enough. In he goes, and they are chambered. Then sends she for her husband, or her friend, and there either the farmer's pocket is stripped, or else the crossbiters fall upon him, and threaten him with Bridewell and the law. Then, for fear, he gives them all in his purse, and makes them some bill to pay a sum of money at a certain day.

jet: strut.
guarded: embroidered.
surfling water: sulphur water or similar cosmetic.
Si quis: 'If anyone'; opening words of advertisements posted at St Paul's.
exordium: introduction.

If the poor farmer be bashful, and passeth by one of these shameless strumpets, then will she verse it with him, and claim acquaintance of him, and, by some policy or other, fall aboard on him, and carry him into some house or other. If he but enter in at the doors with her (though the poor farmer never kissed her), yet then the crossbiters, like vultures, will prey upon his purse, and rob him of every penny. If there be any young gentleman that is a novice and hath not seen their trains, to him will some common filth, that never knew love, feign an ardent and honest affection, till she and her crossbiters have versed him to the beggars' estate.

Ah, gentlemen, merchants, yeomen and farmers, let this to you all, and to every degree else, be a caveat to warn you from lust, that your inordinate desire be not a mean to impoverish your purses, discredit your good names, condemn your souls, but also that your wealth got with the sweat of your brows, or left by your parents as a patrimony, shall be a prey to those cozening crossbiters! Some fond men are so far in with these detestable trugs that they consume what they have upon them, and find nothing but a Neapolitan favour for their labour. Read the seventh of Solomon's proverbs, and there at large view the description of a shameless and impudent courtesan.

Yet is there another kind of crossbiting which is most pestilent, and that is this. There lives about this town certain householders, yet mere shifters and cozeners, who, learning some insight in the civil law, walk abroad like 'paritors, summoners and informers, being none at all, either in office or credit; and they go spying about where any merchant, or merchant's prentice, citizen, wealthy farmer, or other of credit, either accompany with any woman familiarly, or else hath gotten some maid with child (as men's natures be prone to sin); straight they come over his fallows thus: they send for him to a tavern, and there open the matter unto him, which they have cunningly learned out, telling him he must be presented to the Arches,[7] and the citation shall be peremptorily served in his parish church. The party, afraid to

Neapolitan favour: venereal disease.

'paritors: apparitors, servants or attendants of civil or ecclesiastical officers.

have his credit cracked with the worshipful of the City and the rest of his neighbours, and grieving highly his wife should hear of it, straight takes composition with this cozener for some twenty marks. Nay, I heard of forty pound crossbitten at one time. And then the cozening informer, or crossbiter, promiseth to wipe him out of the book and discharge him from the matter, when it was neither known nor presented. So go they to the woman, and fetch her off if she be married, and, though they have this gross sum, yet ofttimes they crossbite her for more. Nay, thus do they fear citizens, prentices and farmers, that they find but anyway suspicious of the like fault. The crossbiting bawds, for no better can I term them, in that for lucre they conceal the sin and smother up lust, do not only enrich themselves mightily thereby, but also discredit, hinder and prejudice the Court of the Arches and the officers belonging to the same. There are some poor blind patches of that faculty, that have their tenements purchased and their plate on the board very solemnly, who only get their gains by crossbiting, as is afore rehearsed. But (leaving them to the deep insight of such as be appointed with justice to correct vice) again to the crew of my former crossbiters, whose fee-simple to live upon is nothing but the following of common, dishonest and idle trulls, and thereby maintain themselves brave, and the strumpets in handsome furniture. And to end this art with an English demonstration, I'll tell you a pretty tale of late performed in Bishopsgate Street:

There was there five traffics, pretty, but common housewives, that stood fast by a tavern door, looking if some prey would pass by for their purpose. Anon the eldest of them, and most experienced in that law, called Mall B., spied a master of a ship coming along.

'Here is a simpler,' quoth she, 'I'll verse him, or hang me. Sir,' said she, 'good even. What, are you so liberal to bestow on three good wenches that are dry, a pint of wine?'

'In faith, fair women,' quoth he, 'I was never niggard for so much': and with that he takes one of them by the hand, and

fear: make afraid.
patches: fools.
furniture: apparel and ornaments.
housewives: whores.

carries them all into the tavern. There he bestowed cheer and hippocras upon them, drinking hard till the shot came to a noble, so that they three, carousing to the gentleman, made him somewhat tipsy, and then *et Venus in vinis, ignis in igne fuit!* Well, night grew on, and he would away, but this Mistress Mall B. stopped his journey thus:

'Gentleman,' quoth she, 'this undeserved favour of yours makes us so deeply beholden to you, that our ability is not able anyway to make sufficient satisfaction; yet, to show us kind in what we can, you shall not deny me this request, to see my simple house before you go.'

The gentleman, a little whittled, consented, and went with them. So the shot was paid, and away they go: without the tavern door stood two of their husbands, J.B. and J.R., and they were made privy to the practice. Home goes the gentleman with these lusty housewives, stumbling. At last he was welcome to Mistress Mall's house, and one of the three went into a chamber, and got to bed, whose name was A.B. After they had chatted a while, the gentleman would have been gone, but she told him that, before he went, he should see all the rooms of her house, and so led him up into the chamber where the party lay in bed.

'Who is here?' said the gentleman.

'Marry,' saith Mall, 'a good pretty wench, sir; and if you be not well, lie down by her; you can take no harm of her.'

Drunkenness desires lust; and so the gentleman begins to dally; and away goes she with the candle! And at last he put off his clothes and went to bed. Yet he was not so drunk, but he could after a while remember his money, and, feeling for his purse, all was gone, and three links of his whistle broken off. The sum that was in his purse was in gold and silver twenty nobles. As thus he was in a maze, though his head were well laden, in comes J.B., the goodman of the house, and two other with him, and speaking somewhat loud.

'Peace, husband,' quoth she, 'there is one in bed, speak not so loud.'

shot: bill.
et Venus . . . fuit: 'and Venus was in the wine, the heat of lust in the fire'.
whittled: drunk.

'In bed?' saith he, 'Gog's Nownes! I'll go see.'

'And so will I,' saith the other.

'You shall not,' saith his wife, but strove against him; but up goes he, and his crossbiters with him, and, seeing the gentleman in bed, out with his dagger, and asked what base villain it was that there sought to dishonest his wife. Well, he sent one of them for a constable, and made the gentleman rise, who, half drunk, yet had that remembrance to speak fair and to entreat him to keep his credit. But no entreaty could serve, but to the Counter he must, and the constable must be sent for. Yet, at the last, one of them entreated that the gentleman might be honestly used, and carried to a tavern to talk of the matter till a constable come.

'Tut!' said J.B. 'I will have law upon him.'

But the base crossbiter at last stooped, and to the tavern they go, where the gentleman laid his whistle to pawn for money, and there bestowed as much of them as came to ten shillings, and sat drinking and talking until the next morrow. By that the gentleman had stolen a nap, and waking, it was daylight, and then, seeing himself compassed with these crossbiters, and remembering his night's work, soberly smiling, asked them if they knew what he was. They answered: 'Not well.'

'Why then,' quoth he, 'you base cozening rogues! You shall ere we part': and with that drawing his sword, kept them into the chamber, desiring that the constable might be sent for.

But this brave of his could not dismay Mistress Mall; for she had bidden a sharper brunt before – witness the time of her martyrdom, when upon her shoulders was engraven the history of her whorish qualities. But she replying, swore, sith he was so lusty, her husband should not put it up by no means.

'I will tell thee, thou base crossbiting bawd,' quoth he, 'and you cozening companions, I serve a nobleman, and for my credit with him, I refer me to the penalty he will impose on you; for, by God, I will make you an example to all crossbiters ere I end with you! I tell you, villains, I serve —'; and with that he named his lord.

When the guilty whores and cozeners heard of his credit and

Gog's Nownes! : God's wounds!
upon her shoulders : i.e., by whipping or branding.

service, they began humbly to entreat him to be good to them.

'Then,' quoth he, 'first deliver me my money.'

They upon that gladly gave him all, and restored the links of his chain. When he had all, he smiled, and sware afresh that he would torment them for all this, that the severity of their punishment might be a caveat to others to beware of the like cozenage, and upon that knocked with his foot and said he would not let them go till he had a constable. Then in general they humbled themselves, so recompensing the party, that he agreed to pass over the matter, conditionally beside, that they would pay the sixteen shillings he had spent in charges, which they also performed. The gentleman stepped his way, and said: 'You may see the old proverb fulfilled: *Fallere fallentem non est fraus.*'

Thus have I deciphered an odious practice, not worthy to be named. And now, wishing all, of what estate soever, to beware of filthy lust and such damnable stales as draws men on to inordinate desires, and rather to spend their coin amongst honest company, than to bequeath it to such base crossbiters as prey upon men, like ravens upon dead carcases, I end with this prayer, that crossbiting and cony-catching may be as little known in England, as the eating of swines' flesh was amongst the Jews. Farewell!

Nascimur pro patria

FINIS

A Pleasant Discovery of the Cozenage of Colliers

Although, courteous readers, I did not put in amongst the laws of cozening, the law of legering, which is a deceit wherewith colliers abuse the commonwealth in having unlawful sacks,[8] yet take it for a petty kind of craft or mystery, as prejudicial to the poor as any of the other two. For I omitted divers other devilish vices: as the nature of the lift, the black art, and the curbing law, which is the filchers and thieves that come into houses or shops and lift away anything; or picklocks, or hookers at windows,

Fallere . . . fraus: 'To deceive the deceiver is no fraud.'

though they be as species and branches to the table before rehearsed. But, leaving them, again to our law of legering.

Know, therefore, that there be inhabiting in and about London, certain caterpillars (colliers, I should say) that term themselves, among themselves, by the name of legers, who, for that the honourable the Lord Mayor of the City of London and his officers look straitly to the measuring of coals, do (to prevent the execution of his justice) plant themselves in and about the suburbs of London, as Shoreditch, Whitechapel, Southwark and such places, and there they have a house or yard that hath a back gate, because it is the more convenient for their cozening purpose, and the reason is this: the leger (the crafty collier, I mean) riseth very early in the morning, and either goeth towards Croydon, Whetstone, Greenwich or Romford, and there meeteth the country colliers, who bring coals to serve the market. There, in a forestalling manner,[9] this leger bargaineth with the country collier for his coals, and payeth for them nineteen shillings or twenty at the most, but commonly fifteen and sixteen. And there is in the load thirty-six sacks; so that they pay for every couple about fourteen pence.

Now, having bought his coals, every sack containing full four bushels, he carryeth the country collier home to his legering place, and there at the back gate causeth him to unload and, as they say, shoot the coals down. As soon as the country collier hath despatched and is gone, then the leger, who hath three or four hired men under him, bringeth forth his own sacks, which be long and narrow, holding at the most not three bushels, so that they gain in the change of every sack a bushel for their pains. Tush! yet this were somewhat to be borne withal, although the gain is monstrous; but this sufficeth not, for they fill not these sacks full by far, but put into them some two bushels and a half, laying in the mouth of the sack certain great coals, which they call fillers, to make the sack show fair, although the rest be small willow-coals, and half dross. When they have thus, not filled their sacks, but thrust coals into them, that which they lay uppermost is best filled, to make the greater show. Then [comes] a tall, sturdy knave, that is all ragged, and dirty on his legs, as though he came out of the country, for they dirty their hose and shoes on purpose to make themselves seem country colliers. Thus with two sacks apiece they either go out at the back gate, or steal out at the street side, and so go up and down the suburbs and sell their coals, in summer for fourteen and sixteen pence a couple, and in winter for eighteen or twenty. The poor cooks and other citizens that buy them think they be country colliers that have left some coals of their load and would gladly have money, supposing (as the statute is) they be good and lawful sacks, are thus cozened by the legers and have but two bushels and a half for four bushels, and yet are extremely racked in the price, which is not only a great hinderance to Her Majesty's poor commons, but greatly prejudicial to the master-colliers, that bring true sacks and measure out of the country. Then consider, gentle readers, what kind of cozenage these legers use, that make of thirty sacks some fifty-six, which I have seen, for I have set down with my pen how many turns they have made of a load, and they make twenty-eight, every turn being two sacks, so that they have got an intolerable gains by their false measure.

I could not be silent, seeing this abuse, but thought to reveal it for my country's commodity, and to give light to the worshipful justices, and other Her Majesty's officers in Middlesex, Surrey and elsewhere, to look to such a gross cozenage as, contrary to a direct statute, doth defraud and impoverish Her Majesty's poor commons. Well may the honourable and worshipful of London flourish, who carefully look to the country coals, and if they find out four bushels in every sack, do sell them to the poor as forfeit, and distribute the money to them that have need, burning the sack and honouring, or rather dishonouring, the pillory with the colliers' dirty faces! And well may the honourable and worshipful of the suburbs prosper, if they look in justice to these legers who deserve more punishment than the statute appoints for them, which is whipping at a cart's tail, or, with favour, the pillory!

A Plain Discovery

For fuel or firing being a thing necessary in a commonwealth, and charcoal used more than any other, the poor, not able to buy by the load, are fain to get in their fire by the sack, and so are greatly cozened by the retail. Seeing therefore the careful laws Her Majesty hath appointed for the wealth of her commons and succour of the poor, I would humbly entreat all Her Majesty's officers, to look into the life of these legers, and to root them out, that the poor feel not the burden of their inconscionable gains. I heard with my ears a poor woman of Shoreditch, who had bought coals of a leger, with weeping tears complain and rail against him in the street, in her rough eloquence calling him 'cozening knave', and saying: ' 'Tis no marvel, villain (quoth she), if men compare you colliers to the devil, seeing your consciences are worser than the devil's; for he takes none but those souls whom God hates; and you undo the poor whom God loves.'

'What is the matter, good wife,' quoth I, 'that you use such invective words against the collier?'

'A collier, sir!' saith she. 'He is a thief and a robber of the common people. I'll tell you, sir: I bought of a country collier two sacks for thirteen pence, and I bought of this knave three sacks, which cost me twenty-two pence. And, sir, when I measured both their sacks, I had more in the two sacks by three pecks, than I had in the three. I would,' quoth she, 'the justices would look into this abuse, and that my neighbours would join with me in a supplication, and, by God, I would kneel before the queen, and entreat that such cozening colliers might not only be punished with the bare pillory (for they have such black faces that no man knows them again, and so are they careless), but that they might leave their ears behind them for a forfeit; and if that would not mend them, that Bull with a fair halter might root them out of the world, that live in the world by such gross and dishonest cozenage.'

The collier, hearing this, went smiling away, because he knew his life was not looked into, and the woman wept for anger that she had not some one by that might with justice revenge her quarrel.

There be also certain colliers that bring coals to London in barges, and they be called gripers. To these comes the leger, and bargains with him for his coals, and sells by retail with the like

Bull: London hangman at this time.

cozenage of sacks as I rehearsed before. But these mad legers, not content with this monstrous gain, do besides mix among their other sacks of coals store of shruff dust and small coal to their great advantage. And, for proof hereof, I will recite you a matter of truth, lately performed by a cook's wife upon a cozening collier.

How a Cook's Wife in London did lately serve a Collier for his Cozenage

It chanced this summer that a load of coals came forth of Kent to Billingsgate, and a leger bought them, who thinking to deceive the citizens as he did those in the suburbs, furnished himself with a couple of sacks, and comes up St Marys Hill to sell them. A cook's wife bargained with the collier and bought his coals, and they agreed upon fourteen pence for the couple; which being done, he carried the coals into the house and shot them. And when the wife saw them, and perceiving there was scarce five bushels for eight, she calls a little girl to her, and bade her go for the constable; 'For thou cozening rogue,' quoth she, speaking to the collier, 'I will teach thee how thou shalt cozen me with thy false sacks, whatsoever thou dost to others, and I will have thee before my Lord Mayor.' With that she caught a spit in her hand and swore if he offered to stir she would therewith broach him; at which words the collier was amazed, and the fear of the pillory put him in such fright that he said he would go to his boat, and return again to answer whatsoever she durst object against him. 'And for pledge hereof,' quoth the collier, 'keep my sacks, your money, and the coals also.' Whereupon the woman let him go; but as soon as the collier was out of doors, it was needless to bid him run, for down he gets to his boat, and away he thrusts from Billingsgate, and so immediately went down to Wapping, and never after durst return to the cook's wife to demand either money, sacks or coals.

shruff: mineral.

How a Flaxwife and her Neighbours Used a Cozening Collier

Now, Gentlemen, by your leave, and hear a merry jest: there was in the suburbs of London a flaxwife that wanted coals, and, seeing a leger come by with a couple of sacks, that had before deceived her in like sort, cheaped, bargained and bought them, and so went in with her to shoot them in her coalhouse. As soon as she saw her coals, she easily guessed there was scarce six bushels; yet, dissembling the matter, she paid him for them, and bade him bring her two sacks more. The collier went his way, and in the meantime the flaxwife measured the coals, and there was just five bushels and a peck. Hereupon she called to her neighbours, being a company of women, that before time had also been pinched in their coals, and showed them the cozenage, and desired their aid to her in tormenting the collier, which they promised to perform. And thus it fell out: she conveyed them into a back room (some sixteen of them), every one having a good cudgel under her apron.

Straight comes the collier and saith: 'Mistress, here be your coals.'

'Welcome, good collier,' quoth she. 'I pray thee follow me into the back-side, and shoot them in another room.'

The collier was content, and went with her. But as soon as he was in the goodwife locked the door, and the collier, seeing such a troop of wives in the room, was amazed, yet said: 'God speed you all, shrews!'

'Welcome,' quoth one jolly dame, being appointed by them all to give sentence against him; who, so soon as the collier had shot his sacks, said: 'Sirrah collier, know that we are here all assembled as a grand jury, to determine of thy villainies, for selling us false sacks of coals, and know that thou art here indicted upon cozenage. Therefore, hold up thy hand at the bar, and either say "guilty" or "not guilty", and by whom thou wilt be tried, for thou must receive condign punishment for the same ere thou depart.'

cheaped: traded, haggled.
condign: well-deserved.

The collier, who thought they had but jested, smiled and said: 'Come on. Which of you shall be my judge?'

'Marry,' quoth one jolly dame, 'that is I; and, by God, you knave, you shall find I will pronounce sentence against you severely, if you be found guilty.'

When the collier saw they were in earnest, he said: 'Come, come; open the door and let me go.'

With that five or six started up and fell upon the collier and gave unto him half a score of sound lambecks with their cudgels and bade him speak more reverently to their principal. The collier, feeling it smart, was afraid, and thought mirth and courtesy would be the best mean to make amends for his villainy, and therefore said he would be tried by the verdict of the smock. Upon this, they panelled a jury, and the flaxwife gave evidence; and, because this unaccustomed jury required witness, she measured the coals before the collier's face, upon which he was found guilty, and she that sat as principal to give judgement upon him, began as followeth:

'Collier, thou art condemned here, by proof, of flat cozenage, and I am now appointed in conscience to give sentence against thee, being not only moved thereunto because of this poor woman, but also for the general commodity of my country; and therefore this is my sentence: we have no pillory for thee, nor cart to whip thee at; but here I do award that thou shalt have as many bastinados as thy bones will bear, and then to be turned out of doors without sacks or money.' This sentence being pronounced, she rose up, and gave no respite of time for the execution; but, according to the sentence before expressed, all the women fell upon him, beating him extremely, among whom he lent some lusty buffets. But might overcomes right, and therefore *Ne Hercules contra duos*. The women so crushed him, that he was not able to lift his hands to his head, and so with a broken pate or two he was paid, and, like Jack Drum, fair and orderly thrust out of doors.

This was the reward that the collier had, and I pray God all such colliers may be so served, and that goodwives, when they

lambecks: blows (lam + back).
Ne . . . duos: 'Let not (even) Hercules (strive) against two.'

buy such sacks, may give them such payments, and that the honourable and worshipful of this land may look into this gross abuse of colliers, as well for charity sake, as also for the benefit of the poor. And so, wishing colliers to amend their deceitful and disordered dealings herein, I end.

FINIS

THE
SECOND

and laſt part of Conny-catching.

*With new additions containing many merry tales of
all lawes worth the reading, becauſe they are worthy to be remembred.*

Diſcourſing ſtrange cunning in Coolnage, which if you reade without laughing, Ile giue you my cap for a Noble.

Mallem mori quam non proſeſſe patriæ.

R. G.

LONDON.
Printed by Iohn Wolfe for William Wright.
1 5 9 2.

A Table of the Laws Contained in this Second Part[1]

1. *Black art* (picking of locks).
2. *Curbing law* (hooking at windows).
3. *Vincent's law* (cozenage at bowls).
4. *Prigging law* (horse-stealing).
5. *Lifting law* (stealing of any parcels).

The Discovery of the Words of Art Used in these Laws

IN BLACK ART

The gains gotten, *pelfry*.
The picklock is called a *charm*.
He that watcheth, a *stand*.
Their engines, *wresters*.
Picking the lock, *farcing*.

IN CURBING LAW

He that hooks, the *curber*.
He that watcheth, the *warp*.
The hook, the *curb*.
The goods, *snappings*.
The gin to open the window, the *tricker*.

IN LIFTING LAW

He that first stealeth, the *lift*.
He that receives it, the *marker*.
He that standeth without and carries it away, the *santer*.
The goods gotten, *garbage*.

---

farcing: original 'farsing' (=amplifying, interpolation).

IN VINCENT'S LAW

They which play booty, the *bankers*.
He that betteth, the *gripe*.
He that is cozened, the *vincent*.
Gains gotten, *termage*.

IN PRIGGING LAW

The horse-stealer, the *prigger*.
The horse, the *prancer*.
The tolling-place, *All Hallows'*.
The toller, the *rifler*.
The sureties, *quitteries*.
    For the *foist* and the *nip*, as in the first book.

To All Young Gentlemen, Merchants, Citizens, Apprentices,
Yeomen, and plain Country Farmers, Health.

When Scaevola, Gentlemen, saw his native city besieged by
Porsena, and that Rome, the mistress of the world, was ready to
be mastered by a professed foe to the public estate, he entered
boldly into the enemy's camp, and in the tent of the king (taking
him for the king), slew the king's secretary; whereupon con-
demnèd, brought to the fire, he thrust his right hand into the
flame, burning it off voluntarily, because it was so unfortunate
to miss the fatal stab he had intended to his country's enemies,
and then with an honourable resolution, breathed out this:
Mallem non esse quam non prodesse patria. This instance of
Scaevola greatly hath emboldened me to think no pains nor
danger too great that groweth to the benefit of my country; and
though I cannot, as he, manage with my curtal-axe, nor attempt
to unleaguer Porsena, yet with my pen I will endeavour to display the nature and secrets of divers cozenages more prejudicial
to England than the invasion of Porsena was to Rome. For when

---

the first book: i.e. *A Notable Discovery of Cozenage.*
    Mallem ... patria: 'I would rather not be than that (my) country should
not benefit.'
    unleaguer: dislodge.

that valiant king saw the resolution of Scaevola, as one dismayed at the honour of his thoughts, he sorrowed so brave a man had so desperately lost his hand, and thereupon grew friends with the Romans. But, Gentlemen, these cony-catchers, these vultures, these fatal harpies, that putrify with their infections this flourishing estate of England, as if they had their consciences sealed with a hot iron, and that as men delivered up into a reprobate sense, grace were utterly exiled from their hearts; so with the deaf adder they not only stop their ears against the voice of the charmer, but dissolutely, without any spark of remorse, stand upon their bravados, and openly in words and actions maintain their palpable and manifest cozenages, swearing by no less than their enemies' blood, even by God Himself, that they will make a massacre of his bones, and cut off my right hand for penning down their abominable practices. But alas for them, poor snakes! Words are wind, and looks but glances: every thunderclap hath not a bolt, nor every cony-catcher's oath an execution. I live still, and I live to display their villainies, which, Gentlemen, you shall see set down in most ample manner in this small treatise.

But here, by the way, give me leave to answer an objection that some inferred against me; which was, that I showed no eloquent phrases, nor fine figurative conveyance in my first book, as I had done in other of my works, to which I reply that το πρέπον, a certain decorum is to be kept in every thing, and not to apply a high style in a base subject, beside the faculty is so odious, and the men so servile and slavish-minded; that I should dishonour that high mystery of eloquence, and derogate from the dignity of our English tongue, either to employ any figure or bestow one choice English word upon such disdained rakehells as those cony-catchers. Therefore, humbly I crave pardon, and desire I may write basely of such base wretches, who live only to live dishonestly. For they seek the spoil and ruin of all, and like drones eat away what others labour for.

I have set down divers other laws untouched in the first, as their vincent's law, a notable cozenage at bowls, when certain idle companions stand and make bets, being compacted with the bowlers, who look like honest-minded citizens, either to win or

το πρέπον : the fitting thing.

lose, as their watchword shall appoint; then the prigger, or
horse-stealer, with all his gins belonging to his trade, and their
subtle cautels to amend the statute;[2] next, the curbing law,
which some call but too basely hookers, who either dive in at
windows, or else with a hook, which they call a curb, do fetch out
whatsoever, either apparel, linen or woollen, that be left abroad.
Beside I can set down the subtlety of the black art, which is
picking of locks, a cozenage as prejudicial as any of the rest; and
the nature of the lift, which is he that stealeth any parcels, and
slyly taketh them away. This, Gentlemen, have I searched out for
your commodities, that I might lay open to the world the villainy of these cozening caterpillars, who are not only abhorred
of men, but hated of God, living idly to themselves and odiously
to the world. They be those foolish children that Solomon speaks
of, that feeds themselves fat with iniquity, those untamed heifers,
that will not brook the yoke of labour, but get their livings by
the painful thrift of other men's hands. I cannot better compare
them than unto vipers, who while they live are hated and shunned
of all men as most prejudicial creatures; they feed upon hemlock
and aconiton, and such fatal and empoisoned herbs; but the
learned apothecaries takes them, cuts off their heads, and after
they be embowelled of their flesh, they make the most precious
mithridate. So these cony-catchers, foists, nips, priggers, and
lifts, while they live are most improfitable members of the commonwealth; they glut themselves as vipers upon the most loathsome and detestable sins, seeking after folly with greediness,
never doing anything that is good, till they be trussed up at
Tyburn; and then is a most wholesome mithridate made of them,
for by their deaths others are forewarned for falling into the
like enormities. And as the gangrena is a disease incurable by the
censure of the surgeons, unless the member where it is fixed be
cut off, so this untoward generation of loose libertines can by no
wholesome counsels nor advised persuasions be dissuaded from

cautels: crafty devices.
brook: original 'break'.
aconiton: aconite, monkshood, a poisonous plant.
mithridate: antidote.
censure: judgement, skill.

their loathsome kind of life, till by death they be fatally and finally cut off from the commonwealth, whereof spake Ovid well in his *Metamorphoses*:

> *Inmedicabile vulnus,*
> *Ense resecandum est, ne pars sincera trahatur.*[3]

Sith then, this cursed crew, these Machiavellians – that neither care for God nor devil, but set, with the epicures, gain, and ease, their *summum bonum* – cannot be called to any honest course of living, if the honourable and worshipful of this land look into their lives, and cut off such upstarting suckers that consume the sap from the root of the tree, they shall neither lose their reward in Heaven, nor pass over any day wherein there will not be many faithful prayers of the poor exhibited for their prosperous success and welfare – so deeply are these monstrous cozeners hated in the commonwealth. Thus, Gentlemen, I have discovered in brief what I mean to prosecute at large; though not eloquently, yet so effectually, that, if you be not altogether careless, it may redound to your commodity: forewarned, forearmed: burnt children dread the fire; and such as neither counsel, nor other men's harms may make to beware, are worthy to live long, and still by the loss. But hoping these secrets I have set abroach, and my labours I have taken in searching out those base villainies, shall not be only taken with thanks, but applied with care, I take my leave with this farewell. God either confound, or convert, such base-minded cozeners.

Yours, R.G.

A Tale of a Nip

I will tell you, Gentlemen, a pleasant tale of a most singular, experienced, and approved nip, and yet I will not name any, although I could discourse of one that is *magister in artibus*, both a nip and a foist and a crossbiter. But I will tell you a merry jig of a notable nip, named — no more of that if you love me! Who, taking a proper youth, by St Davy, to his prentice, to teach him the order of striking and foisting, so well instructed him in

magister in artibus: Master of Arts (M.A.).

his mystery that he could as well skill of a cuttle-bung as a barber of a razor, and, being of a prompt wit, knew his places, persons, and circumstances, as if he had been a moral philosopher.

The old colt, this grand cutpurse – by St Laurence, let that suffice – did, as the tale was told to me, supply Mannering's place at the burial of the old Lady Rich,[4] and coming thither very devout to hear the sermon, thrust with his apprentice amidst the throng, and lighted upon a rich parson in Essex, not far off from Rochford Hundred. The priest was faced afore with velvet, and had a good bung, which, the nip espying, began to jostle the priest very hard at the entrance of the door, and his apprentice struck the strings, and took his bung clear. The priest little suspecting it, fell to his prayers, and yet, for all his other meditations, he felt for his purse, which, when he missed, he fetched a great sigh, and said, 'Lord have mercy upon me.' – 'What ail you, sir?' said one that stood by. 'Nothing,' said the priest, 'but I think upon the sins of the people'; and so passed it over with silence. Well, it so fell out that when the bung came to sharing, the prentice and his master fell out, and the master controlled him and said, 'Art not my prentice, and hast not bound thyself to me for three years? Is not thy gettings my gains? Then why dost thou stand upon the snap?' – 'Why,' says the prentice, 'brag you so of my years! Shall I be made a slave because I am bound to you? No, no! I can quittance my indenture when I list.' His master in a great rage asked how. – 'Marry!' says the prentice: 'I will nip a bung, or draw a pocket, openly, and so be taken, arraigned and condemned; and then Bull shall cancel my indentures at Tyburn, and so I will not serve you a day after.' At this, his master laughed and was glad for further advantage to yield the bucklers to his prentice, and to become friends. For approving the truth of this, myself conferred with the priest, and he told me thus much.

by St Laurence: perhaps a sly dig at Laurence Pickering (see p. 270).
controlled: reproved.
quittance . . . indenture: cancel clause binding apprentice to master.
cancel . . . Tyburn: hang (me).

The Discovery of the Prigging Law, or Nature of Horse-Stealing

To the effecting of this base villainy of prigging, or horse-stealing, there must of necessity be two at the least, and that is the prigger and the marter. The prigger is he that steals the horse, and the marter is he that receives him, and chops and changeth him away in any fair, mart, or other place where any good rent for horses is. And their method is thus: the prigger, if he be a lance-man, that is, one that is already horsed, then he hath more followers with him, and they ride like gentlemen, and commonly in the form of drovers, and so, coming into pasture grounds or enclosures, as if they meant to survey for cattle, do take an especial and perfect view, where prancers or horses be, that are of worth, and whether they have horse-locks or no. Then lie they hovering about till fit opportunity serve, and in the night they take him or them away; and are skilful in the black art, for picking open the trammels or locks and so make haste till they be out of those quarters. Now if the priggers steal a horse in Yorkshire, commonly they have vent for him in Surrey, Kent, or Sussex, and their marters that receive them at his hand, chops them away in some blind fairs after they have kept them a month or two, till the hue and cry [5] be ceased and passed over. Now if their horse be of any great value, and sore sought after, and so branded or earmarked that they can hardly sell him without extreme danger, either they brand him with a cross-brand upon the former, or take away his ear-mark, and so keep him at hard-meat till he be whole, or else sell him in Cornwall or Wales, if he be in Cumberland, Lincolnshire, Norfolk or Suffolk. But this is if the horse be of great value and worthy the keeping. Marry, if he be only coloured and without brands, they will straight spot him by sundry policies, and in a black horse, mark saddle-spots, or star him in the forehead, and change his tail, which secrets I omit,

vent: sale.
hard-meat: dry fodder.

lest I should give too great a light to others to practise such lewd villainies.

But again to our lance-men priggers, who, as before I said, cry with the lapwing farthest from their nest,[6] and from their place of residence, where their most abode is, furthest from thence they steal their horses, and then in another quarter as far off, they make sale of them by the marter's means, without it be some base prigger that steals of mere necessity, and, beside, is a trailer. The trailer is one that goeth on foot, but meanly attired like some plain gran of the country, walking in a pair of boots without spurs, or else without boots; having a long staff on his neck, and a black buckram bag at his back, like some poor client that had some writing in it; and there he hath his saddle, bridle and spurs, stirrups and stirrup-leathers, so quaintly and artificially made that it may be put in the slop of a man's hose; for his saddle is made without any tree, yet hath it cantle and bolsters, only wrought artificially of cloth and bombast, with folds to wrap up in a short room; his stirrups are made with vices and gins, that one may put them in a pair of gloves, and so are his spurs, and then a little white leather headstall and reins, with a small Scottish brake or snaffle, all so featly formed that, as I said before, they may be put in a buckram bag. Now, this trailer he bestrides the horse which he priggeth, and saddles and bridles him as orderly as if he were his own, and then carryeth him far from the place of his breed, and there sells him.

'Oh!' will some man say, 'it is easier to steal a horse than to sell him, considering that Her Majesty and the honourable Privy Council hath in the last act of Parliament made a strict statute [7] for horse-stealing and the sale of horses, whose proviso is this: that no man may buy a horse untolled, nor the toll be taken without lawful witnesses that the party that selleth the horse is the true owner of him, upon their oath and special knowledge, and that who buyeth a horse without this certificate or proof shall be within the nature of felony, as well as the party that stealeth him.'

To this I answer, that there is no act, statute, nor law so strict conveyed but there be straight found starting-holes to avoid it, as in this. The prigger, when he hath stolen a horse, and hath

gran: old codger.

agreed with his marter, or with any other his confederate, or with an honest person, to sell his horse, bringeth to the toller, which they call the rifler, two honest men, either apparelled like citizens or plain country yeomen, and they not only affirm, but offer to depose, that they know the horse to be his, upon their proper knowledge, although perhaps they never saw man nor horse before, and these perjured knaves be commonly old knights of the post, that are foisted off from being taken for bail at the King's Bench or other places, and seeing for open perjuries they are refused, there they take that course of life, and are wrongly called querries. But it were necessary, and very much expedient for the commonwealth, that such base rogues should be looked into, and be punished as well with the pillory, as the other with the halter. And thus have I revealed the nature of priggers, or horse-stealers, briefly, which if it may profit, I have my desire, but that I may recreate your minds with a pleasant history, mark the sequel.

A Pleasant Story of a Horse-Stealer

Not far from T[ru]ro in Cornwall, a certain prigger, a horse-stealer, being a lance-man, surveying the pastures thereabouts, spied a fair black horse without any white spot at all about him. The horse was fair and lusty, well proportioned, of a high crest, of a lusty countenance, well buttocked, and strongly trussed, which set the prigger's teeth a-water to have him. Well he knew the hardest hap was but a halter, and therefore he ventured fair, and stole away the prancer; and, seeing his stomach was so good as his limbs, he kept him well, and by his policy seared him in the forehead, and made him spotted in the back, as if he had been saddle-bitten, and gave him a mark in both ears, whereas he had but a mark in one.

Dealing thus with his horse, after a quarter of a year, that all hurly-burly was past for the horse, he came riding to T[ru]ro to the market, and there offered him to be sold. The gentleman that lost the horse was there present, and looking on him with other gentlemen, liked him passing well, and commended him,

knight of the post : noted perjurer.
Truro : original 'Tenro' throughout.

insomuch that he bet the price of him, bargained, and bought him. And so when he was tolled, and the horse-stealer clapped him good luck: 'Well, my friend,' quoth the gentleman, 'I like the horse the better, in that once I lost one, as like him as might be, but mine wanted these saddle spots and this star in the forehead.' – 'It may be so, sir,' said the prigger. And so the gentleman and he parted. The next day after, he caused a letter to be made, and sent the gentleman word that he had his horse again that he lost, only he had given him a mark or two, and for that he was well rewarded, having twenty mark for his labour. The gentleman, hearing how he was cozened by a horse-stealer, and not only robbed, but mocked, let it pass till he might conveniently meet with him to revenge it.

It fortuned, not long after, that this lance-man prigger was brought to T[ru]ro jail for some such matter, and indeed it was about a mare that he had stolen. But as knaves have friends, especially when they are well moneyed, he found divers that spake for him, and who said it was the first fault, and the party plaintiff gave but slender evidence against him, so that the judge spake favourably in his behalf. The gentleman as then sat on the bench, and, calling to mind the prigger's countenance, how he had stolen his horse and mocked him, remembered he had the letter in his pocket that he sent him, and therefore, rising up, spake in his behalf, and highly commended the man, and desired the judges for one fault he might not be cast away.

'And, besides, may it please you,' quoth he, 'I had this morning a certificate of his honesty and good behaviour sent me'; and with that he delivered them the letter, and the Judge, with the rest of the bench, smiled at this conceit, and asked the fellow if he never stole horse from that gentleman.

'No,' quoth the prigger, 'I know him not. Your honours mistakes me.'

Said the gentleman, 'He did borrow a black horse of me, and marked him with a star in the forehead, and asked twenty mark of me for his labour'; and so discoursed the whole matter. Whereupon the quest went upon him, and condemned him, and so the prigger went to heaven in a string, as many of his faculty had done before.

The Vincent's Law, with the Discovery Thereof

The vincent's law is a common deceit or cozenage used in bowl-ing-alleys, amongst the baser sort of people that commonly haunt such lewd and unlawful places. For, although I will not dis-commend altogether the nature of bowling, if the time, place, person, and such necessary circumstances be observed, yet, as it is now used, practised and suffered, it groweth altogether to the maintenance of unthrifts, that idly and disorderly make that recreation a cozenage.

Now the manner and form of their device is thus effected: the bawkers – for so the common haunters of the alley are termed – apparelled like very honest and substantial citizens, come to bowl, as though rather they did it for sport than gains, and under that colour of carelessness, do shadow their pretended knavery. Well, to bowls they go, and then there resort of all sorts of people to behold them, some simple men brought in of purpose by some cozening companions to be stripped of his crowns; others, gentle-men, or merchants, that delighted with the sport, stand there as beholders to pass away the time. Amongst these are certain old soakers, which are lookers-on, and listen for bets, either even or odd, and these are called gripes. And these fellows will refuse no lay, if the odds may grow to their advantage. For the gripes and the bawkers are confederate, and their fortune at play ever sorts according as the gripes have placed their bets, for the bawker, he marketh how the lays goes, and so throws his casting. So that note this: the bowlers cast ever booty, and doth win or lose as the bet of the gripe leadeth them; for suppose seven be up for the game, and the one hath three and the other none, then the vincent – for that is the simple man that stands by, and not acquainted with their cozenage, nor doth so much as once imagine that the bawkers, that carry the countenance of honest substantial men, would by any means, or for any gains, be per-suaded to play booty – well, this vincent (for so the cozeners or gripes please to term him), seeing three to none, beginneth to offer odds on that side that is fairest to win. 'What odds?' says the gripe. – 'Three to one,' says the vincent. – 'No,' says the gripe, 'it is more.' And with that they come to four for none. Then the vincent offers to lay four to one. 'I take six to one,' says the gripe. – 'I lay it,' says the vincent; and so they make a bet of some six crowns, shillings, or pence, as the vincent is of ability to lay, and thus will sundry take their odds of him. Well, then the bawkers go forward with their bowls, and win another cast, which is five. Then the vincent grows proud, and thinks, both by the odds and goodness of the play, that it is impossible for his side to lose, and therefore takes and lays bets freely. Then the bawker's fortune begins to change, and perhaps they come to three for five; and still, as their luck changes, diversity of bets grows on, till at last it comes to five and five; and then the gripe comes upon the vincent and offers him odds, which, if the vincent take, he loseth all, for upon what side the gripe lays, that side ever wins, how great soever the odds be at the first in the contrary part, so that the cozenage grows in playing booty, for the gripe and the bawker meet together at night, and there they share whatsoever termage they have gotten – for so they call the money that the poor vincent loseth unto them. Now, to shadow the matter the more, the bawker that wins and is aforehand with the game, will lay frankly that he shall win, and will bet hard, and lay great odds – but with whom? Either with them which play with him, that are as crafty knaves as himself, or else with the gripe: and this makes the vincent stoop to the blow, and to lose all the money in his purse. Besides, if any honest men that holds themselves skilful in bowling, offer to play any set match against these common bawkers, if they fear to have the worse, or suspect the others' play to be better than theirs, then they have a trick in watering of the alley, to give such a moisture to the bank, that he that offers to strike a bowl with a shore, shall never hit it whilst he lives, because the moisture of the bank hinders the proportion of his aiming.

Divers other practices there are in bowling, tending unto cozenage, but the greatest is booty, and therefore would I wish all men that are careful of their coin, to beware of such cozeners, and none to come in such places, where a haunt of such hell-

shore : ? 'A slant stroke that reaches its mark by a curve' (Grosart).

rakers are resident, and not in any wise to stoop to their bets, lest he be made a vincent, for so manifest and palpable is their cozenage that I have seen men stone-blind offer to lay bets frankly, although they can see a bowl no more than a post, but only hearing who plays, and how the old gripes make their lays. Seeing then as the game is abused to a deceit, that is made for an honest recreation, let this little be a caveat for men to have an insight into their knavery.

For the Foist and the Nip, as in the First Book [i.e. Cony-Catching]

The professors of this law, being somewhat dashed, and their trade greatly impoverished, by the late editions of their secret villainies, seek not a new means of life, but a new method how to fetch in their conies and to play their pranks; for as grievous is it for them to let slip a country farmer come to the Term, that is well apparelled, and in a dirty pair of boots (for that is a token of his new coming up), and a full purse, as it was for the boys of Athens to let Diogenes [8] pass by without a hiss. But the countrymen, having had partly a caveat for their cozenage, fear their favourable speeches and their courteous salutations, as deadly as the Greeks did the whistle of Polyphemus.[9]

The cony-catcher now no sooner cometh in company, and calleth for a pair of cards, but straight the poor cony smokes him, and says: 'Masters, I bought a book of late for a groat, that warns me of card-play, lest I fall among cony-catchers.'

'What, dost thou think us to be such?' says the verser.

'No, Gentlemen,' says the cony, 'you may be men of honest disposition, but yet, pardon me, I have forsworn cards ever since I read it.'

At this reply, God wot, I have many a cozening curse at these cony-catchers' hands, but I solemnly stick to the old proverb: the fox, the more he is cursed, the better he fares. But yet I will discover some of their newest devices, for these caterpillars resemble the Sirens, who, sitting with their watching eyes upon the rocks to allure sea-passengers, to their extreme prejudice, sound out most heavenly melody in such pleasing chords, that whoso listens to their harmony, lends his ear unto his own bane and ruin; but if any wary Ulysses pass by and stop his ears against their enchantments, then have they most delightful jewels to show him, as glorious objects, to inveigle his eye with such pleasant vanities that, coming more nigh to behold them, they may dash their ship against a rock and so utterly perish. So these cony-catchers, for that I smoked them in my last book, and laid open their plots and policies, wherewith they drew poor conies into their hay, seeking, with the orators, *benevolentiam captare*, and as they use rhetorical tropes and figures, the better to draw their hearers with the delight of variety, so these moths of the commonwealth apply their wits to wrap in wealthy farmers with strange and uncouth conceits. Tush, it was so easy for the setter to take up a cony before I discovered their cozenage, that one stigmatical shameless companion amongst the rest would in a bravery wear parsley in his hat, and said, he wanted but *aqua vitae* to take a cony with; but since, he hath looked upon his feet, and vailed his plumes with the peacock, and swears by all the shoes in his shop I shall be the next man he means to kill, for spoiling of his occupation. But I laugh at his bravados, and though he speaks with his eunuch's voice, and wears a long sword like a morris-pike, were it not I think he would, with Bathyllus,[10] hang himself at my invective, his name should be set down, with the nature of his follies. But let him call himself home from this course of life, and this cozenage, and I shall be content to shadow what he is with pardon. But from this digression again to the double diligence of these cony-catchers, whose new sleights, because you shall the more easily perceive, I will tell you a story pleasant and worth the noting.

A Pleasant Tale of a Horse[-Stealer], how at Uxbridge he Cozened a Cony-Catcher and had Like to have Brought him to his Neck-Verse.[11]

It fortuned that, not long since, certain cony-catchers met by hap a pranker or horse-stealer at Uxbridge, who took up his

benevolentiam captare : to ensure goodwill.
vailed : let fall.

inn where those honest crew lodged, and, as one vice follows
another, was as ready to have a cast at cards as he had a hazard
at a horse. The cony-catchers who supped with him, feeling him
pliant to receive the blow, began to lay the plot how they might
make him stoop all the money in his purse, and so for a pint of
wine drew him in at cards by degrees. As these rakehells do,
lento gradu, measure all things by minutes, he fell from wine to
money, and from pence to pounds, that he was stripped of all
that ever he had, as well crowns, apparel, as jewels; that at last
to maintain the main, and to check vies with revies, he laid his
horse in the hazard and lost him.

When the prigger had smoked the game, and perceived he was
bitten of all the bite in his bung, and turned to walk penniless
in Mark Lane,[12] as the proverb is, he began to chafe, and to
swear, and to rap out Gog's Nouns – and pronouns! – while at
voluntary he had sworn through the eight parts of speech in the
accidence, avowing they had cozened him both of his money and
horse. Whereupon the gross ass, more hardy than wise, understanding the cony-catchers were gone, went to the Constable and
made hue and cry after them, saying they had robbed him of his
horse. At this the headboroughs followed amain, and by chance
met with another hue and cry that came for him that had stolen,
which hue and cry was served upon the horse-stealer.

And at that time, as far as I can either conjecture or calculate,
the cony-catchers were taken suspicious for the same horse, and
the rather for that they were found loose livers, and could yield
no honest method or means of their maintenance. Upon this, for
the horse they were apprehended, and bound over to the sessions
at Westminster, to answer what might be objected against them
in Her Majesty's behalf. Well, the horse-stealer brake from his
keepers, and got away, but the rest of the rascal crew, the cony-
catchers I mean, were brought to the place of judgement, and
there, like valiant youths, they thrust twelve men into a corner,
who found them guiltless for the fact, but if great favour had
not been shown, they had been condemned, and burnt in the ears
for rogues. Thus the horse-stealer made hue and cry after the
cony-catchers; and the man that had lost the horse, he pursued

lento gradu: 'by slow steps'.

the horse-stealer, so that a double hue and cry passed on both sides, but the cony-catchers had the worse; for what they got in the bridle they lost in the saddle, what they cozened at cards had like to cost them their necks at the sessions, so that, when they were free and acquitted, one of the cony-catchers in a merry vein said, he had catched many conies, but now a horse had like to [have] caught him: 'And so deeply,' quoth he, 'that *Miserere mei* had like to have been my best matins.'

Thus we may see, *fallere fallentem non est fraus*: every deceit hath his due: he that maketh a trap falleth into the snare himself; and such as covet to cozen all are crossed themselves oftentimes almost to the cross, and that is the next neighbour to the gallows. Well, Gentlemen, thus have I bewrayed much and got little thanks, I mean of the dishonest sort, but I hope such as measure virtue by her honours will judge of me as I deserve. Marry! the goodmen cony-catchers, those base excrements of dishonesty, report they have got one — — I will not bewray his name, but a scholar they say he is – to make an invective against me, in that he is a favourer of those base reprobates. But let them, him, and all know, the proudest peasant of them all dare not lift his plumes in disparagement of my credit, for, if he do, I will for revenge only appoint the jakes-farmers of London, who shall case them in their filthy vessels, and carry them as dung to manure the barren places of Tyburn. And so for cony-catchers an end.

A Discourse, or Rather Discovery, of a Nip and the Foist, Laying Open the Nature of the Cutpurse and Pickpocket

Now, Gentlemen, merchants, farmers, and termers, yea, whatsoever he be that useth to carry money about him, let him attentively hear what a piece of new-found philosophy I will lay open to you, whose opinions, principles, aphorisms, if you carefully note and retain in memory, [may] perhaps save some crowns in your purse ere the year pass; and therefore thus. The nip and the

jakes-farmers: collectors of night-soil.

foist, although their subject is one which they work on, that is, a well-lined purse, yet their manner is different, for the nip useth his knife, and the foist his hand; the one cutting the purse, the other drawing the pocket. But of these two scurvy trades, the foist holdeth himself of the highest degree, and therefore they term themselves gentlemen foists, and so much disdain to be called cutpurses as the honest man that lives by his hand or occupation, insomuch that the foist refuseth even to wear a knife about him to cut his meat withal, lest he might be suspected to grow into the nature of the nip. Yet, as I said before, is their subject and haunt both alike, for their gains lies by all places of resort and assemblies; therefore their chief walks is Paul's, Westminster, the Exchange,[13] plays, bear-garden,[14] running at tilt, the Lord Mayor's day, any festival meetings, frays, shootings, or great fairs. To be short, wheresoever is any extraordinary resort of people, there the nip and the foist have fittest opportunity to show their juggling agility.

Commonly, when they spy a farmer or merchant whom they suspect to be well moneyed, they follow him hard until they see him draw his purse, then spying in what place he puts it up, the stall, or shadow, being with the foist or nip, meets the man at some strait turn, and jostles him so hard that the man, marvelling, and perhaps quarrelling with him, the whilst the foist hath his purse, and bids him farewell. In Paul's, especially in the termtime, between ten and eleven, then is their hours and there they walk, and, perhaps, if there be great press, strike a stroke in the middle walk, but that is upon some plain man that stands gazing about, having never seen the church before; but their chiefest time is at divine service, when men devoutly given do go up to hear either a sermon, or else the harmony of the choir and the organs. There the nip and the foist, as devoutly as if he were some zealous person, standeth soberly, with his eyes elevated to heaven, when his hand is either on the purse or in the pocket, surveying every corner of it for coin. Then, when the service is done, and the people press away, he thrusteth amidst the throng, and there worketh his villainy. So likewise in the markets, they note how every one putteth up his purse, and there, either in a

Westminster: centre of legal administration at this time.

great press, or while the party is cheapening of meat, the foist is in their pocket, and the nip hath the purse by the strings, or sometimes cuts out the bottom, for they have still their stalls following them, who thrusteth or jostleth him or her whom the foist is about to draw. So likewise at plays, the nip standeth there leaning like some mannerly gentleman against the door as men go in, and there finding talk with some of his companions, spyeth what every man hath in his purse, and where, in what place, and in which sleeve or pocket he puts the bung, and, according to that, so he worketh, either where the thrust is great within, or else as they come out at the doors. But suppose that the foist is smoked, and the man misseth his purse, and apprehendeth him for it, then straight, he either conveyeth it to his stall, or else droppeth the bung, and with a great brave he defyeth his accuser; and though the purse be found at his feet, yet because he hath it not about him, he comes not within compass of life.

Thus have they their shifts for the law, and yet at last so long the pitcher goeth to the brook that it cometh broken home; and so long the foists put their villainy in practice that westward they go, and there solemnly make a rehearsal sermon at Tyburn.[15] But again, to the places of resort, Westminster, ay, marry, that is their chiefest place that brings in their profit; the term-time is their harvest, and therefore, like provident husbandmen, they take time while time serves, and make hay while the sun shines, following their clients, for they are at the Hall very early, and there work like bees, haunting every court, as the Exchequer Chamber, the Star Chamber, the King's Bench, Common Pleas, and every place where the poor client standeth to hear his lawyer handle his matter, for the poor man is so busied with his causes, and so careful to see his counsel, and to ply his attorney, that he thinketh least of his purse. But the foist or nip, he watcheth, and, seeing the client draw his purse to pay some charges or fees necessary for the court, marketh where he putteth it, and then when he thrusteth into the throng, either to answer for himself, or to stand by his counsellor to put him in mind of his cause, the foist draws his pocket and leaves the poor client penniless. This do they in all courts, and go disguised like servingmen, wringing the simple people by this juggling subtlety. Well might, therefore, the honourable and worshipful of those courts do, to take order for such vile and base-minded cutpurses, that as the law hath provided death for them, if they be taken, so they might be rooted out, especially from Westminster, where the poor clients are undone by such roguish catchers.

It boots not to tell their course at every remove of Her Majesty, when the people flock together, nor at Bartholomew Fair,[16] on the Queen's day at the Tilt-yard,[17] and at all other places of assembly; for let this suffice, at any great press of people or meeting, there the foist and the nip is in his kingdom. Therefore let all men take this caveat, that when they walk abroad amid any of the forenamed places, or like assemblies, that they take great care for their purse, how they place it, and not leave it careless in their pockets or hose, for the foist is so nimble-handed, that he exceeds the juggler for agility, and hath his legerdemain as perfectly. Therefore an exquisite foist must have three properties that a good surgeon should have, and that is, an eagle's eye, a lady's hand, and a lion's heart; an eagle's eye, to spy out a purchase, to have a quick insight where the bung lies, and then a lion's heart, not to fear what the end will be, and then a lady's hand to be little and nimble, the better and the more easy to dive into any man's pocket.

These are the perfect properties of a foist. But you must note that there be diversities of this kind of people, for there be city nips, and country nips which haunt from fair to fair, and never come in London, unless it be at Bartholomew Fair, or some other great and extraordinary assemblies. Now there is a mortal hate between the country foist and the city foist: for if the city foist spy one of the country foists in London, straight he seeks by some means to smoke him; and so the country nip, if he spy a city nip in any fair, then he smokes him straight, and brings him in danger, if he flee not away the more speedily. Beside, there be women foists and women nips, but the woman foist is the most dangerous, for commonly there is some old bawd or snout-fair strumpet, who inveigleth either some ignorant man or some young youth to folly; she hath straight her hand in the pocket, and so foists him of all that he hath. But let all men take heed of

remove of Her Majesty: royal progess.

such common harlots, who either sit in the streets in evenings, or else dwell in bawdy-houses, and are pliant to every man's lure. Such are always foists and pickpockets, and seek the spoil of all such as meddle with them, and, in cozening of such base-minded lechers as give themselves to such lewd company, are worthy of whatsoever befalls, and sometimes they catch such a Spanish pip, that they have no more hair on their heads than on their nails.

But, leaving such strumpets to their souls' confusion and bodies' correction in Bridewell, again to our nips and foists, who have a kind of fraternity or brotherhood amongst them, having a hall or place of meeting, where they confer of weighty matters touching their workmanship, for they are provident in that every one of them hath some trusty friend whom he calleth his treasurer, and with him he lays up some rateable portion of every purse he draws, that when need requires, and he is brought in danger, he may have money to make composition with the party. But of late there hath been a great scourge fallen among them; for now if a purse be drawn of any great value, straight the party maketh friends to some one or other of the Council, or other inferior Her Majesty's Justices, and then they send out warrants, if they cannot learn who the foist is, to the keepers of Newgate, that take up all the nips and foists about the City, and let them lie there while the money be re-answered unto the party, so that some pay three pound, nay, five pound at a time, according as the same loss did amount unto, which doth greatly impoverish their trade, and is likewise an hindrance to their figging law.

Therefore about such causes grow their meetings, for they have a kind of corporation, as having wardens of their company, and a hall. I remember their hall was once about Bishopsgate, near unto Fisher's Folly, but because it was a noted place, they have removed it to Kent Street, and as far as I can learn, it is kept at one Laurence Pickering's house, one that hath been, if he be not still, a notable foist. A man of good calling he is, and well allied, brother-in-law to Bull the hangman. There keep they their feasts and weekly meetings fit for their company.

Spanish pip : venereal disease.
Fisher's Folly : a large house in Bishopsgate.
Kent Street : now Tabard Street, Southwark.

Thus have I partly set down the nature of the foist, and the nip, with their special haunts, as a caveat to all estates to beware of such wicked persons, who are as prejudicial unto the commonwealth as any other faculty whatsoever; and although they be by the great discretion of the Judges and Justices daily trussed up, yet still there springeth up young, that grow in time to bear fruit fit for the gallows. Let then every man be as careful as possibly he may, and by this caveat take heed of his purse, for the prey makes the thief, and there an end.

A Merry Tale, how a Miller had his Purse Cut in Newgate Market

It fortuned that a nip and his stall, drinking at the 'Three Tuns' in Newgate Market, sitting in one of the rooms next to the street, they might perceive where a meal-man stood selling of meal, and had a large bag by his side, where by conjecture was some store of money. The old cole, the old cutpurse I mean, spying this, was delighted with the show of so glorious an object, for a full purse is as pleasing to a cutpurse's eye, as the curious physiognomy of Venus was to the amorous god of war; and, entering to a merry vein, as one that counted that purchase his own, discovered it to the novice and bade him go and nip it. The young toward scholar, although perhaps he had stricken some few strokes before, yet seeing no great press of people, and the meal-man's hand often upon his bag, as if he had in times past smoked some of their faculty, was half afraid, and doubted of his own experience, and so refused to do it.

'Away, villain!' said the old nip. 'Art thou faint-hearted? Belongs it to our trade to despair? If thou wilt only do common work and not make experience of some hard matters to attempt, thou wilt never be master of thine occupation. Therefore try thy wits and do it.'

At this the young stripling stalks me out of the tavern, and feeling if his cuttle-bung were glib and of a good edge, went to this meal-man to enter combat hand to hand with his purse. But, seeing the meal-man's eye was still abroad, and for want of other sport that he played with his purse, he was afraid to trust either to his wit or fortune, and therefore went back again without any act achieved.

'How now!' saith the old nip, 'what hast thou done?'

'Nothing,' quoth he. 'The knave is so wary, that it is unpossible to get any purchase there, for he stands playing with his purse, for want of other exercise.'

At this his fellow looks out and smiles, making this reply: 'And doest thou count it impossible to have the meal-man's bung? Lend me thy knife, for mine is left at home, and thou shalt see me strike it straight, and I will show thee a method, how perhaps hereafter to do the like by my example, and to make thee a good scholar. And therefore go with me, and do as I shall instruct thee. Begin but a feigned quarrel, and when I give thee a watchword, then throw flour in my face, and, if I do miss his purse, let me be hanged for my labour.'

With that he gave him certain principles to observe, and then paid for the wine, and out they went together. As soon as they were come unto the meal-man, the old nip began to jest with the other about the miller's sack, and the other replied as knavishly. At last the elder called the younger rogue.

'Rogue, thou swain,' quoth he, 'dost thou, or darest thou dishonour me with such a base title?' And with that, taking a whole handful of meal out of the sack, threw it full in the old nip's neck, and his breast, and then ran his way.

He, being thus dusted with meal, entreated the meal-man to wipe it out of his neck, and stooped down his head. The meal-man, laughing to see him so rayed and whited, was willing to shake off the meal, and the whilst he was busy about that, the nip had strucken the purse and done his feat, and both courteously thanked the meal-man, and closely went away with his purchase. The poor man, thinking little of this cheat, began again to play with his purse strings, and suspected nothing till he had sold a peck of meal, and offered for to change money, and then he found his purse bottomless, which struck such a quandary to his stomach as if in a frosty morning he had drunk a draught of small-beer next his heart. He began then to exclaim against such villains, and called to mind how in shaking the dust out of the gentleman's neck, he shaked his money out of his purse, and so the poor meal-man fetched a great sigh, knit up his sack and went sorrowing home.

A Kind Conceit of a Foist Performed in Paul's

While I was writing this discovery of foisting, and was desirous of any intelligence that might be given me, a gentleman, a friend of mine, reported unto me this pleasant tale of a foist, and as I well remember it grew to this effect:

There walked in the middle walk a plain country farmer, a man of good wealth, who had a well-lined purse, only barely thrust up in a round slop, which a crew of foists having perceived, their hearts were set on fire to have it, and every one had a fling at him, but all in vain, for he kept his hand close in his pocket, and his purse fast in his fist like a subtle churl, that either had been forewarned of Paul's, or else had aforetime smoked some of that faculty. Well, howsoever it was impossible to do any good with him, he was so wary. The foists spying this, strained their wits to the highest string how to compass this bung, yet could not all their politic conceits fetch the farmer over, for jostle him, chat with him, offer to shake him by the hand, all would not serve to get his hand out of his pocket. At last one of the crew, that for his skill might have been doctorate in his mystery, amongst them all chose out a good foist, one of a nimble hand and great agility, and said to the rest thus:

'Masters, it shall not be said such a base peasant shall slip away from such a crew of gentlemen-foists as we are, and not have his purse drawn, and therefore this time I'll play the stall myself, and if I hit him not home, count me for a bungler for ever'; and so left them and went to the farmer and walked directly before him and next him three or four turns. At last, standing still, he cried, 'Alas, honest man, help me. I am not well'; and with that sunk down suddenly in a swoon. The poor farmer, seeing a proper young gentleman, as he thought, fall dead afore him, stepped to him, held him in his arms, rubbed him and chafed him.

At this, there gathered a great multitude of people about him,

middle walk: central aisle of St Paul's.

and the whilst the foist drew the farmer's purse and away. By that the other thought the feat was done, he began to come something to himself again, and so half staggering, stumbled out of Paul's, and went after the crew where they had appointed to meet, and there boasted of his wit and experience.

The farmer, little suspecting this villainy, thrust his hand into his pocket and missed his purse, searched for it, but lining and shells and all was gone, which made the countryman in a great maze, that he stood still in a dump so long that a gentleman, perceiving it, asked what he ailed.

'What ail I, sir?' quoth he. 'Truly I am thinking how men may long as well as women.'

'Why dost thou conjecture that, honest man?' quoth he.

'Marry! sir,' answers the farmer. 'The gentleman even now that swooned here, I warrant him breeds his wife's child, for the cause of his sudden qualm, that he fell down dead, grew of longing!'

The gentleman demanded how he knew that.

'Well enough, sir,' quoth he, 'and he hath his longing too, for the poor man longed for my purse, and thanks be to God he hath it with him.'

At this all the hearers laughed, but not so merrily as the foist and his fellows, that then were sharing his money.

A Quaint Conceit [18] of a Cutler and a Cutpurse

A nip, having by fortune lost his cuttle-bung, or having not one fit for his purpose, went to a cunning cutler to have a new made, and prescribed the cutler such a method and form to make his knife, and the fashion to be strong, giving such a charge of the fineness of the temper and setting of the edge, that the cutler wondered what the gentleman would do with it. Yet, because he offered so largely for the making of it, the cutler was silent and made few questions, only he appointed [him] the time to come for it, and that was three days after. Well, the time being expired, the gentleman-nip came, and, seeing his knife, liked it passing well, and gave him his money with advantage. The cutler desirous to know to what use he would put it, said to the cut-purse thus:

'Sir,' quoth he, 'I have made many knives in my days, and yet I never saw any of this form, fashion, temper, or edge, and there-fore, if without offence, I pray you tell me how or to what will you use it?'

While thus he stood talking with the nip, *he*, spying the purse in his apron, had cut it passing cunningly, and then, having his purchase close in his hand, made answer: 'In faith, my friend, to dissemble is a folly. 'Tis to cut a purse withal, and I hope to have good handsel.'

'You are a merry gentleman,' quoth the cutler.

'I tell true,' quoth the cutpurse, and away he goes.

No sooner was he gone from the stall, but there came another and bought a knife, and should have single money again. The cutler, thinking to put his hand in his bag, thrust it quite through at the bottom. All his money was gone, and the purse cut. Perceiving this, and remembering how the man prayed he might have good handsel, he fetched a great sigh, and said:

'Now I see: he that makes a snare, first falls into it himself. I made a knife to cut other men's purses, and mine is the first handsel. Well, revenge is fallen upon me, but I hope the rope will fall upon him.' And so he smoothed up the matter to himself, lest men should laugh at his strange fortune.

The Discovery of the Lifting Law

The lift is he that stealeth or prowleth any plate, jewels, bolts of satin, velvet, or such parcels from any place, by a sleight con-veyance under his cloak, or so secretly that it may not be espied. Of lifts there be divers kinds as their natures be different, some base rogues, that lift, when they come into ale-houses, quart pots, platters, cloaks, swords, or any such paltry trash which com-monly is called pilfering or petulacery, for, under the colour of spending two or three pots of ale, they lift away anything that

good handsel: auspicious beginning in trade.
single money: change.

cometh within the compass of their reach, having a fine and nimble agility of the hand, as the foist had.

These are the common and rascal sort of lifts; but the higher degrees and gentlemen-lifts have to the performance of their faculty three parties of necessity, the lift, the marker and the santer. The lift, attired in the form of a civil country gentleman, comes with the marker into some mercer's shop, haberdasher's, goldsmith's, or any such place where any particular parcels of worth are to be conveyed, and there he calls to see a bolt of satin, velvet, or any such commodity, and, not liking the pile, colour, or brack, he calls for more, and the whiles he begins to resolve which of them most fitly may be lifted, and what garbage (for so he calls the goods stolen) may be most easily conveyed. Then he calls to the mercer's man and says, 'Sirrah, reach me that piece of velvet or satin, or that jewel, chain, or piece of plate'; and whilst the fellow turns his back, he commits his garbage to the marker; for note, the lift is without his cloak, in his doublet and hose, to avoid the more suspicion. The marker, which is the receiver of the lift's luggage, give[s] a wink to the santer, that walks before the window, and then, the santer going by in great haste, the marker calls him and says, 'Sir, a word with you. I have a message to do unto you from a very friend of yours, and the errand is of some importance.'

'Truly, sir,' says the santer, 'I have very urgent business in hand, and as at this time I cannot stay ...'

'But one word, and no more,' says the marker. And then he delivers him whatsoever the lift hath conveyed unto him; and then the santer goes his way, who never came within the shop, and is a man unknown to them all.

Suppose he is smoked, and his lifting looked into, then are they upon their pantofles, because there is nothing found about them. They defy the world for their honesty, because they be as dishonest as any in the world, and swear, as God shall judge them, they never saw the parcel lost. But oaths with them are like wind out of a bellows, which being cool kindleth fire; so their vows are without conscience, and so they call for revenge. There-

brack: flaw in cloth.
pantofles: footwear (i.e. 'on their dignity').

fore, let this be a caveat to all occupations, sciences and mysteries that they beware of the gentleman-lift, and to have an eye to such as cheapen their wares, and not, when they call to see new stuff, to leave the old behind them, for the fingers of lifts are formed of adamant: though they touch not, yet they have virtue attractive to draw any pelf to them, as the adamant doth the iron.

But yet these lifts have a subtle shift to blind the world, for this close kind of cozenage they have when they want money: one of them apparels himself like a country farmer, and with a memorandum drawn in some legal form, comes to the chamber of some counsellor or Serjeant-at-Law, with his marker and his santer, and there tells the lawyer his case and desires his counsel, the whilst the marker and the santer lay the platform for any rapier, dagger, cloak, gown, or any other parcel of worth that is in the withdrawing or outer chamber, and as soon as they have it they go their way. Then when the lawyer hath given his opinion of the case the lift requires, then he puts in some demur or blind, and says he will have his cause better discovered, and then he will come to his worship again. So, taking his leave without his ten shillings fee, he goes his ways to share what his companions had gotten. The like method they use with scriveners, for coming by the shop, and, seeing any garbage worth the lifting, one starteth in to have an obligation or bill made in haste, and, while the scrivener is busy, the lift bringeth the marker to the blow, and so the luggage is carried away. Now, these lifts have their special receivers of their stolen goods, which are two sundry parties: either some notorious bawds, in whose houses they lie, and they keep commonly tapping-houses, and have young trugs in their house, which are consorts to these lifts, and love them so dear that they never leave them till they come to the gallows; or else they be brokers, a kind of idle sort of lewd livers, as pernicious as the lift, for they receive at their hands whatsoever garbage is conveyed, be it linen, woollen, plate, jewels, and this they do by a bill of sale, making the bill in the name of John a' Nokes or John a' Stiles, so that they shadow the lift, and yet keep themselves without the danger of the law. Thus are these brokers and bawds,

cheapen: bargain for.
adamant: here 'magnet'.

as it were efficient causes of the lifter's villainy, for, were it not their alluring speeches and their secret concealings, the lift for want of receivers should be fain to take a new course of life, or else be continually driven into great extremes for selling his garbage. And thus much briefly for the nature of the lift.

The Discovery of the Curbing Law

The curber, which the common people call the hooker, is he that with a curb, as they term it, or hook, doth pull out of a window any loose linen cloth, apparel, or else any other household stuff whatsoever, which stolen parcels they in their art call snappings. To the performance of this law there be required duly two persons, the curber and the warp. The curber, his office is to spy in the day-time fit places where his trade may be practised at night, and, coming unto any window, if it be open, then he hath his purpose; if shut, then growing into the nature of the black art, [he] hath his trickers, which are engines of iron, so cunningly wrought, that he will cut a bar of iron in two with them so easily, that scarcely shall the standers-by hear him. Then, when he hath the window open and spies any fat snappings worth the curbing, then straight he sets the warp to watch, who hath a long cloak to cover whatsoever he gets. Then doth the other thrust in a long hook some nine foot in length, which he calleth a curb, that hath at the end a crook, with three tines turned contrary, so that 'tis unpossible to miss, if there be any snappings abroad. Now this long hook they call a curb, and, because you shall not wonder how they carry it for being spied, know this, that it is made with joints like an angle-rod, and can be conveyed into the form of truncheon, and worn in the hand like a walking-staff until they come to their purpose, and then they let it out at the length, and hook or curb whatsoever is loose and within the reach; and then he conveys it to the warp, and from thence, as they list, their snappings go to the broker or to the bawd, and there they have as ready money for it, as merchants have for their ware in the Exchange. Beside, there is a diver, which is in the

angle-rod : fishing rod.

very nature of the curber, for as he puts in a hook, so the other puts in at the window some little figging boy, who plays his part notably; and perhaps the youth is so well instructed, that he is a scholar in the black art, and can pick a lock if it be not too cross-warded, and deliver to the diver what snappings he finds in the chamber. Thus you hear what the curber doth, and the diver, and what inconvenience grows to many by their base villainies. Therefore I wish all men-servants and maids to be careful for their masters' commodities, and to leave no loose ends abroad, especially in chambers where windows open to the street, lest the curber take them as snappings, and convey them to the cozening broker. Let this suffice; and now I will recreate your wits with a merry tale or two.

Of a Curber, and how Cunningly he was Taken

It fortuned of late that a curber and his warp went walking in the dead of the night to spy out some window open for their purpose, and by chance came by a nobleman's house about London, and saw the window of the porter's lodge open, and looking in, spied fat snappings, and bade his warp watch carefully, for there would be purchase, and, with that, took his curb, and thrust it into the chamber. And the porter, lying in his bed, was awake and saw all, and so was his bedfellow that was yeoman of the wine-cellar. The porter stole out of his bed to see what would be done.

The first snapping the curber light[ed] on was his livery coat. As he was drawing it unto the window, the porter easily lifted it off, and so the curber drew his hook in vain, the whilst his bedfellow stole out of the chamber, and raised up two or three more, and went about to take them. But still the rogue plied his business, and lighted on a gown, that he used to sit in in the porter's lodge, and warily drew it, but when it came to the window, the porter drew it off so lightly, that the hooker perceived it not. Then, when he saw his curb would take no hold, he swore and chafed and told the warp he had hold of two good snaps, and yet missed them both, and that the fault was in the curb. Then he fell to sharping and hammering of the hook, to make it hold better, and in again he thrusts it, and lights upon a pair of buff hose; but when he had drawn them to the window, the porter took them off again, which made the curber almost mad, and swore he thought the devil was abroad tonight, he had such hard fortune.

'Nay,' says the yeoman of the cellar, 'there is three abroad, and we are come to fetch you and your hooks to hell.'

So they apprehended these base rogues and carried them into the porter's lodge, and made that their prison. In the morning a crew of gentlemen in the houses, sat for judges – in that they would not trouble their lord with such filthy caterpillars – and by them they were found guilty, and condemned to abide forty blows apiece with a bastinado, which they had solemnly paid, and so went away without any further damage.

Of the Subtlety of a Curber in Cozening a Maid

A merry jest and as subtle was reported to me of a cunning curber, who had apparelled himself marvellous brave, like some good well-favoured young gentleman, and, instead of a man, had his warp to wait upon him. This smoothfaced rogue comes into Moorfields,[19] and caused his man to carry a pottle of hippocras under his cloak, and there had learned out, amongst others that was drying of clothes, of a very well-favoured maid that was there with her flasket of linen, what her master was, where she dwelt, and what her name. Having gotten this intelligence, to this maid he goes, courteously salutes her, and after some pretty chat, tells her how he saw her sundry times at her master's door, and was so besotted with her beauty, that he had made inquiry what her qualities were, which by the neighbours he generally heard to be so virtuous, that his desire was the more inflamed, and thereupon in sign of good will, and in further acquaintance, he had brought her a pottle of hippocras. The maid, seeing him a good proper man, took it very kindly, and thanked him, and so they drunk the wine, and, after a little lovers' prattle, for that time they parted.

The maid's heart was set on fire that a gentleman was become a suitor to her, and she began to think better of herself than ever she did before, and waxed so proud that her other suitors were counted too base for her, and there might be none welcome but this new-come gentleman her lover. Well, divers times they appointed meetings, that they grew very familiar, and he often-times would come to her master's house, when all but she and her fellow maids were in bed, so that he and the warp his man did almost know every corner of the house. It fortuned that so long he dallied, that at length he meant earnest, but not to marry the maid (whatsoever he had done else), and coming into the fields to her on a washing day, saw a mighty deal of fine linen, worth twenty pound as he conjectured. Whereupon he thought this night to set down his rest, and therefore he was very pleasant with his lover, and told her that that night after her master and mistress were in bed, he would come, and bring a bottle of sack with him and drink with her. The maid, glad at these news, promised to sit up for him; and so they parted till about ten o'clock at night, when he came, and brought his man with him, and one other curber with his tools, who should stand without the doors. To be brief, welcome he came, and so welcome as a man might be to a maid. He, that had more mind to spy the clothes than to look on her favour, at last perceived them in a parlour that stood to the streetward, and there would the maid have had him sit. 'No, sweeting,' quoth he, 'it is too near the street. We can neither laugh nor be merry, but every one that passeth by must hear us.' Upon that they removed into another room, and pleasant they were, and tippled the sack round till all was out, and the gentleman swore that he would have another pottle, and so sent his man, who told the other curber, that stood without, where the window was he should work at, and away goes he for more sack and brings it very orderly, and then to their cups they fall again, while the curber without had not left one rag of linen behind. Late it grew, and the morn-ing began to wax grey, and away goes this curber and his man, leaving the maid very pleasant with his flattering promises until such time as, poor soul, she went into the parlour, and missed all her mistress's linen. Then what a sorrowful heart she had I refer to them that have grieved at the like loss.

The Discovery of the Black Art

The black art is picking of locks; and to this busy trade two persons are required, the charm and the stand. The charm is he that doth the feat, and the stand is he that watcheth. There be more that do belong to the burglary for conveying away the goods, but only two are employed about the lock. The charm hath many keys and wrests, which they call picklocks, and for every sundry fashion they have a sundry term; but I am ignorant of their words of art, and therefore I omit them: only this, they have such cunning in opening a lock, that they will undo the hardest lock though never so well warded, even while a man may turn his back. Some have their instruments from Italy, made of steel; some are made here by smiths, that are partakers in their villainous occupations. But, howsoever, well may it be called the black art, for the devil cannot do better than they in their faculty.

I once saw the experience of it myself, for, being in the Counter upon commandment, there came in a famous fellow in the black art, as strong in that quality as Samson. The party now is dead, and by fortune died in his bed. I, hearing that he was a charm, began to enter familiarity with him, and to have an insight into his art. After some acquaintance he told me much, and one day, being in my chamber, I showed him my desk, and asked him if he could pick that little lock that was so well warded, and too little, as I thought, for any of his gins.

'Why, sir,' says he, 'I am so experienced in the black art, that if I do but blow upon the lock, it shall fly open; and therefore let me come to your desk, and do but turn five times about, and you shall see my cunning.' With that I did as he bade me, and ere I had turned five times, his hand was rifling in my desk very orderly. I wondered at it, and thought verily that the devil and his dam was in his fingers. Much discommodity grows by this black art in shops and noblemen's houses for their plate. Therefore are they most severely to be looked into by the honourable and worshipful of England. And to end this discourse as pleasantly as the rest, I will rehearse you a true tale done by a most worshipful knight in Lancashire against a tinker that professed the black art.

A True and Merry Tale of a Knight and a Tinker that was a Picklock

Not far off from Bolton-in-the-moors, there dwelled an ancient knight, who for courtesy and hospitality was famous in those parts. Divers of his tenants, making repair to his house, offered divers complaints to him, how their locks were picked in the night, and divers of them utterly undone by that means; and who it should be they could not tell, only they suspected a tinker, that went about the country, and in all places did spend very lavishly. The knight willingly heard what they exhibited, and promised both redress and revenge, if he or they could learn out the man.

It chanced not long after their complaints but this jolly tinker, so expert in the black art, came by the house of this knight, as the old gentleman was walking before the gate, and cried for work. The knight, straight conjecturing this should be that famous rogue that did so much hurt to his tenants, called in and asked if they had any work for the tinker. The cook answered, there was three or four old kettles to mend.

'Come in, tinker.' So this fellow came in, laid down his budget and fell to his work. 'A black jack of beer for the tinker,' says the knight, 'I know tinkers have dry souls.' The tinker he was pleasant and thanked him humbly. The knight sat down with him and fell a ransacking his budget, and asked wherefore this tool served and wherefore that. The tinker told him all. At last as he tumbled among his old brass, the knight spied three or four bunches of picklocks. He turned them over quickly as though he had not seen them, and said: 'Well, tinker, I warrant thou art a passing cunning fellow and well skilled in thine occupation by the store of thy tools thou hast in thy budget.'

'In faith, if it please your worship,' quoth he, 'I am, thanks be to God, my craft's master.'

'Ay, so much I perceive that thou are a passing cunning fellow,' quoth the knight. 'Therefore let us have a fresh jack of beer, and that of the best and strongest, for the tinker.'

Thus he passed away the time pleasantly, and when he had done his work, he asked what he would have for his pains.

'But two shillings – of your worship,' quoth the tinker.

'Two shillings?' says the knight. 'Alas, tinker, it is too little! For I see by thy tools thou art a passing cunning workman. Hold, there is two shillings. Come in, thou shalt drink a cup of wine before thou goest. But I pray thee tell me, which way travellest thou?'

'Faith, sir,' quoth the tinker, 'all is one to me. I am not much out of my way wheresoever I go; but now I am going to Lancaster.'

'I pray thee, tinker,' then quoth the knight, 'carry me a letter to the jailer, for I sent in a felon thither the other day and I would send word to the jailer he should take no bail for him.'

'Marry, that I will, in most dutiful manner,' quoth he, 'and much more for your worship than that.'

'Give him a cup of wine,' quoth the knight. 'And sirrah (speaking to his clerk) make a letter to the jailer.' But then he whispered to him and bade him make a *mittimus*[20] to send the tinker to prison.

The clerk answered, he knew not his name.

'I'll make him tell it thee himself,' says the knight; 'and therefore fall you to your pen.'

The clerk began to write his *mittimus*, and the knight began to ask what countryman he was, where he dwelt, what was his name. The tinker told him all, and the clerk set it in with this proviso to the jailer, that he should keep him fast bolted, or else he would break away. As soon as the *mittimus* was made, sealed and subscribed in form of a letter, the knight took it, and delivered it to the tinker, and said, 'Give this to the chief jailer of Lancaster; and here is two shillings more for thy labour.'

So the tinker took the letter and the money, and with many a cap and knee thanked the old knight and departed, and made haste till he came at Lancaster, and stayed not in the town so much as to taste one cup of nappy ale before he came to the

nappy: foaming, heady.

jailer, and to him very briefly he delivered his letter. The jailer took it and read it, and smiled agood, and said:

'Tinker, thou art welcome for such a knight's sake. He bids me give thee the best entertainment I may.'

'Ay, sir,' quoth the tinker, 'the knight loves me well; but, I pray you, hath the courteous gentleman remembered such a poor man as I?'

'Ay, marry, doth he, tinker. And therefore, sirrah,' quoth he to one of his men, 'take the tinker into the lowest ward; clap a strong pair of bolts on his heels, and a basil of twenty-eight pound weight. And then, sirrah, see if your picklocks will serve the turn to bail you hence!'

At this the tinker was blank, but yet he thought the jailer had but jested. But, when he heard the *mittimus*, his heart was cold, and had not a word to say; his conscience accused him. And there he lay while the next sessions, and was hanged at Lancaster, and all his skill in the black art could not serve him.

FINIS

THIRDE

and last Part of Conny-catching.

WITH THE NEW DEVISED
knauish Art of Foole-taking.

The like Cosenages and Villenies neuer before
discouered.

By R. G.

Imprinted at London by *Thomas Scarlet* for
Cutberd Burbie, and are to be solde at his shoppe in the
Poultrie, by S. Mildreds Church. 1592.

To All Such as have Received either Pleasure or Profit by the Two Former Published Books of this Argument, and to All Beside that Desire to Know the Wonderful Sly Devices of this Hellish Crew of Cony-Catchers.

IN the time of King Henry the Fourth, as our English chroniclers have kept in remembrance, lived divers sturdy and loose companions in sundry places about the City of London, who gave themselves to no good course of life, but because the time was somewhat troublesome, watched diligently, when by the least occasion of mutiny offered, they might prey upon the goods of honest citizens, and so by their spoil enrich themselves. At that time likewise lived a worthy gentleman, whose many very famous deeds (whereof I am sorry I may here make no rehearsal, because neither time nor occasion will permit me) renown his name to all ensuing posterities; he being called Sir Richard Whittington, the founder of Whittington College[1] in London, and one that bear the office of Lord Mayor of this City three several times. This worthy man, well noting the dangerous disposition of that idle kind of people, took such good and discreet order (after he had sent divers of them to serve in the king's wars, and they, loath to do so well returned to their former vomit) that in no place of or about London they might have lodging or entertainment, except they applied themselves to such honest trades and exercises as might witness their maintaining was by true and honest means. If any to the contrary were found, they were in justice so sharply proceeded against, as the most hurtful and dangerous enemies to the commonwealth.

In this quiet and most blissful time of peace, when all men, in course of life, should show themselves most thankful for so great a benefit, this famous City is pestered with the like or rather worse kind of people, that bear outward show of civil, honest, and gentlemanlike disposition, but in very deed their behaviour is most infamous to be spoken of. And, as now, by their close villainies they cheat, cozen, prig, lift, nip, and suchlike tricks now used in their cony-catching trade, to the hurt and undoing of many an honest citizen, and other: so if God should in justice be angry with us, as our wickedness hath well deserved, and, as the Lord forfend, our peace should be molested as in former time, even as they did, so will these be the first in seeking domestical spoil and ruin; yea, so they may have it, it skills not how they come by it. God raise such another as was worthy Whittington, that in time may bridle the headstrong course of this hellish crew, and force them live as becometh honest subjects, or else to abide the reward due to their looseness.

By reading this little treatise ensuing, you shall see to what marvellous subtle policies these deceivers have attained, and how daily they practise strange drifts for their purpose. I say no more, but, if all these forewarnings may be regarded, to the benefit of the well-minded, and just control of these careless wretches, it is all I desire, and no more than I hope to see.

Yours in all he may, R.G.

The Third and Last Part of Cony-Catching, with the New-Devised Knavish Art of Fool-Taking

Being by chance invited to supper, where were present divers both of worship and good account, as occasion served for intercourse of talk, the present treacheries and wicked devices of the world was called in question. Amongst other most hateful and well worthy reprehension, the wondrous villainies of loose and lewd persons, that bear the shape of men, yet are monsters in condition, was specially remembered and not only they, but their complices, their confederates, their base-natured women and close compacters were noted; namely, such as term themselves cony-catchers, crossbiters, with their appertaining names to their several cozening qualities, as already is made known to the world by two several imprinted books, by means whereof the present kind of conference was occasioned.

Quoth a gentleman sitting at the table, whose deep step into age deciphered his experience, and whose gravity in speech reported his discretion, quoth he: 'By the two published books of

two several imprinted books: Greene's two previous tracts.

cony-catching I have seen divers things whereof I was before ignorant. Notwithstanding, had I been acquainted with the author, I could have given him such notes of notorious matters that way intenting as in neither of the pamphlets are the like set down. Beside, they are so necessary to be known, as they will both forearm any man against such treacherous vipers, and forewarn the simpler sort from conversing with them.'

The gentleman being known to be within Commission of the Peace, and that what he spake of either came to him by examinations, or by riding in the circuits as other like officers do, was entreated by one man above the rest, as his leisure served him, to acquaint him with those notes, and he would so bring it to pass as the writer of the other two books should have the sight of them, and if their quantity would serve, that he should publish them as a third, and more necessary, part than the former were.

The gentleman replied: 'All such notes as I speak are not of mine own knowledge. Yet from such men have I received them, as I dare assure their truth; and but that by naming men wronged by such mates, more displeasure would ensue than were expedient, I could set down both time, place and parties. But the certainty shall suffice without any such offence. As for such as shall see their injuries discovered, and, biting the lip, say to themselves, "Thus was I made a cony", their names being shadowed, they have no cause of anger, in that the example of their honest simplicity beguiled may shield a number more endangered from tasting the like. And, seeing you have promised to make them known to the author of the former two books, you shall the sooner obtain your request; assuring him thus much upon my credit and honesty, that no one untruth is in the notes, but every one credible, and to be justified, if need serve.'

Within a fortnight or thereabout afterward, the gentleman performed his promise, in several papers sent the notes, which here are in our book compiled together. When thou hast read, say, if ever thou heardest more notable villainies discovered. And if thou or thy friends receive any good by them, as it cannot be but they will make a number more careful of themselves, thank the

by examinations: i.e. by interrogating those who came up before him.

honest gentleman for his notes, and the writer that published both the other and these for general example.

A Pleasant Tale how an Honest Substantial Citizen was Made a Cony, and Simply Entertained a Knave that Carried Away his Goods very Politicly

What laws are used among this hellish crew, what words and terms they give themselves and their copesmates, are at large set down in the former two books. Let it suffice ye then in this, to read the simple true discourses of such as have by extraordinary cunning and treachery been deceived, and remembering their subtle means there, and sly practices here, be prepared against the reaches of any such companions.

Not long since, a crew of cony-catchers meeting together, and in conference laying down such courses as they severally should take to shun suspect, and return a common benefit among them, the carders received their charge, the dicers theirs, the hangers-about-the-Court theirs, the followers of sermons theirs, and so the rest to their offices; but one of them especially, who at their wonted meetings, when report was made how every purchase was gotten, and by what policy each one prevailed, this fellow in a kind of priding scorn, would usually say:

'In faith masters, these things are prettily done – common sleights, expressing no deep reach of wit. And I wonder men are so simple to be so beguiled. I would fain see some rare artificial feat indeed, that some admiration and fame might ensue the doing thereof. I promise ye, I disdain these base and petty paltries, and, may my fortune jump with my resolution, ye shall hear, my boys, within a day or two, that I will accomplish a rare stratagem indeed, of more value than forty of yours, and when it is done shall carry some credit with it!'

They, wondering at his words, desired to see the success of them, and so, dispersing themselves as they were accustomed, left this frolic fellow pondering on his affairs. A citizen's house in London, which he had diligently eyed and aimed at for a fortnight's space, was the place wherein he must perform this exploit; and, having learned one of the servant-maid's name of the house, as also where she was born and her kindred, upon a Sunday in the afternoon, when it was her turn to attend on her master and mistress to the garden in Finsbury Fields, to regard the children while they sported about, this crafty mate, having duly watched their coming forth, and seeing that they intended to go down St Laurence Lane, stepped before them, ever casting an eye back, lest they should turn some contrary way. But, their following still fitting his own desire, near unto the conduit in Aldermanbury he crossed the way and came unto the maid, and kissing her said: 'Cousin Margaret, I am very glad to see you well. My uncle your father, and all your friends in the country are in good health, God be praised!'

The maid, hearing herself named, and not knowing the man, modestly blushed, which he perceiving, held way on with her amongst her fellow apprentices, and thus began again: 'I see, cousin, you know me not, and I do not greatly blame you, it is so long since you came forth of the country; but I am such a one's son' – naming her uncle right, and his son's name, which she very well remembered, but had not seen him in eleven years. Then, taking forth a bowed groat, and an old penny bowed, he gave it her as being sent from her uncle and aunt, whom he termed to be his father and mother. 'Withal,' quoth he, 'I have a gammon of bacon and a cheese from my uncle your father, which are sent to your master and mistress, which I received of the carrier, because my uncle enjoined me to deliver them, when I must entreat your mistress that at Whitsuntide next she will give you leave to come down into the country.' The maid, thinking simply all he said was true, and as they, so far from their parents, are not only glad to hear of their welfare, but also rejoice to see any of their kindred, so this poor maid, well knowing her uncle had a son so named as he called himself, and thinking from a boy, as he was at her leaving the country, he was now grown such a proper handsome young man, was not a little joyful to see him. Beside, she seemed proud that her kinsman was so neat a youth, and so she held on questioning with him about her friends, he soothing each matter so cunningly, as the maid was confidently persuaded of him.

In this time, one of the children stepped to her mother and

said, 'Our Marget, mother, hath a fine cousin come out of the country, and he hath a cheese for my father and you.' Whereon she, looking back, said: 'Maid, is that your kinsman?' – 'Yea forsooth, mistress,' quoth she, 'my uncle's son, whom I left a little one when I came forth of the country.'

The wily treacher, being master of his trade, would not let slip this opportunity, but courteously stepping to the mistress – who, loving her maid well, because indeed she had been a very good servant, and from her first coming to London had dwelt with her, told her husband thereof – coined such a smooth tale unto them both, fronting it with the gammon of bacon and the cheese sent from their maid's father, and hoping they would give her leave at Whitsuntide to visit the country, as they with very kind words entertained him, inviting him the next night to supper, when he promised to bring with him the gammon of bacon and the cheese. Then, framing an excuse of certain business in the town, for that time he took his leave of the master and mistress and his new cousin Margaret, who gave many a look after him, poor wench, as he went, joying in her thoughts to have such a kinsman.

On the morrow he prepared a good gammon of bacon, which he closed up in a soiled linen cloth, and sewed an old card upon it, whereon he wrote a superscription unto the master of the maid, and at what sign it was to be delivered, and afterward scraped some of the letters half out, that it might seem they had been rubbed out in the carriage. A good cheese he prepared likewise, with inscription accordingly on it, that it could not be discerned but that some unskilful writer in the country had done it, both by the gross proportion of the letters, as also the bad orthography, which amongst plain husbandmen is very common, in that they have no better instruction. So, hiring a porter to carry them, between five and six in the evening he comes to the citizen's house, and entering the shop, receives them of the porter, whom the honest-meaning citizen would have paid for his pains, but this his maid's new-found cousin said he was satisfied already, and so, straining courtesy, would not permit him.

Well, up are carried the bacon and the cheese, where God knows Margaret was not a little busy to have all things fine and neat against her cousin's coming up. Her mistress likewise, as one well affecting her servant, had provided very good cheer, set all her plate on the cupboard for show, and beautified the house with cushions, carpets, stools, and other devices of needlework, as at such times divers will do, to have the better report made of their credit amongst their servant's friends in the country, albeit at this time, God wot, it turned to their own aftersorrowing. The master of the house, to delay the time while supper was ready, he likewise shows this dissembler his shop, who, seeing things fadge so pat to his purpose, could question of this sort, and that well enough I warrant you, to discern the best from the worst and their appointed places, purposing a further reach than the honest citizen dreamed of. And to be plain with ye, such was this occupier's trade, as, though I may not name it, yet thus much I dare utter, that the worst thing he could carry away was worth about twenty nobles, because he dealt altogether in whole and great sale, which made this companion forge this kindred and acquaintance, for an hundred pound or twain was the very least he aimed at.

At length the mistress sends word supper is on the table, whereupon up he conducts his guest, and, after divers welcomes, as also thanks for the cheese and bacon, to the table they sit, where, let it suffice, he wanted no ordinary good fare, wine and other knacks, besides much talk of the country, how much his friends were beholden for his cousin Margaret, to whom by her mistress's leave he drank twice or thrice, and she, poor soul, doing the like again to him, with remembrance of her father and other kindred, which he still smoothed very cunningly. Countenance of talk made them careless of the time, which slipped from them faster than they were aware of, nor did the deceiver hasten his departing, because he expected what indeed followed, which was, that, being past ten of the clock, and he feigning his lodging to be at St Giles in the Field, was entreated both by the goodman and his wife to take a bed there for that night. For fashion sake, though very glad of this offer, he said he would not trouble them, but giving them many thanks, would to his lodging though it

fadge : fall out.
occupier's : merchant's.

were further. But wonderful it was to see how earnest the honest citizen and his wife laboured to persuade him, that was more willing to stay than they could be to bid him, and what dissembled willingness of departure he used on the other side, to cover the secret villainy intended. Well, at the length, with much ado, he is contented to stay, when Margaret and her mistress presently stirred to make ready his bed, which the more to the honest man's hard hap, but all the better for this artificial cony-catcher, was in the same room where they supped, being commonly called their hall, and there indeed stood a very fair bed, as in such sightly rooms it may easily be thought citizens use not to have anything mean or simple.

The mistress, lest her guest should imagine she disturbed him, suffered all the plate to stand still on the cupboard, and when she perceived his bed was warmed, and everything else according to her mind, she and her husband, bidding him good night, took themselves to their chamber, which was on the same floor, but inward, having another chamber between them and the hall, where the maids and children had their lodging. So, desiring him to call for anything he wanted, and charging Margaret to look it should be so, to bed are they gone; when the apprentices having brought up the keys of the street door, and left them in their master's chamber as they were wont to do, after they had said prayers, their evening exercise, to bed go they likewise, which was in a garret backward over their master's chamber. None are now up but poor Margaret and her counterfeit cousin, whom she, loath to offend with long talk, because it waxed late, after some few more speeches, about their parents and friends in the country, she, seeing him laid in bed, and all such things by him as she deemed needful, with a low courtesy I warrant ye commits him to his quiet, and so went to bed to her fellows the maidservants.

Well did this hypocrite perceive the keys of the doors carried into the goodman's chamber, whereof he, being not a little glad, thought now they would imagine all things sure, and therefore doubtless sleep the sounder. As for the keys, he needed no help of them, because such as he go never unprovided of instruments fitting their trade, and so at this time was this notable treacher.

sightly: liable to be seen (by visitors). Also handsome.

In the dead time of the night, when sound sleep makes the ear unapt to hear the very least noise, he forsaketh his bed, and, having gotten all the plate bound up together in his cloak, goeth down into the shop, where, well remembering both the place and parcels, maketh up his pack with some twenty pounds' worth of goods more. Then settling to his engine, he getteth the door off the hinges, and being forth, lifteth close to again, and so departs, meeting within a dozen paces, three or four of his companions that lurked thereabouts for the purpose. Their word for knowing each other, as is said, was *quest*, and this villain's comfortable news to them was *twag*, signifying he had sped. Each takes a fleece for easier carriage, and so away to bellbrow, which, as I have heard is, as they interpret it, the house of a thief-receiver, without which they can do nothing; and this house, with an apt porter to it, stands ready for them all hours of the night. Too many such are there in London, the masters whereof bear countenance of honest substantial men, but all their living is gotten in this order. The end of such, though they 'scape awhile, will be sailing westward in a cart to Tyburn. Imagine these villains there in their jollity, the one reporting point by point his cunning deceit, and the other, fitting his humour, extolling the deed with no mean commendations.

But, returning to the honest citizen, who, finding in the morning how dearly he paid for a gammon of bacon and a cheese, and how his kind courtesy was thus treacherously requited, blames the poor maid, as innocent herein as himself, and imprisoning her, thinking so to regain his own, grief with ill cherishing there shortens her life. And thus ensueth one hard hap upon another, to the great grief both of master and mistress, when the truth was known, that they so wronged their honest servant. How it may forewarn others I leave to your own opinions, that see what extraordinary devices are nowadays to beguile the simple and honest liberal-minded.

Of a Notable Knave, who for his Cunning Deceiving a
Gentleman of his Purse, Scorned the Name of a Cony-Catcher,
and would Needs be Termed a Fool-Taker, as Master and
Beginner of that New-Found Art

A crew of these wicked companions being one day met together
in Paul's Church, as that is a usual place of their assembly, both
to determine on their drifts, as also to speed of many a booty,
seeing no likelihood of a good afternoon (so they term it either
forenoon or after- when ought is to be done), some dispersed
themselves to the plays, other to the bowling-alleys, and not past
two or three stayed in the church.

Quoth one of them, 'I have vowed not to depart, but something or other I'll have before I go. My mind gives me that this
place yet will yield us all our suppers this night.' The other,
holding like opinion with him, there likewise walked up and
down, looking when occasion would serve for some cash.

At length they espied a gentleman toward the law entering in
at the little north door, and a country client going with him in
very hard talk; the gentleman holding his gown open with his
arms on either side as very many do, gave sight of a fair purple
velvet purse, which was half put under his girdle, which I
warrant you the resolute fellow that would not depart without
something, had quickly espied. 'A game,' quoth he to his fellows.
'Mark the stand'; and so, separating themselves, walked aloof,
the gentleman going to the nether step of the stairs that ascend
up into the choir, and there he walked still with his client. Oft
this crew of mates met together, and said there was no hope of
nipping the bung because he held open his gown so wide, and
walked in such an open place. 'Base knaves,' quoth the frolic
fellow, 'if I say I will have it, I must have it, though he that owes
it had sworn the contrary.' Then, looking aside, he spied his
trug, or quean, coming up the church. 'Away,' quoth he to the
other. 'Go look you for some other purchase; this wench and I
are sufficient for this.'

They go; he lessons the drab in this sort, that she should go to
the gentleman, whose name she very well knew, in that she had

holpen to cozen him once before, and, pretending to be sent to him from one he was well acquainted with for his counsel, should give him his fee for avoiding suspicion, and so frame some wrong done her, as well enough she could. When her mate, taking occasion as it served, would work the mean, she should strike, and so they both prevail. The quean, well inured with such courses, because she was one of the most skilful in that profession, walked up and down alone in the gentleman's sight, that he might discern she stayed to speak with him, and as he turned toward her, he saw her take some money out of her purse, whereby he gathered some benefit was toward him; which made him the sooner dispatch his other client, when she, stepping to him, told such a tale of commendations from his very friend, that had sent her to him (as she said), that he entertained her very kindly, and giving him his fee, which before her face he put up into his purse, and thrust it under his girdle again, she proceeded to a very sound discourse, whereto he listened with no little attention.

The time serving fit for the fellow's purpose, he came behind the gentleman, and, as many times one friend will familiarly with another, clap his hands over his eyes to make him guess who he is, so did this companion, holding his hands fast over the gentleman's eyes, said, 'Who am I?' twice or thrice, in which time the drab had gotten the purse and put it up. The gentleman, thinking it had been some merry friend of his, reckoned the names of three or four, when, letting him go, the crafty knave, dissembling a bashful shame of what he had done, said:

'By my troth, sir, I cry ye mercy. As I came in at the church door, I took ye for such a one (naming a man), a very friend of mine, whom you very much resemble. I beseech ye, be not angry; it was very boldly done of me, but in penance of my fault, so please ye to accept it, I will bestow a gallon or two of wine on ye,' and so laboured him earnestly to go with him to the tavern, still alleging his sorrow for mistaking him.

The gentleman, little suspecting how 'Who-am-I?' had handled him, seeing how sorry he was, and seeming to be a man of no such base condition, took all in good part, saying, 'No harm, sir, to take one for another, a fault wherein any man may easily err,' and so excusing the acceptation of his wine, because he was busy there with a gentlewoman his friend.

The treacher with a courtesy departed, and the drab, having what she would, shortening her tale (he desiring her to come to his chamber the next morning), went to the place where her copesmate and she met, and not long after, divers other of the crew, who, hearing in what manner this act was performed, smiled agood thereat, that she had both got the gentleman's purse her own money again, and his advice for just nothing. He that had done this tall exploit, in a place so open in view, so hardly to be come by, and on a man that made no mean esteem of his wit, bids his fellows keep the worthless name of a cony-catcher to themselves; for he henceforth would be termed a fool-taker, and such as could imitate this quaint example of his, which he would set down as an entrance into that art, should not think scorn to become his scholars.

Night drawing on apace, the gentleman returned home, not all this while missing his purse, but being set at supper, his wife entreated a pint of sack, which he minding to send for, drew to his purse, and seeing it gone, what strange looks, besides sighs, were between him and his wife, I leave to your supposing. And blame them not; for, as I have heard, there was seven pound in gold, beside thirty shillings and odd white money in the purse. But in the midst of his grief, he remembered him that said, 'Who am I?' Wherewith he brake forth into a great laughter, the cause whereof his wife being desirous to know, he declared all that passed between him and the deceiver, as also how soon afterward the quean abbreviated her discourse and followed. 'So by troth wife,' quoth he, 'between "Who-am-I," and the drab, my purse is gone.' Let his loss teach others to look better to theirs.

Another Tale of a Cozening Companion who would Needs Try his Cunning in this New-Invented Art, and how by his Knavery at One Instant he Beguiled Half a Dozen and More

Of late time there hath a certain base kind of trade been used, who, though divers poor men, and doubtless honest, apply themselves to [it], only to relieve their need, yet are there some notorious varlets do the same, being compacted with such kind of people as this present treatise manifesteth to the world, and, what with outward simplicity on the one side and cunning close treachery on the other, divers honest citizens and day-labouring men, that resort to such places as I am to speak of, only for recreation as opportunity serveth, have been of late sundry times deceived of their purses. This trade, or rather unsufferable loitering quality, in singing of ballads and songs at the doors of such houses where plays are used, as also in open markets and other places of this City, where is most resort; which is nothing else but a sly fetch to draw many together, who, listening unto an harmless ditty, afterward walk home to their houses with heavy hearts. From such as are hereof true witnesses to their cost, do I deliver this example.

A subtle fellow, belike emboldened by acquaintance with the former deceit, or else being but a beginner to practise the same, calling certain of his companions together, would try whether he could attain to be master of his art or no, by taking a great many of fools with one train. But let his intent and what else beside remain to abide the censure after the matter is heard, and come to Gracious Street, where this villainous prank was performed. A roguing mate, and such another with him, were there got upon a stall singing of ballads, which belike was some pretty toy, for very many gathered about to hear it, and divers buying, as their affections served, drew to their purses and paid the singers for them. The sly mate and his fellows, who were dispersed among them that stood to hear the songs, well noted where every man that bought put up his purse again, and to such as would not buy, counterfeit warning was sundry times given by the rogue and his associate, to beware of the cutpurse, and look to their purses, which made them often feel where their purses were, either in sleeve, hose, or at girdle, to know whether they were safe or no.

Thus the crafty copesmates were acquainted with what they most desired, and as they were scattered, by shouldering, thrusting, feigning to let fall something, and other wily tricks fit for their purpose, here one lost his purse, there another had his pocket picked, and, to say all in brief, at one instant, upon the

quality : occupation.
Gracious Street : Gracechurch Street.

complaint of one or two that saw their purses were gone, eight more in the same company found themselves in like predicament. Some angry, others sorrowful, and all greatly discontented, looking about them, knew not who to suspect or challenge, in that the villains themselves that had thus beguiled them, made show that they had sustained like loss. But one angry fellow, more impatient than all the rest, he falls upon the ballad-singer, and, beating him with his fists well favouredly, says, if he had not listened his singing, he had not lost his purse, and therefore would not be otherwise persuaded, but that they two and the cutpurses were compacted together. The rest that had lost their purses likewise, and saw that so ma[n]y complain together, they jump in opinion with the other fellow, and begin to tug and hale the ballad singers, when, one after one, the false knaves began to shrink away with the purses. By means of some officer then being there present, the two rogues were had before a Justice, and upon his discreet examination made, it was found, that they and the cutpurses were compacted together, and that by this unsuspected villainy, they had deceived many. The fine fooltaker himself, with one or two more of that company, was not long after apprehended, when I doubt not but they had their reward answerable to their deserving; for I hear of their journey westward, but not of their return. Let this forewarn those that listen [to] singing in the streets.

Of a Crafty Mate that Brought Two Young Men unto a Tavern, where, Departing with a Cup, he Left them to Pay Both for the Wine and Cup

A friend of mine sent me this note, and assuring me the truth thereof, I thought necessary to set it down amongst the rest, both for the honest simplicity on the one side, and most cunning knavery used on the other; and thus it was.

Two young men of familiar acquaintance, who delighted much in music, because themselves therein were somewhat expert, as on the virginals, bandora, lute and suchlike, were one evening at a common inn of this town, as I have heard, where the one of

bandora: stringed instrument resembling lute or guitar.

them showed his skill on the virginals, to the no little content-
ment of the hearers. Now, as divers guests of the house came into
the room to listen, so among the rest entered an artificial cony-
catcher, who, as occasion served, in the time of ceasing between
the several toys and fancies he played, very much commended
his cunning, quick hand, and such qualities praiseworthy in
such a professor. The time being come when these young men
craved leave to depart, this politic varlet, stepping to them, desired that they would accept a quart of wine at his hand, which
he would, most gladly he would, bestow upon them. Besides, if
it liked him that played on the virginals to instruct, he would
help him to so good a place, as happily might advantage him for
ever.

These kind words, delivered with such honest outward show,
caused the young men, whose thoughts were free from any other
opinion than to be as truly and plainly dealt withal as themselves
meant, accepted his offer, because he that played on the virginals
was desirous to have some good place of service, and hereupon
to the tavern they go, and being set, the wily companion calleth
for two pints of wine, a pint of white, and a pint of claret, casting his cloak upon the table, and falling to his former communication of preferring the young man. The wine is brought, and
two cups withal, as is the usual manner. When drinking to them
of the one pint, they pledge him, not unthankful for his gentleness. After some time spent in talk, and, as he perceived, fit for
his purpose, he takes the other cup, and tastes the other pint of
wine, wherewith he finding fault, that it drank somewhat hard,
said that rose-water and sugar would do no harm; whereupon
he leaves his seat, saying he was well acquainted with one of the
servants of the house, of whom he could have twopennyworth
of rose-water for a penny, and so of sugar likewise, wherefore he
would step to the bar unto him. So, taking the cup in his hand,
he did, the young man never thinking on any such treachery as
ensued, in that he seemed an honest man, and beside left his cloak
lying on the table by them.

artificial: cunning.
instruct: authorize.
preferring: recommending.

No more returns the younker with rose-water and sugar, but stepping out of doors, unseen of any, goes away roundly with the cup. The young men, not a little wondering at his long tarrying, by the coming of the servants to see what they wanted, who took no regard of his sudden departure, find themselves there left, not only to pay for the wine, but for the cup also, being rashly supposed by the master and his servants to be co-partners with the treacherous villain. But their honest behaviour well known, as also their simplicity too much abused, well witnessed their innocency; notwithstanding they were fain to pay for the cup, as afterward they did, having nothing towards their charge but a threadbare cloak not worth two shillings. Take heed how you drink wine with any such companions.

Of an Honest Householder which was Cunningly Deceived by a Subtle Companion that Came to Hire a Chamber for his Master

Not far from Charing Cross dwelleth an honest young man, who, being not long since married, and having more rooms in his house than himself occupieth, either for term-time, or the Court lying so near, as divers do, to make a reasonable commodity, and to ease house-rent, which, as the world goeth now is none of the cheapest, letteth forth a chamber or two, according as it may be spared. In an evening but a while since, came one in the manner of a servingman to this man and his wife, and he must needs have a chamber for his master, offering so largely, as the bargain was soon concluded between them. His intent was to have fingered some booty in the house, as by the sequel it may be likeliest gathered. But, belike no fit thing lying abroad, or he better regarded than haply he would be, his expectation that way was frustrate. Yet as a resolute cony-catcher indeed, that scorneth to attempt without some success, and rather will prey upon small commodity than return to his fellows disgraced with a lost labour, he summons his wits together, and by a smooth tale overreached both the man and his wife. He tells them that his master was a captain late come from the sea, and had costly apparel to bring thither, which, for more easy carriage, he entreats them

regarded: observed.

lend him a sheet to bind it up in. They suspecting no ill, because he required their boy should go with him to help him carry the stuff, the good wife steps unto her chest, where her linen lay finely sweetened with roseleaves and lavender, and lends him a very good sheet indeed.

This success made him bold to venture a little further, and then he tells them his master had a great deal of broken sugar and fine spices, that lay negligently abroad in his lodging as it was brought from the ship, all which he was assured his master would bestow on them, so he could devise how to get it brought thither.

These liberal promises, prevailing with them that lightly believed and withal were somewhat covetous of the sugar and spices, the woman demanded if a couple of pillow-beres would not serve to bring the sugar and spices in. 'Yes, marry,' quoth he, 'so the sugar may best be kept by itself, and the spices by themselves. And,' quoth he, 'because there are many crafty knaves abroad' – grieving that any should be craftier than himself – 'and in the evening the linen might quickly be snatched from the boy,' for the more safety, he would carry the sheet and pillow-beres himself, and within an hour or little more, return with the boy again, because he would have all things ready before his master came, who, as he said, was attending on the Council at the Court.

The man and his wife, crediting his smooth speeches, sends their boy with him, and so along toward Ivy Bridge go they. The cony-catcher, seeing himself at free liberty, that he had gotten a very good sheet, and two fine pillow-beres, steps to the wall, as though he would make water, bidding the boy go fair and softly on before. The boy, doubting nothing, did as he willed him, when presently he stepped into some house hard by fit to entertain him. And never since was he, his master, the sugar, spices, or the linen heard of. Many have been in this manner deceived, as I hear. Let this then give them warning to beware of any such unprofitable guests.

pillow-beres: pillow-cases.

Of One that Came to buy a Knife, and made First Proof of his Trade on him that Sold it

One of the cunning nips about the town came unto a poor cutler to have a cuttle made according unto his own mind, and not above three inches would he have both the knife and the haft in length; yet of such pure metal, as possible may be. Albeit the poor man never made the like before, yet, being promised four times the value of his stuff and pains, he was contented to do this, and the day being come that he should deliver it, the party came, who, liking it exceedingly, gave him the money promised, which the poor man gladly put up into his purse, that hung at a button-hole of his waistcoat before his breast, smiling that he was so well paid for so small a trifle. The party perceiving his merry count-enance, and imagining he guessed for what purpose the knife was, said, 'Honest man, whereat smile you?' – 'By my troth, sir,' quoth the cutler, 'I smile at your knife, because I never made one so little before; and, were it not offensive unto you, I would request to know to what use you will put it to.' – 'Wilt thou keep my counsel?' quoth the nip. 'Yea, on mine honesty,' quoth the cutler. 'Then hearken in thy ear,' said the nip, and so rounding with him, cut the poor man's purse that hung at his bosom, he never feeling when he did it. 'With this knife,' quoth the nip, 'mean I to cut a purse.' – 'Marry, God forbid!' quoth the cutler: 'I cannot think you to be such a kind of man. I see you love to jest'; and so they parted.

The poor man, not so wise as to remember his own purse, when by such a warning he might have taken the offender doing the deed, but rather proud, as it were, that his money was so easily earned, walks to the ale-house, which was within a house or two of his own, and, finding there three or four of his neigh-bours, with whom he began to jest very pleasantly, swears by cock and pie he would spend a whole groat upon them, for he had gotten it and more clearly by a good bargain that morning.

Though it was no marvel to see him so liberal, because indeed he was a good companion, yet they were loath to put him unto such cost. Nothwithstanding he would needs do it, and so far as promise stretched, was presently filled in and set upon the board. In the drinking time often he wished to meet with more such customers as he had done that morning, and commended him for a very honest gentleman, I warrant you. At length, when the reckoning was to be paid, he draws to his purse, where, finding nothing left but a piece of the string in the buttonhole, I leave to your judgement whether he was now as sorry as he was merry before.

Blank and all amort sits the poor cutler, and with such a pitiful countenance as his neighbours did not a little admire his solemn alteration, and desirous to know the cause thereof, from point to point he discourseth the whole manner of the tragedy, never naming his new customer, but with such a far-fetched sigh, as soul and body would have parted in sunder. And in midst of all his grief, he brake forth into these terms:

'I'll believe a man the better by his word while I know him. The knife was bought to cut a purse indeed, and I thank him for it he made the first proof of the edge with me.'

The neighbours grieving for his loss, yet smiling at his folly to be so overreached, were fain to pay the groat the cutler called in, because he had no other money about him, and spent as much more beside to drive away his heaviness.

This tale, because it was somewhat misreported before,[2] upon talk had with the poor cutler himself, is set down now in true form and manner how it was done. Therefore is there no offence offered, when by better consideration, a thing may be enlarged or amended, or at least the note be better confirmed.

Let the poor cutler's mishap example others, that they brag not over-hastily of gain easily gotten, lest they chance to pay as dearly for it as he did.

Of a Young Nip that Cunningly Beguiled an Ancient Professor of that Trade, and his Quean with him, at a Play

A good fellow that was newly entered into the nipping craft, and had not as yet attained to any acquaintance with the chief and cunning masters of that trade, in the Christmas holidays last

amort: dispirited.

came to see a play at the 'Bull within Bishopsgate',[3] there to take
his benefit as time and place would permit him. Not long had
he stayed in the press, but he had gotten a young man's purse
out of his pocket, which when he had, he stepped into the stable
to take out the money, and to convey away the purse. But looking
on his commodity he found nothing therein but white counters,
a thimble and a broken threepence, which belike the fellow that
ought it, had done of purpose to deceive the cutpurse withal, or
else had played at the cards for counters, and so carried his
winnings about him till his next sitting to play. Somewhat dis-
pleased to be so overtaken, he looked aside, and spied a lusty
youth entering at the door, and his drab with him. This fellow
he had heard to be one of the finest nippers about the town, and
ever carried his quean with him, for conveyance when the stratagem was performed. He puts up the counters into the purse again,
and follows close to see some piece of their service. Among a
company of seemly men was this lusty companion and his minion
gotten, where both they might best behold the play, and work for
advantage, and ever this young nip was next to him, to mark
when he should attempt any exploit, standing as it were more
than half between the cunning nip and his drab, only to learn
some part of their skill. In short time the deed was performed,
but how, the young nip could not easily discern, only he felt him
shift his hand toward his trug, to convey the purse to her, but
she, being somewhat mindful of the play, because a merriment
was then on the stage, gave no regard, whereby, thinking he had
pulled her by the coat, he twitched the young nip by the cloak,
who, taking advantage of this offer, put down his hand and received the purse of him. Then, counting it discourtesy to let
him lose all his labour, he softly plucked the quean by the coat,
which she feeling, and imagining it had been her companion's
hand, received of him the first purse with the white counters in
it. Then, fearing lest his stay should hinder him, and seeing the
other intended to have more purses ere he departed, away goes
the young nip with the purse he got so easily, wherein, as I have
heard was thirty-seven shillings and odd money, which did so
much content him, as that he had beguiled so ancient a stander

ought: owned.

252

in that profession. What the other thought when he found the purse, and could not guess how he was cozened, I leave to your censures. Only this makes me smile, that one false knave can beguile another, which bids honest men look the better to their purses.

How a Gentleman was Craftily Deceived of a Chain of Gold and his Purse in Paul's Church in London

A gentleman of the country, who, as I have heard since the time of his mishap, whereof I am now to speak, had about half a year before buried his wife, and, belike thinking well of some other gentlewoman, whom he meant to make account of as his second choice, upon good hope or otherwise persuaded, he came up to London to provide himself of such necessaries as the country is not usually stored withal. Besides silks, velvets, cambrics and suchlike, he bought a chain of gold that cost him fifty-seven pounds and odd money, whereof, because he would have the maidenhead or first wearing himself, he presently put it on in the goldsmith's shop, and so walked therewith about London as his occasions served. But let not the gentleman be offended, who, if this book come to his hands, can best avouch the truth of this discourse, if here by the way I blame his rash pride, or simple credulity; for between the one and other, the chain he paid so dear for about ten of the clock in the morning, the cony-catchers the same day ere night shared amongst them, a matter whereat he may well grieve, and I be sorry, in respect he is my very good friend. But to the purpose. This gentleman walking in Paul's, with his chain fair glittering about his neck, talking with his man about some business, was well viewed and regarded by a crew of cony-catchers, whose teeth watered at his goodly chain, yet knew not how to come by it, hanging as it did, and therefore entered into secret conspiration among themselves, if they could not come by all the chain, yet how they might make it lighter by half a score pounds at the least. Still had they their eyes on the honest gentleman, who little doubted any such treason intended against his so late bought bargain; and they, having laid their plot, each one to be assistant in this enterprise, saw when the gentleman dismissed his servant to go about such affairs as he had appointed him, himself still walking there up and down the middle aisle.

One of these mates, that stood most on his cunning in these exploits, followed the servingman forth of the church calling him by divers names as John, Thomas, William, etc., as though he had known his right name, but could not hit on it. Which whether he did or no I know not, but well I wot the servingman turned back again, and seeing him that called him seemed a gentleman, booted and cloaked after the newest fashion, came with his hat in his hand to him, saying, 'Sir, do you call me?' – 'Marry do I, my friend,' quoth the other, 'dost not thou serve such a gentleman?' – and named one as himself pleased. 'No, truly, sir,' answered the servingman. 'I know not any such gentleman as you speak of.' – 'By my troth,' replied the cony-catcher, 'I am assured I knew thee and thy master, though now I cannot suddenly remember myself.' The servingman, fearing no harm, yet fitting the humour of this treacherous companion, told right his master's name whom he served, and that his master was even then walking in Paul's. 'O' God's will,' quoth the cony-catcher, repeating his master's name, 'a very honest gentleman. Of such a place is he not?' naming a shire of the country – for he must know both name, country, and sometimes what gentlemen dwell near the party that is to be overreached, ere he can proceed. 'No indeed sir,' answered the servingman, with such reverence as it had been to an honest gentleman indeed, 'my master is of such a place, a mile from such a town, and hard by such a knight's house.' By which report the deceiver was half instructed, because, though he was ignorant of the fellow's master, yet well he knew the country and the knight named. So craving pardon that he had mistaken him, he returns again into the church, and the servingman trudgeth about his assigned business.

Being come to the rest of the crew, he appoints one of them, whom he knew to be expert indeed, to take this matter in hand, for himself might not do it, lest the servingman should return and know him. He schooled the rest likewise what every man should do when the pinch came, and, changing his cloak with one of his fellows, walked by himself attending the feat. And everyone being as ready, the appointed fellow makes his sally forth, and coming to the gentleman, calling him by his name, gives him the courtesy and embrace, likewise thanking him for good cheer he had at his house, which he did with such seemly behaviour and protestation, as the gentleman, thinking the other to be no less, used like action of kindness to him. Now as country gentlemen have many visitors both with near-dwelling neighbours and friends that journey from far, whom they can hardly remember, but some principal one that serves as countenance to the other; so he, not discrediting the cunning mate's words, who still at every point alleged his kindred to the knight, neighbour to the gentleman, which the poor servingman had, doubting no ill, revealed before, and that both there and at his own house in hawking-time with that knight and other gentlemen of the country he had liberally tasted his kindness; desiring pardon that he had forgotten him, and offered him the courtesy of the City. The cony-catcher excused himself for that time, saying, at their next meeting he would bestow it on him. Then, seeming to have espied his chain, and commending the fairness and workmanship thereof, says: 'I pray ye, sir, take a little counsel of a friend. It may be you will return thanks for it. I wonder,' quoth he, ' you dare wear such a costly jewel so open in sight, which is even but a bait to entice bad men to adventure time and place for it, and nowhere sooner than in this city, where, I may say to you, are such a number of cony-catchers, cozeners and such like, that a man can scarcely keep any thing from them, they have so many reaches and sleights to beguile withal; which a very especial friend of mine found too true not many days since.'

Hereupon he told a very solemn tale of villainies and knaveries in his own profession, whereby he reported his friend had lost a watch of gold; showing how closely his friend wore it in his bosom, and how strangely it was gotten from him, that the gentleman by that discourse waxed half afraid of his chain, and giving him many thanks for this good warning, presently takes the chain from about his neck, and tying it up fast in a handkerchief, put it up into his sleeve, saying: 'If the cony-catcher get it here, let him not spare it.'

Not a little did the treacher smile in his sleeve, hearing the rash security but indeed simplicity of the gentleman, and no sooner saw he it put up but presently he counted it sure his own, by the assistance of his complices, that lay in an ambuscado for the purpose. With embraces and courtesies on either side, the cony-catcher departs, leaving the gentleman walking there still. Whereat the crew were not a little offended that he still kept in the church, and would not go abroad. Well, at length, belike remembering some business, the gentleman, taking leave of another that talked with him, hasted to go forth at the furthest west door of Paul's, which he that had talked with him, and gave him such counsel, perceiving, hied out of the other door, and got to the entrance ere he came forth, the rest following the gentleman at an inch. As he was stepping out, the other stepped in, and let fall a key, having his hat so low over his eyes that he could not well discern his face, and, stooping to take up the key, kept the gentleman from going backward or forward, by reason his leg was over the threshold. The foremost cony-catcher behind, pretending a quarrel unto him that stooped, rapping out an oath, and drawing his dagger, said, 'Do I meet the villain? Nay, he shall not 'scape me now,' and so made offer to strike him.

The gentleman at his standing up, seeing it was he that gave him so good counsel, and pretended himself his very friend, but never imagining this train was made for him, stepped in his defence, when the other following tripped up his heels; so that he and his counsellor were down together, and two more upon them, striking with their daggers very eagerly. Marry, indeed the gentleman had most of the blows, and both his handkerchief with the chain, and also his purse with three and fifty shillings in it, were taken out of his pocket in this struggling, even by the man that himself defended.

It was marvellous to behold how, not regarding the villain's words uttered before in the church, nor thinking upon the charge about him, which after he had thus treacherously lost unwittingly, he stands pacifying them that were not discontented but only to beguile him. But they, vowing that they would presently go for their weapons, and so to the field, told the gentleman he laboured but in vain, for fight they must and would, and so, going down by Paul's Chain,[4] left the gentleman made a cony going up toward Fleet Street, sorry for his new counsellor and friend, and wishing him good luck in the fight; which indeed was with nothing but wine pots, for joy of their late-gotten booty. Near to St Dunstan's Church, the gentleman remembered himself, and feeling his pocket so light, had suddenly more grief at his heart than ever happen to him or any man again. Back he comes to see if he could espy any of them, but they were far enough from him. God send him better hap when he goes next a-wooing, and that this his loss may be a warning to others!

How a Cunning Knave got a Trunk Well-Stuffed with Linen and Certain Parcels of Plate out of a Citizen's House, and how the Master of the House Holp the Deceiver to Carry away his Own Goods

Within the City of London dwelleth a worthy man who hath very great dealing in his trade, and his shop very well frequented with customers, had such a shrewd mischance of late by a cony-catcher, as may well serve for an example to others lest they have the like.

A cunning villain, that had long time haunted this citizen's house, and gotten many a cheat which he carried away safely, made it his custom when he wanted money, to help himself ever where he had sped so often. Divers things he had which were never missed, especially such as appertained to the citizen's trade, but when any were found wanting, they could not devise which way they were gone, so politicly this fellow always behaved himself. Well knew he what times of greatest business this citizen had in his trade, and when the shop is most stored with chapmen. Then would he step up the stairs (for there was and is another door to the house besides that which entereth into the shop), and what was next hand came ever away with. One time above the rest, in an evening about Candlemas, when daylight shuts in about six of the clock, he watched to do some feat in the house, and seeing the mistress go forth with her maid, the goodman and his folks very busy in the shop, up the stairs he goes as he was wont to do, and lifting up the latch of the hall

cheat: article, thing.
chapmen: petty traders, pedlars.

portal door, saw nobody near to trouble him, when stepping into the next chamber, where the citizen and his wife usually lay, at the bed's feet there stood a handsome trunk, wherein was very good linen, a fair gilt salt, two silver French bowls for wine, two silver drinking pots, a stone jug covered with silver, and a dozen of silver spoons. This trunk he brings to the stairs' head, and, making fast the door again, draws it down the steps so softly as he could, for it was so big and heavy, as he could not easily carry it. Having it out at the door, unseen of any neighbour or anybody else, he stood struggling with it to lift it up on the stall, which by reason of the weight troubled him very much.

The goodman coming forth of his shop, to bid a customer or two farewell, made the fellow afraid he should now be taken for all together, but, calling his wits together to escape if he could, he stood gazing up at the sign belonging to the house, as though he were desirous to know what sign it was, which the citizen perceiving, came to him and asked him what he sought for.

'I look for the sign of the "Blue Bell", sir,' quoth the fellow, 'where a gentleman having taken a chamber for this term-time hath sent me hither with this his trunk of apparel.'

Quoth the citizen, 'I know no such sign in this street, but in the next (naming it) there is such a one indeed, and there dwelleth one that letteth forth chambers to gentlemen.'

'Truly sir,' quoth the fellow,' that's the house I should go to. I pray you, sir, lend me your hand but to help the trunk on my back, for I, thinking to ease me a while upon your stall, set it short, and now I can hardly get it up again.'

The citizen, not knowing his own trunk, but indeed never thinking on any such notable deceit, helps him up with the trunk, and so sends him away roundly with his own goods. When the trunk was missed, I leave to your conceits what household grief there was on all sides, especially the goodman himself, who, remembering how he helped the fellow up with a trunk, perceived that hereby he had beguiled himself, and lost more than in haste he should recover again. How this may admonish others I leave to the judgement of the indifferent opinion, that see when honest meaning is so craftily beleaguered, as good foresight must be used to prevent such dangers.

How a Broker was Cunningly Overreached by as Crafty a Knave as himself, and Brought in Danger of the Gallows

It has been used as a common byword: *a crafty knave needeth no broker*, whereby it should appear that there can hardly be a craftier knave than a broker. Suspend your judgements till you have heard this discourse ensuing, and then, as you please, censure both the one and the other.

A lady of the country sent up a servant whom she might well put in trust, to provide her of a gown answerable to such directions as she had given him, which was of good price, as may appear by the outside and lace, whereto doubtless was every other thing agreeable. For the tailor had seventeen yards of the best black satin could be got for money, and so much gold lace, beside spangles, as valued thirteen pound. What else was beside, I know not, but let it suffice thus much was lost, and therefore let us to the manner how.

The satin and the lace being brought to the tailor that should make the gown, and spread abroad on the shop-board to be measured, certain good fellows of the cony-catching profession chanced to go by, who, seeing so rich lace and so excellent good satin, began to commune with themselves how they might make some purchase of what they had seen. And quickly it was to be done, or not at all. As ever in a crew of this quality, there is some one more ingenious and politic than the rest, or at least-wise that covets to make himself more famous than the rest, so this instant was there one in this company that did swear his cunning should deeply deceive him, but he would have both the lace and satin. When having laid the plot with his companions, how and which way their help might stand him in stead, this way they proceeded.

Well noted they the servingman that stood in the shop with the tailor, and gathered by his diligent attendance that he had some charge of the gown there to be made. Wherefore by him

broker: middleman, secondhand dealer, fence.

must they work their treachery intended, and use him as an instrument to beguile himself. One of them sitting on a seat near the tailor's stall could easily hear the talk that passed between the servingman and the tailor, where among other communication, it was concluded that the gown should be made of the self-same fashion in every point, as another lady's was, who then lay in the City; and that measure being taken by her, the same would fitly serve the lady for whom the gown was to be made. Now the servingman intended to go speak with the lady, and upon a token agreed between them (which he carelessly spake so loud that the cony-catcher heard it), he would, as her leisure served, certify the tailor, and he should bring the stuff with him, to have the lady's opinion both of the one and the other.

The servingman being gone about his affairs, the subtle mate that had listened to all their talk acquaints his fellows both with the determination and token appointed for the tailor's coming to the lady. The guide and leader to all the rest for villainy – though there was no one but was better skilled in such matters than honesty – he appoints that one of them should go to the tavern, which was not far off, and laying two faggots on the fire in a room by himself, and a quart of wine filled, for countenance of the treachery. Another of that crew should give attendance on him, as if he were his master, being bareheaded, and 'Sir' humbly answering at every word. To the tavern goes this counterfeit gentleman, and his servant waiting on him, where everything was performed as is before rehearsed, when the master-knave, calling the drawer, demanded if there dwelt near at hand a skilful tailor, that could make a suit of velvet for himself. Marry, it was to be done with very great speed!

The drawer named the tailor that we now speak of, and upon the drawer's commending his cunning, the man in all haste was sent for, to a gentleman for whom he must make a suit of velvet forthwith. Upon talk had of the stuff, how much was to be bought of everything appertaining thereto, he must immediately take measure of this counterfeit gentleman, because he knew not when to return that way again. Afterward they would go to the mercer's.

As the tailor was taking measure on him bareheaded, as if he had been a substantial gentleman indeed, the crafty mate had cunningly gotten his purse out of his pocket, at the one string whereof was fastened a little key, and at the other his signet ring. This booty he was sure of already, whether he should get anything else or no of the mischief intended. Stepping to the window, he cuts the ring from the purse, and by his supposed man, rounding him in the ear, sends it to the plotlayer of this knavery, minding to train the tailor along with him, as it were to the mercer's, while he the meantime took order for the other matter.

Afterward, speaking aloud to his man, 'Sirrah,' quoth he, 'dispatch what I bade you, and about four of the clock meet me in Paul's. By that time I hope the tailor and I shall have dispatched.' To Cheapside goeth the honest tailor with this notorious dissembler, not missing his purse for the space of two hours after, in less than half which time the satin and gold lace was gotten likewise by the other villain from the tailor's house in this order:

Being sure the tailor should be kept absent, he sends another mate home to his house, who abused his servants with this device: that the lady's man had met their master abroad, and had sent him to the other lady to take measure of her, and, lest they should delay the time too long, he was sent for the satin and lace, declaring the token appointed, and withal giving their master's signet ring for better confirmation of his message. The servants could do no less than deliver it, being commanded, as they supposed, by so credible testimony. Neither did the leisure of any one serve to go with the messenger, who seemed an honest young gentleman, and carried no cause of distrust in his countenance. Wherefore they delivered him the lace and satin, folded up together as it was, and desired him to will their master to make some speed home, both for cutting out of work and other occasions.

To a broker fit for their purpose goes this deceiver with the satin lace, who, knowing well they could not come honestly by it, nor anything else he bought of that crew, as often before he

train: take.

had dealt much with them, either gave them not so much as they would have, or at least as they judged they could have in another place, for which the ringleader of this cozenage vowed in his mind to be revenged on the broker. The master-knave, who had spent two hours and more in vain with the tailor, and would not like of any velvet he saw, when he perceived that he missed his purse, and could not devise how or where he had lost it, showed himself very sorry for his mishap, and said in the morning he would send the velvet home to his house, for he knew where to speed of better than any he had seen in the shops. Home goes the tailor very sadly, where he was entertained with a greater mischance, for there was the lady's servingman, swearing and stamping that he had not seen their master since the morning they parted, neither had he sent for the satin and lace, but, when the servants justified their innocency, beguiled both with the true token rehearsed, and their master's signet ring, it exceedeth my cunning to set down answerable words to this exceeding grief and amazement on either part, but most of all the honest tailor, who sped the better by the broker's wilfulness, as afterward it happened, which made him the better brook the loss of his purse. That night all means were used that could be, both to the mercer's, broker's, goldsmith's, gold-finer's, and such like, where haply such things do come to be sold. But all was in vain. The only help came by the inventer of this villainy, who scant sleeping all night, in regard of the broker's extreme gaining, both by him and those of his profession, the next morning he came by the tailor's house, at what time he espied him with the lady's servingman, coming forth of the doors; and into the tavern he went to report what a mishap he had upon the sending for him thither the day before.

As he was but newly entered his sad discourse, in comes the party offended with the broker, and having heard all, whereof none could make better report than himself, he takes the tailor and servingman aside, and pretending great grief for both their causes, demands what they would think him worthy of that could help them to their good again. On condition to meet with such a friend, offer was made of five pound, and after sundry

speed of: obtain.

speeches passing between them alone, he, seeming that he would work the recovery thereof by art, and they promising not to disclose the man that did them good, he drew forth a little book out of his bosom, whether it were Latin or English[5] it skilled not, for he could not read a word on it; then desiring them to spare him alone awhile, they should perceive what he would do for them. Their hearts encouraged with some good hope, kept all his words secret to themselves; and not long had they sitten absent out of the room, but he called them in again, and seeming as though he had been a scholar indeed, said he found by his figure that a broker in such a place had their goods lost, and in such a place of the house they should find it, bidding them go thither with all speed, and as they found his words, so (with reserving to themselves how they came to knowledge thereof) to meet him there again in the evening, and reward him as he had deserved.

Away in haste goes the tailor and the servingman, and entering the house with the constable, found them in the place where he that revealed it knew the broker alway laid such gotten goods. Of their joy again I leave you to conjecture, and think you see the broker with a good pair of bolts on his heels, ready to take his farewell of the world in a halter, when time shall serve. The counterfeit cunning man, and artificial cony-catcher, as I heard, was paid his five pound that night. Thus one crafty knave beguiled another. Let each take heed of dealing with any such kind of people.

FINIS

A DISPVTATION,

Betweene a Hee Conny-catcher, and a

Shee Conny-catcher, whether a Theefe or a Whoore, is
most hurtfull in Cousonage, to the Com-
mon-wealth.

DISCOVERING THE SECRET VILLA-
nies of alluring Strumpets.

With the Conuersion of an English Courtizen, reformed
this present yeare, 1592.

Reade, laugh, and learne.

Nascimur pro patria.

R. G.

Imprinted at London, by A. I. for T. G. and are to be solde at
the Westende of Paules. 1592.

To all Gentlemen, Merchants, Apprentices, and Country Farmers, Health

GENTLEMEN, countrymen, and kind friends (for so I value all that are honest and enemies of bad actions), although in my books of cony-catching I have discovered divers forms of cozenings, and painted out both the sacking and crossbiting laws which strumpets use to the destruction of the simple, yet, willing to search all the substance, as I have glanced at the shadow, and to enter into the nature of villainy, as I have broached up the secrets of vice, I have thought good to publish this dialogue or disputation between a he-cony-catcher and a she-cony-catcher, whether of them are most prejudicial to the commonwealth, discoursing the base qualities of them both, and discovering the inconvenience that grows to men through the lightness of inconstant wantons, who, being wholly given to the spoil, seek the ruin of such as light into their company. In this dialogue, loving countrymen, shall you find what prejudice ensues by haunting of whore-houses, what dangers grows by dallying with common harlots, what inconvenience follows the inordinate pleasures of unchaste libertines, not only by their consuming of their wealth, and impoverishment of their goods and lands, but to the great endangering of their health. For in conversing with them they aim not simply at the loss of goods, and blemish of their good names, but they fish for diseases, sickness, sores incurable, ulcers bursting out of the joints, and salt rheums, which by the humour of that villainy, leapt from Naples into France and from France into the bowels of England; which makes many cry out in their bones, whilst goodman Surgeon laughs in his purse; a thing to be feared as deadly while men live, as Hell is to be dreaded after death, for it not only infecteth the body, consumeth the soul, and waste[th] wealth and worship, but engraves a perpetual shame in the forehead of the party so abused. Whereof Master Huggins [1] hath well written in his *Mirror of Magistrates*, in the person of Mempricius, exclaiming against harlots. The verses be these:

Eschew vile Venus' toys; she cuts off age:
And learn this lesson oft, and tell thy friends,
By pox, death sudden, begging, harlots end.

Besides, I have here laid open the wily wisdom of overwise
courtezans, that with their cunning can draw on, not only poor
novices, but such as hold themselves masters of their occupation.
What flatteries they use to bewitch, what sweet words to inveigle,
what simple holiness to entrap, what amorous glances, what
smirking œillades, what cringing curtsies, what stretching 'adios',
following a man like a bloodhound, with their eyes white, laying
out of hair, what frouncing of tresses, what paintings, what ruffs,
cuffs and braveries – and all to betray the eyes of the innocent
novice, whom when they have drawn on to the bent of their
bow, they strip like the prodigal child, and turn out of doors
like an outcast of the world! The crocodile hath not more
tears, Proteus more shape, Janus more faces, the hieria [2] more
sundry tunes to entrap the passengers, than our English courtezans – to be plain, our English whores – to set on fire the hearts
of lascivious and gazing strangers. These common, or rather
consuming, strumpets, whose throats are softer than oil, and
yet whose steps lead unto death. They have their ruffians to
rifle, when they cannot fetch over with other cunning, their
crossbiters attending upon them, their foists, their buffs, their
nips, and suchlike. Being waited on by these villains, as by
ordinary servants, so that who thinks himself wise enough to
escape their flatteries, him they crossbite; who holds himself
to rule, to be bitten with a counterfeit apparitor, him they rifle;
if he be not so to be versed upon, they have a foist or a nip
upon him, and so sting him to the quick. Thus he that meddles
with pitch cannot but be defiled, and he that acquainteth himself or converseth with any of these cony-catching strumpets,
cannot but by some way or other be brought to confusion. For
either he must hazard his soul, blemish his good name, lose his
goods, light upon diseases, or at the least have been tied to the
humour of an harlot, whose quiver is open to every arrow, who
likes all that have fat purses, and loves none that are destitute

buffs: original 'bufts': bum-bailiffs.

of pence. I remember a monk *in diebus illis* writ his opinion of the end of an adulterer thus:

> *Quattuor his casibus sine dubio cadet adulter,*
> *Aut hic pauper erit, aut hic subito morietur,*
> *Aut cadet in causum qua debet judice vinci,*
> *Aut aliquod membrum casu vel crimine, perdet.*

Which I Englished thus:

> *He that to harlots' lures do yield him thrall,*
> *Through sour misfortune to bad end shall fall:*
> *Or sudden death, or beggary shall him chance,*
> *Or guilt before a judge his shame enhance:*
> *Or else by fault or fortune he shall leese,*
> *Some member sure escape from one of these.*

Seeing then such inconvenience grows from the caterpillars of the commonwealth, and that a multitude of the monsters here about London, particularly and generally abroad in England, to the great overthrow of many simple men that are inveigled by their flatteries, I thought good not only to discover their villainies in a dialogue, but also to manifest by an example how prejudicial their life is to the state of the land, that such as are warned by an instance, may learn and look before they leap. To that end, kind countrymen, I have set down at the end of the disputation the wonderful life of a courtezan; not a fiction, but a truth of one that yet lives, but now in another form repentant; in the discourse of whose life, you shall see how dangerous such trulls be to all estates that be so simple as to trust their feigned subtleties. Here shall parents learn how hurtful it is to cocker up their youth in their follies, and have a deep insight how to bridle their daughters, if they see them anyways grow wantons. Wishing therefore my labours may be a caveat to my countrymen to avoid the company of such cozening courtezans,

Farewell. R.G.

leese: lose, destroy.

A Disputation between Laurence, a Foist, and Fair Nan, a Traffic, Whether a Whore or a Thief is Most Prejudicial.

LAURENCE. Fair Nan, well met! What news about your Vine Court [3] that you look so blithe? Your cherry cheeks discovers your good fare, and your brave apparel bewrays a fat purse. Is Fortune now a-late grown so favourable to foists, that your husband hath lighted on some large purchase, or hath your smooth looks linked in some young novice to sweat for a favour all the bite in his bung, and to leave himself as many crowns as thou hast good conditions, and then he shall be one of Pierce Penilesse's [4] fraternity? How is it, sweet wench? Goes the world on wheels, that you tread so daintily on your tiptoes?

NAN. Why, Laurence, are you pleasant or peevish that you quip with such brief girds? Think you a quartern-wind cannot make a quick sail, that easy lists cannot make heavy burthens, that women have not wiles to compass crowns as well as men; yes, and more, for though they be not so strong in the fists, they be more ripe in their wits, and 'tis by wit that I live and will live, in despite of that peevish scholar, that thought with his cony-catching books to have crossbit our trade. Dost thou marvel to see me thus brisked? Fair wenches cannot want favours, while the world is so full of amorous fools. Where can such girls as myself be blemished with a threadbare coat, as long as country farmers have full purses, and wanton citizens pockets full of pence?

LAURENCE. Truth, if fortune so favour thy husband, that he be neither smoked nor cloyed, for I am sure all thy bravery comes by his nipping, foisting and lifting.

NAN. In faith, sir, no! Did I get no more by mine own wit than I reap by his purchase, I might both go bare and penniless the whole year. But mine eyes are stalls, and my hands lime-

girds: biting remarks.
brisked: dolled up.
cloyed: obstructed.

twigs, else were I not worthy the name of a she-cony-catcher.
Circe had never more charms, Calypso [5] more enchantment, the
sirens more subtle tunes, than I have crafty sleights to inveigle
a cony and fetch in a country farmer. Laurence, believe me, you
men are but fools, your gettings is uncertain, and yet you still
fish for the gallows. Though by some great chance you light
upon a good bung, yet you fast a great while after; whereas
[as] we mad wenches have our tenants – for so I call every
simple lecher and amorous fox – as well out of term as in
term to bring us our rents. Alas! were not my wits and my
wanton pranks more profitable than my husband's foisting, we
might often go to bed supperless for want of surfeiting, and yet,
I dare swear, my husband gets a hundred pounds a year by
bungs.

LAURENCE. Why, Nan, are you grown so stiff, to think that
your fair looks can get as much as our nimble fingers, or that
your sacking can gain as much as our foisting? No, no, Nan,
you are two bows down the wind. Our foist will get more than
twenty the proudest wenches in all London.

NAN. Lie a little further and give me some room. What,
Laurence, your tongue is too lavish; all stands upon proof, and
sith I have leisure and you no great business, as being now
when Paul's is shut up, and all purchases and conies in their
burrows, let us to the tavern and take a room to ourselves, and
there, for the price of our suppers, I will prove that women, I
mean of our faculty, a traffic, or, as base knaves term us,
strumpets, are more subtle, more dangerous in the commonwealth, and more full of wiles to get crowns, than the cun-
ningest foist, nip, lift, prags, or whatsoever that lives at this
day.

LAURENCE. Content. But who shall be moderator in our con-
troversies, sith in disputing *pro* and *contra* betwixt ourselves,
it is but your Yea and my Nay, and so neither of us will yield to
other's victories.

NAN. Trust me Laurence; I am so assured of the conquest,
offering so in the strength of mine own arguments, that when I
have reasoned, I will refer it to your judgement and censure.

lime-twigs: twigs spread with wet lime to trap birds.

LAURENCE. And trust me as I am an honest man, I will be indifferent.

NAN. Oh swear not so deeply, but first let me hear what you can say for yourself.

LAURENCE. What? Why more, Nan, than can be painted out in a great volume; but briefly this: I need not describe the laws of villainy, because R.G. hath so amply penned them down in the *First Part of Cony-Catching*, that though I be one of the faculty, yet I cannot discover more than he hath laid open.

Therefore first to the gentleman-foist. I pray you what finer quality, what art is more excellent, either to try the ripeness of the wit, or the agility of the hand, than that for him that will be master of his trade must pass the proudest juggler alive the points of legerdemain; he must have an eye to spy the bung, or purse, and then a heart to dare to attempt it – for this by the way, he that fears the gallows shall never be good thief while he lives. He must as the cat watch for a mouse, and walk Paul's, Westminster, the Exchange, and such common-haunted places, and there have a curious eye to the person, whether he be gentleman, citizen, or farmer, and note, either where his bung lies, whether in his hose or pockets, and then dog the party into a press where his stall with heaving and shoving shall so molest him, that he shall not feel when we strip him of his bung, although it be never so fast or cunningly couched about him. What poor farmer almost can come to plead his case at the bar, to attend upon his lawyer's at the bench, but, look he never so narrowly to it, we have his purse, wherein sometime there is fat purchase, twenty or thirty pounds. And I pray you, how long would one of your traffics be earning so much with your chamber work? Besides, in fairs and markets, and in the circuits after judges, what infinite money is gotten from honest-meaning men, that either busy about their necessary affairs, or carelessly looking to their crowns, light amongst us that be foists? Tush, we dissemble in show, we go so neat in apparel, so orderly in outward appearance, some like lawyers' clerks, others like servingmen, that attended there about their masters' business, that we are hardly smoked, versing upon all men with kind courtesies and fair

First Part: i.e. *A Notable Discovery of Cozenage.*

words, and yet being so warily watchful, that a good purse cannot be put up in a fair, but we sigh if we share it not amongst us. And though the books of cony-catching hath somewhat hindered us, and brought many brave foists to the halter, yet some of our country farmers, nay, of our gentlemen and citizens, are so careless in a throng of people, that they show us the prey, and so draw on a thief, and bequeath us their purses, whether we will or no, for who loves wine so ill, that he will not eat grapes if they fall into his mouth, and who is so base, that if he see a pocket fair before him, will not foist it if he may, or, if foisting will not serve, use his knife and nip; for, although there be some foists that will not use their knives, yet I hold him not a perfect workman or master of his mystery that will not cut a purse as well as foist a pocket, and hazard any limb for so sweet a gain as gold. How answer you me this brief objection, Nan? Can you compare with either our cunning to get o[u]r gains in purchase?

NAN. And have you no stronger arguments, Goodman Laurence, to argue your excellency in villainy but this? Then in faith put up your pipes, and give me leave to speak. Your choplogic hath no great subtlety, for simple you reason of foisting, and appropriate that to yourselves, to you men I mean, as though there were not women foists and nips as neat in that trade as you, of as good an eye, as fine and nimble a hand, and of as resolute a heart, yes Laurence, and your good mistresses in that mystery, for we without like suspicion can pass in your walks under the colour of simplicity to Westminster, with a paper in our hand, as if we were distressed women that had some supplication to put up to the judges, or some bill of information to deliver to our lawyers, when, God wot, we shuffle in for a bung as well as the best of you all, yea, as yourself, Laurence, though you be called King of Cutpurses, for though they smoke you, they will hardly mistrust us, and suppose our stomach stand against it to foist, yet who can better play the stall or the shadow than we, for in a thrust or throng, if we shove hard, who is he that will not favour a woman, and in giving place to us, give you free passage for his purse? Again,

our stomach stand against it : we are disinclined to.

in the market, when every wife hath almost her hand on her bung, and that they cry, 'Beware the cutpurse and cony-catchers!' then I as fast as the best, with my hand-basket as mannerly as if I were to buy great store of butter and eggs for provision of my house, do exclaim against them with my hand on my purse, and say the world is bad when a woman cannot walk safely to market for fear of these villainous cut-purses, whenas the first bung I come to, I either nip or foist, or else stall another while he hath strucken, dispatched, and gone. Now I pray you, gentle sir, wherein are we inferior to you in foisting? And yet this is nothing to the purpose, for it is one of our most simplest shifts. But yet I pray you, what think you when a farmer, gentleman, or citizen, come to the term? Perhaps he is wary of his purse, and watch him never so warily, yet he will never be brought to the blow. Is it not possible for us to pinch him ere he pass? He that is most chary of his crowns abroad, and will cry, ' 'Ware the cony-catchers', will not be afraid to drink a pint of wine with a pretty wench, and perhaps go to a trugging-house to ferry out one for his purpose. Then with what cunning we can feed the simple fop, with what fair words, sweet kisses, feigned sighs, as if at that instant we fell in love with him that we never saw before! If we meet him in an evening in the street, if the farmer or other whatsoever be not so forward as to motion some courtesy to us, we straight insinuate into his company, and claim acquaintance of him by some means or other, and if his mind be set for lust, and the devil drive him on to match himself with some dishonest wanton, then let him look to his purse, for if he do but kiss me in the street, I'll have his purse for a farewell, although he never commit any other act at all. I speak not this only by myself, Laurence, for there be a hundred in London more cunning than myself in this kind of cony-catching. But if he come into a house, then let our trade alone to verse upon him, for first we feign ourselves hungry, for the benefit of the house, although our bellies were never so full, and no doubt the good pander or bawd she comes forth like a sober matron, and sets store of cates on the table, and then I

house: brothel.
cates: sweetmeats.

fall aboard on them, and though I can eat little, yet I make havoc of all. And let him be sure every dish is well sauced, for he shall pay for a pippin-pie that cost in the market fourpence, at one of the trugging-houses eighteenpence. Tush! what is dainty if it be not dear bought, and yet he must come off for crowns besides, and when I see him draw to his purse, I note the putting up of it well, and ere we part, that world goes hard if I foist him not of all that he hath. And then, suppose the worst, that he miss it, am I so simply acquainted or badly provided, that I have not a friend, which with a few terrible oaths and countenance set, as if he were the proudest soldado that ever bare arms against Don John of Austria, will face him quite out of his money, and make him walk like a woodcock homeward by weeping cross, and so buy repentance with all the crowns in his purse? How say you to this, Laurence, whether are women-foists inferior to you in ordinary cozenage or no?

LAURENCE. Excellently well reasoned, Nan. Thou hast told me wonders, but wench, though you be wily and strike often, your blows are not so big as ours.

NAN. Oh, but note the subject of our disputation, and that is this: which are more subtle and dangerous in the commonwealth, and to that I argue.

LAURENCE. Ay, and beshrew me, but you reason quaintly. Yet will I prove your wits are not so ripe as ours, nor so ready to reach into the subtleties of kind cozenage, and though you appropriate to yourself the excellency of cony-catching, and that you do it with more art than we men do, because of your painted flatteries and sugared words that you flourish rhetorically like nets to catch fools, yet will I manifest with a merry instance a feat done by a foist, that exceeded any that ever was done by any mad wench in England.

A Pleasant Tale of a Country Farmer, that Took it in Scorn to have his Purse Cut or Drawn from him, and how a Foist Served Him

It was told me for a truth that not long since, here in London, there lay a country farmer, with divers of his neighbours, about

quaintly: ingeniously.

law matters, amongst whom, one of them going to Westminster Hall, was by a foist stripped of all the pence in his purse, and, coming home, made great complaint of his misfortune. Some lamented his loss, and others exclaimed against the cutpurses, but this farmer he laughed loudly at the matter, and said such fools as could not keep their purses no surer were well served. 'And for my part,' quoth he, 'I so much scorn the cutpurses, that I would thank him heartily that would take pains to foist mine.' – 'Well,' says his neighbour, 'then you may thank me, sith my harms learns you to beware. But if it be true that many things fall out between the cup and the lip, you know not what hands Fortune may light in your own lap.' – 'Tush,' quoth the farmer, 'here's forty pounds in this purse in gold. The proudest cutpurse in England win it and wear it.' As thus he boasted, there stood a subtle foist by and heard all, smiling to himself at the folly of the proud farmer, and vowed to have his purse or venture his neck for it, and so went home and bewrayed it to a crew of his companions, who taking it in dudgeon that they should be put down by a peasant, met either at Laurence Pickering's [6] or at Lambeth. Let the blackamoor take heed I name him not, lest an honourable neighbour of his frown at it, but wheresoever they met they held a convocation, and both consulted and concluded all by a general consent to bend all their wits to be possessors of this farmer's bung; and for the execution of this their vow, they haunted about the inn where he lay, and dogged him into divers places, both to Westminster Hall and other places, and yet could never light upon it. He was so watchful and smoked them so narrowly, that all their travail was in vain. At last one of them fled to a more cunning policy, and went and learned the man's name and where he dwelt, and then hied him to the Counter and entered an action against him of trespass,[7] damages two hundred pounds. When he had thus done, he feed two sergeants, and carried them down with him to the man's lodging, wishing them not to arrest him till he commanded them. Well agreed they were, and down to the farmer's lodging they came, where were a crew of foists, whom he had made privy to the end of his practice, stood waiting. But he took no knowledge at all of them, but walked up and down. The farmer came out and went to Paul's. The cutpurse bade stay, and would not yet suffer the officers to meddle with him, till he came into the west end of Paul's Churchyard, and there he willed them to do their office, and they, stepping to the farmer, arrested him. The farmer amazed, being amongst his neighbours, asked the sergeant at whose suit he was troubled.

'At whose suit soever it be,' said one of the cutpurses that stood by, 'you are wronged, honest man, for he hath arrested you here in a place of privilege,[8] where the Sheriffs nor the officers have nothing to do with you, and therefore you are unwise if you obey him.'

'Tush,' says another cutpurse, 'though the man were so simple of himself, yet shall he not offer the Church so much wrong, as by yielding to the mace, to imbolish Paul's liberty, and therefore I will take his part.' And with that he drew his sword.

Another took the man and haled him away. The officer, he stuck hard to him, and said he was his true prisoner, and cried 'Clubs!' The prentices arose, and there was a great hurlyburly, for they took the officer's part, so that the poor farmer was mightily turmoiled amongst them, and almost haled in pieces. Whilst thus the strife was, one of the foists had taken his purse away, and was gone, and the officer carried the man away to a tavern, for he swore he knew no such man, nor any man that he was indebted to. As then they sat drinking of a quart of wine, the foist that had caused him to be arrested sent a note by a porter to the officer that he should release the farmer, for he had mistaken the man; which note the officer showed him, and bade him pay his fees and go his ways. The poor countryman was content with that, and put his hand in his pocket to feel for his purse, and, God wot, there was none, which made his heart far more cold than the arrest did, and with that, fetching a great sigh he said:

'Alas! masters, I am undone! My purse in this fray is taken out of my pocket and ten pounds in gold in it besides white money.'

'Indeed,' said the sergeant, 'commonly in such brawls the

imbolish: interfere with.
Clubs!: traditional rallying-cry of London apprentices.

cutpurses be busy, and I pray God the quarrel was not made upon purpose by the pickpockets.'

'Well,' says his neighbour, 'who shall smile at you now? The other day when I lost my purse you laughed at me.'

The farmer brook all, and sat malcontent, and borrowed money of his neighbours to pay the sergeant, and had a learning I believe ever after to brave the cutpurse.

How say you to this, Mistress Nan? Was it not well done? What choice-witted wench of your faculty, or the foist, hath ever done the like? Tush Nan, if we begin once to apply our wits, all your inventions are follies towards ours.

NAN. You say good, Goodman Laurence, as though your subtleties were sudden as women's are. Come but to the old proverb, and I put you down: 'Tis as hard to find a hare without a muse, as a woman without a 'scuse; and that wit that can devise a cunning lie, can plot the intent of deep villainies. I grant this fetch of the foist was pretty, but nothing in respect of that we wantons can compass. And, therefore, to quit your tale with another, hear what a mad wench of my profession did alate to one of your faculty.

A Passing Pleasant Tale how a Whore Cony-Catched a Foist

There came out of the country a foist, to try his experience here in Westminster Hall, and struck a hand or two, but the devil a snap he would give to our citizen-foists, but wrought warily, and could not be fetched off by no means; and yet it was known he had some twenty pounds about him; but he had planted it so cunningly in his doublet, that it was sure enough for finding. Although the city foist[s] laid all the plots they could, as well by discovering him to the jailers as otherways, yet he was so politic that they could not verse upon him by any means, which grieved them so, that one day at a dinner they held a council amongst themselves how to cozen him, but in vain; till at last a good wench that sat by undertook it, so they would swear to let her have all that he had. They confirmed it solemnly, and she put it in practice thus: she subtly insinuated herself into this

muse: meuse, loophole, gap in hedge.

foist's company, who seeing her a pretty wench, began, after twice meeting, to wax familiar with her, and to question about a night's lodging. After a little nice loving and bidding, she was content for her supper and what else he would of courtesy bestow upon her, for she held it scorn, she said, to set a salary price on her body. The foist was glad of this, and yet he would not trust her, so that he put no more but ten shillings in his pocket; but he had above twenty pounds twilted in his doublet. Well, to be short, supper-time came, and thither comes my gentle foist, who making good cheer, was so eager of his game, that he would straight to bed by the leave of Dame Bawd, who had her fee too; and there he lay till about midnight, when three or four old hacksters whom she had provided upon purpose came to the door and rapped lustily.

'Who is there?' says the bawd, looking out of the window.

Marry, say they, such a Justice, and named one about the City that is a mortal enemy to cutpurses – 'who is come to search your house for a Jesuit and other suspected persons'.

'Alas sir,' says she; 'I have none here.'

'Well,' quoth they, 'ope the door.'

'I will,' says she, and with that she came into the foist's chamber, who heard all this, and was afraid it was some search for him, so that he desired the bawd to help him that he might not be seen.

'Why then,' quoth she, 'step into this closet.'

He whipped in hastily, and never remembered his clothes. She locked him in safe, and then let in the crew of rakehells, who, making as though they searched every chamber, came at last into that where his leman lay, and asked her what she was. She, as if she had been afraid, desired their worships to be good to her. She was a poor country maid come up to the term.

'And who is that,' quoth they, 'that was in bed with you?'

'None forsooth!' says she.

'No?' says one. 'That is a lie. Here is the print of two; and, besides, wheresoever the fox is, here is his skin, for this is his doublet and hose.'

twilted: ? 'twitched', tightly secured.
hacksters: bully boys.

Then down she falls upon her knees, and says, indeed it was her husband.

'Your husband?' quoth they. 'Nay, that cannot be so, minion, for why then would you have denied him at the first.' With that one of them turned to the bawd, and did question with her what he was and where he was.

'Truly, sir,' says she, 'they came to my house, and said they were man and wife, and for my part I know them for no other, and he, being afraid, is indeed, to confess the truth, shut up in the closet.'

'No doubt, if it please your worships,' says one rakehell, 'I warrant you he is some notable cutpurse or pickpocket, that is afraid to show his face. Come and open the closet, and let us look on him.'

'Nay, sir,' says she. 'Not for tonight, I beseech your worship; carry no man out of my house, I will give my word he shall be forthcoming tomorrow morning.'

'Your word, Dame Bawd,' says one. ''Tis not worth a straw. You, housewife, that says ye are his wife, ye shall go with us; and for him, that we may be sure he may not start, I'll take his doublet, hose and cloak, and tomorrow I'll send them to him by one of my men. Were there a thousand pounds in them, there shall not be a penny diminished.'

The whore kneeled down on her knees and feigned to cry pitifully, and desired the Justice (which was one of her companions) not to carry her to prison.

'Yes, housewife,' quoth he, 'your mate and you shall not tarry together in one house, that you may make your tales all one. And therefore bring her away. And after ye, dame Bawd! See you lend him no other clothes, for I will send his in the morning betimes; and come you with him to answer for lodging him.'

'I will, sir,' says she. And so away goes the wench and her companions laughing, and left the bawd and the foist. As soon as the bawd thought good, she unlocked the closet, and cursed the time that ever they came in her house. 'Now,' quoth she, 'here will be a fair ado. How will you answer for yourself? I fear me I shall be in danger of the cart.'

'Well,' quoth he, 'to be short, I would not for forty pounds come afore the Justice.'

'Marry, no more would I,' quoth she. 'Let me shift if you were conveyed hence, but I have not a rag of man's apparel in the house.'

'Why,' quoth he, 'seeing it is early morning, lend me a blanket to put about me, and I will 'scape to a friend's house of mine.'

'Then leave me a pawn,' quoth the bawd.

'Alas! I have none,' says he, 'but this ring on my finger.'

'Why that,' quoth she; 'or tarry while the Justice comes.'

So he gave it her, took the blanket and went his ways, whither I know not, but to some friend's house of his. Th[u]s was this wily foist by the wit of a subtle wench cunningly stripped of all that he had, and turned to grass to get more fat.

How say you to this device, Laurence? Was it not excellent? What think you of a woman's wit if it can work such wonders?

LAURENCE. Marry, I think my mother was wiser than all the honest women of the parish besides.

NAN. Why then, belike she was of our faculty, and a matron of my profession, nimble of her hands, quick of tongue and light of her tail; I should have put in 'sir reverence', but a foul word is good enough for a filthy knave.

LAURENCE. I am glad you are so pleasant, Nan. You were not so merry when you went to Dunstable. But, indeed, I must needs confess that women-foists, if they be careful in their trades, are, though not so common yet more dangerous than men-foists. Women have quick wits, as they have short heels, and they can get with pleasure what we fish for with danger. But now, giving you the bucklers at this weapon, let me have a blow with you at another.

NAN. But before you induce any more arguments, by your leave in a little by-talk. You know, Laurence, that, though you can foist, nip, prig, lift, curb, and use the black art, yet you cannot crossbite without the help of a woman, which crossbiting nowadays is grown to a marvellous profitable exercise; for some cowardly knaves that, for fear of the gallows, leave nipping and foisting, become crossbites, knowing there is no danger therein

have short heels: are lascivious.

but a little punishment, at the most the pillory, and *that* is saved with a little *unguentum aureum*. As, for example, Jack Rhodes is now a reformed man. Whatsoever he hath been in his youth, now in his latter days he is grown a corrector of vice, for whomsoever he takes suspicious with his wife, I warrant you he sets a sure fine on head, though he hath nothing for his money but a bare kiss. And in this art we poor wenches are your surest props and stay. If you will not believe me, ask poor A.B. in Turnmill Street what a saucy signor there is, whose purblind eyes can scarcely discern a louse from a flea, and yet he hath such insight into the mystical trade of crossbiting, that he can furnish his board with a hundred pounds' worth of plate. I doubt the sand-eyed ass will kick like a western pug if I rub him on the gall. But 'tis no matter if he find himself touched, and stir, although he boasts of the chief of the clergy's favour. Yet I'll so set his name out, that the boys at Smithfield Bars [9] shall chalk him on the back for a crossbite. Tush, you men are fops in fetching novices over the coals. Hearken to me, Laurence. I'll tell thee a wonder.

Not far off from Hogsdon (perhaps it *was* there) – and if you think I lie, ask Master Richard Chot and Master Richard Strong, two honest gentlemen, that can witness as well as I this proof of a woman's wit – there dwelt here sometimes a good ancient matron, that had a fair wench to her daughter, as young and tender as a morrow-mass priest's leman. Her she set out to sale in her youth, and drew on sundry to be suitors to her daughter, some wooers, and some speeders. Yet none married her, but of her beauty they made a profit, and inveigled all, till they had spent upon her what they had, and then, forsooth, she and her young pigeon turn them out of doors like prodigal children. She was acquainted with Dutch and French, Italian and Spaniard, as well as English, and at last, as so often the pitcher goes to the brook that it comes broken home, my fair daughter was hit on the master-vein and gotten with child. Now the mother, to colour this matter to save her daughter's mar-

unguentum aureum : literally salve of gold; hence 'greasing the palm'.
Hogsdon : Hoxton, at this time an area of ill repute.
morrow-mass : day's first mass.

riage, begins to wear a cushion under her own kirtle, and to feign herself with child, but let her daughter pass as though she ailed nothing. When the forty weeks were come, and that my young mistress must needs cry out forsooth, this old B. had gotten housewives answerable to herself, and so brought her daughter to bed, and let her go up and down the house; and the old crone lay in childbed as though she had been delivered, and said the child was hers, and so saved her daughter's scape. Was not this a witty wonder, Master Laurence, wrought by an old witch, to have a child in her age, and make a young whore seem an honest virgin? Tush! this is little to the purpose. If I should recite all, how many she had cozened under the pretence of marriage! Well, poor plain signor, see, you were not stiff enough for her, although it cost you many crowns and the loss of your service. I'll say no more. Perhaps she will amend her manners.

Ah, Laurence, how like you of this gear? In crossbiting we put you down; for God wot it is little looked to in and about London, and yet I may say to thee, many a good citizen is crossbit in the year by odd walkers abroad. I heard some named the other day as I was drinking at the 'Swan' in Lambeth Marsh. But let them alone; 'tis a foul bird that defiles the own nest, and it were a shame for me to speak against any good wenches or boon companions, that by their wits can wrest money from a churl. I fear me R.G. will name them too soon in his *Black Book*. A pestilence on him! They say he hath there set down my husband's pedigree, and yours too, Laurence. If he do it, I fear me your brother-in-law Bull[10] is like to be troubled with you both.

LAURENCE. I know not what to say to him, Nan. Hath plagued me already. I hope he hath done with me. And yet I heard say he would have about at my nine-holes. But, leaving him as an enemy of our trade, again to our disputation. I cannot deny, Nan, but you have set down strange precedents of women's prejudicial wits, but yet, though you be crossbites, foists and nips, yet you are not good lifts, which is a great help to our faculty, to filch a bolt of satin or velvet.

scape: transgression.
my nine-holes: i.e. my game.

NAN. Stay thee a word. I thought thou hadst spoken of R.B. of Long Lane and his wife. Take heed, they be parlous folks, and greatly acquainted with keepers and jailers. Therefore meddle not you with them, for I hear say, R.G. hath sworn, in despite of the Brazil staff, to tell such a foul tale of him in his *Black Book*, that it will cost him a dangerous joint.

LAURENCE. Nan, Nan, let R.G. beware! For had not an ill fortune fallen to one of R.B. his friends, he could take little harm.

NAN. Who is that, Laurence?

LAURENCE. Nay, I will not name him.

NAN. Why then I prithee what misfortune befell him?

LAURENCE. Marry, Nan, he was strangely washed alate by a French barber, and had all the hair of his face miraculously shaven off by the scythe of God's vengeance, insomuch that some said he had that he had not, but, as hap was, howsoever his hair fell off, it stood him in some stead when the brawl was alate, for if he had not cast off his beard, and so being unknown, it had cost him some knocks, but it fell out to the best.

NAN. The more hard fortune that he had such ill hap. But hasty journeys breed dangerous sweats, and the physicians call it the Ale Peria. Yet omitting all this, again to where you left.

LAURENCE. You have almost brought me out of my matter. But I was talking about the lift, commending what a good quality it was, and how hurtful it was, seeing we practise it in mercers' shops, with haberdashers of small wares, haberdashers of hats and caps, amongst merchant tailors for hose and doublets, and in such places, getting much gains by lifting, when there is no good purchase abroad by foisting.

NAN. Suppose you are good at the lift, who be more cunning than we women, in that we are more trusted, for they little suspect us, and we have as close conveyance as you men. Though you have cloaks, we have skirts or gowns, hand-baskets, the crowns of our hats, our plackets, and, for a need, false bags

Brazil staff : Brazil wood was used for clubs and staffs.
washed . . . barber : i.e. caught the pox.
Ale Peria : for alopecia or mange.
plackets : slits in petticoats or skirts.

under our smocks, wherein we can convey more closely than you.

LAURENCE. I know not where to touch you, you are so witty in your answers, and have so many starting-holes. But let me be pleasant with you a little. What say you to prigging or horse-stealing? I hope you never had experience in that faculty?

NAN. Alas, simple sot! Yes, and more shift to shun the gallows than you.

LAURENCE. Why, 'tis impossible!

NAN. In faith, sir, no. And for proof I will put you down with a story of a mad merry little dapper fine wench, who at Spilsby Fair had three horse of her own or another man's to sell. As she, her husband, and another good fellow walked them up and down the fair, the owner came and apprehended them all, and clapped them in prison. The jailer not keeping them close prisoners, but letting them lie all in a chamber, by her wit she so instructed them in a formal tale, that she saved all their lives thus. Being brought the next morrow after their apprehension before the Justices, they examined the men how they came by those horses, and they confessed they met her with them, but where she had them they knew not. Then was my pretty piece brought in, who, being a handsome trull, blushed as if she had been full of grace, and, being demanded where she had the horses, made this answer:

'May it please your worships, this man being my husband, playing the unthrift as many more have done, was absent from me for a quarter of a year, which grieved me not a little; insomuch that, desirous to see him, and having intelligence he would be at Spilsby Fair, I went thither even for pure love of him on foot, and, being within some ten miles of the town, I waxed passing weary and rested me often and grew very faint. At last there came riding by me a servingman in a blue coat, with three horses tied one at another's tail, which he led, as I guessed, to sell at the fair. The servingman, seeing me so tired, took pity on me, and asked me if I would ride on one of his empty horses, for his own would not bear double. I thanked him heartily, and at the next hill got up, and rode till we came

Spilsby Fair: held at Whitsuntide in Spilsby, Lincolnshire.

to a town within three miles of Spilsby, where the servingman
alighted at a house, and bade me ride on afore, and he would
presently overtake me. Well, forward I rode half a mile, and
looking behind me could see nobody. So, being alone, my heart
began to rise, and I to think of my husband. As I had rid a little
farther, looking down a lane, I saw two men coming lustily up
as if they were weary, and marking them earnestly, I saw one of
them was my husband, which made my heart as light as before
it was sad. So staying for them, after a little unkind greeting betwixt us, for I chid him for his unthriftiness, he asked me where
I had the horse, and I told him how courteously the servingman had used me. "Why then," says he, "stay for him." – "Nay,"
quoth I, "let's ride on, and get you two up on the empty horses,
for he will overtake us ere we come at the town. He rides on a
stout lusty young gelding." So forward we went, and looked
often behind us; but our servingman came not. At last we coming to Spilsby alighted, and broke out fast, and tied our horses
at the door, that if he passed by, seeing them, he might call in.
After we had broke our fast, thinking he had gone some other
way, we went into the horse fair, and there walked our horses
up and down to meet with the servingman, not for the intent
to sell them. Now may it please your worship, whether he had
stolen the horses from this honest man or no, I know not. But
alas! simply I brought them to the horse fair, to let him that delivered me them have them again, for I hope your worships doth
imagine, if I had stolen them as it is suspected, I would never
have brought them into so public a place to sell. Yet if the law
be any way dangerous for the foolish deed, because I know not
the servingman, it is I must bide the punishment, and as guiltless as any here.'

And so, making a low curtsy, she ended, the Justice holding
up his hand and wondering at the woman's wit, that had cleared
her husband and his friend, and saved herself without compass
of law. How like you of this, Laurence? Cannot we wenches
prig well?

LAURENCE. By God, Nan: I think I shall be fain to give you
the bucklers.

NAN. Alas! good Laurence, thou art no logician. Thou canst

not reason for thyself, nor hast no witty arguments to draw me to an exigent. And therefore give me leave at large to reason for this supper. Remember the subject of our disputation is this positive question, whether whores or thieves are most prejudicial to the commonwealth. Alas! you poor thieves do only steal and purloin from men, and the harm you do is to imbolish men's goods, and bring them to poverty. This is the only end of men's thievery, and the greatest prejudice that grows from robbing or filching. So much do we by our theft, and more by our lechery, for what is the end of whoredom but consuming of goods and beggary, and, besides, perpetual infamy? We bring young youths to ruin and utter destruction. I pray you, Laurence, whether had a merchant's son, having wealthy parents, better light upon a whore than a cutpurse, the one only taking his money, the other bringing him to utter confusion; for if the foist light upon him, or the cony-catcher, he loseth at the most some hundred pounds; but if he fall into the company of a whore, she flatters him, she inveigles him, she bewitcheth him, that he spareth neither goods nor lands to content her, that is only in love with his coin. If he be married, he forsakes his wife, leaves his children, despiseth his friends, only to satisfy his lust with the love of a base whore, who, when he hath spent all upon her and he brought to beggary, beateth him out like the prodigal child, and for a small reward, brings him, if to the fairest end, to beg, if to the second, to the gallows, or at the last and worst, to the pox, or as prejudicial diseases.

I pray you, Laurence, when any of you come to your confession at Tyburn, what is your last sermon that you make? – that you were brought to that wicked and shameful end by following of harlots. For to that end do you steal, to maintain whores, and to content their bad humours. Oh, Laurence! enter into your own thoughts, and think what the fair words of a wanton will do, what the smiles of a strumpet will drive a man to act, into what jeopardy a man will thrust himself for her that he loves, although for his sweet villainy he be brought to loathsome leprosy. Tush, Laurence, they say the pox came from Naples, some from Spain, some from France, but wheresoever it first grew, it is so surely now rooted in England, that by S.

(*Syth*) it may be called a *morbus Anglicus* than *Gallicus*! And I hope you will grant all these French favours grew from whores. Besides in my high loving, or rather creeping, I mean where men and women do rob together, there always the woman is most bloody, for she always urgeth unto death, and, though the men would only satisfy themselves with the party's coin, yet she endeth her theft in blood, murdering parties, so deeply as she is malicious.

I hope, gentle Laurence, you cannot contradict these reasons: they be so openly manifestly probable. For mine own part, I hope you do not imagine but I have had some friends besides poor George my husband. Alas! he knows it, and is content like an honest simple suffragan, to be co-rival with a number of other good companions; and I have made many a good man, I mean a man that hath a household, for the love of me to go home and beat his poor wife, when, God wot, I mock him for the money he spent, and he had nothing for his pence but the waste beleavings of other's beastly labours. Laurence, Laurence, if concubines could inveigle Solomon, if Delilah could betray Samson, then wonder not if we, more nice in our wickedness than a thousand such Delilahs, can seduce poor young novices to their utter destructions! Search the jails. There you shall hear complaints of whores. Look into the spitals and hospitals. There you shall see men diseased of the French marbles, giving instruction to others that are said to beware of whores. Be an auditor or ear-witness at the death of any thief, and his last testament is, 'Take heed of a whore.' I dare scarce speak of Bridewell, because my shoulders tremble at the name of it, I have so often deserved it. Yet look but in there, and you shall hear poor men with their hands in their pigeon-holes cry, 'Oh fie upon whores!' when Fowler [11] gives them the terrible lash. Examine beggars that lie lame by the highway, and they say they came to that misery by whores; some threadbare citizens that from merchants and other good trades grow to be base informers and knights of the post, cry out when they dine with Duke Humphrey,[12] 'Oh what wickedness comes from whores!'

morbus anglicus: the English disease.
suffragan: deputy, assistant.
French marbles: pox.

Prentices that runs from their masters, cries out upon whores. Tush, Laurence! What enormities proceeds more in the commonwealth than from whoredom? But sith 'tis almost suppertime, and mirth is the friend to digestion, I mean a little to be pleasant. I pray you how many bad profits again grows from whores? Bridewell would have very few tenants, the hospital would want patients, and the surgeons much work; the apothecaries would have surfling water and potato roots lie dead on their hands, the painters could not despatch and make away their vermilion, if tallow-faced whores used it not for their cheeks. How should Sir John's broadsmen[13] do, if we were not? Why, Laurence, the Galley would be moored and the Blue Boar so lean that he would not be man's meat, if we of the trade were not to supply his wants! Do you think in conscience the Peacock could burnish his fair tail, were it not the whore of Babylon and suchlike makes him lusty with crowns? No, no, though the Talbot hath bitten some at the game, yet new fresh huntsmen shake the she-crew out of the couples. What should I say more, Laurence? The suburbs should have a great miss of us, and Shoreditch would complain to Dame Anne a Cleare,[14] if we of the sisterhood should not uphold her jollity. Who is that, Laurence, comes in to hear our talk?

LAURENCE. Oh 'tis the boy, Nan, that tells us supper is ready.

NAN. Why then, Laurence, what say you to me? Have I not proved that in foisting and nipping we excel you; that there is none so great inconvenience in the commonwealth as grows from whores, first for the corrupting of youth, infecting of age, for breeding of brawls, whereof ensues murder, insomuch that the ruin of many men comes from us, and the fall of many youths of good hope, if they were not seduced by us, do proclaim at Tyburn that we be the means of their misery? You men-thieves touch the body and wealth; but we ruin the soul, and endanger that which is more precious than the world's treasure. You make work only for the gallows; we both for the gallows and the devil, ay, and for the surgeon too, that some lives like loathsome lazars, and die with the French marbles. Whereupon I conclude that I have won the supper.

LAURENCE. I confess it, Nan, for thou hast told me such wondrous villainies, as I thought never could have been in women (I mean of your profession). Why, you are crocodiles when you weep, basilisks when you smile, serpents when you devise, and the Devil's chiefest brokers to bring the world to destruction. And so, Nan, let's sit down to our meat and be merry.

Thus, countrymen, you have heard the disputation between these two cozening companions, wherein I have shaked out the notable villainy of whores, although Mistress Nan, this good oratress, hath sworn to wear a long Hamburg knife to stab me, and all the crew have protested my death, and to prove they meant good earnest, they beleaguered me about in the 'St John's Head' within Ludgate, being at supper. There were some fourteen or fifteen of them met, and thought to have made that the fatal night of my overthrow, but that the courteous citizens and apprentices took my part, and so two or three of them were carried to the Counter, although a gentleman in my company was sore hurt. I cannot deny but they begin to waste away about London, and Tyburn, since the setting out of my book, hath eaten up many of them; and I will plague them to the extremity. Let them do what they dare with their Bilbao blades! I fear them not. And to give them their last adieu, look shortly countrymen for a pamphlet against them, called *The Black Book*, containing four new laws never spoken of yet: *the creeping law* of petty thieves, that rob about the suburbs; *the limiting law*, discoursing the orders of such as follow judges in their circuits, and go about from fair to fair; *the jugging law*, wherein I will set out the disorders at nine-holes and rifling, how they are only for the benefit of the cutpurses; *the stripping law*, wherein I will lay open the lewd abuses of sundry jailers in England. Beside, you shall see there what houses there be about the suburbs and town's end, that are receivers of cutpurses' stolen goods, lifts, and such like. And, lastly, look for a be[a]d-roll or catalogue of all the names of the foists, nips, lifts and priggers, in and about London. And although some say

basilisks: mythical birds whose glance turned observers to stone.
St John's Head: a well-known tavern.

I dare not do it, yet I will shortly set it abroach, and whosoever I name or touch, if he think himself grieved, I will answer him before the Honourable Privy Council.

The Conversion of an English Courtezan

Sith to discover my parentage would double the grief of my living parents, and revive in them the memory of my great amiss, and that my untoward fall would be a dishonour to the house from whence I came; sith to manifest the place of my birth would be a blemish, through my beastly life so badly misled, to the shire where I was born; sith to discourse my name might be holden a blot in my kindred's brow, to have a sinew in their stock of so little grace, I will conceal my parents, kin and country, and shroud my name with silence, lest envy might taunt others for my wantonness. Know, therefore, I was born, about three score miles from London, of honest and wealthy parents, who had many children, but I their only daughter, and therefore the jewel wherein they most delighted, and more, the youngest of all, and therefore the more favoured; for being gotten in the waning of my parents' age, they doted on me above the rest, and so set their hearts the more on fire. I was the fairest of all, and yet not more beautiful than I was witty, insomuch that, being a pretty parrot, I had such quaint conceits and witty words in my mouth, that the neighbours said, I was too soon wise to be long old. Would to God, either the proverb had been authentical, or their sayings prophecies! Then had I, by death in my nonage, buried many blemishes that my riper years brought me to. For the extreme love of my parents was the very efficient cause of my follies, resembling herein the nature of the ape, that ever killeth that young one which he loveth most, with embracing it too fervently. So my father and mother, but she most of all, although he too much, so cockered me up in my wantonness, that my wit grew to the worst, and I waxed upward with the ill weeds. Whatsoever I did, were it never so bad, might not be found fault withal. My father would smile at it and say, 'twas but the trick of a child; and my mother allowed of my unhappy parts, alluding to this profane and old proverb: an untoward girl makes a good woman.

But now I find, in sparing the rod, they hated the child; that over-kind fathers make unruly daughters. Had they bent the wand while it had been green, it would have been pliant; but I, ill-grown in my years, am almost remediless. The hawk that is most perfect for the flight and will, seldom proveth haggard; and children that are virtuously nurtured in youth, will be honestly natured in age. Fie upon such as say, 'Young saints, old devils'! It is no doubt a devilish and damnable saying; for what is not bent in the cradle, will hardly be bowed in the saddle. Myself am an instance, who after I grew to be six years old, was set to school, where I profited so much that I writ and read excellently well, played upon the virginals, lute and cithern, and could sing prick-song at the first sight; insomuch as by that time I was twelve years old, I was holden for the most fair and best qualitied young girl in all that country; but, with this, bewailed of my well-wishers, in that my parents suffered me to be so wanton.

But they so tenderly affected me, and were so blinded with my excellent qualities, that they had no insight into my ensuing follies. For I, growing to be thirteen year old, feeling the rein of liberty loose on mine own neck, began with the wanton heifer to aim at mine own will, and to measure content by the sweetness of mine own thoughts, insomuch that, pride creeping on, I began to prank myself with the proudest, and to hold it in disdain that any in the parish should exceed me in bravery. As my apparel was costly, so I grew to be licentious, and to delight to be looked on, so that I haunted and frequented all feasts and weddings, and other places of merry meetings, where, as I was gazed on of many, so I spared no glances to surview all with a curious eye-favour. I observed Ovid's rule right: *Spectatum veniunt, veniunt spectentur ut ipsae.*[15]

I went to see and be seen, and decked myself in the highest degree of bravery, holding it a glory when I was waited on with

haggard : wild, untamed (a hawking term).
prick-song : melody set down by pricking paper.
bravery : finery, ostentation.

many eyes, to make censure of my birth. Beside, I was an ordinary dancer, and grew in that quality so famous, that I was noted as the chiefest thereat in all the country. Yea, and to soothe me up in these follies, my parents took a pride in my dancing, which afterward proved my overthrow, and their heartbreaking.

Thus as an unbridled colt, I carelessly led forth my youth, and wantonly spent the flower of my years, holding such maidens as were modest, fools, and such as were not as wilfully wanton as myself, puppies, ill brought up and without manners. Growing on in years, as tide nor time tarrieth no man, I began to wax passion-proud, and think her not worthy to live that was not a little in love, that as divers young men began to favour me for my beauty, so I began to censure of some of them partially, and to delight in the multitude of many wooers, being ready to fall from the tree before I was come to the perfection of a blossom, which an uncle of mine seeing, who was my mother's brother, as careful of my welfare as nigh to me in kin, finding fit opportunity to talk with me, gave me this wholesome exhortation.

A Watchword to Wanton Maidens

'Cousin, I see the fairest hawk hath oftentimes the sickest feathers, that the hottest day hath the most sharpest thunders, the brightest sun, the most sudden shower, and the youngest virgins, the most dangerous fortunes; I speak as a kinsman, and wish as a friend. The blossom of a maiden's youth, such as yourself, hath attending upon it many frosts to nip it, and many cares to consume it, so that if it be not carefully looked unto, it will perish before it come to any perfection.

'A virgin's honour consisteth not only in the gifts of nature, as to be fair and beautiful. Though they be favours that grace maidens much, for as they be glistering, so they be momentary, ready to be worn with every winter's blast, and parched with every summer's sun; there is no face so fair, but the least mole, the slenderest scar, the smallest brunt of sickness will quickly blemish.

'Beauty, cousin, as it flourisheth in youth, so it fadeth in age:

ordinary: i.e. conformable to order, having a good sense of rhythm.
censure . . . partially: look favourably on.

it is but a folly that feedeth man's eye, a painting that Nature lends for a time, and men allow on for a while, insomuch that such as only aim at your fair looks, tie but their loves to an apprenticeship of beauty, which broken either with cares, misfortune or years, their destinies are at liberty, and they begin to loath you, and like of others.

> *Forma bonum fragile est; quantumque accredit ad annos,*
> *Fit minor; et spatio carpitur ipsa suo.*[16]

'Then cousin, stand not too much on such a slippery glory, that is as brittle as glass; be not proud of beauty's painting, that, hatched by time, perisheth in short time. Neither are women the more admirable of wise men for their gay apparel, though fools are fed with guards; for a woman's ornaments is the excellency of her virtues; and her inward good qualities, are of far more worth than her outward braveries. Embroidered hair, bracelets, silks, rich attire and such trash do rather bring the name of a young maid in question, than add to her fame any title of honour.

'The Vestal Virgins were not reverenced of the senators for their curious clothing, but for their chastity. Cornelia[17] was not famoused for ornaments of gold, but for excellent virtues. Superfluity in apparel showeth rather lightness of mind, than it importeth any other inward good quality; and men judge of maidens' rareness by the modesty of their raiment, holding it rather garish than glorious to be tricked up in superfluous and exceeding braveries. Neither, cousin, is it seemly for maids to jet abroad, or to frequent too much company.

'For she that is looked on by many, cannot choose but be hardly spoken of by some; for report hath a blister on her tongue, and maidens' actions are narrowly measured. Therefore would not the ancient Romans suffer their daughters to go any further than their mothers' looks guided them. And therefore Diana is painted with a tortoise under her feet, meaning that a maid should not be a straggler, but, like the snail, carry her house on her head, and keep at home at her work, so to keep

guards: ornaments, trimmings.
Diana: goddess of chastity.

her name without blemish, and her virtues from the slander of envy.

'A maid that hazards herself in much company may venture the freedom of her heart by the folly of her eye, for so long the pot goes to the water, that it comes broken home; and such as look much must needs like at last. The fly dallies with a flame, but at length she burneth: flax and fire put together will kindle. A maid in company of young men shall be constrained to listen to the wanton allurements of many cunning speeches. If she hath not either with Ulysses tasted of moly,[18] or stopped her ears warily, she may either be enticed with the sirens, or enchanted by Circes. Youth is apt to yield to sweet persuasions, and therefore, cousin, think nothing more dangerous than to gad abroad. Neither, cousin, do I allow this wanton dancing in young virgins. 'Tis more commendation for them to moderate their manners than to measure their feet, and better to hear nothing than to listen unto unreverent music. Silence is a precious jewel, and nothing so much worth as a countenance full of chastity; light behaviour is a sign of lewd thoughts, and men will say, there goes a wanton that will not want one, if a place and person were agreeable to her desires. If a maiden's honour be blemished or her honesty called in question, she is half defloured, and therefore had maidens need to be chary, lest envy report them for unchaste.

'Cousin, I speak this generally, which if you apply particularly to yourself, you shall find in time my words were well said.'

I gave him slender thanks, but with such a frump that he perceived how light I made of his counsel; which he perceiving, shaked his head, and with tears in his eyes departed. But I, whom wanton desires had drawn in delight, still presumed in my former follies, and gave myself either to gad abroad, or else at home to read dissolute pamphlets, which bred in me many ill-affected wishes, so that I gave leave to love and lust to enter into the centre of my heart, where they harboured till they wrought my final and fatal prejudice.

frump: derisive snort.
prejudice: injury.

Thus leading my life loosely, and being soothed up with the applause of my too kind and loving parents, I had many of every degree that made love unto me, as well for my beauty, as for the hope of wealth that my father would bestow upon me. Sundry suitors I had, and I allowed of all, though I particularly granted love to none, yielding them friendly favours, as being proud I had more wooers than any maid in the parish beside. Amongst the rest there was a wealthy farmer that wished me well, a man of some forty years of age, one too worthy for one of so little worth as myself, and him my father, mother, and other friends would have had me match myself withal. But I, that had had the reins of liberty too long in mine own hands, refused him and would not be ruled by their persuasions, and though my mother with tears entreated me to consider of mine own estate, and how well I sped if I wedded with him, yet carelessly I despised her counsel, and flatly made answer that I would none of him. Which, though it pinched my parents at the quick, yet rather than they would displease me, they left me in mine own liberty to love. Many there were beside him, men's sons of no mean worth, that were wooers unto me, but in vain. Either my fortune or destiny drove me to a worser end, for I refused them all, and, with the beetle, refusing to light on the sweetest flowers all day, nestled at night in a cowshard.

It fortuned that, as many sought to win me, so amongst the rest there was an odd companion that dwelt with a gentleman hard by, a fellow of small reputation, and of no living; neither had he any excellent qualities but thrumming on the gittern. But of pleasant disposition he was, and could gawl out many quaint and ribaldrous jigs and songs, and so was favoured of the foolish sect for his foppery. This shifting companion, suitable to myself in vanity, would ofttimes be jesting with me, and I so long dallying with him, that I began deeply – Oh, let me blush at this confession! – to fall in love with him, and so construed of all his actions, that I consented to mine own overthrow. For as smoke will hardly be concealed, so love will not be long smothered, but will bewray her own secrets; which was manifest in me, who in my sporting with him, so bewrayed my affec-

gawl out : bawl out.

tion, that he, spying I favoured him, began to strike when the iron was hot, and to take opportunity by the forehead, and one day, finding me in a merry vein, began to question with me of love, which although at the first I slenderly denied him, yet at last I granted, so that not only I agreed to plight him my faith, but that night meeting to have farther talk, I lasciviously consented that he cropped the flower of my virginity. When thus I was spoiled by such a base companion, I gave myself to content his humour, and to satisfy the sweet of mine own wanton desires. Oh, here let me breathe and with tears bewail the beginning of my miseries, and to exclaim against the folly of my parents, who, by too much favouring me in my vanity in my tender youth, laid the first plot of my ensuing repentance! Had they with due correction chastised my wantonness, and suppressed my foolish will with their grave advice, they had made me more virtuous and themselves less sorrowful. A father's frown is a bridle to the child, and a mother's check is a stay to the stubborn daughter. Oh, had my parents in overloving me not hated me, I had not at this time cause to complain! Oh, had my father regarded the saying of the wise man, I had not been thus woebegone!

If thy daughter be not shamefast hold her straitly, lest she abuse herself through overmuch liberty.

Take heed of her that hath an unshamefast eye, and marvel not if she trespass against thee.

The daughter maketh the father to watch secretly, and the carefulness he hath for her taketh away his sleep:

In her virginity, lest she should be deflowered in her father's house.

If therefore thy daughter be unshamefast in her youth, keep her straitly, lest she cause thine enemies to laugh thee to scorn, and make thee a common talk in the city, and defame thee among the people, and bring thee to public shame.

Had my parents with care considered of this holy counsel, and levelled my life by the loadstone of virtue, had they looked narrowly into the faults of my youth, and bent the tree while it was a wand, and taught the hound while he was a puppy, this

If . . . against thee: Ecclesiastes 26, xiii, xiv.
The daughter . . . shame: ibid., 43, ix–xi.

blemish had never befortuned me, nor so great dishonour had not befallen them. Then, by my example, let all parents take heed, lest in loving their children too tenderly, they subvert them utterly; lest in manuring the ground too much with the unskilful husbandman, it wax too fat, and bring forth more weeds than flowers; lest cockering their children under their wings without correction, they make them careless, and bring them to destruction: as their nurture is in youth, so will their nature grow in age. If the palm-tree be suppressed while it is a scion, it will contrary to nature be crooked when it is a tree.

> *Quo semel est imbuta recens servabit odorem*
> *Testa diu.*[19]

If then virtue be to be engrafted in youth, lest they prove obstinate in age, reform your children betimes both with correction and counsel. So shall you that are parents glory in the honour of their good endeavours. But, leaving this digression, again to the looseness of mine own life, who now having lost the glory of my youth, and suffered such a base slave to possess it, which many men of worth had desired to enjoy, I waxed bold in sin and grew shameless, insomuch he could not desire so much as I did grant, whereupon, seeing he durst not reveal it to my father to demand me in marriage, he resolved to carry me away secretly, and therefore wished me to provide for myself, and to furnish me every way both with money and apparel, hoping, as he said, that after we were departed, and my father saw we were married, and that no means was to amend it, he would give his free consent, and use us as kindly, and deal with us as liberally as if we had matched with his good will. I, that was apt to any ill, agreed to this, and so wrought the matter, that he carried me away into a strange place, and then using me a while as his wife, when our money began to wax low, he resolved secretly to go into the country where my father dwelt, to hear not only how my father took my departure, but what hope we had of his ensuing favour. Although I was loath to be left alone in a strange place, yet I was willing to hear from my friends, who no doubt conceived much heart-sorrow for my unhappy fortunes; so that

scion: shoot, twig.

I parted with a few tears, and enjoined him to make all the haste he might to return. He being gone, as the eagles always resort where the carrion is, so the bruit being spread abroad of my beauty, and that at such an inn lay such a fair young gentlewoman, there resorted thither many brave youthful gentlemen and cutting companions, that, tickled with lust, aimed at the possession of my favour, and by sundry means sought to have a sight of me, which I easily granted to all, as a woman that counted it a glory to be wondered at by many men's eyes, insomuch that coming amongst them, I set their hearts more and more on fire, that there rose divers brawls who should be most in my company. Being thus haunted by such a troop of lusty rufflers, I began to find mine own folly, that had placed my first affection so loosely, and therefore began as deeply to loath him that was departed, as erst I liked him when he was present, vowing in myself, though he had the spoil of my virginity, yet never after should he triumph in the possession of my favour, and therefore began I to affection these new-come guests, and one above the rest, who was a brave young gentleman, and no less addicted unto me than I devoted unto him; for daily he courted me with amorous sonnets and curious proud letters, and sent me jewels, and all that I might grace him with the name of my servant. I returned him as loving lines at last, and so contented his lusting desire, that secretly, and unknown to all the rest, I made him sundry nights my bedfellow, where I so bewitched him with sweet words, that the man began deeply to dote upon me, insomuch that, selling some portion of land that he had, he put it into ready money, and providing horse and all things convenient, carried me secretly away, almost as far as [the] Bath. This was my second choice and my second shame.

Thus I went forward in wickedness, and delighted in change, having left mine old love to look after some other mate more fit for [his] purpose. How he took my departure when he returned, I little cared, for now I had my content, a gentleman, young, lusty, and endued with good qualities, and one that loved me more tenderly than himself. Thus lived this new entertained friend and I together unmarried, yet as man and wife for a

cutting: swaggering.
[*his*]: original 'her'.

while, so lovingly, as was to his content and my credit, but as the tiger, though for a while she hide her claws, yet at last she will reveal her cruelty, and as the *agnus castus* leaf, when it looks most dry is then most full of moisture, so women's wantonness is not qualified by their wariness, nor do their chariness for a month warrant their chastity for ever; which I proved true, for my supposed husband, being every way a man of worth, could not so covertly hide himself in the country, though a stranger, but that he fell in acquaintance with many brave gentlemen, whom he brought home to his lodging, not only to honour them with his liberal courtesy, but also to see me, being proud [if] any man of worth applauded my beauty. Alas, poor gentleman! Too much bewitched by the wiliness of a woman, had he deemed my heart to be a harbour for every new desire, or mine eye a suitor to every new face, he would not have been so fond as to have brought his companions into my company, but rather would have mewed me up as a hen, to have kept that several to himself by force which he could not retain by kindness. But the honest-minded novice little suspected my change, although I, God wot, placed my delight in nothing more than the desire of new choice, which fell out thus:

Amongst the rest of the gentlemen that kept him company, there was one that was his most familiar, and he reposed more trust and confidence in him than in all the rest. This gentleman began to be deeply enamoured of me, and showed it by many signs which I easily perceived, and I, whose ear was pliant to every sweet word, and who so allowed of all that were beautiful, affected him no less, so that, love prevailing above friendship, he broke the matter with me, and made not many suits in vain before he obtained his purpose, for he had what he wished, and I had what contented me. I will not confess that any of the rest had some seldom favours, but this gentleman was my second self, and I loved him more for the time at the heel, than the other at the heart, so that though the other youth bare the charges and was made Sir Pay-for-all, yet this new friend was

agnus castus : also called Abraham's balm or chaste tree.
several : particular, private.
time at the heel : time spent in lechery.

he that was master of my affections, which kindness betwixt us was so unwisely cloaked that in short time it was manifest to all our familiars, which made my supposed husband to sigh and others to smile. But he that was hit with the horn was pinched at the heart; yet so extreme was the affection he bare to me, that he had rather conceal his grief than any way make me discontent, so that he smothered his sorrow with patience, and brooked the injury with silence, till our loves grew so broad before, that it was a wonder to the world. Whereupon one day at dinner, I being very pleasant with his chosen friend and my choice lover, I know not how, but either by fortune, or it may be some set match, there was by a gentleman there present a question popped in about women's passions, and their mutability in affection, so that the controversy was defended, *pro* and *contra*. Which arguments, whether a woman might have a second friend or no, at last it was concluded, that love and lordship brooks no fellowship, and therefore none so base-minded to bear a rival. Hereupon arose a question about friends that were put in trust, how it was a high point of treason for one to betray another, especially in love, insomuch that one gentleman at the board protested by a solemn oath, that if any friend of his, made privy and favoured with the sight of his mistress whom he loved, whether it were his wife or no, should secretly seek to encroach into his room and offer him that dishonour to partake his love, he would not use any other revenge, but at the next greeting stab him with his poynado, though he were condemned to death for the action.

All this fitted for the humour of my supposed husband, and struck both me and my friend into a quandary, but I scornfully jested at it, whenas my husband, taking the ball before it fell to the ground, began to make a long discourse what faithless friends they were that would fail in love, especially where a resolved trust of the party beloved was committed unto them, and hereupon, to make the matter more credulous, and to quip my folly, and to taunt the baseness of his friend's mind, that, so he might with courtesy both warn us of our wantonness, and

hit with the horn: cuckolds were supposed to grow (invisible?) horns.
fellowship: rivalry.

CONY-CATCHERS AND BAWDY BASKETS

reclaim us from ill, he promised to tell a pleasant story, performed, as he said, not long since in England, and it was to this effect:

A Pleasant Discourse, how a Wife Wanton by her Husband's Gentle Warning Became to Be a Modest Matron

There was a gentleman, to give him his due, an esquire, here in England, that was married to a young gentlewoman, fair and of a modest behaviour, virtuous in her looks, howsoever she was in her thoughts, and one that every way with her dutiful endeavour and outward appearance of honesty did breed her husband's content, insomuch that the gentleman so deeply affected her, as he counted all those hours ill spent which he passed not away in her company, besotting so himself in the beauty of his wife, that his only care was to have her every way delighted. Living thus pleasantly together, he had one special friend amongst the rest, whom he so dearly affected, as ever Damon did his Pythias, Pylades his Orestes, or Titus his Gisippus.[20] He unfolded all his secrets in his bosom, and what passion he had in his mind that either joyed him or perplexed him, he revealed unto his friend, and directed his actions according to the sequel of his counsels, so that they were two bodies and one soul. This gentleman, for all the inward favour shown him by his faithful friend, could not so withstand the force of fancy, but he grew enamoured of his friend's wife, whom he courted with many sweet words and fair promises, charms that are able to enchant almost the chastest ears, and so subtly couched his arguments, discovered such love in his eyes, and such sorrow in his looks, that despair seemed to sit in his face, and swore that, if she granted not him *le don du merci*, the end of a lover's sighs, then would present his heart as a tragic sacrifice to the sight of his cruel mistress. The gentlewoman, waxing pitiful, as women are kind-hearted and are loath gentlemen should die for love, after a few excuses, let him dub her husband knight of the forked order, and so, to satisfy his humour, made forfeit of her own honour.

Thus these two lovers continued by a great space in such plea-

le don du merci: the gift of kindness, 'the last favour'.
knight of the forked order: see 1st note, p. 301.

sures as unchaste wantons count their felicity, having continually fit opportunity to exercise their wicked purpose, sith the gentleman himself did give them free liberty to love, neither suspecting his wife, or suspecting his friend. At last, as such traitorous abuses will burst forth, it fell so out, that a maid who had been an old servant in the house, began to grow suspicious that there was too much familiarity between her mistress and her master's friend, and upon this watched them divers times so narrowly, that at last she found them more private than either agreed with her master's honour or her own honesty, and thereupon revealed it one day unto her master. He, little credulous of the light behaviour of his wife, blamed the maid, and bade her take heed lest she sought to blemish her virtues with slander, whom he loved more tenderly than his own life. The maid replied that she spake not of envy to him, but of mere love she bare unto him, and the rather that he might shadow such a fault in time, and by some means prevent it, lest if others should note it as well as she, his wife's good name and his friend's should be called in question. At these wise words, spoken by so base a drudge as his maid, the gentleman waxed astonished and listened to her discourse, wishing her to discover how she knew or was so privy to the folly of her mistress, or by what means he might have assured proof of it. She told him that to her, her own eyes were witnesses, for she saw them unlawfully together. 'And please it you, sir,' quoth she, 'to feign yourself to go from home, and then in the back-house to keep you secret, I will let you see as much as I have manifested unto you.' Upon this the master agreed, and warned his maid not so much as to make it known to any of her fellows. Within a day or two after, the gentleman said he would go a-hunting, and so rise very early, and, causing his men to couple up his hounds, left his wife in bed and went abroad. As soon as he was gone a mile from the house, he commanded his men to ride afore and to start the hare and follow the chase, 'and we will come fair and softly after.' They, obeying their master's charge, went their ways, and he returned by a back way to his house, and went secretly to the place where his maid and he had appointed. In the meantime, the mistress, thinking her husband safe with his hounds, sent for her friend to her bedchamber, by a trusty servant of hers in whom she assured, that was a secret pander in such affairs, and the gentleman was not slack to come, but, making all the haste he could, came and went into the chamber, asking for the master of the house very familiarly. The old maid noting all this, as soon as she knew them together, went and called her master and carried him up by a secret pair of stairs to her mistress's chamber door, where, peeping in at a place that the maid before had made for the purpose, he saw more than he looked for, and so much as pinched him at the very heart, causing him to accuse his wife for a strumpet, and his friend for a traitor. Yet, for all this, valuing his own honour more than their dishonesty, thinking if he should make an uproar, he should but aim at his own discredit, and cause himself to be a laughing game to his enemies, he concealed his sorrow with silence, and taking the maid apart, charged her to keep all secret, whatsoever she had seen, even as she esteemed of her own life, for if she did bewray it to any, he himself would with his sword make an end of her days, and with that, putting his hand in his sleeve, gave the poor maid six angels to buy her a new gown. The wench, glad of this gift, swore solemnly to tread it underfoot, and, sith it pleased him to conceal it, never to reveal it as long as she lived.

Upon this they parted, she to her drudgery, and he to the field to his men, where, after he had killed the hare, he returned home, and finding his friend in the garden, that in his absence had been grafting horns in the chimneys, and entertained him with his wonted familiarity, and showed no bad countenance to his wife, but dissembled all his thoughts to the full. As soon as dinner was done, and that he was gotten solitary by himself, he began to determine of revenge, but not as every man would have done, how to have brought his wife to shame, and her love to confusion, but he busied his brains how he might reserve his honour inviolate, reclaim his wife, and keep his friend, meditating a long time how he might bring all this to pass. At last a humour fell into his head, how cunningly to compass all three, and therefore he went and got him certain slips, which are counterfeit pieces of money, being brass and covered over with silver, which the common people call slips. Having furnished himself with these, he put them in his purse, and at night went to bed as he was wont to do, yet not using the kind of familiarity that he accustomed, notwithstanding he abstained not from the use of her body, but knew his wife as aforetimes, and every time he committed the act with her, he laid the next morning in the window a slip, where he was sure she might find it, and so many times as it pleased him to be carnally pleasant with his wife, so many slips he still laid down upon her cushnet.

This he used for the space of a fortnight, till at last, his wife finding every day a slip, or sometime more or less, wondered how they came there, and examining her waiting-maids, none of them could tell her anything touching them. Whereupon she thought to question with her husband about it, but being out of her remembrance, the next morning as he and she lay dallying in bed, it came into her mind, and she asked her husband if he laid those slips on her cushnet, that she of late found there, having never seen any before.

'Ay, marry, did I,' quoth he, 'and I have laid them there upon special reason, and it is this. Ever since I have been married to thee, I have deemed thee honest, and therefore used and honoured thee as my wife, parting coequal favours betwixt us as true loves, but alate finding the contrary, and with these eyes seeing thee play the whore with my friend, in whom I did repose all my trust, I sought not, as many would have done, to have revenged in blood, but for the safety of mine own honour, which otherwise would have been blemished by thy dishonesty, I have been silent, and have neither wronged my quondam friend, nor abused thee, but still do hold bed with thee, that the world should not suspect anything; and to quench the desire of lust I do use thy body, but not so lovingly as I would a wife, but carelessly as I would a strumpet, and, therefore, even as to a whore, so I give thee hire, which is for every time a slip, a counterfeit coin, which is good enough for such a slippery wanton, that will wrong her husband that loved her so tenderly. And thus will I use thee for the safety of mine own honour, till I have assured proof that thou becomest honest.'

And thus, with tears in his eyes, and his heart ready to burst with sighs, he was silent, when his wife, stricken with remorse of conscience, leaping out of her bed in her smock, humbly confessing all, craved pardon, promising if he should pardon this offence which was new begun in her, she would become a new reformed woman, and never after so much as in thought, give him any occasion of suspicion of jealousy. The patient husband, not willing to urge his wife, took her at her word, and told her that when he found her so reclaimed, he would, as afore he had done, use her lovingly and as his wife, but till he was so persuaded of her honesty, he would pay her still slips for his pleasure, charging her not to reveal any thing to his friend, or to make it known to him that he was privy to their loves.

Thus the debate ended, I guess in some kind greeting, and the gentleman went abroad to see his pastures, leaving his wife in bed full of sorrow and almost renting her heart asunder with sighs.

As soon as he was walked abroad, the gentleman his friend came to the house and asked for the goodman. The pander that was privy to all their practices, said that his master was gone abroad to see his pastures, but his mistress was in bed. 'Why then,' says he, 'I will go and raise her up.' So coming into the chamber and kissing her, meaning as he was wont to have used other accustomed dalliance, she desired him to abstain, with broken sighs and her eyes full of tears. He, wondering what should make her thus discontent, asked her what was the cause of her sorrow, protesting with a solemn oath that if any had done her injury, he would revenge it, were it with hazard of his life. She then told him, scarce being able to speak for weeping, that she had a suit to move him in, which if he granted unto her, she would hold him in love and affection without change next her husband for ever. He promised to do whatsoever it were. 'Then,' says she, 'swear upon a Bible you will do it without exception.' With that he took a Bible that lay in the window and swore that whatsoever she requested him to do, were it to the loss of his life, he would without exception perform it. Then she, holding down her head and blushing, began thus:

'I need not', quoth she, 'make manifest how grossly and grievously you and I have both offended God, and wronged the honest gentleman my husband and your friend, he putting a special trust in us both, and assuring such earnest affiance in your unfeigned friendship, that he even committeth me, his wife, his love, his second life, into your bosom. This love have I requited with inconstancy, in playing the harlot. That faith that he reposeth in you, have you returned with treachery and falsehood, in abusing mine honesty and his honour. Now a remorse of conscience toucheth me for my sins, that I heartily repent, and vow ever hereafter to live only to my husband, and therefore my suit is to you, that from henceforth you shall never so much as motion any dishonest question unto me, nor seek any unlawful pleasure or conversing at my hands. This is my suit, and hereunto I have sworn you, which oath if you observe as a faithful gentleman, I will conceal from my husband what is past, and rest in honest sort your faithful friend for ever.'

At this she burst afresh into tears, and uttered such sighs, that he thought for very grief her heart would have clave asunder. The gentleman, astonished at this strange metamorphosis of his mistress, sat a good while in a maze, and at last taking her by the hand, made this reply:

'So God help me, fair sweeting, I am glad of this motion, and wondrous joyful that God hath put such honest thoughts into your mind, and hath made you the means to reclaim me from my folly. I feel no less remorse than you do, in wronging so honest a friend as your husband, but this is the frailness of man, and therefore to make amends, I protest anew, never hereafter so much as in thought, as to motion you of dishonesty. Only I crave you be silent.'

She promised that, and so they ended. And so for that time they parted. At noon the gentleman came home and cheerfully saluted his wife and asked if dinner were ready, and sent for his friend, using him wonderfully familiarly, giving him no occasion of mistrust, and so pleasantly they passed away the day together. At night when his wife and he went to bed, she told him all, what had passed between her and his friend, and how she had bound him with an oath, and that he voluntarily of himself swore as much, being heartily sorry that he had so deeply offended so kind a friend. The gentleman commended her wit, and found her afterward a reclaimed woman, she living so honestly that she never gave him any occasion of mistrust. Thus the wise gentleman reclaimed with silence a wanton wife, and retained an assured friend.

At this pleasant tale all the board was at a mutiny, and they said the gentleman did passing wisely that wrought so cunningly for the safety of his own honour, but highly exclaiming against such a friend as would to his friend offer such villainy, all condemning her that would be false to so loving a husband. Thus they did diversely descant and passed away dinner. But this tale wrought little effect in me, for as one past grace, I delighted in change. But the gentleman that was his familiar, and my paramour, was so touched, that never after he would touch me dishonestly, but reclaimed himself, abstained from me and became true to his friend. I wondering that according to his wonted custom he did not seek my company, he and I being one day in the chamber alone, and he in his dumps, I began to dally with him, and to ask him why he was so strange, and used not his accustomed favours to me. He solemnly made answer that, though he had played the fool in setting his fancy upon another man's wife, and in wronging his friend, yet his conscience was now touched with remorse, and ever since he heard the tale afore rehearsed, he had vowed in himself never to do my husband the like wrong again. 'My husband?' quoth I. 'He is none of mine. He hath brought me from my friends and keeps me here unmarried, and therefore am I as free for you as for him'; and thus began to grow clamorous, because I was debarred of my lust.

The gentleman seeing me shameless, wished me to be silent, and said: 'Although you be but his friend, yet he hold you as dear as his wife, and therefore I will not abuse him, neither would I wish you to be familiar with any other, seeing you have a friend that loves you so tenderly.'

Much good counsel he gave me, but all in vain, for I scorned it, and began to hate him, and resolved both to be rid of him and my supposed husband; for, falling in another familiar of my husband's, I so inveigled him with sweet words, that I caused him to make a piece of money to steal me away, and so carry me to London, where I had not lived long with him, ere he, seeing my light behaviour, left me to the world, and to shift for myself.

Here by my example may you note the inconstant life of courtezans and common harlots, who, after they have lost their honesty,
care not who grow into their favour, nor what villainy they
commit. They fancy all as long as crowns last, and only aim at
pleasure and ease. They cleave like caterpillars to the tree, and
consume the fruit where they fall; they be vultures that prey on
men alive, and like the serpent sting the bosom wherein they are
nourished. I may best discourse their nature, because I was one
of their profession, but now, being metamorphosed, I hold it
meritorious for me to warn women from being such wantons, and
to give a caveat to men, lest they addict themselves to such
straggling strumpets, as love none, though they like all, but affec-
tionate only for profit, and when he hath spent all, they beat him
out of doors with the prodigal child. But stopping here, till
occasion serve me fitter to discover the manner of courtezans, to
myself, who now being brought to London, and left here at
random, was not such a house-dove while any friend stayed with
me, but that I had visit some houses in London that could harbour as honest a woman as myself, whenas, therefore, I was left
to myself, I removed my lodging, and gat me into one of those
houses of good hospitality whereunto persons resort, commonly
called a trugging-house, or to be plain, a whore-house, where I
gave myself to entertain all companions, sitting or standing at the
door like a stale, to allure or draw in wanton passengers, refusing
none that would with his purse purchase me to be his, to satisfy
the disordinate desire of his filthy lust. Now I began not to
respect personage, good qualities, to the gracious favour of the
men, when eye had no respect of person, for the oldest lecher
was as welcome as the youngest lover, so he brought meat in his
mouth; otherwise I pronounce[d] against him, *Si nihil attuleris,
ibis, Homere foras.*[21]

I waxed thus in this hell of voluptuousness daily worse and
worse, yet having, as they term it, a respect to the main chance,
as near as I could to avoid diseases, and to keep myself brave in
apparel, although I paid a kind of tribute to the bawd, according
as the number and benefit of my companions did exceed; but
never could I be brought to be a pickpocket or thievish by any of
their persuasions, although I wanted daily no instructions to allure

me to that villainy, for I think nature had wrought in me a contrary humour, otherwise my bad nurture, and conversing with such bad company had brought me to it. Marry, in all their vices I carried a brazen face and was shameless, for what ruffian was there in London that would utter more desperate oaths than I in mine anger, what to spit, quaff or carouse more devilishly, or rather damnably, than myself, and for beastly communication Messalina[22] of Rome might have been waiting-maid. Besides, I grew so grafted in sin, that *consueto peccandi tollebat sensum peccati*, custom of sin took away the feeling of the sin, for I so accustomably use myself to all kind of vice, that I accounted swearing no sin. Whoredom – why, I smile at that, and could profanely say, that it was a sin which God laughed at. Gluttony I held good-fellowship, and wrath, honour and resolution. I despised God, nay, in my conscience I might easily have been persuaded there was no God. I contemned the preachers, and when any wished me to reform my life, I bade, away with the Puritan; and if any young woman refused to be as vicious every way as myself, I would then say: 'Gip, fine soul, a young saint will prove an old devil.' I never would go to the church and sermons. I utterly refused, holding them as needless tales told in a pulpit. I would not bend mine ears to the hearing of any good discourse, but still delighted in jangling ditties of ribaldry.

Thus to the grief of my friends, hazard of my soul, and consuming of my body, I spent a year or two in this base and bad kind of life, subject to the whistle of every desperate ruffian, till on a time, there resorted to our house a clothier, a proper young man, who by fortune, coming first to drink, espying me, asked me if I would drink with him. There needed no great entreaty, foras then I wanted company, and so clapped me down by him, and began very pleasantly then to welcome him. The man being of himself modest and honest, noted my personage, and judicially reasoned of my strumpetlike behaviour, and inwardly, as after he reported unto me, grieved that so foul properties were hidden in so good a proportion, and that such rare wit and excellent beauty was blemished with whoredom's base deformity, insomuch that he began to think well of me, and to wish that I were as honest as I was beautiful. Again, see how God wrought for my conversion! Since I gave myself to my loose kind of life, I never liked any so well as him, insomuch that I began to judge of every part, and methought he was the properest man that ever I saw. Thus we sat both amorous of other, I lasciviously, and he honestly. At last he questioned with me what countrywoman I was, and why, being so proper a woman, I would beseem to dwell or lie in a base ale-house, especially in one that had a bad name. I warrant you he wanted no knavish reply to fit him, for I told him the house was as honest as his mother's. Marry, if there were in it a good wench or two, that would pleasure their friends at a need, I guess by his nose what porridge he loved, and that he hated none such. Well, seeing me in that voice, he said little, but shaked his head, paid for the beer and went his way, only taking his leave of me with a kiss, which methought was the sweetest that ever was given me. As soon as he was gone, I began to think what a handsome man he was, and wished that he would come and take a night's lodging with me, sitting in a dump to think of the quaintness of his personage, till other companions came in, that shaked me out of that melancholy. But as soon again as I was secret to myself, he came into my remembrance.

Passing over thus a day or two, this clothier came again to our house, whose sight cheered me up, for that spying him out at a casement, I ran down the stairs and met him at the door, and heartily welcomed him, and asked him if he would drink.

'I come for that purpose,' says he; 'but I will drink no more below but in a chamber.'

'Marry, sir,' quoth I, 'you shall,' and so brought him into the fairest room.

In there sitting there together drinking, at last the clothier fell to kissing and other dalliance, wherein he found me not coy. At last told me that he would willingly have his pleasure of me, but the room was too lightsome, for of all things in the world, he could not in such actions away with a light chamber. I consented unto him, and brought him into a room more dark, but still he said it was too light. Then I carried him into a farther chamber, where, drawing a buckram curtain afore the window, and closing the curtains of the bed, I asked him, smiling, if that were close enough.

'No, sweet love,' says he. 'The curtain is thin, and not broad enough for the window. Peradventure some watching eye may espy us. My heart misdoubts, and my credit is my life. Good love if thou has a more close room than this, bring me to it.'

'Why then,' quoth I, 'follow me'; and with that I brought him into a back loft, where stood a little bed only appointed to lodge suspicious persons, so dark that at noondays it was impossible for any man to see his own hands. 'How now, sir?' quoth I. 'Is not this dark enough?'

He, sitting him down on the bed-side, fetched a deep sigh, and said indifferent, 'So so, but there is a glimpse of light in at the tiles. Somebody may by fortune see us.'

'In faith, no,' quoth I, 'none but God.'

'God?' says he. 'Why, can God see us here?'

'Good sir,' quoth I, 'why I hope you are not so simple, but God's eyes are so clear and penetrating, that they can pierce through walls of brass, and that were we enclosed never so secretly, yet we are manifestly seen to him.'

'And alas!' quoth he, 'sweet love, if God see us, shall we not be more ashamed to do such a filthy act before him than before men? I am sure thou art not so shameless but thou wouldst blush and be afraid to have the meanest commoner in London see thee in the action of thy filthy lust. And dost thou not shame more to have God, the maker of all things, see thee, who revengeth sin with death, he whose eyes are clearer than the sun, who is the searcher of the heart, and holdeth vengeance in his hands to punish sinners? Consider, sweet love, that if man and wife would be ashamed to have any of their friends see them in the act of generation, or performing the rights of marriage which is lawful and allowed before God, yet for modesty do it in the most covert they may, then how impudent or graceless should we be, to fulfil our filthy lust before the eyes of the Almighty, who is greater than all kings or princes on the earth. Oh, let us tremble that we but once durst have such wanton communication in the hearing of his divine majesty, who pronounceth damnation for such as give themselves over to adultery. It is not possible, saith the Lord, for any whore-master or lascivious wanton to enter into the kingdom of God. For such sins whole cities have sunk, kingdoms have been destroyed; and though God suffereth such wicked livers to escape for a while, yet at length he payeth home, in this world with beggary, shame, diseases, or infamy, and in the other life with perpetual damnation. Weigh but the inconvenience that grows through thy loose life. Thou art hated of all that are good, despised of the virtuous, and only well thought of of reprobates, rascals, ruffians, and such as the world hates, subject to their lust, and gaining thy living at the hands of every diseased lecher. Oh, what a miserable trade of life is thine, that livest of the vomit of sin, in hunting after maladies! But suppose, while thou art young, thou art favoured of thy companions; when thou waxest old, and that thy beauty is vaded, then thou shalt be loathed and despised, even of them that professed most love unto thee. Then, good sister, call to mind the baseness of thy life, the heinous outrage of thy sin, that God doth punish it with the rigour of his justice. Oh, thou art made beautiful, fair and well-formed! And wilt thou then by thy filthy lust make thy body, which, if thou be honest, is the temple of God, the habitation of the devil? Consider this, and call to God for mercy, and amend thy life. Leave this house, and I will become thy faithful friend in all honesty, and use thee as mine own sister.'

At this, such a remorse of conscience, such a fearful terror of my sin struck into my mind, that I kneeled down at his feet, and with tears besought him he would help me out of that misery – for his exhortation had caused in me a loathing of my wicked life – and I would not only become a reformed woman, but hold him as dear as my father that gave me life; whereupon he kissed me with tears, and so we went down together, where we had further communication, and presently he provided me another lodging, where I not only used myself so honestly, but also was so penitent, every day in tears for my former folly, that he took me to his wife, and how I have lived since and loathed filthy lust, I refer myself to the majesty of God, who knoweth the secrets of all hearts.

Thus, countrymen, I have published the conversion of an English courtezan, which, if any way it be profitable either to forewarn youth, or withdraw bad persons to goodness, I have

vaded: faded.

the whole end of my desire, only craving every father would bring up his children with careful nurture, and every young woman respect the honour of her virginity.

But amongst all these blithe and merry jests, a little by your leave! if it be no further than Fetter Lane. Oh take heed, that's too nigh the Temple! What then? I will draw as near the sign of the 'White Hart' as I can, and breathing myself by the bottle ale-house, I'll tell you a merry jest, how a cony-catcher was used.

A Merry Tale Taken not far from Fetter Lane End, of a New-found Cony-Catcher, that was Cony-Catched himself

So it fell out, that a gentleman was sick and purblind, and went to a good honest man's house to sojourn, and taking up his chamber, grew so sick, that the goodman of the house hired a woman to keep and attend day and night upon the gentleman. This poor woman, having a good conscience, was careful of his welfare and looked to his diet, which was so slender, that the man, although sick, was almost famished, so that the woman would no longer stay, but bade his host provide him of some other to watch with him, sith it grieved her to see a man lie and starve for want of food, especially being set on the score for meat and drink, in the space of a fortnight, four pounds.

The goodman of the house at last, hearing how that poor woman did find fault with his scoring, the gentleman not only put her out of doors without wages, but would have arrested her for taking away his good name, and defaming and slandering him, and with that, calling one of his neighbours to him, said, 'Neighbour, whereas such a bad-tongued woman hath reported to my discredit that the gentleman that lies sick in my house wants meat, and yet runs very much on the score, I pray you judge by his diet whether he be famished or no. First in the morning, he hath a caudle next his heart, half an hour after that, a quart of sugar sops, half an hour after that, a neck of mutton in broth, half an hour after that, chickens in sorrel sops, and an hour

score : bill.
caudle : warm spiced drink.
next his heart : most desired by him.

after that, a joint of roast meat for his dinner. Now, neighbour, having this provision, you may judge whether he be spoiled for lack of meat or no, and to what great charges his diet will arise.' Whereas in truth, the poor gentleman would have been glad of the least of these, for he could get none at all, but the cozening knave thought to verse upon him, and one day, seeing money came not briefly to the gentleman, took some of his apparel, his cloak I guess, and pawned it for forty shillings, whereas, God wot, all he ate in that time was not worth a crown.

Well, the gentleman seeing how the knave went about to cony-catch him, and that he had taken his cloak, smothered all for revenge, and watched opportunity to do it; and on a time, seeing the goodman out, borrowed a cloak far better than his own of the boy, saying that he would go to a friend of his to fetch money for his master and discharge the house. The boy lending it him, away walks the gentleman, though weak after this great diet, and never came at the tailor's house to answer him cloak or money. And thus was he cony-catched himself, that thought to have versed upon another.

FINIS

THE
BLACKE BOOKES
MESSENGER.

Laying open the Life and Death
of *Ned Browne* one of the moſt notable Cutpurſes,
Croſbiters, and Conny-catchers, that
euer liued in England.

Heerein hee telleth verie plea-
ſantly in his owne perſon ſuch ſtrange prancks and
monſtrous villanies by him and his Conſorte
performed, as the like was yet neuer
heard of in any of the former
bookes of Conny-
catching.

Read and be warnd, Laugh as you like,
Iudge as you find.

Naſcimur pro Patria.
by R. G.

Printed at London by Iohn Danter, for *Thomas*
Nelſon dwelling in Siluer ſtreete, neere to the
ſigne of the Red-Croſſe. 1592.

To the Courteous Reader, Health

GENTLEMEN, I know you have long expected the coming forth of my *Black Book*, which I long have promised, and which I had many days since finished, had not sickness hindered my intent. Nevertheless, be assured it is the first thing I mean to publish after I am recovered. This *Messenger* to my *Black Book* I commit to your courteous censures, being written before I fell sick, which I thought good in the meantime to send you as a fairing, discoursing Ned Browne's villainies, which are too many to be described in my *Black Book*.

I had thought to have joined with this treatise a pithy discourse of the repentance of a cony-catcher lately executed out of Newgate, yet forasmuch as the method of the one is so far differing from the other, I altered my opinion, and the rather for that the one died resolute and desperate, the other penitent and passionate. For the cony-catcher's repentance, which shall shortly be published, it contains a passion of great importance, first, how he was given over from all grace and godliness, and seemed to have no spark of the fear of God in him; yet, nevertheless, through the wonderful working of God's spirit, even in the dungeon at Newgate the night before he died, he so repented him from the bottom of his heart, that it may well beseem parents to have it for their children, masters for their servants, and to be perused of every honest person with great regard.

And for Ned Browne, of whom my *Messenger* makes report, he was a man infamous for his bad course of life and well known about London. He was in outward show a gentlemanlike companion, attired very brave, and to shadow his villainy the more would nominate himself to be a marshal-man,[1] who when he had nipped a bung or cut a good purse, he would steal over into the Low Countries, there to taste three or four stoups of Rhenish wine, and then come over forsooth a brave soldier. But at last he leapt at a daisy[2] for his loose kind of life. And therefore imagine

fairing: complimentary gift.
passion: passionate outburst.

you now see him in his own person, standing in a great bay window with a halter about his neck ready to be hanged, desperately pronouncing this his whole course of life, and confesseth as followeth.

Yours in all courtesy, R.G.

A Table of the Words of Art Lately Devised by Ned Browne and his Associates to Crossbite the Old Phrases Used in the Manner of Cony-Catching

He that draws the fish to the bait, *the beater*.
The tavern where they go, *the bush*.
The fool that is caught, *the bird*.
Cony-catching to be called *bat-fowling*.
The wine to be called *the shrap*.
The cards to be called *the lime-twigs*.
The fetching in a cony, *beating the bush*.
The good ass if he be won: *stooping to the lure*.
If he keep aloof: *a haggard*.
The verser in cony-catching is called *the retriever*.
And the barnacle *the pot-hunter*.

The Life and Death of Ned Browne, a Notable Cutpurse and Cony-Catcher

If you think, Gentlemen, to hear a repentant man speak, or to tell a large tale of his penitent sorrows, ye are deceived. For as I have ever lived lewdly, so I mean to end my life as resolutely, and not by a cowardly confession to attempt the hope of a pardon. Yet, in that I was famous in my life for my villainies, I will at my death profess myself as notable, by discoursing to you all merrily the manner and method of my knaveries, which, if you hear without laughing, then after my death call me base knave, and never have me in remembrance.

Know therefore, Gentlemen, that my parents were honest, of good report and no little esteem amongst their neighbours, and sought (if good nurture and education would have served) to have made me an honest man. But as one selfsame ground brings forth flowers and thistles, so of a sound stock proved an untoward scion; and of a virtuous father, a most vicious son. It boots little to rehearse the petty sins of my nonage, as disobedience to my parents, contempt of good counsel, despising of mine elders, filching, pettilashery, and such trifling toys. But with these follies I inured myself, till, waxing in years, I grew into greater villainies. For when I came to eighteen years old, what sin was it that I would not commit with greediness, what attempt so bad, that I would not endeavour to execute! Cutting of purses, stealing of horses, lifting, picking of locks, and all other notable cozenages. Why, I held them excellent qualities, and accounted him unworthy to live, that could not, or durst not, live by such damnable practices. Yet, as sin too openly manifested to the eye of the magistrate is either sore revenged or soon cut off, so I, to prevent that, had a net wherein to dance, and divers shadows to colour my knaveries withal, as I would title myself with the name of a fencer, and make gentlemen believe that I picked a living out by that mystery, whereas, God wot, I had no other fence but with my short knife and a pair of purse strings, and with them in troth many a bout have I had in my time. In troth? Oh, what a simple oath was this to confirm a man's credit withal! Why, I see the halter will make a man holy, for whilst God suffered me to flourish, I scorned to disgrace my mouth with so small an oath as *In faith*; but I rent God in pieces, swearing and forswearing by every part of his body, that such as heard me rather trembled at mine oaths, than feared my braves, and yet for courage and resolution I refer myself to all them that have ever heard of my name.

Thus animated to do wickedness, I fell to take delight in the company of harlots, amongst whom, as I spent what I got, so I suffered not them I was acquainted withal to feather their nests, but would at my pleasure strip them of all that they had. What bad woman was there about London, whose champion I would not be for a few crowns, to fight, swear, and stare in her behalf, to the abuse of any that should do justice upon her! I still had one or two in store to crossbite withal, which I used as snares to trap simple men in. For if I took but one suspiciously in her company, straight I versed upon him, and crossbit him for all the money in his purse. By the way, sith sorrow cannot help to save me, let me tell you a merry jest how once I crossbit a malt-man, that would needs be so wanton as when he had shut his malt to have a wench, and thus the jest fell out.

pettilashery: see p. 219.

A Pleasant Tale how Ned Browne Crossbit a Maltman

This *senex fornicator*, this old lecher, using continually into Whitechapel, had a haunt into Petticoat Lane to a trugging-house there, and fell into great familiarity with a good wench that was a friend of mine, who one day revealed unto me how she was well thought on by a maltman, a wealthy old churl, and that ordinarily twice a week he did visit her, and therefore bade me plot some means to fetch him over for some crowns. I was not to seek for a quick invention, and resolved at his coming to crossbite him, which was, as luck served, the next day. Monsieur the maltman, coming according to his custom, was no sooner secretly shut in the chamber with the wench, but I came stepping in with a terrible look, swearing as if I meant to have challenged the earth to have opened and swallowed me quick, and presently fell upon her and beat her. Then I turned to the maltman, and lent him a blow or two, for he would take no more. He was a stout stiff old tough churl, and then I railed upon them both, and objected to him how long he had kept my wife, how my neighbours could tell me of it, how the Lane thought ill of me for suffering it, and now that I had myself taken them together, I would make both him and her smart for it before we parted.

The old fox that knew the ox by the horn, was subtle enough to spy a pad in the straw, and to see that we went about to crossbite him, wherefore he stood stiff, and denied all, and although the whore cunningly on her knees weeping did confess it, yet the maltman faced her down, and said she was an honest woman for all him, and that this was but a cozenage compacted between her and me to verse and crossbite him for some piece of money for amends, but, sith he knew himself clear, he would never grant to pay one penny.

I was straight in mine oaths, and braved him with sending for the constable, but in vain. All our policies could not draw one cross from this crafty old carl, till I, gathering my wits together, came over his fallows thus. I kept him still in the chamber, and sent, as though I had sent for the constable, for a friend of mine, an ancient cozener, and one that had a long time been a knight of the post. Marry, he had a fair cloak and a damask coat, that served him to bail men withal. To this perjured companion I sent to come as a constable, to make the maltman stoop, who, ready to execute any villainy that I should plot, came speedily like an ancient wealthy citizen, and, taking the office of a constable in hand, began very sternly to examine the matter, and to deal indifferently, rather favouring the maltman than me. But I complained how long he had kept my wife. He answered, I lied, and that it was a cozenage to crossbite him of his money. Mas[ter] Constable cunningly made this reply to us both:

'My friends, this matter is bad, and truly I cannot in conscience but look into it. For you, Browne, you complain how he hath abused your wife a long time, and she partly confesseth as much. He, who seems to be an honest man, and of some countenance amongst his neighbours, forswears it, and saith it is but a device to strip him of his money. I know not whom to believe, and therefore this is my best course because the one of you shall not laugh the other to scorn. I'll send you all three to the Counter, so to answer it before some justice that may take examination of the matter.'

The maltman, loath to go to prison, and yet unwilling to part from any pence, said he was willing to answer the matter before any man of worship, but he desired the constable to favour him that he might not go to ward, and he would send for a brewer a friend of his to be his bail.

'In faith,' says this cunning old cozener, 'you offer like an honest man, but I cannot stay so long till he be sent for, but if you mean, as you protest, to answer the matter, then leave some pawn, and I will let you go whither you will while tomorrow, and then come to my house here hard by at a grocer's shop, and you and I will go before a justice, and then clear yourself as you may.' The maltman, taking this crafty knave to be some substantial citizen, thanked him for his friendship and gave him a seal-ring that he wore on his forefinger, promising the next morning to meet him at his house.

As soon as my friend had the ring, away walks he, and while we stood brabbling together, he went to the brewer's house with whom this maltman traded and delivered the brewer the ring as a token from the maltman, saying he was in trouble, and that he desired him by that token to send him ten pound. The brewer, seeing an ancient citizen bringing the message, and knowing the maltman's ring, stood upon no terms, sith he knew his chapman would and was able to answer it again if it were a brace of hundred pounds, delivered him the money without any more ado; which ten pound at night we shared betwixt us, and left the maltman to talk with the brewer about the repayment. Tush, this was one of my ordinary shifts, for I was holden in my time the most famous crossbiter in all London.

Well, at length as wedding and hanging comes by destiny, I would, to avoid the speech of the world, be married forsooth, and keep a house. But, Gentlemen, I hope you that hear me talk of marriage, do presently imagine that sure she was some virtuous matron that I chose out. Shall I say, my conscience, she was a little snout-fair, but the commonest harlot and hackster that ever made fray under the shadow of Coleman Hedge. Wedded to this trull, what villainy could I devise but she would put in practice, and yet, though she could foist a pocket well, and get me some pence, and lift now and then for a need, and with the lightness of her heels bring me in some crowns, yet I waxed weary, and stuck to the old proverb, that change of pasture makes fat calves. I thought that in living with me two years she lived a year too long, and therefore, casting mine eye on a pretty wench, a man's wife well known about London, I fell in love with her, and that so deeply that I broke the matter to her husband, that I loved his wife, and must needs have her, and confirmed it with many oaths, that if he did not consent to it, I would be his death. Whereupon her husband, a kind knave, and one every way as base a companion as myself, agreed to me, and we bet a bargain, that I should have his wife, and he should have mine, conditionally that I should give him five pounds to boot, which I promised, though he never had it. So we, like two good horse-coursers, made a chop and change, and swapped up a roguish bargain, and

Coleman Hedge: garden near the church of St Catherine Coleman.
lightness . . . heels: unchastity.

so he married my wife and I his. Thus, Gentlemen, did I neither fear God nor his laws, nor regarded honestly, manhood, or conscience.

But these be trifles and venial sins. Now, sir, let me boast of myself a little, in that I came to the credit of a high lawyer, and with my sword freebooted abroad in the country like a cavalier on horseback, wherein I did excel for subtlety. For I had first for myself an artificial hair, and a beard so naturally made, that I could talk, dine, and sup in it, and yet it should never be spied. I will tell you there rests no greater villainy than in this practice, for I have robbed a man in the morning, and come to the same inn and baited, yea, and dined with him the same day; and for my horse that he might not be known I could ride him one part of the day like a goodly gelding with a large tail hanging to his fetlocks, and the other part of the day I could make him a cut, for I had an artificial tail so cunningly counterfeited, that the ostler when he dressed him could not perceive it. By these policies I little cared for hues and cries, but straight with disguising myself would outslip them all, and as for my cloak, it was tarmosind, as they do term it, made with two outsides that I could turn it how I list, for howsoever I wore it the right side still seemed to be outward. I remember how prettily once I served a priest, and because one death dischargeth all, and is as good as a general pardon, hear how I served him.

A Merry Tale how Ned Browne Used a Priest

I chanced as I rode into Berkshire to light in the company of a fat priest that had hanging at his saddle-bow a cap-case well stuffed with crowns that he went to pay for the purchase of some lands. Falling in talk with him, as communication will grow betwixt travellers, I behaved myself so demurely that he took me for a very honest man, and was glad of my company, although ere we parted it cost him very dear. And amongst other chat he questioned me if I would sell my horse, for he was a fair large gelding well spread and foreheaded, and so easily and swiftly paced, that I could well ride him seven mile an hour. I made him answer that I was loath to part from my gelding, and so shaped him a slightly reply, but before we came at our bait he was so in love with him that I might say him no nay, so that when we came at our inn and were at dinner together we swapped a bargain. I had the priest's, and twenty nobles to boot, for mine.

Well, as soon as we had changed I got me into the stable, and there secretly I knit a hair about the horse['s] fetlock so straight upon the vein that he began a little to check of that foot, so that when he was brought forth the horse began to halt; which the priest espying, marvelled at it, and began to accuse me that I had deceived him.

'Well,' quoth I, ''tis nothing but a blood, and as soon as he is warm he will go well, and if in riding you like him not, for twenty shillings loss, I'll change with you at night.'

The priest was glad of this, and caused his saddle to be set on my gelding, and so, having his cap-case on the saddle pommel, rode on his way, and I with him. But still his horse halted, and by that time we were two miles out of the town he halted right down. At which the priest chafed, and I said I wondered at it, and thought he was pricked, bade him alight, and I would see what he ailed, and wished him to get up of my horse that I had of him for a mile or two, and I would ride of his, to try if I could drive him from his halt. The priest thanked me, and was sorrowful, and I, feeling about his foot cracked the hair asunder, and when I had done, got up on him, smiling to myself to see the cap-case hang so mannerly before me, and putting spurs to the horse, made him give way a little, but being somewhat stiff, he halted for half a mile, and then began to fall into his old pace, which the priest spying, said: 'Methinks my gelding begins to leave his halting.'

'Ay, marry, doth he Master Parson,' quoth I, 'I warrant you he'll gallop too fast for you to overtake. And so, good priest, farewell, and take no thought for the carriage of your cap-case.'

With that I put spurs to him lustily, and flung I like the wind. The parson called to me, and said he hoped that I was but in jest, but he found it in earnest, for he never had his horse nor his cap-case after.

Gentlemen, this is but a jest to a number of villainies that I have acted, so graceless hath my life been. The most expert and skilful alchemist never took more pains in experience of his metals, the physician in his simples, the mechanical man in the mystery of his occupation, than I have done in plotting precepts, rules, axioms and principles, how smoothly and neatly to foist a pocket, or nip a bung.

It were too tedious to hold you with tales of the wonders I have acted, seeing almost they be numberless, or to make report how desperately I did execute them, either without fear of God, dread of the law, or love to my country. For I was so resolutely, or rather reprobately given, that I held death only as nature's due, and howsoever ignominiously it might happen unto me, that I little regarded. Which careless disdain to die, made me thrust myself into every brawl, quarrel and other bad action whatsoever, running headlong into all mischief, neither respecting the end, nor foreseeing the danger, and that secure life hath brought me to this dishonourable death.

But what should I stand here preaching? I lived wantonly, and therefore let me end merrily, and tell you two or three of my mad pranks and so bid you farewell. Amongst the rest I remember once walking up and down Smithfield, very quaintly attired in a fustian doublet and buff hose, both laid down with gold lace, a silk stock and a new cloak. I traced up and down very solemnly, as having never a cross to bless me withal, where being in my dumps there happened to me this accident following.

A Pleasant Tale how Ned Browne Kissed a Gentlewoman and Cut her Purse

Thus, Gentlemen, being in my dumps, I saw a brave country gentlewoman coming along from St Bartholomew's in a satin gown, and four men attending upon her. By her side she had hanging a marvellous rich purse embroidered, and not so fair without but it seemed to be as well lined within. At this my teeth watered, and, as the prey makes the thief, so necessity and the sight of such a fair purse began to muster a thousand inventions in my head how to come by it. To go by her and nip it I could

cross: silver coin.

not, because she had so many men attending on her: to watch her into a press, that was in vain, for, going towards St John's Street, I guessed her about to take horse to ride home, because all her men were booted. Thus perplexed for this purse, and yet not so much for the bung as the shells, I at last resolutely vowed in myself to have it, though I stretched a halter for it. And so, casting in my head how to bring my fine mistress to the blow, at last I performed it thus. She standing and talking a while with a gentleman, I stepped before her and leaned at the bar till I saw her leave him, and then stalking towards her very stoutly as if I had been some young cavalier or captain, I met her, and courteously saluted her, and not only greeted her, but, as if I had been acquainted with her, I gave her a kiss, and so in taking acquaintance closing very familiarly to her I cut her purse. The gentlewoman seeing me so brave, used me kindly, and blushing said, she knew me not. 'Are you not, mistress,' quoth I, 'such a gentlewoman, and such a man's wife?' – 'No truly sir,' quoth she, 'you mistake me.' – 'Then I cry you mercy,' quoth I, 'and am sorry that I was so saucily bold.' – 'There is no harm done, sir,' said she, 'because there is no offence taken.' And so we parted, I with a good bung, and my gentlewoman with a kiss, which I dare safely swear, she bought as dear as ever she did a thing in her life, for what I found in the purse that I keep to myself.

Thus did I plot devices in my head how to profit myself, though it were to the utter undoing of any one. I was the first that invented the letting fall of the key, which had like to cost me dear, but it is all one, as good then as now. And thus it was.

How Ned Browne Let Fall a Key

Walking up and down Paul's, I saw where a nobleman's brother in England came with certain gentlemen his friends in at the west door, and how he put up his purse, as having bought something in the Churchyard. I, having an eagle's eye, spied a good bung containing many shells as I guessed, carelessly put up into his sleeve, which drave me straight into a mutiny with myself how to come by it. I looked about me if I could see any of my fellow friends walking there, and straight I found out three or

bung . . . shells: see p. 177.

four trusty foists with whom I talked and conferred about this purse. We all concluded it was necessary to have it, so we could plot a means how to catch it. At last I set down the course thus: as soon as the throng grew great, and that there was jostling in Paul's for room, I stepped before the gentleman and let fall a key, which stooping to take up, I stayed the gentleman that he was fain to thrust by me, while in the press two of my friends foisted his purse, and away they went withal, and in it there was some twenty pound in gold. Presently, putting his hand in his pocket for his handkercher, he missed his purse, and suspected that he that let fall the key had it; but suppositions are vain, and so was his thinking, seeing he knew me not, for till this day he never set eye of his purse.

There are a number of my companions yet living in England, who, being men for all companies, will by once conversing with a man, so draw him to them, that he shall think nothing in the world too dear for them, and never be able to part from them, until he hath spent all he hath.

If he be lasciviously addicted, they have Aretine's tables at their fingers' ends, to feed him on with new kind of filthiness; they will come in with Rous, the French painter, and what an usual vein in bawdry he had! Not a whore or quean about the town but they know, and can tell you her marks, and where and with whom she hosts.

If they see you covetously bent, they will tell you wonders of the philosophers' stone, and make you believe they can make gold of goose-grease; only you must be at some two or three hundred pounds' cost, or such trifling matter, to help to set up their stills, and then you need not care where you beg your bread, for they will make you do little better if you follow their prescriptions.

Discourse with them of countries, they will set you on fire with travelling. Yea, what place is it they will not swear they have been in, and, I warrant you, tell such a sound tale, as if it were all Gospel they spake. Not a corner in France but they can describe. Venice? Why it is nothing; for they have intelli-

Aretine's tables: obscene illustrations to Aretino's erotic poems. I have been unable to identify Rous.

gence from it every hour, and at every word will come in with *Strado Curtizano*,[3] and tell you such miracles of Madame Padilia and Romana Imperia, that you will be mad till you be out of England. And if he see you are caught with that bait, he will make as though he would leave you, and feign business about the Court, or that such a nobleman sent for him, when you will rather consent to rob all your friends, than be severed from him one hour. If you request his company to travel, he will say:

'In faith, I cannot tell. I would sooner spend my life in your company than in any man's in England, but at this time I am not so provided of money as I would. Therefore I can make you no promise. And if a man should adventure upon such a journey without money, it were miserable and base, and no man will care for us.'

'Tut, money?' say you, like a liberal young master, 'take no care for that, for I have so much land, and I will sell it. My credit is so much, and I will use it. I have the keeping of a cousin's chamber of mine, which is an old counsellor, and he this vacation time is gone down into the country. We will break up his study, rifle his chests, dive into the bottom of his bags, but we will have to serve our turn. Rather than fail, we will sell his books, pawn his bedding and hangings, and make riddance of all his household stuff to set us packing.'

To this he listens a little, and says: 'These are some hopes yet.' But if he should go with you, and you have money and he none, you will domineer over him at your pleasure, and then he were well set up to leave such possibilities in England, and be made a slave in another country! With that you offer to part halves with him, or put all you have into his custody, before he should think you meant otherwise than well with him. He takes you at your offer, and promiseth to husband it so for you, that you shall spend with the best and yet not waste so much as you do. Which makes you (meaning simply) put him in trust and give him the purse. Then all a boon voyage into the Low Countries you trudge, so to travel up into Italy, but *per varios casus et tot discrimina rerum*, in a town of garrison he leaves you, runs away with your money, and makes you glad to betake your-

per varios ... rerum: 'through diverse chances and many perils' (Virgil).

self to provant, and to be a gentleman of a company. If he fear you will make after him, he will change his name, and if there be any better gentleman than other in the country where he sojourns, his name he will borrow, and creep into his kindred, or it shall cost him a fall, and make him pay sweetly for it in the end, if he take not the better heed. Thus will he be sure to have one ass or other afoot on whom he may prey, and ever to have new inventions to keep himself in pleasing.

There is no art but he will have a superficial sight into, and put down every man with talk, and, when he hath uttered the most he can, makes men believe that he knows ten times more than he will put into their heads, which are secrets not to be made common to every one.

He will persuade you he hath twenty receipts of love powders; that he can frame a ring with such a quaint device, that if a wench put it on her finger, she shall not choose but follow you up and down the streets.

If you have an enemy that you would fain be rid of, he'll teach you to poison him with your very looks; to stand on the top of Paul's with a burning-glass in your hand, and cast the sun with such a force on a man's face that walks under, that it shall strike him stark dead more violently than lightning; to fill a letter full of needles, which shall be laid after such a mathematical order, that when he opens it to whom it is sent, they shall all spring up and fly into his body as forcibly as if they had been blown up with gunpowder, or sent from a caliver's mouth like small shot.

To conclude, he will have such probable reasons to procure belief to his lies, such a smooth tongue to deliver them, and set them forth with such a grace, that a very wise man he should be that did not swallow the gudgeon at his hands.

In this sort have I known sundry young gentlemen of England trained forth to their own destruction, which makes me the more willing to forewarn other of such base companions.

Wherefore, for the rooting out of these sly insinuating moth-

provant: soldier's allowances.
be a . . . company: enlist as a soldier.
caliver: arquebus, portable gun.

worms, that eat men out of their substance unseen, and are the decay of the forwardest gentlemen and best wits, it were to be wished that Amasis' law[4] were revived, who ordained that every man at the year's end should give account to the magistrate how he lived, and he that did not so, or could not make an account of an honest life, to be put to death as a felon without favour or pardon.

Ye have about London, that (to the disgrace of gentlemen) live gentleman-like of themselves, having neither money nor land, nor any lawful means to maintain them; some by play, and they go a-mumming into the country all Christmas time with false dice, or, if there be any place where gentlemen or merchants frequent in the city or town corporate, thither will they, either disguised like young merchants or substantial citizens, and draw them all dry that ever deal with them.

There are some do nothing but walk up and down Paul's, or come to men's shops to buy wares, with budgets of writings under their arms, and these will talk with any man about their suits in law, and discourse unto them how these and these men's bands they have for money, that are the chiefest dealers in London, Norwich, Bristol and suchlike places, and complain that they cannot get one penny. 'Why, if such a man doth owe it you,' will some man say that knows him, 'I durst buy the debt of you, let me get it of him as I can.' 'Oh,' saith my budget-man, 'I have his hand and seal to show. Look here else.' And with that plucks out a counterfeit band, as all his other writings are, and reads it to him. Whereupon, for half in half they presently compound, and after he hath that ten pound paid him for his band of twenty, besides the forfeiture, or so forth. He says, 'Faith, these lawyers drink me as dry as a sieve, and I have money to pay at such a day, and I doubt I shall not be able to compass it. Here are all the leases and evidences of my land lying in such a shire. Could you lend me forty pound on them till the next term, or for some six months, and it shall then be repaid with interest, or I'll forfeit my whole inheritance, which is better worth than a hundred marks a year.'

The wealthy gentleman, or young novice, that hath store of

band: bond.

crowns lying by him, greedy of such a bargain, thinking, perhaps, by one clause or other to defeat him of all he hath, lends him money, and takes a fair statute merchant[5] of his lands before a judge. But when all comes to all, he hath no more land in England than a younger brother's inheritance, nor doth any such great occupier as he feigneth know him, much less owe him any money; whereby my covetous master is cheated forty or fifty pound thick at one clap.

Not unlike to these are they that, coming to ordinaries about the Exchange, where merchants do table for the most part, will say they have two or three ships of coals new come from Newcastle, and wish they could light on a good chapman, that would deal for them altogether. 'What's your price?' saith one. 'What's your price?' saith another. He holds them at the first at a very high rate, and sets a good face on it, as though he had such traffic indeed, but afterwards comes down so low, that every man strives who shall give him earnest first, and ere he be aware, he hath forty shillings clapped in his hand, to assure the bargain to some one of them. He puts it up quietly, and bids them inquire for him at such a sign and place, where he never came, signifying also his name, when in troth he is but a cozening companion, and no such man to be found. Thus goes he clear away with forty shillings in his purse for nothing, and they unlike to see him any more.

A Merry Jest how Ned Browne's Wife was Crossbitten in her Own Art

But here note, gentlemen, though I have done many sleights, and crossbitten sundry persons, yet so long goes the pitcher to the water,[6] that at length it comes broken home. Which proverb I have seen verified. For I remember once that I, supposing to crossbite a gentleman who had some ten pound in his sleeve, left my wife to perform the accident, who in the end was crossbitten herself. And thus it fell out. She compacted with a hooker, whom some call a curber, and having before bargained with the gentleman to tell her tales in her ear all night, he came according to promise, who, having supped and going to bed, was advised by my wife to lay his clothes in the window, where the hooker's crome might crossbite them from him, yet secretly intending before in the night-time to steal his money forth of his sleeve. They, being in bed together, slept soundly; yet such was his chance, that he suddenly wakened long before her, and, being sore troubled with a lask, rose up and made a double use of his chamber-pot. That done, he intended to throw it forth at the window, which the better to perform, he first removed his clothes from thence; at which instant the spring of the window rose up of the own accord. This suddenly amazed him so, that he leapt back, leaving the chamber-pot still standing in the window, fearing that the Devil had been at hand. By and by he espied a fair iron crome come marching in at the window, which, instead of the doublet and hose he sought for, suddenly took hold of that homely service in the member vessel, and so plucked goodman jordan with all his contents down pat on the curber's pate. Never was gentle angler so dressed, for his face, his head, and his neck were all besmeared with the soft Sir Reverence, so as he stunk worse than a jakes-farmer. The gentleman, hearing one cry out, and seeing his mess of altogether so strangely taken away, began to take heart to him, and looking out perceived the curber lie almost brained, almost drowned, and well near poisoned therewith; whereat, laughing heartily to himself, he put on his own clothes, and got him secretly away, laying my wife's clothing in the same place, which the gentle angler soon after took. But never could she get them again till this day.

This, Gentlemen, was my course of life, and thus I got much by villainy, and spent it amongst whores as carelessly. I seldom or never listened to the admonition of my friends, neither did the fall of other men learn me to beware, and therefore am I brought now to this end. Yet little did I think to have laid my bones in France. I thought, indeed, that Tyburn would at last have shaked me by the neck. But having done villainy in England, this was always my course, to slip over into the Low

crome : hook.
lask : diarrhoea.

Countries, and there for a while play the soldier, and partly that was the cause of my coming hither. For, growing odious in and about London, for my filching, lifting, nipping, foisting and crossbiting, that everyone held me in contempt and almost disdained my company, I resolved to come over into France, by bearing arms to win some credit, determining with myself to become a true man. But as men, though they change countries, alter not their minds, so, given over by God into a reprobate sense, I had no feeling of goodness, but with the dog fell to my old vomit, and here most wickedly I have committed sacrilege, robbed a church, and done other mischievous pranks, for which justly I am condemned and must suffer death: whereby I learn that revenge deferred is not quittanced; that though God suffer the wicked for a time, yet he pays home at length. For while I lasciviously led a careless life, if my friends warned me of it, I scoffed at them, and if they told me of the gallows, I would swear it was my destiny, and now I have proved myself no liar: yet must I die more basely, and be hanged out at a window.

O countrymen and Gentlemen, I have held you long, as good at the first as at the last. Take then this for a farewell: trust not in your own wits, for they will become too wilful oft, and so deceive you. Boast not in strength, nor stand not on your manhood, so to maintain quarrels: for the end of brawling is confusion. But use your courage in defence of your country, and then fear not to die; for the bullet is an honourable death. Beware of whores, for they be the sirens that draw men on to destruction; their sweet words are enchantments, their eyes allure, and their beauties bewitch. Oh, take heed of their persuasions, for they be crocodiles, that when they weep, destroy. Truth is honourable, and better is it to be a poor honest man, than a rich and wealthy thief. For the fairest end is the gallows; and what a shame is it to a man's friends, when he dies so basely! Scorn not labour, Gentlemen, nor hold not any course of life bad or servile, that is profitable and honest, lest in giving yourselves over to idleness, and having no yearly maintenance, you fall into many prejudicial mischiefs. Contemn not the virtuous counsel of a friend, despise not the hearing of God's ministers, scoff not at the magistrates; but fear God, honour your Prince, and love your country. Then God will bless you, as I hope he will do me, for all my manifold offences. And so, Lord, into thy hands I commit my spirit. – And with that he himself sprung out at the window and died.

Here, by the way, you shall understand, that, going over into France, he near unto Aix robbed a church, and was therefore condemned, and, having no gallows by, they hanged him out a window, fastening the rope about the bar. And thus this Ned Browne died miserably, that all his life time had been full of mischief and villainy, slightly at his death regarding the state of his soul. But note a wonderful judgement of God showed upon him after his death. His body being taken down and buried without the town, it is verified that in the night-time there came a company of wolves, and tore him out of his grave, and ate him up, whereas there lay many soldiers buried and many dead carcases, that they might have preyed on to have filled their hungry paunches. But the judgements of God, as they are just, so they are inscrutable. Yet thus much we may conjecture, that as he was one that delighted in rapine and stealth in his life, so at his death the ravenous wolves devoured him, and plucked him out of his grave, as a man not worthy to be admitted to the honour of any burial. Thus have I set down the life and death of Ned Browne, a famous cutpurse and cony-catcher, by whose example, if any be profited, I have the desired end of my labour.

FINIS

THE DEFENCE OF
Conny catching.
OR

A CONFVTATION OF THOSE
two iniurious Pamphlets publiſhed by *R.G.* againſt
the practitioners of many Nimble-witted
and myſticall Sciences.

By Cuthbert Cunny-catcher, Licenciate in Whittington Colledge.

*Qui bene latuit bene vixit, dominatur enim
fraus in omnibus.*

Printed at London by *A. I.* for *Thomas Gubbins*
and are to be ſold by *Iohn Busbie*, 1592.

To All my Good Friends, Health

As Plato (my good friends) travelled from Athens to Egypt, and from thence through sundry climes to increase his knowledge: so I, as desirous as he to search the depth of those liberal arts wherein I was professor, left my study in Whittington College and traced the country to grow famous in my faculty, so that I was so expert in the Art of Cony-catching by my continual practice, that that learned philosopher Jacke Cuttes, whose deep insight into this science had drawn him thrice through every gaol in England, meeting of me at Maidstone, gave me the bucklers, as the subtlest that ever he saw in that quaint and mystical form of Foolosophie: for if ever I brought my cony but to crush a pot of ale with me, I was as sure of all the crowns in his purse, as if he had conveyed them into my proper possession by a deed of gift with his own hand.

Newgate builded by one Whittington.

At Decoy, Mumchance, Catch-dolt, Oure le bourse, Non est possible, Dutch Noddie, or Irish one and thirty, none durst ever make compare with me for excellence: but as so many heads so many wits, so some that would not stoop a farthing as cards, would venture all the bite in their bung at dice. Therefore had I cheats for the very sise, of the squariers, langrets, gourds, stop-dice, high men, low men, and dice barde for all advantages: that if I fetched in any novice either at tables, or any other game of hazard, I would be sure to strip him of all that his purse had *in esse*, or his credit *in posse*, ere the simple cony and I parted.

The names of such games as cony-catchers use.

All the money in their purse.

When neither of these would serve, I had consorts that could verse, nip, and foist, so that I had a superficial sight into every profitable faculty. Insomuch that my principles grew authentical, and I so famous, that had I not been crossed by those two peevish pamphlets, I might at the next midsummer have worn

sise: size, portion of food and/or drink.

in esse . . . in posse: actually and potentially.

341

Doctor Storey's cap[3] for a favour. For I travelled almost throughout all England, admired for my ingenious capacity: till coming about Exeter, I began to exercise my art, and drawing in a tanner for a tame cony, as soon as he had lost two shillings he made this reply. 'Sirrah, although you have a livery on your back, and a cognisance to countenance you withal, and bear the port of a gentleman, yet I see you are a false knave and a cony-catcher, and this your companion your setter, and that before you and I part I'll prove.'

Some cony-catch[ers] dare wear noblemen's liver[ies] as W. Bickerton and others.

At these words cony-catcher and setter, I was driven into as great a maze, as if one had dropped out of the clouds, to hear a peasant cant the words of art belonging to our trade: yet I set a good face on the matter and asked him what he meant by cony-catching. 'Marry,' quoth he, 'although it is your practice, yet I have for three pence bought a little pamphlet, that hath taught me to smoke such a couple of knaves as you be.' When I heard him talk of smoking, my heart waxed cold, and I began to gather into him gently. 'No, no, sir,' quoth he, 'you cannot verse upon me, this book hath taught me to be beware of crossbiting.' And so, to be brief, he used me courteously, and that night caused the constable to lodge me in prison, and the next morning I was carried before the justice, where likewise he had this cursed book of cony-catching, so that he could tell the secrets of mine art better than my self: whereupon after strict examination I was sent to the gaol, and at the Sessions by good hap and some friend that my money procured me, I was delivered. As soon as I was at liberty, I got one of these books, and began to toss it over very devoutly, wherein I found [our] art so perfectly anatomized, as if he had been practitioner in our faculty forty winters before: then with a deep sigh I began to curse this R.G. that had made a public spoil of so noble a science, and to exclaim against that palpable ass whosoever, that would make any pen-man privy to our secret sciences. But see the sequel, I smothered my sorrow in silence, and away I trudged out of Devonshire, and went towards Cornwall, and coming to a simple

cognisance: distinguishing crest or device.
[*our*]: original 'one'.

ale-house to lodge, I found at a square table hard by the fire half a dozen country farmers at cards. The sight of these penny-fathers at play, drove me straight into a pleasant passion, to bless fortune that had offered such sweet opportunity to exercise my wits, and fill my purse with crowns: for I counted all the money they had mine by proper interest. As thus I stood looking on them playing at cross-ruff, one was taken revoking, whereat the other said: 'What, neighbour, will you play the cony-catcher with us? No, no, we have read the book as well as you.' Never went a cup of small beer so sorrowfully down an ale-knight's belly in a frosty morning, as that word struck to my heart, so that for fear of trouble I was fain to try my good hap at square play, at which fortune favouring me, I won twenty shillings, and yet do as simply as I could, I was not only suspected, but called cony-catcher and crossbiter.

But away I went with the money, and came presently to London, where I no sooner arrived amongst the crew, but I heard of a second part worse than the first, which drove me into such a great choler, that I began to inquire what this R.G. should be. At last I learned that he was a scholar, and a Master of Arts, and a cony-catcher in his kind, though not at cards, and one that favoured good fellows, so they were not palpable offenders in such desperate laws: whereupon reading his books, and surveying every line with deep judgement, I began to note folly in the man, that would strain a gnat, and let pass an elephant: that would touch small scapes, and let gross faults pass without any reprehension. Insomuch that I resolved to make an apology, and to answer his libellous invectives, and to prove that we cony-catchers are like little flies in the grass, which live: or little leaves and do no more harm: whereas there be in England other professions that be great cony-catchers and caterpillars, that make barren the field wherein they bait.

Therefore all my good friends vouch of my pains, and pray for my proceedings, for I mean to have about with this R.G. and to give him such a veny, that he shall be afraid hereafter to disparage that mystical science of cony-catching: if not, and

revoking: at cards, not following suit when able to.
veny: pungent retort.

that I prove too weak for him in sophistry, I mean to borrow Will Bickerton's blade, of as good a temper as Morglay King Arthur's sword was, and so challenge him to the single combat: but desirous to end the quarrel with the pen if it be possible, hear what I have learned in Whittington College.

Yours in cards and dice,
Cuthbert Cony-Catcher.

Morglay: sword wielded by Sir Bevis of Hampton.

I cannot but wonder, Master R.G., what poetical fury made you so fantastic, to write against cony-catchers? Was your brain so barren that you had no other subject? or your wits so dried with dreaming of love pamphlets that you had no other humour left, but satirically with Diogenes, to snarl at all men's manners? You never found in Tully nor Aristotle, what a setter or a verser was.

It had been the part of a scholar, to have written seriously of some grave subject, either philosophically to have shown how you were proficient in Cambridge, or divinely to have manifested your religion to the world. Such trivial trinkets and threadbare trash had better seemed T.D., whose brains, beaten to the yarking up of ballads, might more lawfully have glanced at the quaint conceits of cony-catching and crossbiting.

But to this my objection, me thinks I hear your mastership learnedly reply, *Nascimur pro patria*: Every man is not born for himself, but for his country: and that the end of all studious endeavours ought to tend to the advancing of virtue, o[r] suppressing of vice in the commonwealth. So that you have herein done the part of a good subject, and a good scholar, to anatomize such secret villainies as are practised by cozening companions, to the overthrow of the simple people: for by the discovery of such pernicious laws you seek to root out of the commonwealth such ill and licentious living persons as do *Ex alieno succo vivere*, live of the sweat of other men's brows, and under subtle shifts of wit abused, seek to ruin the flourishing estate of England. These you call vipers, moths of the commonwealth, caterpillars worse than God rained down on Egypt, rotten flesh which must be divided from the whole.

Ense resecandum est ne pars sincera trahatur.

T.D.: Thomas Dekker.
o[r]: original 'of'.
Ense . . . trahatur: see additional note to p. 199.

This, Master R.G., I know will be your answer, as it is the pretended cause of your injurious pamphlets. And indeed it is very well done, but greater had your praise been, if you had entered into the nature of more gross abuses, and set down the particular enormities that grow from such palpable villainies. For truth it is, that this is the Iron Age,[4] wherein iniquity hath the upper hand, and all conditions and estates of men seek to live by their wits, and he is counted wisest that hath the deepest insight into the getting of gains: every thing now that is found profitable is counted honest and lawful: and men are valued by their wealth, not by their virtues. He that cannot dissemble cannot live, and men put their sons nowadays apprentices, not to learn trades and occupations, but crafts and mysteries.

If then wit in this age be counted a great patrimony, and subtlety an inseparable accident to all estates, why should you be so spiteful, Master R.G., to poor cony-catchers above all the rest, sith they are the simplest souls of all in shifting to live in this over-wise world?

But you play like the spider that makes her web to entrap and snare little flies, but weaves it so slenderly that the great ones break through without any damage. You strain gnats, and pass over elephants; you scour the pond of a few croaking frogs, and leave behind an infinite number of most venomous scorpions. You decipher poor cony-catchers, that perhaps with a trick at cards win forty shillings from a churl that can spare it, and never talk of those caterpillars that undo the poor, ruin whole lordships, infect the commonwealth, and delight in nothing but in wrongful extorting and purloining of pelf, when as such be the greatest cony-catchers of all, as by your leave, Master R.G., I will make manifest.

Sir-reverence on your worship, had you such a mote in your eye, that you could not see those fox-furred gentlemen that hide under their gowns faced with foins more falsehood than all the cony-catchers in England beside, those miserable usurers I mean, that like vultures prey upon the spoil of the poor, sleeping with his neighbour's pledges all night in his bosom, and

accident to: concomitant of.
foins: marten's fur.

feeding upon forfeits and penalties, as the ravens do upon carrion? If his poor neighbour want to supply his need, either for his household necessaries, or his rent at the day, he will not lend a penny for charity, all his money is abroad: but if he offer him either cow or sow, mare or horse, or the very corn scarce sprouted out of the ground to sell, so the bargain may be cheap, though to the beggary of the poor man, he chops with him straight, and makes the poor cony fare the worse all the year after. Why write you not of these cony-catchers, Master R.G.?

Besides if pawns come, as the lease of a house, or the fee simple in mortgage, he can out of his furred cassock draw money to lend: but the old cole hath such quirks and quiddities in the conveyance, such provisoes, such days, hours, nay minutes of payments, that if his neighbour break but a moment, he takes the forfeit, and like a pink-eyed ferret so claws the poor cony in the burrow, that he leaves no hair on his breach nor on his back ere he parts with him. Are not these vipers of the commonwealth, and to be exclaimed against, not in small pamphlets, but in great volumes?

You set down how there be requisite setters and versers in cony-catching, and be there not so I pray you in usury? For when a young youthful gentleman, given a little to lash out liberally, wanteth money, makes he not his moan first to the broker, as subtle a knave to induce him to his overthrow, as the wiliest setter or verser in England? And he must be feed to speak to the usurer, and have so much in the pound for his labour: then he shall have grant of money and commodities together, so that if he borrow a hundred pound, he shall have forty in silver, and threescore in wares, dead stuff God wot; as lute strings, hobby horses, or (if he be greatly favoured) brown paper or cloth, and that shoots out in the lash. Then his land is turned over in statute or recognizance for six months and six months, so that he pays some thirty in the hundred to the usurer, beside the scrivener he hath a blind share: but when he comes to sell his threescore pound commodities, 'tis well if he get five and thirty.

Thus is the poor gentleman made a mere and simple cony,

and versed upon to the uttermost, and yet if he break his day, loseth as much land as cost his father a thousand marks.

Is not this cozenage and cony-catching, Master R.G.? and more daily practised in England, and more hurtful than our poor shifting at cards, and yet your mastership can wink at the cause? They be wealthy, but Cuthbert Cony-Catcher cares for none of them no more than they care for him, and therefore will reveal all. And because, Master R.G., you were pleasant in examples, I'll tell you a tale of an usurer, done within a mile of a knave's head, and since the cuckoo sung last, and it fell out thus.

A Pleasant Tale of an Usurer

It fortuned that a young gentleman not far off from Cockermouth, was somewhat slipt behind hand, and grown in debt, so that he durst hardly show his head for fear of his creditors, and having wife and children to maintain, although he had a proper land, yet wanting money to stock his ground, he lived very bare: whereupon he determined with himself to go to an old penny-father that dwelt hard by him, and to borrow some money of him, and so to lay his land in mortgage for the repayment of it.

He no sooner made the motion but it was accepted, for it was a goodly Lordship, worth in rent of assize seven score pound by the year, and did abut upon the usurer's ground, which drew the old churl to be marvellous willing to disburse money, so that he was content to lend him two hundred marks for three year according to the statute, so that he might have the land for assurance of his money.

The gentleman agreed to that, and promised to acknowledge a statute staple to him, with letters of defeasance.[5] The usurer, although he liked this well, and saw the young man offered more than reason required, yet had a further fetch to have the land his whatsoever should chance, and therefore he began to verse upon the poor cony thus:

'Sir,' quoth he, 'if I did not pity your estate, I would not lend you my money at such a rate: for whereas you have it after ten pounds in the hundred, I can make it worth thirty. But seeing the distress you, your wife and children are in, and considering all grows through your own liberal nature, I compassionate you the more, and would do for you as for mine own son: therefore if you shall think good to follow it, I will give you fatherly advice. I know you are greatly indebted, and have many unmerciful creditors, and they have you in suit, and I doubt ere long will have some extent against your lands, so shall you be utterly undone, and I greatly encumbered. Therefore to avoid all this, in my judgement it were best for you to make a deed of gift of all your lands, without condition or promise, to some one faithful friend or other, in whom you may repose credit, so shall your enemies have no advantage against you: and seeing they shall have nothing but your bare body liable to their executions, they will take the more easy and speedy composition. I think this the surest way, and if you durst repose your self in me, God is my witness, I would be to you as your father if he lived.' How say you to this compendious tale, Master R.G., could the proudest setter or verser in the world have drawn on a cony more cunningly?

Well, again to our young gentleman, who simply, with tears in his eyes to hear the kindness of the usurer, thanked him heartily, and deferred not to put in practice his counsel, for he made an absolute deed of gift from wife and children to this usurer of all his Lordship, and so had the two hundred marks upon the plain forfeit of a band.

To be short, the money made him and his merry, and yet he did husband it so well, that he not only duly paid the interest, but stocked his grounds, and began to grow out of debt, so that his creditors were willing to bear with him. Against the three years were expired, he made shift by the help of his friends for the money, and carried it home to the usurer, thanking him greatly, and craving a return of his deed of gift. 'Nay soft, sir,' saith the old churl, 'that bargain is yet to make, the land is mine to me and mine heirs for ever, by a deed of gift from your own hand, and what can be more sure: take the money if you please, and there is your band, but for the Lordship I will enter on it tomorrow: yet if you will be my tenant, you shall have it before another, and that is all the favour you shall have of me.'

At this the gentleman was amazed, and began to plead conscience with him, but in vain: whereupon he went sorrowfully home and told his wife, who as a woman half lunatic ran with her little children to his house, and cried out, but bootless: for although they called him before the chief of the country, yet sith the law had granted him the fee simple thereof he would not part withal: so that this distressed gentleman was fain to become tenant to this usurer, and for two hundred marks to lose a Lordship worth six or seven thousand pounds. I pray you was not this an old cony-catcher, Mr R.G., that could lurch a poor cony of so many thousands at one time? Whether is our crossing at cards more perilous to the commonwealth than this cozenage for land? You wink at it, but I will tell all, yet hear out the end of my tale, for as fortune fell out, the usurer was made a cony himself.

The gentleman and his wife smothering this with patience, she that had a reaching wit, and hair-brain revenge in her head, counselled her husband to make a voyage from home, and to stay a week or two: 'and,' quoth she, 'before you come again you shall see me venture fair for the land.' The gentleman willing to let his wife practise her wits, went his way, and left all to his wife's discretion. She, after her husband was four or five days from home, was visited by the usurer, who used her very kindly, and sent victuals to her house, promising to sup with her that night, and that she should not want any thing in her husband's absence. The gentlewoman with gracious acceptance thanked him, and bade divers of her neighbours to bear him company, having a further reach in her head than he suspected. For the old churl coming an hour before supper-time, even as she herself would wish, for an amorous wehe or two, as old jades whinny when they cannot wag the tail, began to be very pleasant with his tenant, and desired her to shew him all the rooms in her house, and 'Happily,' saith he, 'if I die without issue, I may give it to your children, for my conscience bids me be favourable to you.'

lurch: defraud.
wehe: conventional representation of horse neighing.

The gentlewoman led him through every part, and at last brought him into a back room much like a backhouse, where she said thus unto him:

'Sir, this room is the most unhandsomest in all the house, but if there were a dormer built to it, and these shut windows made bay windows and glazed, it would make the properest parlour in all the house: for,' saith she, 'put your head out at this window, and look what a sweet prospect belongs unto it.'

The usurer mistrusting nothing, thrust out his crafty sconce, and the gentlewoman shut to the window, and called her maids to help, where they bound and pinioned the caterpillar's arms fast, and then stood he with his head into a backyard, as if he had been on a pillory, and struggle durst not for stifling himself. When she had him thus at the vantage, she got a couple of six-penny nails and a hammer, and went into the yard, having her children attending upon her, every one with a sharp knife in their hands, and then coming to him with a stern countenance, she looked as Medea did when she attempted revenge against Jason.[6] The usurer seeing this tragedy, was afraid of his life, and cried out, but in vain, for her maids made such a noise, that his shrieking could not be heard, whilst she nailed one ear fast to the window, and the other to the stanshel; then began she to use these words unto him:

'Ah, vile and injurious caterpillar, God hath sent thee to seek thine own revenge, and now I and my children will perform it. For sith thy wealth doth so countenance thee, that we cannot have thee punished for thy cozenage, I myself will be justice, judge, and executioner: for as the pillory belongs to such a villain, so have I nailed thy ears, and they shall be cut off to the perpetual example of such purloining reprobates, and the executors shall be these little infants, whose right without conscience or mercy thou so wrongfully detainest. Look on this old churl, little babes, this is he that with his cozenage will drive you to beg and want in your age, and at this instant brings your father to all this present misery; have no pity upon him, but you two cut off his ears, and thou,' quoth she to the eldest, 'cut off his nose, and so be revenged on the villain, whatsoever fortune

stanshel: stanchion, upright supporting bar.

me for my labour.' At this the usurer cried out, and bade her stay her children, and he would restore the house and land again to her husband. 'I cannot believe thee, base churl,' quoth she, 'for thou that wouldst perjure thyself against so honest a gentleman as my husband, will not stick to forswear thyself were thou at liberty and therefore I will mangle thee to the uttermost.' As thus she was ready to have her children fall upon him, one of her maids came running in, and told her, her neighbours were come to supper. 'Bid them come in', quoth she, 'and behold this spectacle.' Although the usurer was passing loath to have his neighbours see him thus tyrannously used, yet in they came, and when they saw him thus mannerly in a new-made pillory, and his ears fast nailed, some wondered, some laughed, and all stood amazed, till the gentlewoman discoursed to them all the cozenage, and how she meant to be revenged: some of them persuaded her to let him go, others were silent, and some bade him confess. He hearing them debate the matter, and not to offer to help him, cried out: 'Why, and stand you staring on me, neighbours, and will not you save my life?' 'No,' quoth the gentlewoman, 'he or she that stirs to help thee shall pay dearly for it, and therefore, my boys, off with his ears.' Then he cried out, 'But stay,' and he would confess all, when from point to point he rehearsed how he had cozened her husband by a deed of gift only made to him in trust, and there was content to give him the two hundred marks freely for amends, and to yield up before any men of worship the land again into his possession, and upon that he bade them all bear witness. Then the gentlewoman let loose his ears, and let slip his head, and away went he home with his bloody lugs, and tarried not to take part of the meat he had sent, but the gentlewoman and her neighbours made merry therewith, and laughed heartily at the usage of the usurer. The next day it was bruited abroad, and came to the ears of the worshipful of the country, who sat in commission upon it, and found out the cozenage of the usurer, so they praised the wit of the gentlewoman, restored her husband to the land, and the old churl remained in discredit, and was a laughing stock to all the country all his life after.

I pray you what say to Mounser the miller with the gilden thumb, whether think you him a cony-catcher or no? that robs every poor man of his meal and corn, and takes toll at his own pleasure, how many conies doth he take up in a year? For when he brings them wheat to the mill, he sells them meal of their own corn in the market. I omit Miles the miller's cozenage for wenching affairs, as no doubt in these causes they be mighty cony-catchers, and mean to speak of their policy in filching and stealing of meal. For you must note, that our jolly miller doth not only verse upon the poor and rich for their toll, but hath false hoppers conveyed under the fall of his mill, where all the best of the meal runs by; this is, if the party be by that bringeth the corn: but because many men have many eyes, the miller will drive them off for their grist for a day or two, and then he plays his pranks at his own pleasure. I need not tell that stale jest of the gentleman's miller that kept court and leet once every week, and used to set in every sack a candle, and so summon the owners to appear by their names, if they came not, as they were far enough from that place, then he amerced them, and so took triple toll of every sack. One night amongst the rest, the gentleman his master was under the mill, and heard all his knavery, how every one was called, and paid his amercement; at last he heard his own name called, and then stepping up the ladder, he bade stay, for he was there to make his appearance. I do imagine that the miller was blank, and perhaps his master called him knave, but the fox the more he is cursed the better he fares, and the oftener the miller is called thief, the richer he waxeth: and therefore do men rightly by a byword bid the miller put out, and if he asketh what, they say a thief's head and a thief's pair of ears: for such grand cony-catchers are these millers, that he that cannot verse upon a poor man's sack, is said to be born with a golden thumb. But that you may see more plainly their knavery, I'll tell you a pleasant tale, performed not many years since by a miller in Enfield Mill, ten miles from London, and an alewife's boy of Edmonton, but

Mounser: Monsieur.
court and leet: literally, court presided over by lord of manor.
amerced: fined arbitrarily.

because they are all at this present alive, I will conceal their names, but thus it fell out.

A Pleasant Tale of a Miller and an Alewife's Boy of Edmonton

An alewife of Edmonton, who had a great vent for spiced cakes, sent her son often to Enfield Mill for to have her wheat ground, so that the boy who was of a quick spirit and ripe wit, grew very familiar both with the miller and his man, and could get his corn sooner put in the mill than any boy in the country beside. It fortuned on a time, that this good wife wanting meal, bade her boy hie to the mill, and be at home that night without fail, for she had not a pint of flour in the house. Jack her son, for so we will call his name, lays his sack on his mare's back, and away he rides singing towards Enfield: as he rode, he met at the washes with the miller, and gave him the time of the day. 'Godfather,' quoth he, 'whither ride you?' 'To London, Jack,' quoth the miller. 'Oh, good godfather,' quoth the boy, 'tell me what store of grist is at the mill?' 'Marry, great store,' quoth the miller, 'but, Jack, if thou wilt do me an errand to my man, I'll send thee by a token that thou shalt have thy corn cast on and ground as soon as thou comest.' 'I'll say and do what you will to be dispatched, for my mother hath neither cakes nor flour at home.' 'Then, Jack,' saith the miller, 'bid my man grind thy corn next, by that token he look to my bitch and feed her well. 'I will, godfather,' saith the boy, and rides his way, and marvelled with himself what bitch it was that he bade his man feed, considering for two or three years he had used to the mill, and never saw a dog nor bitch, but a little prickeared shault that kept the mill door. Riding thus musing with himself, at last he came to Enfield, and there he had his corn wound up; as soon as he came up the stairs, the miller's man being somewhat sleepy began to ask Jack drowsily what news. 'Marry,' quoth the boy, 'the news is this, that I must have my corn laid on next.' 'Soft, Jack,' quoth the miller's man, 'your turn will not come afore midnight, but ye are always in haste; soft fire makes sweet malt; your betters shall be served afore you this time.' 'Not so,'

shault: ? shelt, a small pony.

quoth the boy, 'for I met my godfather at the washes riding to London, and told him what haste I had, and so he bids my grist shall be laid on next, by that token you must look to his bitch and feed her well.' At that the miller's man smiled, and said he should be the next, and so rose up and turned a pin behind the hopper. Jack marked all this, and being a wily and a witty boy, mused where this bitch should be, and seeing none, began to suspect some knavery, and therefore being very familiar, was bold to look about in every corner, while the man was busy about the hopper. At last Jack, turning up a cloth that hung before the trough, spied under the hopper below, where a great poke was tied with a cord almost full of fine flour, that ran at a false hole underneath, and could not be spied by any means. Jack, seeing this, began to suspect this was the miller's bitch that he commanded his man to feed, and so smiled and let it alone. At last when the corn was ground off that was in the hopper, Jack laid on his, and was very busy about it himself, so that the miller's man set him down and took a nap, knowing the boy could look to the mill almost as well as himself. Jack all this while had an eye to the bitch, and determined at last to slip her halter, which he warily performed, for when his corn was ground and he had put up his meal, he whipst asunder the cord with his knife that held the poke, and thrust it into the mouth of his sack; now there was in the poke a bushel and more of passing fine flour, that the miller's bitch had eaten that day. As soon as Jack had tied up his sack, there was striving who should lay on corn next, so that the miller's man waked, and Jack, desiring one to help him up with his corn, took his leave and went his way, riding merely homeward, smiling to think how he had cozened the miller. As he rode, at that same place where he met the miller outward, he met him homeward. 'How now, Jack,' quoth the miller, 'hast ground?' 'Ay, I thank you, godfather,' quoth the boy. 'But didst remember my errand to my man?' says he, 'didst bid him look to my bitch well?' 'Oh, godfather,' quoth the boy, 'take no care for your bitch; she is well, for I have her here in my sack, whelps and all.' Away rides Jack at this laughing, and the miller grieving, but when he found it true, I leave you to guess how he and his man dealt together, but how the alewife sported at the knavery of her son when he told her all the jest, that imagine; but howsoever for all that, Jack was ever welcome to the mill and ground before any, and whose soever sack fed the bitch, Jack's 'scapt ever toll-free, that he might conceal the miller's subtlety.

Was not this miller a cony-catcher, Master R.G.? What should I talk of the baser sort of men, whose occupation cannot be upholden without craft? There is no mystery nor science almost, wherein a man may thrive, without it be linked to this famous art of cony-catching. The alewife unless she nick her pots and cony-catch her guests with stone pots and petty cans, can hardly pay her brewer; nay and yet that will not serve, the chalk must walk to set up now and then a shilling or two too much, or else the rent will not be answered at the quarter day, besides ostrey, faggots, and fair chambering, and pretty wenches that have no wages, but what they get by making of beds. I know some taphouses about the suburbs, where they buy a shoulder of mutton for two groats, and sell it to their guest for two shillings, and yet have no female friends to sup withal; let such take heed, lest my father's white horse loose saddle and bridle and they go on foot to the devil on pilgrimage. Tush, Master R.G., God is my witness, I have seen chandlers about London, have two pair of weights, and when the searchers come, they shew them those that are sealed, but when their poor neighbours buy ware, they use them that lack weight. I condemn not all, but let such amend as are touched at the quick. And is not this flat cony-catching? Yes, if it please your mastership, and worser. Why, the base sort of ostlers have their shifts, and the crew of St Patrick's costermongers can sell a simple man a crab for a pippin. And but that I have loved wine well, I would touch both the vintner and his bush, for they have such brewing and tunning, such chopping and changing, such mingling and mixing, what of wine with water in the quart pot, and tempering one wine with another in the vessel, that it is hard

ostrey: ? hay for horses.
searchers: official inspectors.
crab: crab-apple.

to get a neat cup of wine and simple of itself in most of our ordinary taverns. And do not they make poor men conies, that for their current money give them counterfeit wine?

What say you [7] to the butcher with his pricks, that hath policies to puff up his meat to please the eye, is not all his craft used to draw the poor cony to rid him of his ware? Hath not the draper his dark shop to shadow the dye and wool of his cloth, and all to make the country gentleman or farmer a cony? What trade can maintain his traffic, what science uphold itself, what man live, unless he grow into the nature of a cony-catcher? Do not the lawyers make long pleas, stand upon their demurs, and have their quirks and quiddities to make his poor client a cony? I speak not generally, for so they be the ministers of justice, and the patrons of the poor men's right, but particularly of such as hold gains their God, and esteem more of coin than of conscience. I remember by the way a merry jest performed by a fool, yet wittily hit home at hazard, as blind men shoot the crow.

A Pleasant Tale of Will Summers

King Henry the Eighth of famous memory, walking one day in his privy garden with Will Summers his fool, it fortuned that two lawyers had a suit unto His Majesty for one piece of ground that was almost out of lease and in the King's gift, and at time put up their supplication to His Highness, and at that instant one of the pantry that had been a long servitor, had spied out the same land, and exhibited his petition for the same gift, so that in one hour, all the three supplications were given to the King, which His Highness noting, and being as then pleasantly disposed, he revealed it to them that were by him, how there were three fishes at one bait, and all gaped for a benefice, and he stood in doubt on whom to bestow it, and so showed them the supplications. The courtiers spoke for their fellow, except two that were feed by the lawyers, and they particularly pleaded for their friends, yielding many reasons to the King on both sides. At last His Majesty said he would refer the matter to Will Summers; which of them his fool thought most worthy of it should have the land.

neat: unadulterated.

Will was glad of this, and loved him of the pantry well, and resolved he should have the ground, but the fool brought it about with pretty jest. 'Marry,' quoth he, 'what, are these two lawyers?' 'Ay, Will,' said the King. 'Then,' quoth the fool, 'I will use them as they use their poor clients. Look here,' quoth he, 'I have a walnut in my hand, and I will divide it among the three.' So Will cracked it, and gave to one lawyer one shell, and to another the other shell, and to him of the pantry the meat. 'So shall thy gift be, Harry,' quoth he, 'this lawyer shall have good [l]ooks, and this fair promises, but my fellow of the pantry shall have the land. For thus deal they with their clients; two men go to two, and spend all that they have upon the law, and at last, have nothing but bare shells for their labour.' At this, the King and his noblemen laughed: the yeoman of the pantry had the gift, and the lawyers went home with fleas in their ears, by a fool's verdict. I rehearsed this act to show how men of law feed on poor men's purses, and makes their country clients oftentimes simple conies. But leaving these common courses and trivial examples, I will show you, Master R.G., of a kind of cony-catchers, that as yet passeth all these.

There be in England, but especially about London, certain quaint picked and neat companions, attired in their apparel, either *à la mode de France*, with a side cloak, and a hat of a high block and a broad brim, as if he could with his head cosmographize the world in a moment, or else *à l'espagnol*, with a straight bombast sleeve like a quail pipe, his short cloak, and his rapier hanging as if he were entering the list to a desperate combat: his beard squared with such art, either with his mustachios after the lash of lion, standing as stiff as if he wore a ruler in his mouth, or else nickt off with the Italian cut, as if he meant to profess one faith with the upper lip, and another with his nether lip; and then he must be marquisadoed, with a side peak pendant, either sharp like the single of a deer, or curtailed like the broad end of a mole spade. This gentleman forsooth, haunteth tabling houses, taverns, and such places, where young novices resort, and can fit his humour to all companies, and openly shadoweth his disguise with the name of a traveller,

[*l*]*ooks*: original 'books'.

so that he will have a superficial insight into certain phrases of every language, and pronounce them in such a grace, as if almost he were that countryman born: then shall you hear him vaunt of his travels, and tell what wonders he hath seen in strange countries: how he hath been at St James of Compostella in Spain, at Madrid in the King's Court: and then drawing out his blade, he claps it on the board, and swears he bought that in Toledo: then will he rove to Venice, and with a sigh, discover the situation of the city, how it is seated two leagues from terra frenia,[8] in the sea, and speak of Rialto Treviso and Murano, where they make glasses: and to set the young gentleman's teeth an edge, he will make a long tale of La Strado Curtizano, where the beautiful courtezans dwell, describing their excellency, and what angelical creatures they be, and how amorously they will entertain strangers. Tush, he will discourse the state of Barbary, and there to Eschites and Alcaires, and from thence leap to France, Denmark, and Germany, after all concluding thus:

'What is a gentleman,' saith he, 'without travel? even as a man without one eye. The sight of sundry countries made Ulysses so famous: bought wit is the sweetest, and experience goeth beyond all patrimonies. Did young gentlemen, as well as I, know the pleasure and profit of travel, they would not keep them at home within their native continent: but visit the world, and win more wisdom in travelling two or three years, than all the wealth their ancestors left them to possess. Ah, the sweet sight of ladies, the strange wonders in cities, and the divers manners of men and their conditions, were able to ravish a young gentleman's senses with the surfeit of content; and what is a thousand pound spent to the obtaining of those pleasures?'

All these novelties doth this pippened braggart boast on, when his only travel hath been to look on a fair day from Dover Cliffs to Calais, never having stept a foot out of England, but surveyed the maps, and heard others talk what they knew by experience. Thus decking himself like the daw with the fair feathers of other birds, and discoursing what he heard other men report, he grew so plausible among young gentlemen, that he got his ordinary at the least, and some gracious thanks for his labour. But happily

pippened: round-faced.

some amongst many, tickled with the desire to see strange countries, and drawn on by his alluring words, would join with him, and question if he meant ever to travel again. He straight after he hath bitten his peak by the end, *alla Neopolitano* begins thus to reply.

'Sir, although a man of my travel and experience might be satisfied in the sight of countries, yet so insatiate is the desire of travelling, that if perhaps a young gentleman of a liberal and courteous nature, were desirous to see Jerusalem or Constantinople, would he well acquit my pains and follow my counsel, I would bestow a year or two with him out of England.' To be brief, if the gentleman jump with him, then doth he cause him to sell some Lordship, and put some thousand or two thousand pound in the bank to be received by letters of exchange: and because the gentleman is ignorant, my young master his guide must have the disposing of it: which he so well sets out, that the poor gentleman never sees any return of his money after. Then must store of suits of apparel be bought and furnished every way: at last, he names a ship wherein they should pass, and so down to Gravesend they go, and there he leaves the young novice, fleeced of his money and woe begone, as far from travel as Miles the merry cobbler of Shoreditch, that swore he would never travel further than from his shop to the ale-house. I pray you call you not these fine-witted fellows cony-catchers, Master R.G.?

But now sir by your leave a little, what if I should prove you a cony-catcher, Master R.G., would it not make you blush at the matter? I'll go as near to it as the friar did to his hostess's maid, when the clerk of the parish took him at Leatem at midnight. Ask the Queen's Players, if you sold them not Orlando Furioso for twenty nobles, and when they were in the country, sold the same play to the Lord Admiral's Men for as much more. Was not this plain cony-catching, Master R.G.?

But I hear when this was objected, that you made this excuse: that there was no more faith to be held with players, than with them that valued faith at the price of a feather: for as they were comedians to act, so the actions of their lives were chameleon-like, that they were uncertain, variable, time-pleasers, men that

Leatem: ? lenten, meagre (i.e. without clothes), or Latin *laitum*, joy.

measured honesty by profit, and that regarded their authors not by desert, but by necessity of time. If this may serve you for a shadow, let me use it for an excuse of our card cony-catching: for when we meet a country farmer with a full purse, a miserable miser, that either racks his tenants' rents, or sells his grain in the market at an unreasonable rate, we hold it a devotion to make him a cony, in that he is a caterpillar to others, and gets that by pilling and polling of the poor, that we strip him of by sleight and agility of wit.

Is there not here resident about London, a crew of terrible hacksters in the habit of gentlemen, well apparelled, and yet some wear boots for want of stockings, with a lock worn at their left ear for their mistress's favour, his rapier *a la revolto*, his poynado pendant ready for the stab, and caviliverst like a warlike magnifico? Yet for all this outward show of pride, inwardly they be humble, and despise worldly wealth, for you shall never take them with a penny in their purse. These soldados, for under that profession most of them wander, have a policy to scourge ale-houses, for where they light in, they never leap out, till they have showed their arithmetic with chalk on every post in the house, figured in ciphers like round Os, till they make the goodman cry O, O, O, as if he should call an Oyez at 'Size or Sessions. Now sir, they have sundry shifts to maintain them in this versing, for either they creep in with the goodwife, and so undo the goodman, or else they bear it out with great brags if the host be simple, or else they trip him in some words when he is tipsy, that he hath spoken against some Justice of Peace or other, or some other great man: and then they hold him at a bay with that, till his back almost break. Thus shift they from house to house, having this proverb amongst them: 'Such must eat as are hungry and they must pay that have money.' Call you not these cony-catchers, Master R.G.?

It were an endless piece of work, to discover the abhominable[9] life of brokers, whose shops are the very temples of the devil, themselves his priests, and their books of account more damnable, than the Alcoran set out by Mahomet: for as they induce

a la revolto : reverse of usual fashion.
caviliverst : ? cavalierest=swaggers.

young gentlemen to pawn their lands, as I said before, so they are ready (the more is the pity that it is suffered) to receive any goods, howsoever it be come by, having their shops, as they say, a lawful market to buy and sell in, so that whence grows so many lifts about London, but in that they have brokers their friends, to buy whatsoever they purloin and steal? And yet is the picklock, lift, or hooker, that brings the stolen goods, made a flat cony, and used as an instrument only of their villainy: for suppose he hath lifted a gown or a cloak, or so many parcels as are worth ten pounds, and ventures his life in hazard for the obtaining of it: the miserable caterpillar the broker will think he dealeth liberally with him if he give him forty shillings, so doth he not only maintain felony, but like a thief cozens the thief. And are not these grand cony-catchers, Master R.G.?

I knew, not far from Fleet Bridge, a haberdasher, it were a good deed to take pain to tell his name, that took of a boy of seven year old a rapier worth forty shillings, and a stitched taffeta hat worth ten, and all for five shillings: the gentleman, father to the child, was sick when necessity drove him thus nigh, to lay his weapon and his bonnet to pawn, and as soon as he recovered, which was within six weeks after, sent the money and twelve pence for the loan, to have the parcels again. But this cutthroat's answer was, the boy had made him a bill of sale of his hand for a month, and the day was broken, and he had made the best of the rapier and hat. Was not this a Jew and a notable cony-catcher, Master R.G.?

It had been well if you had rolled out your rhetoric against such a rakehell. But come to their honest kind of life, and you shall see how they stand upon circumstances: if you borrow but two shillings, there must be a groat for the money, and a groat for the bill of sale, and this must be renewed every month: so that they resemble the box at dice, which being well paid all night, will in the morning be the greatest winner.

Wer't not a merry jest to have a bout again, Master R.G., with your poetical brethren? Amongst the which, one learned hypocrite that could brook no abuses in the commonwealth, was so zealous, that he began to put an English she-saint in the legend, for the holiness of her life: and forgot not so much as her dog, as Tobie's [10] was remembered, that wagged his tail at the sight of his old mistress. This pure Martinist [11] (if he were not worse) had a combat between the flesh and the spirit, that he must needs have a wife, which he cunningly cony-catched in this manner.

A Pleasant Tale how a Holy Brother Cony-Catched for a Wife

First you must understand, that he was a kind of scholastical 'panion, nurst up only at grammar school, lest going to the university, through his nimble wit, too much learning should make him mad. So he had past *As in praesenti*, and was gone a proficient as far as *Carmen Heroicum*: for he pronounced his words like a braggart, and held up his head like a malt-horse, and could talk against bishops, and wish very mannerly the discipline of the Primitive Church were restored. Now sir, this gentleman had espied (I dare not say about Fleet Street) a proper maid, who had given her by the decease of her father four hundred pound in money, besides certain fair houses in the City: to this girl goeth this proper Greek a-wooing, naming himself to be a gentleman of Cheshire, and only son and heir to his father, who was a man of great revenues: and to make the matter more plausible, he had attired his own brother very orderly in a blue coat, and made him his servingman, who, though he were eldest, yet to advance his younger brother to so good a marriage, was content to lie, cog, and flatter, and to take any servile pains, to sooth up the matter: insomuch that when her father-in-law (for her mother was married again, to an honest, virtuous, and substantial man in Fleet Street or thereabouts) heard how this young gentleman was a suitor to his daughter-in-law, careful she should do well, called the servingman aside, which by his outward behaviour seemed to be an honest and discreet man, and began to question with him what his master was, of what parentage, of what possibility of living after his father's decease, and how many children he had beside him.

This fellow, well instructed by his holy brother, without distrust to the man, simply as he thought, said, that he was the son

As in praesenti: tag from Latin text-book.
Carmen Heroicum: opening of Servatius' commentary on Virgil's *Aeneid*.

CONY-CATCHERS AND BAWDY BASKETS

and heir of one Master etc. dwelling in Cheshire, at the Manor of etc. and that he had a younger brother, but this was heir to all, and rehearsed a proper living of some five hundred marks a year. The honest man, knowing divers Cheshire gentlemen of that name, gave credit to the fellow, and made no further inquiry, but gave countenance to my young master, who by his flattering speeches had won, not only the maid's favour unto the full, but also the good will of her mother, so that the match shortly was made up, and married they should be forsooth, and then should she, her father and her mother, ride home to his father in Cheshire, to have sufficient dowry appointed.

To be brief, wedded they were, and bedded they had been three or four nights, and yet for all this fair show the father was a little jealous, and smoked him, but durst say nothing. But at last, after the marriage had been past over three or four days, it chanced that her father and this servingman went abroad, and past through St Paul's Churchyard. Amongst the stationers, a prentice amongst the rest, that was a Cheshire man, and knew this counterfeit servingman and his brother, as being born in the same parish where his father dwelt, called to him, and said: 'What, hey, how doth your brother P., how doth your father, lives he still?' The fellow answered him all were well, and loath his brother's wife's father should hear any thing, made no stay but departed.

This acquaintance naming the fellow by his name and asking for his brother, drove the honest citizen into a great maze, and doubted he, his wife and his daughter were made conies. Well, he smoothed all up, as if he had heard nothing, and let it pass till he had sent the man about necessary business, and then secretly returned again unto the stationer's shop, and began to question with the boy, if he knew the servingman well, that he called to him of late. 'Ay, marry,' quoth he, 'I know both him and his brother P. I can tell you they have an honest poor man to their father, and though now in his old age he be scarce able to live without the help of the parish, yet he is well beloved of all his neighbours.' The man hearing this, although it grieved him that he was thus cozened by a palliard, yet seeing no means to amend

jealous: suspicious.

it, he thought to gird his son pleasantly, and therefore bade divers of his friends and honest wealthy neighbours to a supper. Well, they being at the time appointed come, all welcome, who must sit at the board's end but my young master, and he very coyly, bade them all welcome to his father's house. They all gave him reverent thanks, esteeming him to be a man of worship and worth. As soon as all were set, and the meat served in, and the gentleman's servingman stood mannerly waiting on his brother's trencher, at last the goodman of the house smiling said : 'Son P., I pray you let your man sit down, and eat such part with us as God hath sent us.' – 'Marry,' quoth Master P., 'that were well, to make my man my companion, he is well enough, let him sup with his fellows.' – 'Why, sir,' saith he, 'in faith be plain, call him brother, and bid him sit down. Come cousin. Ay,' quoth he, 'make not strange, I am sure your brother P. will give you leave.' At this Master P. blushed, and asked his father-in-law what he meant by those words, and whether he thought his man his brother or no. 'Ay, by my faith do I, son,' quoth he, 'and account thee no honest man that wilt deny thine own brother and thy father : for, sir, know I have learned your pedigree. Alas, daughter,' quoth he, 'you are well married, for his father lives off the alms of the parish, and this poor fellow which he hath made his slave, is his eldest brother.' At this his wife began to weep, all was dashed, and what she thought God knows. Her mother cried out, but all was bootless. Master P. confest the truth, and his brother sat down at supper, and for all that he had the wench. I pray you was not this a cony-catcher, Master R.G.?

But now to be a little pleasant with you, let me have your opinion what you deem of those Amorosos here in England, and about London, that (because the old proverb saith, change of pasture makes fat calves) will have in every shire in England a sundry wife, as for an instance your countryman R.B. Are not they right cony-catchers? Enter into the nature of them, and see whether your pen had been better employed in discovering their villainies, than a simple legerdemain at cards. For suppose a man hath but one daughter, and hath no other dowry but her beauty and honesty, what a spoil is it for her to light in the hands of such an adulterous and incestuous rascal? Had not her father been better to have lost forty shillings at cards, than to have his daughter so cony-catched and spoiled for ever after? These youths are proper fellows, never without good apparel and store of crowns, well horsed, and of so quaint and fine behaviour, and so eloquent, that they are able to induce a young girl to folly, especially since they shadow their villainy with the honest pretence of marriage; for their custom is this: when they come into the City or other place of credit, or sometime in a country village, as the fortune of their villainy leads them, they make inquiry what good marriages are abroad, and on the Sunday make survey what fair and beautiful maids or widows are in the parish: then, as their licentious lust leads them, whether the eye for favour, or the ear for riches, so they set down their rest, and sojourn either there or thereabouts, having money at will, and their companions to sooth up whatsoever damnably they shall protest, courting the maid or widow with such fair words, and sweet promises, that she is often so set on fire, that neither the report of others, nor the admonition of their friends, can draw them from the love of the Poligamoi or bell-swaggers of the country. And when the wretches have by the space of a month or two satisfied their lust, they wax weary, and either fain some great journey for a while to be absent, and so go and visit some other of his wives, or else if he mean to give her the bag, he selleth whatsoever he can, and so leaves her spoiled both of her wealth and honesty, than which there is nothing more precious to an honest woman. And because you shall see an instance, I will tell you a pleasant tale performed by our villains in Wiltshire not long since. I will conceal the parties' names, because I think the woman is yet alive.

A Pleasant Tale of a Man that was Married to Sixteen Wives, and how Courteously his Last Wife Entreated him

In Wiltshire there dwelt a farmer of indifferent wealth, that had but only one child, and that was a daughter, a maid of excellent beauty and good behaviour, and so honest in her conversation, that the good report of her virtues was well spoken of in all the country, so that what for her good qualities, and sufficient dowry that was like to fall to her, she had many suitors, men's sons of good wealth and honest conversation. But whether this maid had no mind to wed, or she liked none that made love to her, or she was afraid to match in haste lest she might repent at leisure, I know not; but she refused all, and kept her still a virgin. But as we see oftentimes, the coyest maids happen on the coldest marriages, playing like the beetle that makes scorn all day of the daintiest flowers, and at night takes up his lodging in a cowshard. So this maid, whom we will call Marian, refused many honest and wealthy farmers' sons, and at last lighted on a match, that for ever after marred her market: for it fell out thus: one of these notable rogues, by occupation a tailor, and a fine workman, a reprobate given over to the spoil of honest maids, and to the deflowering of virgins, hearing as he travelled abroad of this Marian, did mean to have a fling at her, and therefore came into the town where her father dwelt and asked work. A very honest man of that trade, seeing him a passing proper man, and of a very good and honest countenance, and not simply apparelled, said he would make trial of him for a garment or two, and so took him into service: as soon as he saw him use his needle, he wondered not only at his workmanship, but at the swiftness of his hand. At last the fellow (whom we will name William) desired his master that he might use his shears but once for the cutting out of a doublet, which his master granted, and he used so excellently well, that although his master was counted the best tailor in Wiltshire, yet he found himself a botcher in respect of his new-entertained journeyman, so that from that time forward he was made foreman of the shop, and so pleased the gentlemen of that shire, that who but William talked on for a good tailor in that shire. Well, as young men and maids meet on Sundays and holydays, so this tailor was passing brave, and began to frolic it amongst the maids, and to be very liberal, being full of silver and gold, and for his personage a properer man than any was in all the parish, and made afar off a kind of love to this Marian, who seeing this William to be a very handsome man, began somewhat to affect him, so that in short time she thought well of his favours, and there grew some love between them, insomuch that it came to her father's ears, who began to school his daughter for such foolish affection towards one she knew not what he was, nor whither he would: but in vain, Marian could not but think well of him, so that her father one day sent for his master, and began to question of the disposition of his man. The master told the farmer friendly that what he was he knew not, as being a mere stranger unto him; but for his workmanship, he was one of the most excellent both for needle and shears in England; for his behaviour since he came into his house, he had behaved himself very honestly and courteously; well apparelled he was, and well moneyed, and might for his good qualities seem to be a good woman's fellow. Although this somewhat satisfied the father, yet he was loath a tailor should carry away his daughter, and that she should be driven to live of a bare occupation, whereas she might have landed men to her husbands, so that he and her friends called her aside, and persuaded her from him, but she flatly told them she never loved any but him, and sith it was her first love, she would not now be turned from it, whatsoever hap did afterward befall unto her. Her father that loved her dearly, seeing no persuasions could draw her from the tailor, left her to her own liberty, and so she and William agreed together, that in short time they were married, and had a good portion, and set up shop, and lived together by the space of a quarter of a year very orderly. At last satisfied with the lust of his new wife, he thought it good to visit some other of his wives (for at that instant he had sixteen alive), and made a scuse to his wife and his wife's father to go into Yorkshire, which was his native country, and visit his friends, and crave somewhat of his father towards household. Although his wife was loath to part from her sweet Will[iam] yet she must be content, and so well horsed and provided away he rides for a month or two, that was his furthest day, and down goes he into some other country to solace himself with some other of his wives. In this meanwhile one of his wives that he married in or about Taunton in Somersetshire, had learned of his villainy, and how many wives he had, and by long travel had got a note of their names and dwelling, and the hands and seals of every parish where he was married, and now by fortune she heard that he had married a wife in Wiltshire, not far from Marlborough: thither hies she with warrants from the bishop and divers justices to apprehend him, and coming to the town where he dwelt, very subtly inquired at her host of his estate, who told her that he had married a rich farmer's daughter, but now was gone down to his friends in Yorkshire, and would be at home again within a week, for he had been eight weeks already from home. The woman inquired no further for that time, but the next morning went home to the farmer's house, and desired him to send for his daughter, for she would speak with her from her husband: the man straight did so, and she hearing she should have news from her William, came very hastily. Then the woman said, she was sorry for her, in that their misfortunes were alike, in being married to such a runagate as this tailor: 'For,' quoth she, 'it is not yet a year and a half since he was married to me in Somersetshire.' As this went cold to the old man's heart, so struck it deadly into the mind of Marian, who, desiring her to tell the truth, she out with her testimony, and showed them how he had at that instant sixteen wives alive. When they read the certificate, and saw the hands and seals of every parish, the old man fell a-weeping: but such was the grief of Marian, that her sorrow stopped her tears, and she sat as a woman in a trance, till at last fetching a great sigh, she called God to witness she would be revenged on him for all his wives, and would make him a general example of all such graceless runagates. So she concealed the matter, and placed this her fellow in misfortune in a kinswoman's house of hers, so secretly as might be, attending the coming of her treacherous husband, who returned within a fortnight, having in the space he was absent visited three or four of his wives, and now meant to make a short cut of the matter, and sell all that his new wife had, and to travel into some other shire, for he had heard how his Somersetshire wife had made inquiry after him in divers places. Being come home he was wonderfully welcome to Marian, who entertained him with such courtesies as a kind wife could any ways afford him, only the use of her body she denied, saying her natural disease was upon her. Well, to be brief, a great supper was made, and all her friends was bidden, and he every way so welcome as if it had been the day of his bridal, yea all things was smoothed up so cunningly, that he suspected nothing less than the revenge intended against him. As soon as supper was ended, and all had taken their leave, our tailor would to bed, and his wife with her own hands helped to undress him very lovingly, and being laid down she kissed him, and said she would go to her father's and come again straight, bidding him fall asleep the whilst: he, that was drowsy with travel and drinking at supper, had no need of great entreaty, for he straight fell into a sound slumber, the whilst she had sent for his other wife, and other her neighbours disguised, and coming softly into the parlour where he lay, she turned up his clothes at his feet, and tied his legs fast together with a rope; then waking him, she asked him what reason he had to sleep so soundly. He, new waked out his sleep, began to stretch himself, and galled his legs with the cord, whereat he wondering said: 'How now wife? What's that hurts my legs? What, are my feet bound together?' Marian, looking on him with looks full of death, made him this answer: 'Ay, villain, thy legs are bound, but hadst thou thy just desert, thy neck had long since been stretched at the gallows, but before thou and I part, I will make thee a just spectacle unto the world, for thy abhominable treachery'; and with that she clapped her hand fast on the hair of his head, and held him down to the pillow. William, driven into a wondrous amaze at these words, said trembling: 'Sweet wife, what sudden alteration is this? what mean these words, wife?' 'Traitor,' quoth she, 'I am none of thy wife, neither is this thy wife,' and with that she brought her forth that he was married in Somersetshire, 'although thou art married to her as well as to me, and hast like a villain sought the spoil of fifteen women beside myself, and that thou shalt hear by just certificate'; and with that there was read the bedroll of his wives, where he married them, and where they dwelt. At this he lay mute as in a trance, and only for answer held up his hands, and desired them both to be merciful unto him, for he confessed all was truth, that he had been a heinous offender, and deserved death. 'Tush,' saith Marian, 'but how canst thou make any one of us amends? If a man kill the father, he may satisfy the blood in the son: if a man steal, he may make restitution: but he that robs a woman of her honesty and virginity, can never make any satisfaction: and therefore for all the rest I will be revenged.' With that his other wife and the women clapped hold on him, and held him fast, while Marian with a sharp razor cut off his stones, and made him a gelding. I think she had little respect where the sign was, or observed little art for the string, but off they went, and then she cast them in his face, and said: 'Now lustful whoremaster, go and deceive other women as thou hast done us, if thou canst', so they sent in a surgeon to him that they had provided, and away they went. The man lying in great pain of body and agony of mind, the surgeon looking to his wound, had much ado to stanch the blood, and always he laughed heartily when he thought on the revenge, and bade a vengeance on such sow-gelders as made such large slits: but at last he laid a blood-plaster to him, and stopped his bleeding, and to be brief, in time healed him, but with much pain. As soon as he was whole, and might go abroad without danger, he was committed to the gaol, and after some other punishment, banished out of Wiltshire and Somersetshire for ever after. Thus was this lusty cock of the game made a capon, and as I heard, had little lust to marry any more wives to his dying day.

How like you of this cony-catching, Mr R.G.? But because now we have entered talk of tailors, let me have a bout with them, for they be mighty cony-catchers in sundry kinds. I pray you, what poet hath so many fictions, what painter so many fancies, as a tailor hath fashions, to show the variety of his art? changing every week the shape of his apparel into new forms, or else he is counted a mere botcher. The Venetian and the Gallogascaine is stale, and trunk slop out of use, the round hose bumbasted close to the breech, and ruffed above the neck with a curl, is now common to every cullion in the country, and doublets be they never so quaintly quilted, yet forsooth the swain at plough must have his belly as side as the courtier, that he may piss out at a button hole at the least. And all these strange devices doth the tailor invent to make poor gentlemen conies: for if they were tied to one fashion, then still might they know how much velvet to send to the tailor, and then would his filching abate. But to prevent them, if he have a French belly, he will have a Spanish skirt, and an

Venetian: hose first introduced from Venice.
Gallogascaine: loose breeches (galligaskins).
trunk slop: wide hose reaching to upper thighs.

Italian wing, seamed and quartered at the elbows, as if he were a
soldado ready to put on an armour of proof to fight in Mile-end
under the bloody ensign of the Duke of Shoreditch.[12] Thus will
the fantastic tailor make poor gentlemen conies, and ever ask
more velvet by a yard and a half than the doublet in conscience
requires. But herein lies the least part of their cony-catching: for
those grand tailors that have all the right properties of the mystery, which is to be knavish, thievish, and proud, take this course
with courtiers and courtly gentlemen; they find outside, inside,
lace, drawing out, and making, and then set down their parcels
in a bill, which they so overprice, that some of them with very
pricking up of doublets, have fleeced young gentlemen of whole
Lordships. And call you not this cony-catching, Mr R.G.? To
use the figure *Pleonasmos, Hisce oculis*, with these eyes I have
seen tailors' prentices sell as much vales in a week in cloth of
gold, velvet, satten, taffeta, and lace, as hath been worth thirty
shillings, and these ears hath heard them scorn when their vales
came but to ten shillings, and yet there were four prentices in the
shop. If the prentices could lurch so mightily, then what did the
master? But you must imagine this was a woman's tailor, that
could in a gown put seventeen yards of ell-broad taffeta, blest be
the French sleeves and breech farthingales, that grants them
liberty to cony-catch so mightily. But this I talk of our London
and courtly tailors: but even the poor pricklouse the country
tailor, that hath scarce any more wealth than his thimble, his
needle, his pressing iron, and his shears, will filch as well as the
proudest of that trade in England, they will to snip and snap, that
all the reversion goes into hell. Now sir, this hell is a place that
the tailors have under their shop-board, where all their stolen
shreds is thrust, and I pray you, call you not this pilling and
polling, and flat cony-catching, Master R.G.? But because you
may see whether I speak truth or no, I'll tell you a merry jest of
a tailor in York not far from Petergate, done about fourteen year
ago; and thus it fell out.

mystery: craft, trade.
Pleonasmos: rhetorical figure of redundancy.
vales: perquisites, profits.

A Pleasant Tale of a Tailor, how he Cony-Catched a Gentlewoman, and was Made himself a Cony Afterwards by his Man.

In Yorkshire there dwelt a woman's tailor famous for his art, but noted for his filching, which although he was light-fingered, yet for the excellency of his workmanship, he was much sought too, and kept more journeymen, than any five in that city did: and albeit he would have his share of velvet, satin, or cloth of gold, yet they must find no fault with him, lest he half spoiled their garment in the making. Besides, he was passing proud, and had as haughty a look, as if his father had with devil looked over Lincoln: his ordinary doublets were taffeta cut in the summer upon a wrought shirt, and his cloak faced with velvet, his stockings of the purest granado silk, with a French pained hose of the richest billiment lace, a beaver hat turft with velvet, so quaintly as if he had been some Espagnolo tricked up to go court some quaint courtezan, insomuch that a plain servingman once meeting him in this attire, going through Waingate to take air in the field, thought him at the least some esquire, and off with his hat and gave his worship the time of the day; this clawed this glorioso by the elbow, so that if a tavern had been by, a pottle of wine should have been the least reward for a largesse to the simple servingman: but this bowical huff-snuff, not content to pass away with one worship, began to hold the fellow in prate, and to question whose man he was. The fellow courteously making a low cringe, said, 'May it please your worship, I serve such a gentleman dwelling in such a place.' As thus he answered him, he spied in the gentleman's bosom a needle and a thread, whereupon the fellow simply said to him, 'Fie, your worship's man in looking this morning to your doublet, hath left a needle and a thread on your worship's breast. You had best take it off, lest some think your worship to be a tailor.' The tailor not thinking the fellow had spoken simply, but frumped him, made this reply: 'What, saucy

devil . . . Lincoln: proverbial expression signifying great pride.
billiment: ? elaborately worked (biliment=ornament).
bowical: ? bucket-faced bowey=dial., bucket).

knave, dost thou mock me? What if I be a tailor, what's that to thee? Were't not for shame I would lend thee a box on the ear or two.' The fellow being plain, but peevish and an old knave, gathering by his own words that he was a tailor, said: 'Fie, so God help me I mock you not, but are you a tailor?' 'Ay, marry am I,' quoth he. 'Why then,' says the servingman, 'all my caps, knees, and worships, I did to thy apparel, and therefore master, thank me, for it was against my will, but now I know thee, farewell good honest pricklouse, and look not behind you, for if you do, I'll swinge you in my scabbard of my sword till I can stand over thee.' Away went Monsieur Magnifico frowning, and the servingman went into the city laughing.

But all this is but to describe the nature of the man; now to the secrets of his art. All the gentlewomen of the country cried out upon him, yet could they not part from him, because he so quaintly fitted their humours. At last it so fell out, that a gentlewoman not far from Feroy Bridges, had a taffeta gown to make, and he would have no less at those days than eleven ells of ellbroad taffeta; so she bought so much and ready to send it, she said to her husband in hearing of all her servingmen: 'What a spite is this, seeing that I must send always to yonder knave tailor two yards more than is necessary! But how can we amend us, all the rest are but botchers in respect of him, and yet nothing grieves me but we can never take him with it, and yet I and mine have stood by while he hath cut my gown out.' A pleasant fellow that was new come to serve her husband, one that was his clerk and a pretty scholar, answered: 'Good mistress, give me leave to carry your taffeta and see it cut out, and if I spy not out his knavery laugh at me when I come home.' 'Marry, I prithee do,' quoth his master and mistress, 'but whatsoever thou seest say nothing lest he be angry and spoil my gown.' 'Let me alone mistress,' quoth he, and so away he goes to York, and coming to this tailor found him in his shop, and delivered him the taffeta with this message, that his mistress had charged him to see it cut out, not that she suspected him, but that else he would let it lie long by him and take other work in hand. The tailor scornfully said he should, and asked him if he had any spectacles about him. 'No,' quoth the fellow, 'my sight is young enough, I need no glasses.' 'If you do, put them,' quoth he, 'and see if you can see me steal a yard of taffeta out of your mistress's gown.' And so, taking his shears in hand, he cut it out so nimbly that he cut three foreparts to the gown, and four side pieces, that by computation the fellow guessed he had stolen two ells and a half, but say nothing he durst. As soon as he had done, there came in more gentlemen's men with work, that the tailor was very busy and regarded not the servingmen who, seeing the tailor's cloak lying loose, lifted it away and carried it home with him to his mistress's house, where he discoursed to his master and his mistress what he had seen, and how he had stole the tailor's cloak, not to that intent to filch, but to try an experiment upon him; 'For, master,' quoth he, 'when he brings home my mistress's gown, he will complain of the loss of his cloak, and then see, do you but tell him that I am experienced in magic, and can cast a figure, and will tell him where his cloak is without fail. Say but this sir, and let me alone.' They all agreed, and resolved to try the wit of their young man. But leaving him, again to our tailor: who, when he had dispatched his customers, was ready to walk with one of them to the tavern, and then missed his cloak, searched all about, but find it he could not, neither knew he whom to suspect. So with much grief he passed it over, and when he had ended the gentle-woman's gown (because she was a good customer of his) he himself took his nag and rid home withal. Welcome he was to the gentlewoman and her husband, and the gown was passing fit, so that it could not be amended, insomuch that the gentlewoman praised it, and highly thanked him. 'Oh mistress,' quoth he, 'though it is a good gown to you, 'tis an unfortunate gown to me, for that day your man brought the taffeta, I had a cloak stolen that stood me but one fortnight before in four pound, and never since could I hear any word of it.' – 'Truly,' said the gentleman, 'I am passing sorry for your loss, but that same man that was at your house is passing skilful in negromancy,[13] and if any man in England can tell you where your cloak is, my man can.' – 'Marry,' quoth he, 'and I will give him a brace of angels for his labour.' So the fellow was called and talked withal, and at his mistress's request was content to do it, but he would have his twenty shill-ings in hand, and promised if he told him not where it was, who had it, and caused it to be delivered to him again, for his two angels he would give him ten pounds. Upon this the tailor willingly gave him the money, and up went he into a closet like a learned clerk, and there was three or four hours laughing at the tailor, he thinking he had been all this while at Caurake. At last down comes the fellow with a figure drawn in a paper in his hand, and smiling called for a Bible, and told the tailor he would tell him who had his cloak, where it was, and help him to it again, so that he would be sworn on a Bible to answer to all questions that he demanded of him faithfully. The tailor granted and swore on a Bible, then he commanded all should go out but his master, his mistress, the tailor and himself. Then he began thus: 'Well, you have taken your oath on the holy Bible, tell me,' quoth he, 'did you not cut three foreparts for my mistress's gown?' At this the tailor blushed, and began to be in a chafe, and would have flung out of the door, but the servingman said, 'Nay, never start, man, for before thou goest out of this parlour, if thou deniest it, I will bring the taffeta thou stolest into this place, wrapt in thine own cloak; and therefore answer directly to my question, lest to your discredit I show you the trick of a scholar.' The tailor, half afraid, said he did so indeed. 'And,' quoth he, 'did you not cut four side pieces where you [should] have cut but two?' 'Yes, all is true,' quoth the tailor. 'Why then, as true it is, that to deceive the deceiver is no deceit; for as truly as you stole my mistress's taffeta, so truly did I steal your cloak, and here it is.' At this the tailor was amazed, the gentleman and his wife laughed heartily, and so all was turned to a merriment. The tailor had his cloak again, the gentlewoman her taffeta, and the servingman twenty shillings. Was not this pretty and witty cony-catching, Mr R.G.?

Thus have I proved to your masterships, how there is no estate, trade, occupation, nor mystery, but lives by cony-catching, and that our shift at cards compared to the rest, is the simplest of all, and yet forsooth, you could bestow the pains to write two whole pamphlets against us poor cony-catchers. Think, Mr R.G., it shall not be put up except you grant us our request. It is informed

Caurake: ? misprint for 'oracle'. (Or Latin *caurio*, a religious ceremony.)

us that you are in hand with a book named *The Repentance of a Cony-Catcher*, with a discovery of secret villainies, wherein you mean to discourse at full the nature of *the stripping law*, which is the abuse offered by the keepers of Newgate to poor prisoners, and some that belong to the Marshalsea. If you do so, ye shall do not only a charitable, but a meritorious deed: for the occasion of most mischief, of greatest nipping and foisting, and of all villainies, comes through the extorting bribery of some cozening and counterfeit keepers and companions, that carry unlawful warrants about them to take up men. Will your worship therefore stand to your word, and set out the discovery of that, all we of Whittington College will rest your beadmen. Otherwise look that I will have the crew of cony-catchers swear themselves your professed enemies for ever. Farewell.

Cuthbert Cony-Catcher

FINIS

beadmen: beadsmen, pensioners.

A SERMON

IN PRAISE OF

THIEVES

AND

THIEVERY

A Sermon of Parson Haberdyne,

*which he made at the commandment
of certain thieves, after they
had robbed him besides
Hartley Row in Hampshire,
in the fields there,
standing upon a hill
where [as] a windmill
had been, in the
presence of the
thieves that
robbed him, as
followeth.*

(*The Sermon as Followeth*:)

I GREATLY marvel that any man will presume to dispraise thievery, and think the doers thereof to be worthy of death, considering it is a thing that cometh near unto virtue, being used of many in all countries, and commended and allowed of God himself. The which things, because I cannot compendiously show unto you at so short a warning and in so sharp a weather, I shall desire you, gentle audience of thieves, to take in good part these things that at this time cometh to my mind, not misdoubting that you of your good knowledge are able to add much more unto it than this which I shall now utter unto you.

First, fortitude and stoutness of courage and also boldness of mind, is commended of some men to be a virtue; which being granted, who is it then that will not judge thieves to be virtuous[ed]? For they be of all men most stout and hardy and most without fear. For thievery is a thing most usual among all men; for not only you that be here present, but many other in divers places, both men and women and children, rich and poor, are daily of this faculty (as the hangman of Tyburn can testify).

And that it is allowed of God himself, as it is evident in many stories of [the] Scriptures; for if you look in the whole course of the Bible, you shall find that thieves have been beloved of God. For Jacob, when he came out of Mesopotamia, did steal his uncle Laban's kids. The same Jacob did also steal his brothe[r] Esau's blessing. And yet God said, 'I have chosen Jacob and refused Esau.' The children of Israel, when they came out of Egypt, did steal Egyptians' jewels of silver and gold, as God commanded them so to do. David, in the days of Abiazar [1] the high priest, did come into the temple and did steal the hallowed bread. And yet God said, 'David is a man after mine own heart.'

Christ himself, when he was here on the earth, did take an ass and a colt that was none of his; and you know that God said of him, 'This is my beloved Son, in Whom I delight.'

commended: one version has 'commanded'.

Thus you may see that God delighteth in thieves. But most of all I marvel that men can despise you thieves, whereas in all points (almost) you be like unto Christ himself. For Christ had no dwelling-place; no more have you. Christ went from town to town; and so do you. Christ was hated of all men, saving of his friends; and so are you. Christ was laid wait upon in many places; and so are you. Christ at the length was caught; and so shall you be. He was brought before the judges; and so shall you be. He was condemned; and so shall you be. He was hanged; and so shall you be.

He went down into Hell; and so shall you do. Marry, in this one thing you differ from him, for he rose again and ascended into heaven; and so shall you never do, without God's great mercy, which God grant you! To whom, with the Father, and the Son and the Holy Ghost, be all honour and glory for ever and ever. Amen.

Thus his sermon being ended, they gave him his money again that they took from him, and two shillings to drink, for his sermon.

FINIS

ADDITIONAL NOTES

Walker: A Manifest Detection of Dice-Play

PAGE

34. 1. *of Boulogne:* Boulogne was taken in 1544 after a two-
months' siege. When Henry's ally the Emperor made a separate
treaty with France, England was compelled to cancel plans
for further military action.

38. 2. *Hodge Setter:* this trail-blazer has sunk into undeserved
oblivion.

40. 3. *All the odds ... final purpose:* the difference between
cheaters and thieves or whores lies not in the end, which in
each case is to defraud, but in the means.

49. 4. *alms-knight's room ... Windsor:* ? knight who receives
special award from the king, perhaps of accommodation.

53. 5. *barnard's law:* Greene develops this device in *A Notable
Discovery*, p. 160 ff.

54. 6. *overture of prices:* the expansion of prices following the
debasement of currency was an important issue when Walker
wrote in 1552. Judges points out that when Greene repeated
Walker's words forty years later (see p. 160) the subject was
no longer crucial.

55. 7. *rubber (or rutter):* a member of a gang of cony-catchers
who creates a diversion or quarrel if necessary.

55. 8. *James Ellis:* a celebrated cutpurse hanged at Tyburn on 30
April 1552.

Awdeley: The Fraternity of Vagabonds

61. 1. *Cock Lorel:* a celebrated figure in Elizabethan rogue literature who may have a historical basis. Cock Lorel frequently
appears as the leader of a band of low-life characters resolutely upsetting the status quo wherever and however they
can. The name means 'Villain-in-chief' (Lorel=Losel).

68. 2. *Paul's ... Christ's Hospital ... Royal Exchange:* the aisles
of St Paul's Church were the favourite haunt of loafers, lovers,
con men and others. Christ's Hospital was founded by Edward
VI in 1552 on the site of Greyfriars monastery. The Royal
Exchange had not been erected at the time Awdeley's work

was first published (1561); the allusion must have been inserted in the 1575 edition.

Harman: Caveat for Common Cursitors

81. 1. *Elizabeth, Countess of Shrewsbury:* the celebrated Bess of Hardwick. Her fourth husband was George Talbot, sixth Earl of Shrewsbury. She financed an alms-house at Derby.

83. 2. *keep hospitality in the country:* 'housekeeping' or hospitality was considered part of the social duty of a great man. Its decline is universally lamented in Elizabethan literature.

84. 3. *the last Duke of Buckingham:* Edward Stafford, third Duke of Buckingham, was beheaded on 17 May 1521 for 'imagining the King's death'.

84. 4. *ox sod out in frumenty:* an ox boiled in a mixture of wheat, spiced milk and sugar. The funerals and weddings of the gentry were occasions for widespread hospitality.

85. 5. *Egyptians:* at the time Harman was writing not only gipsies ('Egyptians') but those found in their company faced the death penalty.

95. 6. *Southwark, Kent Street and Bermondsey Street:* districts where stolen goods, especially those of metal and leather, could be easily disposed of.

104. 7. *many Irishmen:* an act of 1572 makes special provision for the deportation of Irish vagrants. There are many references to them in the literature of the period.

108. 8. *Bethlem:* Bethlehem (or Bedlam) Hospital, founded in 1247 in the priory buildings of St Mary of Bethlehem without Bishopsgate.

108. 9. *the Lord Sturton's man:* Charles Sturton, seventh Baron, was hanged at Salisbury for the murder of William Hartgill and his son John. A silken cord was reportedly used for the hanging.

139. 10. *Thistleworth:* Isleworth. The preceding proper names are those of London inns, used as nicknames for isolated barns in the home counties (Judges), or the actual names of inns standing not far from barns.

146. 11. *the Earl of Desmond:* a feud between the Earls of Desmond and Ormonde disturbed Munster, with a pitched battle at Affone in 1565.

149. 12. *the queer cuffin:* Harman glosses the phrase as 'a Justice

of the Peace'. Presumably 'a hoggish and churlish man' is a synonym from the speaker's point of view.
(cf. modern pig = policeman.)

153. 13. *This counterfeit crank:* the 2nd state of the 1567 edition omits the lines from here to the end of the stanza. Instead there is a note identifying the wood-cut as the picture of Nicholas Blunt (alias Jennings) and referring the reader to his story as recorded in the text.

153. 14. *warmed:* Judges amends to 'warned' but perhaps 'warmed' in the sense of 'enkindled' is intended.

Greene: A Notable Discovery of Cozenage

157. 1. *his exile among the Getes:* Ovid spent eight years among a tribe called the Getes in Costanza on the lower Danube, exiled by the Emperor Augustus. In the *Tristia* he expresses regret for the indiscretions which led to his exile.

160. 2. *There was before this, many years ago:* referring to *A Manifest Detection of Dice-Play* (1552). Though Greene claims to write from first-hand experience, it will be noticed that he follows Walker more or less verbatim from here to the end of the paragraph. (See pp. 53 ff.)

161. 3. *a bad commodity:* goods at inflated valuations which needy borrowers were compelled to accept instead of money.

173. 4. *and hereof it riseth:* most of what immediately follows is more unacknowledged pilfering from Walker. (See pp. 39–40.)

175. 5. *Nobles Northward ... Round Robin:* evidently refers to the prison and its jailers.

179. 6. *Polyphemus' cut:* Polyphemus was one of the Cyclops, a race of one-eyed giants. Perhaps the allusion is to a fierce frown with one eye almost closed.

181. 7. *the Arches:* the ecclesiastical court before which cases of adultery would be tried.

185. 8. *unlawful sacks:* the colliers were middlemen between the London public and the charcoal burners of the home counties.

186. 9. *forestalling:* 'cornering the market' by buying up goods beforehand, at this time an indictable offence.

Greene: The Second Part of Cony-Catching

195. 1. *The Second Part:* the original title-page refers to 'The Second and Last Part'. Both *A Notable Discovery* and the

present work were registered and published at about the same
time, which suggests that there was no break in the writing of
the two parts. Greene's elaborate comments about scaring off
the cony-catchers with his earlier work is a puff for himself,
as justified perhaps as such self-advertisements usually are.

198. 2. *the statute:* all horses bought and sold at fairs and markets
had to be certified before the toll-taker by the seller.

199. 3. Immedicabile ... trahatur: 'The wound that will not re-
spond to medicine must be cut away.' (Ovid, *Metamorphoses*
I, 190.) The original Latin has *recidendum* for *resecandum*.
Greene is evidently quoting from memory. The line is quoted
again in *The Defence of Cony-Catching* (p. 345) with the
same alteration.

200. 4. *Mannering's place ... Lady Rich:* Elizabeth, widow of
Robert, Baron Rich, died in December 1591. Mannering was
evidently a well-known thief who, like Walker's Hodge Setter,
appears to have dropped from the annals of roguery but for
this reference.

201. 5. *hue and cry:* when an injured party made a complaint, the
constable could, on the authority of a justice's warrant, call a
hue and cry for which he could insist on the cooperation of
the public.

202. 6. *lapwing ... nest:* this bird was supposed to protect her
young by chirping some distance away from her nest (cf.
Comedy of Errors, IV, ii, 27).

202. 7. *a strict statute:* see note to p. 198 above. Greene is not
strictly accurate in saying that the statute made the buying of a
stolen horse a felony.

207. 8. *Diogenes:* a Greek philosopher who scorned the usual dom-
estic amenities to the extent of taking up residence in a tub.

207. 9. *Whistle of Polyphemus:* Polyphemus, the Cyclops,
whistled as he took his flock to pasture after shutting the cave
door on Odysseus and his companions (see *Odyssey* Book IX l.
315).

208. 10 *Bathyllus:* there are two figures known to classical anti-
quity by this name, one a beautiful youth loved by the poet
Anacreon, the other a celebrated Alexandrian mime; neither
seems to fit Green's context particularly well. Greene is probably thinking of the sculptor Bupalus who mocked the poet
Hipponax and was driven to hang himself when the latter
lampooned him. (See Horace, Epode VI. In Epode XIV,
Horace mentions Bathyllus.)

PAGE

208. 11. *neck-verse:* verse of the Bible (usually the first of Psalm 51) which was kept ready at trials to be read by those who claimed benefit of clergy; hence by extension 'the gallows'.

209. 12. *Mark Lane:* a street in London, running from Fenchurch Street to Great Tower Street where a fair or mart used to be held (hence 'Mart Lane' later Mark Lane).

211. 13. *the Exchange:* built in 1566–7 in Lombard Street, the Royal Exchange was a centre of commerce and fashion.

211. 14. *bear-garden:* there were several of these on the Southwark bank of the river; they are a familiar landmark in contemporary maps and views of London.

212. 15. *sermon at Tyburn:* on their way to the place of execution, the hangman's cart would be stopped for a while, should the condemned man be irresistibly impelled to address the crowd on the wickedness of his past life, etc.

213. 16. *Bartholomew Fair:* a celebrated London fair held annually until the nineteenth century. Ben Jonson immortalized it in his play of the same name.

213. 17. *Queen's day at the Tilt-yard:* joustings in the tilt-yard at Whitehall on the anniversary of the Queen's accession (17 November) were a very popular London attraction.

218. 18. *a quaint conceit:* Greene claims to give a more authentic version of this story in *The Third Part of Cony-Catching* (see p. 250 ff.).

224. 19. *Moorfields:* at this time a stretch of swampy ground just outside the city to the north, often used by laundresses.

228. 20. mittimus: an order to a jailer to hold a named individual in custody.

Greene: *The Third and Last Part of Cony-Catching*

233. 1. *Whittington College:* Sir Richard Whittington (died 1423, immortalized in legend and pantomime) left money in his will for the founding of Whittington College, an almshouse, as well as for Newgate prison; Greene may have the latter in mind.

251. 2. *somewhat misreported before:* see note to p. 218 above.

252. 3. *Bull within Bishopsgate:* a London inn converted to a theatre at this time.

256. 4. *Paul's Chain:* a lane to the south of St Paul's, so named because a chain was hung across it to keep traffic out during service times.

263. 5. *whether it were Latin or English:* Latin was the language used for conjuration and other magical practices.

Greene: A Disputation between a He-Cony-Catcher and a She-Cony-Catcher

267. 1. *Master Huggins:* in 1574 John Higgins brought out a new and enlarged version of the popular collection of tragical-historical-moral-poetical tales *The Mirror for Magistrates,* first published in 1559.

268. 2. *hieria:* perhaps a misprint for 'sirens' or possibly 'hyena', an animal which in myth has a voice which enchants human beings (cf. p. 271).

270. 3. *Vine Court:* in the Middle Temple. The point of the illusion is not clear; perhaps it is a reference to success in litigation or being acquitted at court.

270. 4. *Pierce Penilesse:* the celebrated book by Thomas Nashe, published in the same year as *A Disputation* (available in Penguins). Nash, under the persona of Pierce ('Purse') Pennilesse, enjoys himself hugely at the expense of contemporary social foibles and vices.

271. 5. *Calypso:* a nymph who entertained the shipwrecked Ulysses for several years. (Nan, in addition to her other accomplishments, has evidently had at least a rudimentary classical education.)

276. 6. *at Laurence Pickering's:* the Kent Street house described in *The Second Part of Cony-Catching* (see p. 214).

276. 7. *action ... of trespass:* this was often used in place of an action for custody because the arrested person could be held in custody till the trial came up.

277. 8. *a place of privilege:* the precincts of the cathedral conferred a certain degree of immunity from arrest.

282. 9. *Smithfield Bars:* situated in a disreputable part of London, these bars divided the City precincts from Middlesex.

283. 10. *Bull:* see note on p. 188.

288. 11. *Fowler:* evidently an officer at the house of correction in Bridewell.

288. 12. *dine with Duke Humphrey:* to loaf in an aisle of St Paul's known as Duke Humphrey's walk in the hope of cadging an invitation to dinner.

289. 13. *Sir John's broadsmen:* ? law officers. The proper names which follow may be those of London inns.

289. 14. *Dame Anne a Cleare:* the well of Dame Annis a Cleare at Hoxton, where an alderman's wife was said to have drowned herself.

292. 15. Spectatum ... ipsae: 'They came to see and to be seen themselves.' (Ovid, *Ars Amatoria* I, 99.)

294. 16. Forma bonum ... ipsa suo: 'Beauty is a fragile good, and as it grows it decreases and is devoured by its own years.' (Ovid, *Ars Amatoria* II, 113, 114.)

294. 17. *Cornelia:* mother of the famous tribunes Caius and Tiberius. When a lady boasted about her jewels, Cornelia pointed to her sons, saying 'These are my jewels.' Or so the story goes.

295. 18. *moly:* a fabulous plant with magical properties which, as Homer has it, Hermes gave Ulysses as a charm against Circe.

298. 19. Quo semel ... diu: 'The pitcher, just soaked, will preserve the smell for a long time.' (Horace, *Epistles* I, ii, 70.)

302. 20. *Damon ... Gisippus:* Damon offered his own life to save his friend Pythias. Pylades was the cousin and close friend of Orestes. Gisippus is evidently the Jewish historian Josephus, who accompanied the emperor Vespasian (Titus) during the siege of Jerusalem and was later honoured by him.

309. 21. Si nihil ... foras: 'If you have brought nothing, Homer, out you go!' (Ovid, *Ars Amatoria* II, 280.)

310. 22. *Messalina:* wife of the Emperor Claudius, Messalina was notorious for her profligacy, spectacular even by Roman standards. She was put to death in A.D. 48.

Greene: *The Black Book's Messenger*

319. 1. *marshal-man:* subordinate officer of the Knight Marshal, whose duties included acting as steward during royal processions.

319. 2. *leapt at a daisy:* proverbial expression, meaning 'was hanged'.

331. 3. Strado Curtizano: Courtesans' Street. Perhaps 'Madame Padilia' and 'Romana Imperia' were stars and/or impresarios of establishments on the street.

333. 4. *Amasis' law:* Amasis was king of Egypt from 570 to 526 B.C. (See Herodotus' *History* II, 187.)

334. 5. *statute merchant:* a legal procedure, originally devised for

PAGE

the benefit of merchants, where the borrower acknowledged his debt before a magistrate, and risked imprisonment and forfeiture of his lands if he did not repay the loan by an agreed date.

334. 6. *so long goes the pitcher to the water:* Greene can say that again; in fact he does. This much-used vessel goes to the well at least once in each of the cony-catching pamphlets.

'Cuthbert Cony-Catcher': The Defence of Cony-Catching

339. 1. *Whittington College:* Satirical reference to Newgate prison. See opening sentence of Introductory Epistle and additional note to p. 233.

339. 2. Qui bene ... omnibus; 'He who has lived hidden has lived well; deception rules in all things.' (cf. Ovid, *Tristia*, III, iv, 25.)

342. 3. *Dr Storey's cap:* Grosart suggests that this may be a proverbial expression; cf. 'cap of falsehood'.

346. 4. *Iron Age:* the ancient Romans and Greeks believed themselves to be living in the Iron Age, after the Golden and Silver Ages.

348. 5. *letters of defeasance:* document rendering void a specified right on the fulfilment of an agreed condition.

351. 6. *Medea ... Jason:* as revenge against Jason for deserting her, Medea murdered the two children she had by him and destroyed Jason's new young wife with a poisoned garment.

357. 7. *What say you:* compare this with Walker's remarks on p. 42 of *A Manifest Detection:* 'Though your experience of the world be not so great as mine ...' – a passage Greene also remembered (assuming he is not the author of *A Defence*). See p. 174 'Think you some lawyers could be such purchasers', etc.

359. 8. *terra frenia:* ? from 'fren' = 'foreign'; more probably a misprint for *terra firma*.

361. 9. *abhominable:* misspelling preserved to show the false but popular Elizabethan etymology *ab hominem.*

363. 10. *Tobie's:* the dog who accompanies Raphael and Tobias (in the Book of Tobit), perhaps remembered in the dog Toby of the Punch and Judy show.

363. 11. *Martinist:* Puritan; from Martin Marprelate, pseudonymous author of several sixteenth-century Puritan tracts.

372. 12. *Duke of Shoreditch:* most successful of London archers.

PAGE

375. 13. *negromancy:* the spelling brings out the connection with black magic.

Parson Haberdyne's Sermon

381. 1. *David ... Abiazar:* this Old Testament story is referred to by Christ when the disciples are rebuked for gathering corn on the Sabbath.

THE PENGUIN ENGLISH LIBRARY

Some Recent Volumes